DEFINING US

TAYLOR DELONG

ALSO BY TAYLOR DELONG

The Highway Ride

Loving Rebel

Whiskey Tears

Can't Buy My Love (Girl Power Romance)

Where Forever Leads (Falls Village)

The Lawn Boy (All American Boy)

Up to Fate part of the Steamy Shorts anthology

For my mom, Diane, for your love and support throughout my life. You're the best!

DEFINING US PLAYLIST

Red Ragtop Tim McGraw
Love Like Crazy Lee Brice
I Don't Want This Night to End Luke Bryan
Crazy Girl Eli Young Band
Body Like a Back Road Sam Hunt
Then Brad Paisley
Treat You Better Shawn Mendes
Good Morning Beautiful Steve Holy
A Moment Like This Kelly Clarkson
Die a Happy Man Thomas Rhett
Play That Song Train

PROLOGUE

AINSLEY

*S*topped at the red light on Main Street, Tim McGraw's "Red Ragtop" came on the radio. The irony was not lost on me, and I couldn't help but let out a nervous giggle. Grabbing my phone off the seat next to me, I unlocked it and opened up my text messages. Rereading his last message for the 1000th time, an ounce of the tension I'm feeling released. It didn't help, but at this point, I was fairly certain nothing would. I will continue to convince myself that this was the best option for all involved and not allow the ton of guilt I felt to creep in. Not even a little bit. Nope, not even a tiny bit.

I looked up to see the light changing to green and pushed ahead toward my destination. I knew the building wasn't too far up on the right; I knew the turn was at a light but not exactly sure which one. Coming up to another red light, I spied his car a few cars back. Immediately my lips turned up into a small smile. At least he was punctual, and he followed through with his promise. He said he would come, but a tiny bit of doubt had crept in. It was focus on that or my immense guilt. I chose doubt. Now that he was actually here, the doubt faded, but I was trying to keep the guilt at bay. Knowing I'm not alone in this helped. Although I was pretty sure that the effects of our decision, to some extent, will forever haunt me. Unlike him. He won't ever have to answer "Yes" to that specific question like women have to.

The light turned green, but I didn't realize it until the car behind me started beeping at me, pulling me out of my thoughts and back to the present. Without a glance back, I turned into the parking lot and started to look for a spot. I found one a few rows from the front door. I pulled in and shut off the car. There was a spot right next to mine, and I was hoping he saw it too. I glanced at the clock. Our appointment was in fifteen minutes. I went to grab my bag from the passenger's seat, but before I even had it in my hands, he was parked next to me, hopping out of his car and climbing into mine.

Taking him in, he was a bit disheveled in comparison to his normal put together self. His button-down shirt was untucked and his jeans were wrinkled. The hair that poked out from beneath his baseball cap was sticking out every which way. His face conveyed mixed emotions, one of which was definitely guilt, which honestly surprised me a little.

He was staring straight ahead out the windshield. He seemed nervous, worried almost. Placing my hand on his thigh, he jumped slightly. "Hey, you okay?" I asked, sensing him tense up even more at my touch.

Sighing, he looked over to me. He furrowed his brow. Considering this was his idea, I didn't expect this behavior from him.

I didn't want to ask the question that it looked like he was begging me to ask. I had made my decision; I couldn't allow him to change my mind now, even though I knew the guilt might consume me at some point.

He shook his head. "Are we doing the right thing?" he asked, his voice barely audible.

I glared at him, even though he wasn't looking in my direction. From this angle, his face looked even more worried. "You can't say things like that now," I told him incredulously. "This was your idea. And while I didn't need much convincing, I don't know that I would have come to this decision on my own without your prodding." I couldn't believe he was asking this now. My temperature began to rise as I began to comprehend his reservations.

"Ultimately it's your decision," he told me. "It's your body."

And he just played the woman card. Well, that's fabulous. Such the man thing to do. Too bad he was acting like such a boy right now.

"Look, I'm keeping this appointment. I would like you to join me at it but will understand if you can't or don't want to." Inhaling deeply, I added, "I think deep down, we both know this is for the best."

He turned to face the window. After another audible sigh, he let himself out of the car. I was caught off guard for a split second, wondering what decision he was going to make and what thoughts were racing through his mind.

Before I could ponder what to do, he was around to my side of the car and was opening my door. I quickly grabbed my bag and climbed out of the car. He closed the door behind me and pulled me into him. His arms wrapped around my waist, and he hugged me tightly.

Pulling away, he mumbled, "I'm sorry, Ainsley," and I thought he was going to leave me on my own. Much to my surprise, he grabbed my hand in his, which was clammy to the touch. He led me to the building.

As we walked, I tried to focus on the task at hand, trying to forget his reservations and compartmentalizing my own emotions about what we were about to do.

I was naive to believe that all of the promises we made to one another would be upheld. It wasn't until months later that I realized the true irony in the lyrics of "Red Ragtop."

1

AINSLEY

SIX YEARS LATER

*R*unning late to my first class of the day, I stumble over the uneven pavement, just barely catching myself before I fall. Somehow I manage to keep my bag from slipping completely off my arm, but my travel mug of steaming hot coffee suffers a different fate. It falls from my left hand as I not so gracefully save myself from landing on the ground. "Ah, crap. There goes my day," I stammer aloud to no one but myself, even though there are throngs of people rushing by me. The coffee slowly seeps out through the now open container, staining the sidewalk as it runs down the slight incline.

Realizing I'm going to be even later to class than I originally thought, I grab the mug from the ground, hike my laptop bag up further onto my shoulder and start walking again. Since there were no spots close to my office, I was forced to walk even longer than usual today. It always happens when I'm running late.

"Hey, Professor Bradford," I hear from behind me, as I make my way across the quad. Knowing I will be even later if I stop and turn around to look, I keep trudging toward Manor Hall, which

houses my office and the rest of the English department and class-
rooms, slowing my pace only slightly.

In a moment, the owner of the voice has caught up to me and
is matching me, step for step. I turn to look at one of my sopho-
more students and give him a small smile as I pick my pace back
up. Even though it's a somewhat warm day for spring, he's sporting
his baseball jacket, the one that advertises that the team was last
year's champions. I don't follow baseball too much, especially
since this is the first year I've had some players in my classes. He's
also wearing his fraternity hat. The hat that every time he or one
of his brothers wears it, makes me inwardly cringe.

"I'm running a little late," I start, hoping that he's not going to
want to engage in a conversation now.

"I just wanted to ask you if you've had a chance to read through
the latest draft of my essay," he inquires, not bothering to hide his
persistence.

I don't answer him right away; instead, I keep pushing ahead to
the building, getting closer with each step I take. Unfortunately, he
doesn't miss a beat and keeps up with me. I know I had to cancel
our meeting to discuss his essay, but I politely told him I would
email him with alternate dates to meet. Clearly, that wasn't good
enough for Charles McDonald, the third.

I hear him clear his throat next to me, awaiting my reply.
Normally, I don't mind chatting with my students whenever I'm on
campus, but on top of being late today, Charles is adding to my
irritation of the woes of my life, including a girls' night out with
the queen bitch and her lady-in-waiting later tonight. And well,
add in the fact that I've been sexually frustrated for months,
talking with Charles about the latest draft of his essay that he
swindled me into rewriting for about the fifth time now, is not on
the top of my priority list. Not that I can let him know this, of
course. So, taking in a deep breath, I manage to explain, "As I
wrote to you in response to your email earlier this week, I will
discuss it with you when we meet. Come by my office on Monday
during my office hours, and we can discuss it then." It comes out in

a clipped tone, a little harsher than I mean for it to be delivered. "I've really got to get to class now." I quicken my steps, hoping he will finally get the hint.

"I guess I'll see you Monday then," he huffs out. "Have a nice weekend."

His voice trails off, so I know he's not still next to me, and I let out a sigh of relief. "Entitled brat," I mutter under my breath as I finally get to the building. There are a few late students straggling in as I approach the door, one of them kind enough to hold it open for me. Not wanting to seem ungrateful, I smile at the student and toss out a quick "thanks." She nods her head as I make my way into the building and down the hall to the classroom. Fortunately, it's my Creative Writing class, a class for only upperclassmen so they are less likely to walk out when I'm not on time.

When I walk into the classroom, I'm not surprised to see all the students in their seats, many typing away on their laptops, most likely working on their assignments that are due at the end of next week.

"Sorry I'm late," I begin, walking up to the desk in the front of the room. Once I reach it, I allow my bag to slide down my shoulder and plop down onto the desk. From the corner of my eye, I notice a coffee cup sitting on the edge of the desk. I swipe it up, inhale the scent and then take a long drink, savoring the flavor as it coats my throat. As I swallow the magical concoction, I place the cup back on the desk and peer out into the sea of students, seeking the eyes of my TA. She's sitting in the back row today and when her gaze meets mine, I don't even bother mouthing the words but speak them aloud. "It's too bad I can't give you an A, Maddie. This is just what I needed today." She gives me a quick smile and a wink. With all eyes of my students on me, I can't return the wink, but it's unnecessary at this point. This is her second semester with me, and after finals last semester, we bonded over more than just students' attempts at "creative" writing.

Taking one more sip of pure liquid gold, I shake off my sweater and put my professor hat on and begin class.

* * *

I only teach two classes on Thursdays, and as I head to my office after the second class, I'm in weekend mode since classes have been canceled for tomorrow. Honestly, I'm not even sure for what, but since it means I don't have to come to campus and teach my Freshman 101 class, I'm ever thankful. Even though there are only a few short weeks left in the semester, I'm ready for it to be over.

Inside my tidy office, I drop my bag onto the floor and slump down into my chair. I lean back, resting my head against the back of the chair and close my eyes. Taking a few deep breaths, I allow myself a few minutes to finally breathe after my nonstop morning. When I finally open my eyes, they scan the few piles on my desk. I knew if I went home, I wouldn't get anything done, and I'd really like to be able to enjoy the day off tomorrow. It's with this thought in mind that I grab the top essay off the pile, pull out my red pen from the top drawer, and set to work.

Nearly an hour later, I've read through about six essays, all of them surprisingly less crappy than usual. Glancing over at the clock, I realize I should pack it in and call it a day. I need time to shower and get ready and put on my "party face," as Tara calls it. Already dreading the evening, I sigh as I grab a few essays from the pile of papers and put them into my bag, careful not to let them bend or get crinkled. I'll give myself tomorrow off, but since I have no plans for the weekend, exciting or otherwise, I can get the essays graded on Saturday or Sunday.

Once I've loaded the papers into the bag, I slip my arms back into my sweater that was haphazardly lying on the desk. I hoist the bag up on my shoulder and make my way out of the office, locking the door behind me. In the hall, I'm met with a fellow colleague also leaving for the night.

"Hey, Ainsley, how's it going?" Byron politely asks me. "Looking forward to the day off?" His expression is kind, but ever since we hooked up that one time a few months ago, he's somewhat been keeping his distance and his emotions in check.

It happened only once, shortly after the semester started. This semester was his first one here at the college and when we first met, I could tell that he took an immediate liking to me. I'm not usually one to sleep with colleagues, but his persistence eventually wore me down and one night after a few drinks, I gave in to his advances. I was by no means drunk and was fully aware of the choice I made when he invited me back to his house. Unfortunately, he was just another mediocre lay on my ever-growing list of men I've slept with once. It sucks that I have to constantly see him, but I truly think the experience was worse for him; I've learned how to hide my nonchalance and close off the act of sleeping with someone when there are no emotions on my end.

Not meeting his eyes, I answer, "Yes, I'm thankful for the day off." I keep my gaze on the floor as we walk down the hallway toward the door. Once we reach the door, he goes ahead of me and holds it open for me, careful to stay out of my way lest I somehow make contact with him.

"Well, have a good weekend," he meekly calls out as he goes to the left of the quad as I make my way straight across it.

"Same to you," I mumble. My phone chirps with a text, so I dig it out of my bag. I roll my eyes in disgust at Tara's name in our group text.

TARA

Be ready at seven tonight. I'll pick up Kelcie and then Ainsley. Looking forward to it!

Kelcie responds almost immediately.

Can't wait. See you soon!

I toss my phone back in my bag without even replying. My thoughts drift back to last week when I apparently thought that a girls' night with them sounded like a good idea. I think it came on the heels of some sort of argument with my mother, and the invitation had caught me off guard at first. I agreed without even thinking.

Kelcie and I always got along well enough; we were roommates in college. Once she befriended Tara, I guess I always felt like a third wheel to their duo. Tara and I don't have too much in common and well, she's quite demanding. And controlling. She actually reminds me of a younger version of my mother; she's always judging my actions and choices, especially in regards to guys. Tara didn't even include me in her wedding because in her words, "I can't have you sleeping with one of the groomsmen." I was shocked at first but then relieved because I didn't need to participate in all the stupid activities she forced upon everyone. And just to spite her, I slept with her new husband's brother the night of the wedding. Not going to lie; not my finest moment. I shudder at that memory of him. As far as I know, Tara never found out.

Yesterday, when I realized I truly had no desire to hang out with Tara, because I don't mind when it's just me and Kelcie, and tried to back out, Tara saw through my scheme and decided she would drive us, knowing I couldn't get out of it if she was the designated driver. I'm pretty sure she just tolerates me because I'm friends with Kelcie and Kelcie is always trying to please everyone.

Strolling to the car, I can only hope that wherever we end up, the bartenders will be hot or if I'm really lucky, one of the patrons will be good enough to put an end to my months-long sex dry spell. My lips curl up into a smile at that possibility.

Hey, a girl can dream once in a while, right?

2

GRAYSON

$\mathcal{W}$alking into the bar, I berate myself for getting talked into coming tonight. Even though Dad's Place is my favorite hangout, it's a Thursday night, and I know my buddies won't be here tonight.

I come straight from work, not even stopping at home to change my clothes. As soon as I sit down, the bartender, Dan, puts my obligatory beer in front of me. Nodding my thanks to him, I focus my attention on the dart players. It's been a few months since I've joined in, but truth be told, I don't really miss it.

My attention is diverted from the dart players as the door to the bar opens a few minutes after I am settled on my stool. I watch from the bar as the three women come in. The tallest one seems to be the leader of the group as I notice the other two keep glancing at her, as if they are almost seeking her permission. For what, I can't be sure. She confidently struts to the other end of the bar as the others follow her. She takes a seat on a stool and motions with her hands for her friends to sit next to her. One sits almost immediately, but not the other one. She kind of stands off to the side for a moment, as if not ready to give up total control to her friend.

I take a swig of my beer as I hear the leader demand, "Ainsley, sit down." She glares at her, until Ainsley is practically forced to obey her. She stumbles a bit as she tries to pull out the stool. Once she manages to get seated, the other girl gives her a fake smile. As soon as she's turned her attention to the other girl, Ainsley sticks out her tongue at the back of her head.

Watching from afar, I can't help but chuckle. After a moment, Ainsley glances in my direction. Knowing there's no way she heard me, my heart beats a little faster anyway. Catching my eyes, she waggles her eyebrows at me. I smile back, being kind.

She glances away from me and turns back to her friend who's now talking to her and the other girl. The other girl continuously nods her head up and down as the leader rattles on and on. Ainsley appears bored. She's twirling her finger through her light brown hair, twisting it around her finger and then letting the curl out. She moves to a different spot of hair and starts twirling it again.

I don't know why I'm so mesmerized by what she's doing. Maybe it's the way her fingers curl around the hair and right before she lets it go, she gives it a slight tug. Or the way she keeps rolling her eyes at whatever her friend is talking about. From this far, I can't tell the color of her eyes. I can just about make out how they glitter under the lights of the bar. Well, maybe that's her makeup. Not that she needs it, but it's not so subtle, somewhat caked on her face. Usually that's enough to turn me off completely but not with this girl. And hell if I can explain my curiosity with her, but here I am, watching her every movement. So much so that I don't even realize when Bella sidles up behind me and plants her arms on my shoulders. I jump in response, turning just in time to see her cackling at me.

"Hey!" She laughs. "Didn't mean to startle you. What's got you so worked up?"

Not meaning to, I glance back over to Ainsley. Unfortunately, Bella follows my gaze, her eyes growing wide.

Sitting down on the stool next to me, she questions, "Which of the three caught your eye, Gray? Please don't let it be the tall one."

I shake my head. "Definitely not the tall one," I stammer out and then shudder.

She glances back at the girls. "The blonde?" she questions again.

Again, I shake my head. "The other one."

Taking a more vested interest in ogling the girl across the bar, she looks her up and down, trying to be as discreet as she can. I watch as her eyes take in what she can see of her outfit above the bar: a red V neck top, cut low but not revealing too much. A single charm sits on a silver chain around her neck. Her hair, which she's still twirling, falls in waves around her face, to just below her shoulder. The blonde highlights make the light brown appear even lighter in some areas. Again, she somehow manages to catch me looking at her. This time, she gives me more of a genuine smile. It doesn't quite reach her eyes, yet I can't help feeling the need to smile back at her. Her smile fades as she notices Bella sitting next to me, who has her arms draped over the one I have resting on the bar.

I push Bella's arms off mine but in my haste, I spill the full beer in front of me. "Fuck," I grumble, jumping off the stool as the beer drips down, spilling onto the floor and my pants in the process.

Bella grabs some napkins and starts wiping down the bar. I stop her before she can start wiping my pants. "Give them to me," I sputter at her. I'm grabbing them out of her hands before she can hand them over, but not before I notice she's laughing at me.

"Relax, Gray," she tells me. "It's just beer. One that you weren't going to drink anyway. Don't know why you even pretend anymore or why Dan keeps up the charade." She shakes her head.

Sometimes I wish she would just keep her judgments to herself. Why she has to voice everything is beyond me.

I finish cleaning up my pants as best I can. Dan brings over a rag and wipes up the beer. "You want another one?" he asks, knowing what my answer will be already.

"Nah, I'm good." He gives me a nod.

He looks over to Bella. "The usual?" he asks.

"Please," she says, batting her eyes at him. I roll mine. "Make it two." He raises his eyebrows at her. "Kylie will be here shortly. I told her she can only come if she drinks what I drink." She smiles at him, flashing him her perfect teeth. He knits his brows and walks away to make her drinks.

"Why do you have to do that with him?" I ask her, annoyed with her behavior.

"He knows I don't mean anything by it. He's *so* not my type!" She throws her head back in laughter like the idea of her and Dan is the craziest thing she's ever heard.

"Hello? Can we get some help over here?" I hear quite loudly from the other side of the bar, bringing my attention back to where Ainsley and her friends are sitting. The tall one has an exasperated look on her face, as if she's expecting someone to be waiting on her. Pete, Dan's help behind the bar, strolls over to them.

Settling myself back on the stool, it's just in time for Dan to place Bella's drinks in front of her.

"When will Kylie be here?" I ask Bella as she takes a sip from her martini.

"Right now!" I hear from behind me. Before I can turn myself around, she's throwing her arms around my neck and practically molesting me. As quickly as I can, I push her off of me, spinning on my stool to face her.

"Seriously? Every time?" I respond angrily.

"Oh Gray, you know how much I love you," she answers in return, planting another kiss on my cheek.

"He's just in a mood," Bella says, rolling her eyes and nodding her head over to where Ainsley and her friends sit.

Kylie's gaze follows Bella's head, and she frowns. "Really, Gray? Not the tall one, I hope."

"That's what I said!" Bella exclaims. "He's made it abundantly clear it's not her." She glances back over to the girls. "The one in the red."

Kylie takes a longer look at Ainsley, looking her up and down just like Bella did. "Well, she's got potential."

I shake my head in disbelief that this is really happening.

"Look, Bell. We are embarrassing him." Kylie laughs.

"Oh, look at the time," I say, glancing up at the clock on the wall. "Time for me to go." I start to push off the stool but Kylie's too quick for me. She plants her palms on my chest and shoves me back down. When she's satisfied I will stay sitting, she takes a seat on the stool on the other side of me.

"Dan," Bella beckons him over. Once he's closer to us, she leans over the bar to him and not so subtly whispers, "Send a drink to the brunette in the red dress across the bar. It's on Grayson." She giggles as she lowers herself down to her stool.

My eyes go wide. "Bella!" I spit out, my voice an octave higher than normal. I look at Dan, but he's already moved away from us and has started to pour a drink. I watch, nervously, as he heads down to the other side of the bar, knowing that nothing I say or do will stop this train wreck Bella has set in motion.

Dan tentatively places the drink in front of Ainsley. All three girls stop what they are doing and look first at him, and then over to me. Feeling my face flush, I flash a smile their way. Ainsley looks at the drink questioningly and then back to me. She shrugs her shoulders, although she seems to accept the drink. I watch as she takes a sip. Once she puts the glass back down, she gives me a half smile, a nod of her head, and what appears to be a mouthed "thanks." I nod back at her in return.

Watching the entire exchange, Bella questions, "Now was that so difficult, Gray?" She looks over to me but when my eyes widen in surprise, she quickly turns her head back to the other side of the bar, lets out a tiny gasp, and an "Oh shit!" escapes her mouth.

As it turns out, Ainsley's mouthed thanks wasn't enough. She's off her bar stool and wandering over to the other side of the bar, over to me.

My pulse begins to race, and my palms start to sweat. I run my fingers through my hair and then wipe them down on my jeans. I have about thirty seconds to figure out what I'm going to say to her before she's standing in front of me. Thinking quickly, I come up with either lame pickup lines or my usual "hey." However, I'm let somewhat off the hook when she passes by my stool and stands in back of Bella's. Bella has watched the entire scene from her stool. She only turns to face Ainsley when Ainsley taps her on the shoulder.

I watch the exchange between the two women, Kylie sitting right behind me, almost holding her breath as she scans from Ainsley to Bella and back again.

Ainsley cuts right to the chase. "What's the deal between you and him?" she asks Bella with a glare. Her eyebrows are furled, her eyes, which I can now tell are emerald green, are hard. Confirming what I thought before, she's wearing too much makeup. Despite that fact, I can tell she's pretty.

Bella swallows, her eyes big. "The deal?" she asks hesitantly.

Ainsley nods her head. "You with him?"

Bella bursts out laughing. From behind me, Kylie cackles.

Ainsley looks over at Kylie who's doubled over with laughter. She shoots her eyes back over to Bella.

"No. Definitely not with him," Bella insists.

Ainsley looks back to Kylie. "What about you?" she asks, staring Kylie down.

Kylie about falls off her stool. In between her peals of laughter, she manages to shake her head no.

Ainsley looks to me, not sure of what is so funny.

"My sister," I nod with my head to Bella, "and her girlfriend," motioning to Kylie.

My answer takes a moment to sink in, but when it does, Ainsley's face loses some of the hardness and her eyes light up.

"Well that's good then," she replies, giving me a grin. "I'm Ainsley. Thanks for the drink." She reaches out her hand to mine.

I shake it as politely as I can. "Grayson," I tell her. "You're welcome. Hope it was something you like."

She nods. "You do this often?"

Confused by her question, I don't answer her right away. "Come to the bar?" I ask, taking a guess.

"Well that, and buy drinks for random girls?"

I'm cognizant of the fact Bella and Kylie seem to be not so subtly eavesdropping on our conversation. "I'm here often, but I don't make a habit of buying drinks for women I don't know," I reply.

"Just the special ones?" she asks with a wink.

I don't know what it is about this girl, but her wink causes me to crack a smile.

"Only the special ones."

She chooses that moment to look back at her friends. The tall one is waving her back over to them and her face falls.

"Bitch," I hear her grumble. "Well, I guess I better go back to my friends." There's disappointment in her eyes coupled with annoyance and a hint of sadness.

"Yeah," I agree.

She starts to walk away, gets halfway to her friends, and comes back to me. In a move I'm not expecting, she throws her arms around my neck and plants a kiss smack on my lips. Even though she's small, the force of her hits me and almost knocks me back. And then I give in and kiss her back. She goes to pull away, but I grab the back of her head and bring it back to me. And then she really kisses me. Holy fuck this girl can kiss!

Her tongue forces its way into my mouth but in a gentle way. I part my lips so that her tongue can explore my mouth. She wastes no time in exploring it all. She brings her hands up to my hair and slightly tugs on the back.

I take my tongue and lick her bottom lip, drawing her lip into my mouth, almost forcing her tongue out. The wine she's been drinking transfers from her lips and tongue to mine.

"GRAYSON!" I hear Bella shout.

Annoyed, I pull my mouth away from Ainsley's to find Bella frantically waving her arms at me.

I wipe my lips with the back of my hand and look back at Ainsley. "Shit." She's glancing over at the other end of the bar where her friends are staring, jaws dropped. "Sorry," she replies sheepishly, looking down at the floor.

"I'm not," I tell her, tipping her chin up to look at me.

"Wow! Marry me?" she asks, no hint of sarcasm in her voice.

What. The. Fuck?

Before I can get any words out, she's running back to her friends, leaving me even more confused than I was before.

I slump down on the stool, leaning my back against the bar. My head is spinning. You don't kiss like that, ask someone to marry you, and run away.

Before losing my nerve, in a move so uncharacteristic of who I am, I storm over to the other side of the bar. I ignore my sister's and Kylie's voices calling out to me and make my way over to Ainsley.

When I reach where she is, I grab her arm, practically pulling her off the stool and dragging her behind me. I pull her to the hallway where the bathrooms are, avoiding the people waiting in line for the women's room. Once we have maneuvered past them, I move toward the end of the hall. It's a bit darker here, a perfect place for what I need.

Before I speak, I run my fingers through my hair, contemplating my next move and wondering what the hell I am actually doing. Clearly I haven't thought any of this through. When I look at Ainsley, she's got a wild look to her.

"Grayson," she starts. Before she can say any more, I cut her off.

"What the fuck, Ainsley?" My grumble comes out a little angrier than I actually am. I parrot her question from earlier back to her. "Do you do this often?"

"Do what?" she asks straight-faced.

"This! Kiss random men in bars and ask them to marry you?" I ask, my temper rising a bit.

She shakes her head no.

"No? To which one?"

"Both," she mumbles as her gaze falls down to the floor.

"Good."

She looks back up at me. "You kissed me back," she replies quietly.

I move closer to her. "That was some kiss. You always kiss like that?"

Again, she shakes her head no. "I don't know what came over me," she whispers, moving closer to me. She places her palm on my chest, close to my heart. "Nervous?" she asks with a smirk.

As if my heart isn't beating fast enough, it kicks up into overtime with the combination of her hand on my chest and her smirk. Taking a deep breath, I bring my face down to hers. Knowing what I'm doing, she pushes up onto tippy-toes, meeting me halfway. Her soft lips reach mine and the moment mine touch hers, she starts devouring them. She tilts her head to the side as she puts her arms around my neck. Relieving her from having to stretch so much, I lift her up off the ground. She wraps her legs around my waist as her lips and tongue continue to massage mine. When she pulls my lower lip into her mouth, I'm done for and have to pull away.

Her face falls a bit, and she questions my actions.

"Just need a breather," I assure her. I lower her down to the floor. I twirl my hands through her hair; it's soft and silky to the touch.

Keeping me on my toes, she wraps her hands around my waist and lays her head on my chest. "You smell good," she replies, inhaling my scent.

Not sure how to answer her, I wrap my arms around her and give her a squeeze. I've never felt this close to a woman, let alone a woman I just met. I can't explain it. However, I throw caution to the wind and just take everything in stride. Surprisingly, it's not that difficult to do.

From the corner of my eye, I see her tall friend coming down the hall. Unfortunately, she catches my eye and quickens her pace to get to where Ainsley and I are standing. When she finally reaches us, her look even scares me a little.

"Ainsley, are you ready to go?" she asks, grabbing her arm and tugging her out of my hold.

Ainsley looks from me to the friend and sighs. "Give me five minutes," she finally concedes. When the friend makes no indication of leaving, she snaps, "Alone. Go."

With a huff, the friend turns on her heels and storms off.

"Crap. She's my ride," Ainsley complains, her face taking on a more pissed look.

Thinking fast, I tell her, "I can drive you home."

She shakes her head. "I would love that, but you don't know Tara. She's 'happily married' yet whenever any man shows any interest in me, she's jealous and makes sure I know it." She looks at me, sadness in her eyes.

I choose to focus on the "man" part. "Are there a lot of men interested in you?" I ask tentatively. Although now that I asked it, I'm not sure I want the answer.

She hesitates for a moment, unsure of how to answer me. I get it. We just met, but there's no way she doesn't feel the connection. Heck, she started that kiss!

She pulls her glance away, down to the ground. "No one that matters," she replies. Then in almost a whisper, she adds, "because that's the way Tara wants it."

Treading lightly, I tip her chin up so she can look at me. I don't want to upset her anymore nor judge the friendship. "What do *you* want?"

She takes a deep breath. We both hear shouts of "Let's go, Ainsley!" I take my hands and cover her ears, as if to block it out.

"I have to go." She pulls out of my grasp and starts down the hallway, practically mowing down people in line for the bathroom.

Shocked, I can't even react and don't move for a few minutes. Shaking my head, still in disbelief, I slowly make my way back to the bar. My sister and Kylie have abandoned their spots and are playing darts in the back corner. Glancing up at me, and taking in my shocked look, Bella walks over.

"What the heck, Gray?" she asks, a concerned look on her face.

"Fuck if I know," I reply honestly. "I think I will call it a night now, though. Tell Kylie good night for me, and I will see her soon." I peck her cheek and start to make my way out of the bar.

As I'm walking out of the bar, the cool air hits me, just as my phone signals with an incoming text. Digging my phone out of my pocket, I see the text is from an unknown number. Curiosity getting the better of me, I swipe to unlock my phone and open up Messages.

UNKNOWN

Just know, I hate you. For kissing me back.

What the fuck? I think, for like the fifth time this evening? Who is this girl and why does her text bring a smile to my face?

You don't even know me. You can't hate me. Yet.

After unlocking the doors of my beat-up Explorer, I climb inside. I don't wait for a return text before I drive to my house, my thoughts straying back to the fiery brunette who wants to marry me even though she hates me.

3

AINSLEY

*a*fter I get home from the bar, I shed my bar outfit and throw on my sweats. I couldn't help but giggle when I sent him the text. Honestly, I needed a way to make sure I still had his attention, not that I even doubted it for a minute. I felt that connection; *he* felt that connection. What I get back from him, the "yet" part, has me worried. Not in a bad way, at least I don't think so. But to be on the safe side, I ask him.

> So, when I do get to know you, I will hate you?

But seriously, can we talk about that kiss? I know I started it, but damn, he finished it. Twice! I haven't felt an instant connection to a guy in so long. Not since Jordan. But since I don't allow myself to think about him, I go back to thinking about Grayson while I wait for him to text back.

I'm not sure what came over me to make me kiss him. I had noticed him the minute we walked into the bar. It was pure luck that we ended up at that bar tonight. Tara wanted to go to a different one, but Kelcie convinced her to try that one. And since Kelcie is the only person that Tara will ever agree with, she went

along with her pick. Can't say I'm disappointed in the choice.
Nope, not one single bit.

He looked a bit lonely sitting on the far side of the bar. The
brim of his hat hid most of his face, including his eyes. It's usually
the eyes that draw me in, but since I couldn't see them completely,
it was something else about him. The scruff on his chin was
certainly a plus. When I first spotted him, I noticed it right away,
thought about what it would feel like against my chin. Guess my
mind had already decided I'd kiss him.

Pouring myself a glass of wine, I settle onto my couch and
bring up my Netflix queue. Since I have a rare day off tomorrow,
I'm taking full advantage of staying up late and sleeping in
tomorrow.

Just as I'm about to hit play on my movie, my phone pings with
an incoming text. Hoping it's from the handsome stranger, I reach
over to the end table and pick it up. Disappointed, I see that it's
Tara.

> I had fun tonight, ladies. Let's do it again soon!

I choose not to respond with the first thought that pops into
my head. Taking my time to compose my response, two texts come
in at the same time. One is from Kelcie and the other one is from
Grayson, who I programmed in earlier. When just his first name
comes across the screen, I realize I don't know his last name. I'll
have to remedy that.

> KELCIE
> Yes please! Next week?

Deleting what I was going to say to the girls, I close that thread
out and open up Grayson's.

> If there will be more kisses like tonight, then yes,
> you will most certainly be hating me.

I can't help but crack a smile. Furiously, I type back my response.

> When? When will there be more kisses? And what's your last name?

I watch as the three bubbles appear as he's typing back his response.

> Abbott. Name the time and place, and I'm there.

I add Abbott to his contact information and formulate my next response. *Is tomorrow too soon?* I think. It's Friday night; I bet he already has plans. What the heck? I decide to go for it.

> Tomorrow?

I chew the fingernail of my pointer finger as I await his response, and down some of the wine. After what feels like forever, the phone finally vibrates on my lap.

> I'm out of town tomorrow. I'm back Sunday afternoon.

I so want to know where he's going, but I restrain myself.

> So like Sunday night?

Nothing like being desperate.

> Sure

The three bubbles appear again, then disappear. After a few minutes, I figure he's not responding anymore, but before I put my phone down and turn on my movie, I send a response back to the girls.

> Next week works. Looking forward to it!

I toss my phone on the couch next to me and wonder when I became such the liar to my friends. I would rather gouge my eyes out than go out with Tara two weeks in a row. It's bad enough that we already have plans at the end of the month for Kelcie's birthday. Sighing, I hit play on the movie and sink further down into the couch.

About thirty minutes into the movie, I decide I need some popcorn. Pulling out the box from the pantry, I pop a bag into the microwave. Realizing there's only one bag left, I add "popcorn" to my grocery list on the fridge. While I wait for the popcorn to pop, I pile my hair up on top of my head. The faint sound of my phone vibrates from the couch as the microwave beeps. I grab the popcorn out and make my way back to the couch. Checking my phone, I smile when I see Grayson's name.

Settling back onto the couch with my popcorn, I abandon my movie and open up his message.

> How did you get my number anyway?

> I have my ways. *wink emoji*

He doesn't respond right away. Hope I haven't made him mad. When I left him in the hallway of the bar, shocked shitless, I knew I couldn't leave without at least getting his number. Taking a chance that Bella would actually give it to me, and also hoping that Tara wouldn't be even more pissed at me, I found Bella still sitting at the end of the bar. When I reached her stool, she practically grabbed my phone out of my hands and typed his number in. She had a huge smile on her face as she handed the phone back to me, and then she shocked me by pulling me in for a hug. As I pulled away from her and walked back to my friends, I couldn't help but ponder what the smile and hug were for.

From the short interactions I witnessed, it seemed that she and Grayson were close. I finally settled on that even *she* could see the connection her brother and I had and wanted to help us out. After all, it was her that actually sent the drink over to me, not him. That little fact didn't go unnoticed by me.

> What are you doing right now?

>> Watching a movie on Netflix, complete with popcorn and wine.

> What movie?

>> Draft Day. You know it?

> Yup.

>> That's all you're going to give me?

He's quiet for a bit, so I go back to my movie. I watched this one with my brother when it first came out, but nothing else on my queue looked even remotely entertaining. Talking to my brother on the phone yesterday made me somewhat nostalgic, so when I saw the movie on my recommended list, I hit play automatically.

I'm about halfway through the movie this time when my phone vibrates next to me, making my leg jump a little when I feel it. I don't pause the movie this time; I just grab the phone.

> Bella is really into football so anything even remotely football-related, she attempts to drag me to. Sometimes I go willingly, like to see Draft Day.

>> Which team does she root for?

> She's a Steelers fan. We grew up in rural PA.

His text has opened up a whole new can of worms, and I decide Kevin Costner can wait. I shut off the TV, down my glass of wine, and focus my attention on my phone. Making a split-second decision, I dial his number, not too worried about the consequences.

When he answers, his voice sounds surprised. It's really cute.

"You grew up in Pennsylvania and she doesn't even like the Eagles?" I practically spit in his ear.

Reacting quickly, he comes back with, "Have I hit a nerve, Ainsley?"

I think I hear a faint chuckle on his end.

"I'm a diehard Eagles fan. Always have been. This won't work if you are a Steelers fan." I hold my breath for a minute.

"Well then," he starts, "I guess this isn't going to work out. It's too bad too because I will miss your kisses."

Before he can hang up, I cut him off, thinking fast. "Wait! You said *Bella* was a Steelers fan."

"I did."

Sometimes he's a man of few words. That's not going to work for me.

"How about you?" I ask tentatively. I chew my nails as I wait for his response.

"Personally, I'm more of a baseball guy myself," he replies.

Don't say the Pirates. Don't say the Pirates, I think. When he clears his throat, I realize I said it aloud. *Shit.*

"Actually, I'm a Mariners fan. It's a long story. But right now, I wish I was a Pirates fan." He laughs.

"Shut up! I'll stop hating you."

He's silent for a bit. When I think I've lost him, he says, "Are you into baseball?"

"Not as much as football," I tell him, "but I can't stand the Pirates." I don't give him anything else and decide to change the subject. "So can I ask where you are going this weekend or is that too forward of me?"

He snorts, then goes quiet for a few minutes. "Less than two hours ago you asked me to marry you."

Hmm, he makes a good point. "So then where are you going?"

"On a fishing trip."

"Nice! You like to fish?"

"I do. It's not so much about the fish; I just love being on the boat on the water. Gets me out of my head."

I would like to be in your head.

I pop some popcorn in my mouth before I speak again. "Sounds calming." I sigh.

"Have you ever been?" he asks.

"On a boat, yes, but not specifically for fishing."

"You would love my boat."

"*Your* boat?" I squeal. "You have your own boat?"

"Yup."

"What kind of boat?"

"A big one," he replies. As if that answers the question.

I sit up on the couch. "How big?" I ask hesitantly.

"Sixty feet or so."

I squeal again. "And it's yours? Not like your parents? But yours?"

"Yes," he answers like it's no big deal.

"Are you rich?" I wonder aloud. I figure this isn't the worst question I've asked today.

He's quiet a solid five minutes. In that time, I manage to convince myself that maybe this isn't a good idea. And then silently laugh at the absurdity of that because well, that connection. No denying that. Then he finally speaks. "Rich is a relative term."

"Good point." Sensing he doesn't want to talk about that anymore, I don't push him.

He clears his throat. "As much as I'm enjoying getting to know you, it's late, and I'm up very early for work in the morning."

I glance at the clock. Wow, it's after eleven!

"Yeah, okay," I concede. "Are you like off the grid while on your fishing trip?" I hope he doesn't hear the eagerness in my voice as I ask the question.

"Unfortunately yes," he utters with a sigh. Then in a lower

voice, he adds, "This may be the first time I'm bummed about that."

"You and me both," I concur. "Text me when you get back on Sunday, and we can make plans."

"Will do," he responds. "Ainsley?"

"Yeah?"

"Thanks for the kiss."

The line goes dead before I can respond. Way to leave a girl hanging and wanting more. So much more.

I decide to turn in for the night. After shutting off all the lights in the condo, I walk to my bedroom. I change into PJs, remove my makeup, brush my teeth, and then hop into bed.

I'm asleep before I can even think of getting myself off to the memory of the best first kiss I've ever had.

* * *

*W*hen I wake up, there's a text from Grayson.

Have a good day and rest of the weekend.

Ah, how sweet, I think.

Thanks. You too. See you Sunday. Hope you catch some fish

I spend all day Friday lounging on my couch, alternating between catching up on my shows, napping, and reading. It's nice to have a day off and since I caught up on laundry and housework earlier in the week, I can truly enjoy lounging without feeling guilty that I'm not doing anything.

Saturday passes slowly so when my mother texts me and invites me for dinner at their house with their friends, I reluctantly agree. My dad is an awesome cook, and while I like to think that I've gained some of his skills, I still have a lot to learn to keep up with him. Some of my favorite memories growing up are helping him in the kitchen, gathering ingredients, reading recipes, but mostly just laughing and having a good time.

As soon as I walk in the door, Dad tosses me sweet potatoes. "Grab a knife and cube these for me," he requests, moving to the stove where he's got two pots simmering. He's wearing my mom's apron around his waist even though he's got plenty of his own.

Placing the potatoes on the cutting board on the counter, I grab a knife from the knife block and pop a kiss on his cheek. "Hi, Dad. Good to see you." I laugh.

"Oh, hi back," my dad calls over to me after I've walked back to the counter. "How goes it?"

That's my dad for you.

"Smashing," I reply, chopping the ends off the sweet potatoes. "What are you cooking?"

"Stuffed turkey burgers, roasted veggies, sweet potatoes, and a salad. Mom was in charge of dessert." I look over to him, hoping he says what I've been drooling about since my mom mentioned dinner. Sensing me looking at him, he grins at me. "Like there was any doubt?" he asks.

"Phew." I wipe my arm across my forehead. "You never know. One time, she's going to switch it up on me, and I'll be so disappointed."

My mom makes one dinner and one dessert. That's it. She leaves the rest to my dad, which we are all grateful for.

My dad continues to dance his way around the kitchen, stirring, sautéing, forming turkey burgers. I chop the sweet potatoes and plop them on the cookie tray for him to season, all the while staying out of his way. When I'm done with all of them, I hear Dad say, "Grab me a beer from the fridge, will ya, Agee?"

My dad's been calling me that for as long as I can remember. It's his own nickname for me because I'm Ainsley Grace.

In the fridge, I find a variety of different beers in there. "Which one do you want?" I ask him, peeking my head from behind the door. "And why is there so much beer in here? Who's coming tonight anyway?"

"Newcastle," he states and then continues with, "The usual gang. The Millers, the Stephens, and the Lanes." He garbles the last name.

My breath catches and my heart leaps into my throat. No way I heard him correctly. "What?" I whisper into the fridge. I'm not sure I even want to turn around to face him. Even if it's just his parents, I don't know if I could handle seeing even them. Slowly, I grab the beer from the shelf and manage to shut the fridge door. I place the beer on the counter near my dad and go over to the table and have a seat. Once I sit down, I rest my elbows on the table and my head in my hands.

There's no way I would have agreed to dinner if my mother had told me who was coming, precisely the reason she didn't tell me. She's still holding out hope that Jordan and I will as she likes to say "find our way back to each other." No matter how many times I've tried to tell her it's never going to happen, she insists it will. In my head, I hear my brother's voice. *This is why you stick your tongue down random guy's throats. You've got something to prove to Mom.* I'd like to think he's wrong; it's been *one* random guy I've kissed. Random guys I've slept with? Well, that's another story. Arguing with myself, I know I didn't kiss Grayson to prove anything to anyone. It was about him.

Abandoning his cooking duties, my dad joins me at the table when he sees my reaction. "Agee, don't shut down." He moves my palms out of my face and tips my chin up with his fingers, to really gauge my reaction. My father knows the history with Jordan. All of it. He knows more than my mom, but she doesn't know that nor would she care.

In a quivering voice, I ask, "Why doesn't she get it? Why would she invite me when she knows they are coming?"

He shrugs; he doesn't have an answer. He's tried telling her to back off, but my mother has a mind of her own, especially when it comes to my relationships. Or one in particular.

I want to ask the question I need answered, but I don't want to know the answer. I can't bring myself to ask it.

He shakes his head, as if he knows what I'm going to ask. "He's not coming."

I let go of the breath I was holding. My dad wraps his arm around me and pulls me tightly into his chest. When I don't pull away, he lets go, commenting about finishing dinner. He places a kiss on the top of my head before making his way back to his cooking.

It's at that moment that my mother decides to come into the kitchen. At least I'm not crying.

She takes one look at me and asks, "What's wrong?"

My dad answers for me. "You didn't tell her the Lanes were coming." He doesn't even turn around. It's not necessarily accusatory but of course, that's how my mother takes it.

"Sheila is my friend, and I'm not going to not invite her to our get-togethers." She looks back over to me, a look of uncertainty and a scowl on her face, a look she's perfected over the years. "I hope you're still planning to stay."

"You could have at least mentioned they were coming," I reply to her.

"You wouldn't have come," she retorts. She comes over to the table where I'm sitting. I think she's going to sit down, but she just places her hands on an empty chair and stands there, waiting for my answer.

She's right. There's no way in hell I would have agreed to come, even for my father's cooking. I hate that she didn't tell me on purpose, and if I say I would have come, she would know I was lying. She always knows when I'm lying. My brother got away with shit all the time, practically lying his way through life, and she never once didn't believe him. I'm still not sure if it's because she thinks he walks on water or that she didn't care that he was lying to her. It's probably a combination of both.

I go with the truth, because it's what she wants to hear anyway, but I won't give her the satisfaction of saying she's right. "I wouldn't have come," I confirm, "but now that I'm here, I'm going to enjoy Dad's cooking." I push out of my seat and walk back over to where my dad is still busy tending to dinner. "Anything else I can do to help?" I ask him.

He shakes his head no. He glances up at the clock. "Everyone will be here in about fifteen minutes. Why don't you go outside and make sure the table and chairs are all set up?"

"Will do," I call out as I start outside. He knows everything's all set up; Kim Bradford wouldn't have it any other way. But he also just saved me from anymore of my mother's antics for the time being.

Once outside, I grab myself a beer from the cooler and take a seat at the table. The first swig of beer is always the best, and I relish it as it coats my throat. I lay my head back against the back of the chair and allow my eyes to close. The spring sun feels good on my face.

I hear the sliding doors open behind me. I don't open my eyes, listening for a clue as to who's joining me. When I hear the grill open, I know it's my dad. I open my eyes and tilt my head back down so I can watch him. Grilling is the one thing I hate to do. Every time I try, my food is either charred or undercooked, no matter how many lessons I get from my dad. At this point, I figure I'll just leave it up to him.

"Mom says you spoke to Drew the other day," my dad speaks, even though he's got his back to me.

"He tells her everything," I mumble. At that, my dad turns to face me. I know that he's heard what I've said even though I wasn't clear.

"You can't be surprised," he states, giving me an incredulous look.

"That's why I don't talk to him on regularly."

My brother and I used to be close. It was only the two of us growing up, him older than me by eighteen months. Since there was only a year between us in school, I would hang around him and his friends, and he was totally okay with it. Until Jordan got more than just interested in me. Considering how everything eventually played out, my relationship with Drew never really improved, despite our mother's attempts to rectify it. And by rectify it, I mean for me to smooth things over by taking all the blame. Sensing the pattern, yet? I sometimes wish I could work it out with him, but somehow my mother always gets in the way. If it were up to Drew and me, we could probably work out our differences because we're civil during the few times a year we see each other. Secretly, I love that he lives a plane ride away, and I don't have to see him all that often. We talk on the phone on rare occasions, like the other night, but that's about the extent of our relationship.

My thoughts about my brother are thankfully interrupted by the arrival of my parents' friends. Of course, Sheila and Fletcher Lane are right out in front of the group. I contemplate waiting until they come over to greet me rather than standing up, but I think better of it at the last minute. My mother expects me to always be on my best behavior, even at twenty-five years old.

I stand up and greet them with an awkward hug. I've never been their favorite person, and the feeling is mutual for me.

Sheila opens with, "So good to see you, Ainsley. Have you heard Jordan's engaged?" She fake smiles at me while her husband just stands there looking totally uncomfortable.

I feign enthusiasm back. "No, that's great news. Congratulations."

"It is great news. We just love Maggie so much. She fits right into our family…"

I can't even listen to her bullshit, so I cut her off. "That's wonderful. Excuse me, but I have to help my dad with something inside." I walk away from her, leaving her mid-sentence and mouth agape about Jordan's fiancée.

I huff as I make my way back inside. The rest of the party members have arrived, and I stop to give everyone more awkward hugs. I'm seriously considering forgoing my dad's burgers and feigning an illness. I'm not up to this tonight.

Grabbing my phone off the kitchen counter, I make my way into the living room and throw myself down on the couch. Pretty sure my mother would have a field day if she saw my legs draped over the couch, especially with my shoes on, but I'm beyond caring at this point.

Glancing at my phone, I see a text from Grayson. I immediately sit straight up, and my heart beats faster. I can barely unlock the phone with my sweaty palms. I realize I haven't been this excited for a text message in a long time. Especially from a guy. Opening up Messages, I can't help but smile at his message.

> So, I'm back early. We had a little trouble with the boat. I wondered if you wanted to get breakfast in the morning instead of hanging out tomorrow night.

> Sure, that works. What time and where are you thinking?

I don't expect him to respond right away. His text was sent over an hour ago. However, the alert sounds within a few minutes.

> There's a cool café on Larchmont Ave. Have you ever been? 9 a.m.?

> Never been but that sounds great. See you then.

I don't want to stop texting him, but I also don't want him to think I'm one of those girls requiring constant interaction. I waver back and forth with my decision for a bit before deciding that tomorrow morning will be here soon enough.

I'm just about to get up and go back and join the party— because I'm here so I might as well suck it up and try to enjoy myself, or at least the food—when another text comes through.

> See you then

Thinking I've made the right decision, because there's the brush-off for the night, another text immediately follows.

How was your day?

Debating on how to answer that question, I first settle back in on the couch. I figure that my mother won't come looking for me until it's time to eat.

It wasn't too bad. Not as exciting as being on a boat, but I survived. Now I just have to suffer through a stupid dinner party at my parents' house that I agreed to attend. (Beats head against the wall)

I kick off my shoes and make myself comfortable on the couch while I wait for his response. It takes a few minutes, not that I'm counting or anything. I try to focus on what's going on outside, but from my position, I don't really have a good angle to see.

My phone finally pings.

Wow, that sounds enthralling.

I begin to type my response but before I can finish, another one comes in.

I wish there was a sarcasm font. You should ditch the party and meet me.

I reread his message about five times, unsure if the sarcasm comment applies to the entire message or the one he sent before. I quickly erase what I was going to write, and start another comment. Another text comes in from him. Not so much the man of few words from the other night.

Totally serious about the last part of the message

I really should stay, although thanks for the offer.

I push up off the couch, pop my shoes back on my feet, and

practically run to the back porch. Knowing my dad will take the news better, I hunt the backyard for him. Spotting him showing off the garden, I push open the door and go outside. I ignore the incoming text messages for a minute.

When I get over to my dad, he's talking about his tomatoes. God, he loves his tomatoes.

Waiting for a break in his conversation, once he stops talking, I tell him, "Dad, I'm not feeling so great. I'm going to take off and get some rest. Hope that's okay. Save me a burger please." I place a kiss on his cheek, ignoring the shocked look on his face. As I walk away, without so much as a wave or a goodbye to the others standing there, I call out, "Tell Mom I'll call her soon. Love you."

Once I have made it to my car in the driveway, I climb behind the wheel and read Grayson's message.

> Oh, okay. Well, breakfast it is then. Have a good night.

I smile, pulling down the visor and flipping up the mirror. I look presentable enough, but I contemplate going home to change and put on some makeup. It takes me all of thirty seconds to decide that for once, I'm actually okay with the casual look.

I text him back.

> What, you didn't get the sarcasm in my message? Where am I meeting you?

I wait a few minutes for his response, getting just a little antsier with each minute that passes. Finally the phone pings.

> The billiard hall on White Ave.

I pull away without even responding. A huge smile comes over my face; my night just significantly improved.

4

GRAYSON

*D*riving to the pool hall, I really can't believe she said she'd meet me. I won't lie and say I wasn't hoping she would say yes when I asked, but there was a part of me that didn't really think she would.

I also won't say I'm disappointed the boat had issues, so we had to cut the trip short. Normally, I love being out on the water, away from the daily grind of life. Even my buddy, Caleb, could tell something was off with me. Being a man of few words, he didn't say much. When he did talk, it meant something. And he knows me well enough to be able to read my emotions and call me out on any bullshit I may try to throw his way.

It didn't even faze me that not only would we have to cut the trip short but that the part was going to be ridiculously expensive to fix. When I didn't give a shit about either, he knew.

"Dude, who is she?" he asked me. He was driving the boat, and I was sitting across from him.

I didn't answer him right away. He looked over and stared at me, not in a judgmental way; he just wanted an answer. It was a simple question, but the answer was loaded.

I sighed. "Someone I met on Thursday night." I didn't give anymore.

He would ask or wait for me to give him more. We got along so well because we were so much alike.

He stared straight ahead, keeping his gaze focused on the water. He took a swig of his beer and looked back over at me. "And?" he questioned.

"I can't explain it. She fucking kissed me. Out of nowhere. And damn, that kiss." I took a breath, remembering the way her tongue felt against mine. I felt myself getting hard, so I turned and looked out at the water.

"You gonna see her again?" I heard him ask.

"Tomorrow," I replied, running my hands through my hair. I looked back over to him. He wore a huge smirk on his face. "What?"

"Yeah, like that's going to happen now that you are back early."

I thought about what he said. Of course, it occurred to me to ask her if she was free, but it's last-minute on a Saturday night. What were the odds she wasn't busy?

I realized he was still talking. "Come with us to the pool hall tonight."

"How do you even have plans for tonight? We were supposed to be on the boat still." Caleb might be a man of few words, but he had a social calendar like no one else I knew. Including Bella.

He gave me a crazy look. "If I'm not on the boat, it's a given I'm at the bar or the pool hall," he explained.

"Right."

It couldn't hurt to ask her. I could still join the guys if she couldn't go. It had been a while since I've played.

I realize I'm about to drive past the pool hall and quickly make the turn into the lot. Pulling into a spot, I think about the fact that I have no clue what kind of car Ainsley drives. I look around the lot. There aren't many cars because it's still early for a Saturday night. I spot Caleb's truck right away; it stands out no matter where he parks it. It looks like he's already inside.

Getting out of my car, I'm about to send Ainsley a text when I notice an older model Honda CRV pulling in. Glimpsing at the driver, my heart starts to beat faster, and my palms sweat as I notice it's her driving. She sees me and gives me a small smile and a wave. She pulls into a spot near me. I start to walk over to her, and once she's parked, she hops out of the car and starts walking my way.

She's dressed way more casually tonight, and it suits her. Her hair is pulled back off her face in what looks to be a low ponytail. Her jeans are the skinny, fitted type, and they work well on her. Her light sweater keeps dipping off one shoulder as she walks, but she keeps reaching up to put it back in place. The flats on her feet don't give her any more height, so when she reaches where I'm waiting, I've got about eight inches on her.

Before I can think about making any type of move, she throws her arms around my waist and pulls herself in closer to me. She lays her head on my chest. She murmurs, "Thank you," as she closes her eyes. I wrap my arms around her, pulling her in tighter to me.

"For what?"

Opening her eyes, she pulls her head away from my chest. She looks up at me, her green eyes shining and full of hope. It's then I realize she's barely wearing any makeup. As if to confirm my initial thoughts from the other night, the natural look showcases her beauty more so than all the caked-on makeup. A piece of hair falls in her face, so I brush it away gently as she answers me. "For saving me from my mother and her dinner party. Although I was looking forward to my dad's stuffed burgers..." she replies, then trails off.

"Are you hungry?" I ask her. There's not much food served at the pool hall; mostly only fried appetizers.

"I could go for some food, but let's play pool for a bit and then get food." She smiles at me, this one reaching her eyes.

"Damn, you've got a great smile." The words are out of my mouth before I realize what I'm saying.

"Thanks," she responds, smiling even bigger. She pulls out of my arms completely and grabs my hand and starts walking to the pool hall. Her hand matches the feel of mine, a bit clammy, but neither of us seems to mind.

Once inside, there's no line at the desk, so we reserve a table. Since there's no food or drinks allowed by the tables, we forgo both of those for now and head to the back room. Three of the twelve tables are occupied, Caleb and some of our buddies at one of them.

After sinking his shot, Caleb waves me over. I put down the ball rack on table four and grab Ainsley's hand and walk over.

"So, did you know your friends were going to be here?" she asks nervously, her expression matching her voice. She slows down a bit behind me, as she tries to tug her hand out of mine.

"Yes, but they don't bite," I tell her to calm her nerves, not letting go of her hand. Looking back at her, she gives me a weak smile. I stop walking for a minute and turn my body to face her. Putting my hands on her shoulders, I ask her, "Where's the girl that kissed me when we met?"

"Apparently I left her at home," she counters.

Not knowing where my boldness is coming from, I lean in and whisper in her ear, "Bring her out to play."

She sucks in a breath, mutters "fuck," drawing out the last part of it, and then barrels past me. I watch as she walks over to where my friends are and starts introducing herself. Caleb raises his brows in my direction, and he gives me a slight nod of his approval. When she gets to Natalie, Caleb's girlfriend, Natalie immediately pulls her into a hug. Stumbling ever so slightly, Ainsley returns the hug. I start over to them and walk a little faster when I see Natalie speaking into her ear. Ainsley's smile never fades, so I take that as a good sign.

When I finally make my way over to the group, Natalie pulls me in for a hug. "Good to see you, Gray," she says. She lowers her voice so that no one else overhears. "I've got a good vibe about this one. Make it work." She pulls out of my embrace and gives me a sweet smile.

I love Natalie; she's the other sister I never had. She's such the opposite of Caleb, but for them, it totally works. I've actually known her longer than I've known Caleb; I set them up on a date. Well, it was technically Bella, but I'm pretty sure I suggested it. I trust her judgment implicitly; she's got great people skills, even with first impressions.

"Thanks, Nat," I tell her. "Glad to have your boy back early?" I glance behind me at Caleb. He's focused on his game, pool stick tucked close to him as he watches Rich line up his shot.

Natalie follows my gaze. "I'll be glad later tonight."

After she winks at me, I pop a kiss on the top of her head. "He's ready for you," I quip.

"Oh to be a fly on the wall while you two are out fishing," she retorts with a laugh.

"You know the invitation is always open to you. Come be a fly."

She shakes her head and gags. "No thanks. Well, unless you find me someone to be a fly with." She motions her head over at Ainsley, who has taken a seat on one of the high stools near their table.

I smile at Natalie. "I'll work on it," I say, and then start toward where Ainsley sits. I'm not about to get ahead of myself on the third day of knowing the girl.

As I make my way over, Ainsley pulls her attention from the game to me. She gestures me to her stool. I stand in front of it and put my hands on her knees. Her legs spread open, inviting me closer, and I step in between her legs. She brings her legs into me, squeezing my thighs with her knees.

"I didn't ask if you played pool."

Even though most of her hair is pulled back in the ponytail, she twirls the one strand that's fallen out around her fingers. She lets it fall out of her fingers. "I wouldn't have come if I didn't," she responds.

"Well, let's play then." I take a step back and then lift her off the chair. I let her lead us to the table, where I rack the balls. She picks out a cue for herself and then leans her hip against the table waiting for me. "You want to break?"

"No, I'll leave that up to you."

Grabbing a stick from the holder, I chalk up the tip and then step behind the table. I line up my shot and shoot the cue ball. It hits the pyramid at the angle I want, sending the fifteen balls spiraling out in all different directions. The three-ball slightly bounces off the far left corner before falling into the pocket. Looking for my next shot, I walk around the table, nudging Ainsley as I pass her. She's not fazed at all, just continues to watch me as I line up my next move.

I eye the shot, but at the last minute, the cue ball misses its mark. "Your turn," I call out to her.

I watch her as she moves around the table. As she passes me, her hips sway just a little more than usual as she makes the move more exaggerated. After what seems like five minutes, she gets in position to shoot. I look at her body position and the angle of the shot and am about to comment when she brings back the cue stick and makes contact with the cue ball. I watch as the cue ball hits its intended mark, as two striped balls are struck and make their way to opposite corners, both falling into the pockets.

As she makes her way around to me again to set up her next shot, she stops when she gets to me, and looks up, a wicked gleam in her eyes. "You were going to say?" she asks with a smirk.

My jaw drops, as I realize that not only is she calling me out on the fact that I was going to suggest she not play that move, but also the fact that she's a serious competitor. Or a lucky shot. That's yet to be determined.

I go with the latter. "That was luck. Let's see what else you've got."

As if stepping up to my challenge, she walks to the opposite side of the table. She looks at the different angles of the balls to see which way to play it. Again, she lines up a shot I would never have taken yet somehow manages to sink another ball.

"Still think it's luck?" she questions. "Shall I keep going?" She bats her eyes at me. It's almost enough for me to go up behind her and throw her down on the table. Almost. I still have a tiny bit of restraint left with this girl. For the moment.

"You've got four more stripes to play. Think you can get them all in the pockets?" I ask, goading her.

She stares me down. "Are you asking if I think I can get them all in the pockets before you get to play again or just in general?"

I gulp. Dude, she's got some balls.

Not backing down, I walk over to where she's standing. I lay my cue stick down on the table, careful not to touch any of the balls in play. Looking her in the eyes, in my most gravelly voice, I say, "Four shots. Four stripes in the pockets. Think you can do it?"

She holds my gaze for a few minutes before she speaks. "Yep." She backs away from me slowly, not letting her gaze fall from mine. "Watch me," she hurls my way before pulling her gaze away from mine.

I'm kinda stuck standing where I am, entranced by not only her beauty, but also the confidence she exudes. And suddenly I have to know if she has this confidence in the bedroom. This girl is like no other girl I've known, which is both exciting and fucking terrifying at the same time.

Realizing she hasn't taken a shot yet, I pull myself out of my thoughts and look at her. She's standing with her hands on her hips, a look of exasperation on her face. "Kindly remove your cue stick from the table," she coos when she knows she finally has my attention.

I glance down and realize that I never picked the stick back up. I quickly remove it from the table and as soon as it's out of her way, she sets to work.

She takes one shot from where she stands and sinks two more balls. She makes her way around the table, practically shoving me out of the way when she gets to me. She starts to line up her next shot, but thinks better of it, and moves to a new position. Almost instinctively, I nod.

"Thanks for the approval," she declares, not even taking her eyes off the table. She cranks back the cue stick and hits the cue ball dead center, sending it on its way to barely nudge one of the striped balls into the middle pocket. There's one ball left but really no shot. She eyes the position of the last ball and where the cue ball ended up. Planning out her attack, she steps around the table. It takes her a few minutes to find the right angle, and even after she's decided on the shot, she changes it up one last time.

I glance up to see Natalie watching us from her table. She's not playing, but the guys still are. Her eyes are glued to Ainsley's actions, her jaw dropped in disbelief at what she's witnessing. I shrug my shoulders and give her a crooked smile.

I look back at our table to hear the smack of the cue ball as it makes contact with the last remaining striped ball. The angle appears off, and I think there's no way that it's going to go in. However, at the very last second, the ball finds its way into the pocket.

Without missing a beat, Ainsley lines up the shot for the eight-ball. "Corner pocket," she declares and takes the shot. Color me super impressed when the eight-ball falls into the intended mark.

Ainsley carefully places her cue stick on the table and sidles up to me. She grabs mine out of my hand, places it next to hers, and reaches up to shut my open jaw. Standing on tippy-toes, she pulls my head down a little so she can speak directly in my ear. "Found the girl from the other night. Can you handle it?"

Nope, not even a little.

I crash my lips to hers.

5

AINSLEY

I should have anticipated the kiss. It's not like I didn't want him to kiss me. I so did, so many times before he actually made his move. But when he finally made his move, he caught me off guard. In the best possible way.

His lips crash to mine. He doesn't even hesitate before his tongue finds its way into my mouth. I part my lips for it, almost as if I can't wait for it to get into my mouth. He massages my tongue with his, but not in the way he started the kiss. It's gentler this time, until I kick it up a notch.

Somehow my hands find his neck, and his find my backside, just above the waist, but soon his hands find their way up and he entwines his fingers in my hair. He tugs gently, all the while his tongue is inside my mouth.

He's managed to turn us so that my back is now up against the pool table. I find myself being lifted off the ground, and he sits my ass on the table. He plants himself in between my thighs, like earlier in the night. He pauses the kiss, just enough time to turn his hat around on his head, but then his lips are back on mine. This time, he pulls my bottom lip into his mouth and tugs gently. A small moan escapes my lips, and his dark eyes go a little wilder. He drags his tongue along my lip in his mouth, and then his tongue is back into my mouth. I lick the underside of his tongue with mine as my lip slips out of his.

I pull away for a minute, to catch my breath. My arms are still wrapped loosely around his neck, his exploring my backside, the area around my waist. At first when I pull away, he mumbles, "Fuck," and I think he's mad. I'm about to say something when his face softens the slightest bit and he adds, "Girl, what the hell are you doing to me?" He brings his forehead down to meet mine.

A small giggle escapes me. When my gaze finds his, his face stays serious, so I whisper, "Hell if I know, but the feeling's mutual."

He slowly removes his arms from my backside and backs up the slightest bit, causing my arms to unlatch from his neck and fall to his shoulders. Making no more attempts to move away from me, his face loses some of the seriousness as he begins to speak. "Where the fuck did you learn to play like that?"

I smile. "My brother. We've had a pool table in our basement for as long as I can remember and when he deemed me old enough to play with him, he taught me how to play the game. It probably helps that I can see the different angles as math equations. Even my brother wasn't expecting that part of my talent. He would watch, just as you did, as I would line up shots that he didn't agree with or think wouldn't work. He was more vocal about it than you were, until he realized my shots always worked and learned not to question me." I stop talking. If I continue, I either won't be able to stop or I'll get too reflective about my brother. And I'm not going there with Grayson right now.

He raises his eyebrows at me in disbelief. "You see every shot as a math equation?" I nod. "Are you some sort of math geek?"

There was no judgment in his question, and I think it actually turned him on a bit more.

I contemplate my answer for a minute. "Geek" can be taken in so many ways. I go with, "If the shoe fits."

He lets that sink in for a minute. Then he leans in to me and in that damn gravelly voice I heard for the first time earlier this evening, he rasps, "I bet you were the cutest geek of the bunch."

I wish he weren't standing in between my legs because I really need to close them. He must sense this since he backs himself away from me. He turns his hat back around, and I watch as the wheels appear to be turning in his head.

"You want to play again?" I ask, hopping down from the table.

"I don't know," he replies honestly. Looking down at the ground, he adds, "All you are going to do is kick my ass, although I have to admit, it's quite the turn-on."

I'm glad he sees it as a turn-on. Most guys hate that I can kick their ass. "I can play lefty," I suggest coyly.

He leers over at me. "Sure, why not?" he says with a shrug. "Rack 'em up."

I re-rack the balls and when he makes no motion to break them, I do the honors. Playing lefty isn't as easy as righty, so I only manage to break the balls up; none of them find their way into the pockets. "Your turn."

There's a perfect shot lined up for him; he easily shoots the first ball into the hole. I watch as he walks around the table, contemplating his next move. From my viewpoint, I can easily see a few moves he could start with. Deciding I'd much rather study him than the table, I ogle him up and down. His jeans sit low on his hips, and when he bends down to take the shot, his shirt rides up, revealing a toned stomach. He's wearing long sleeves so it's hard to judge how his arms look. His chiseled jaw sports a few days of scruff, probably because of being on the boat. There's a little more of it than the other night, although it wasn't rough when he kissed me. His hair is hidden beneath his Mariners hat, which also hides his forehead. His face is serious as he lines up his next shot. Again, he easily shoots one into the pocket.

Just as I'm thinking I won't have a shot this game, Natalie comes up to our table and when she begins to speak, it throws him a bit and the cue ball misses its intended mark.

"Shit, sorry Gray," she apologizes when she senses what

happened. She saunters up behind him and wraps her arms around his waist and lays her head on his back. Even though I know she's with Caleb, my body stiffens the slightest bit, although Grayson doesn't flinch. I've never been jealous over a guy before, and this one doesn't even belong to me. Yet, I find my insides start to boil with how comfortable she looks with him and how he allows it.

"What's up, Nat?" he asks her, not bothering to turn around.

"The other guys are almost finished and want to know if you and Ainsley want to go grab some food. Caleb guessed you hadn't eaten anything yet."

Grayson looks over at me. "You hungry?"

"As soon as I clear the table, I will be," I tell him. I look around at the balls, choosing the best position to start. I lean down, line up the cue stick with the ball, and tap the ball with the stick. It moves toward the intended ball, hitting it just as I planned, rolling a few inches before dropping into the pocket.

Natalie unwraps herself from Grayson, staring intently as I set up my next move. I see her look over at Grayson who just shrugs his shoulders and smirks. I can't help but give him a smirk back, as I make my next move. This time, the cue ball hits one of my balls and one of his, but as planned, his just rolls further away from the pocket as mine falls in.

"Wow. I would never have thought that shot would have worked," Natalie says in awe.

"That's nothing," Grayson states. "You should see her play righty."

Natalie's eyes practically bug out of her head. She walks closer to me, careful not to get in my way. She watches as I set up my next shot. She shakes her head, like she knows it's not going to work. What she can't see is that it will work, as long as the cue ball hits the purple one at the exact angle I'm shooting for. It's a little harder to shoot lefty, but I've never let that stop me before, especially with an audience. And well, a guy.

I pull my stick back and let go. The stick hits the ball just where I aimed which causes the reaction I want with the purple ball ending up in the pocket.

"Damn." Then Natalie looks over at me. "You realize Grayson is not only competitive as hell, but he's also a sore loser, right?"

My face falls a bit. I know I don't know the guy well, but he doesn't seem like either of those things. The fact I already kicked his ass once and he agreed to play again tells me that he can't be that competitive nor that much of a sore loser. When she throws her head back and starts cackling, I realize she's totally kidding. She comes over closer to me. She lowers her voice so that he can't hear what she's saying, even though he's watching her with hawk eyes.

"He's really not either of those things." She leans in and continues in my ear, "Until you get him into the bedroom."

What the hell, I think? She's been with him in the bedroom? My eyes shoot over to Grayson, even though he has no clue what she's just told me. I know it shouldn't bother me in the slightest, but for some odd reason, it really does. Obviously he's been with other girls; I'm no virgin by any means. And first impressions of Natalie are favorable. Maybe it was the way she was hanging all over him earlier and looked so comfortable.

Grayson looks over at us, standing with his pool cue tucked against his side. His face has a confused look on it. Before I know what's happening, he's walking over to us. "Whatever she told you, it's most likely not true." He glares over at Natalie.

"Who me?" she asks, putting on an innocent look. She looks back over to her friends at the other table. I follow her gaze and see that they have packed up their table and are getting antsy. "Are you guys almost done? It looks like Caleb and the gang are ready to get going." She motions her head over to point to her friends. Caleb is incessantly beckoning her over.

"We'll meet you. Where are you going? The diner?" Grayson asks. The eight-ball and some stripes are still in play on the table.

"Yep," Natalie answers. She walks back up to me and grabs me into her, wrapping her arms around me. Caught off guard, I hesitantly stiffen but quickly relax as she tightens her grip around me. She pats me on the back before she pulls away. She looks over at Grayson, who is again watching us intently. "He's really a great guy. And I have no idea what he's like in the bedroom, despite what I said before. He's always been like a brother to me. Maybe one day you can fill me in." She winks at me. "See you at the diner."

She walks away from me, leaving me standing there a bit shocked. She hugs Grayson and whispers something in his ear. At her words, a genuine smile creeps onto his face. Seeing his smile makes me smile in return. He really is handsome, especially when he smiles like that.

Once Natalie has walked away, Grayson comes back over to me. I'm leaning on the pool table, and he comes up close next to me. "You ready to call it a game and get some food?"

I nod. He takes the cue stick out of my hand and walks both of the sticks back to the holder on the wall. I start to collect the balls and rack them into the triangle. Once he's back, he sidles up behind me, boxing me in so I can't move. He puts his arms on the table and leans his body into mine, pushing me further into the table. My heart beats a little faster the closer he gets to me. He lays his head on my shoulder and sighs; it about does me in.

I don't know what he's doing, but I don't want him to stop, nor do I want to move, not that I can actually move. My pulse continues to race because not only is he this close to me, but his breathing is labored. It's doing things to my body that I haven't felt in a long time. I like it and at the same time, it scares the shit out of me because I hardly know him. However, none of that stops me from turning my body around.

As soon as I start to move, I feel his head shift and once I'm around, he's got a confused look on his face. "I just needed to see your face," I tell him. His lips turn up into the slightest smile. I run my fingers along his chin, his stubble tickling the tiniest bit.

He drops his forehead and gently leans it on mine but keeps his arms planted on the table, still boxing me in. "I don't want to share you tonight," he voices out of nowhere.

"You mean at the diner?" I ask, somewhat bewildered. He nods. "I know what you mean. But, I'm also curious to get to know your friends. Hell, I want to get to know *you* more." I don't add what I'm really thinking which is that I want to get to know him more intimately. His mind, his body, all of him. I shake my head slightly, to shake away that thought. It's so unlike me to be this interested in getting to know someone intimately this early in the relationship. Because getting to know Grayson involves getting to know all of him; it's not just hooking up.

He must notice my head shaking because he tips my chin up so that I'm looking at him. "What?" he asks. "What are you thinking?"

I decide to go all in. "I'm thinking after our dinner, since we already have plans for breakfast tomorrow, I figure what's the use in going home by myself tonight?" As soon as the words are out of my mouth, I regret them. For about ten seconds. And then I realize there's nothing more I want to do than go home with Grayson. I want to see his house, I want to know where he sleeps, I want to learn what makes him tick. I want to soak him up every which way I can.

His brown eyes go wide. He takes in a deep breath, slowly lets it out, and murmurs, "That can be arranged, darling." He pecks my cheek with his lips and pulls away from me. He grabs the balls and other supplies and starts walking toward the entrance of the pool hall.

It takes me a minute to get my feet to move. Not only did I just tell this man, a man I've known all of forty-eight hours, that I don't want to go home by myself, he agreed to it. As I watch him walk away, his jeans hugging his tight ass, I realize that it's more than just a physical connection we share. It's like he's reached inside of my heart and my soul and grabbed a hold of them both.

I finally will my feet to start moving. I catch up to Grayson as he's paying for our game time. Once he's paid, he grabs my hand in his and we walk out of the pool hall hand-in-hand. In the parking lot, he looks at me. "What should we do about your car?"

I like his take-charge attitude. "My apartment is on the way to the diner. We can drop it off there, I can grab some stuff, and then go meet your friends?" I pose it as a question.

"I'll follow you," he says, nodding.

He walks me to my car, not once letting go of my hand. Once at my car, he brings my hand up to his mouth and ever so gently kisses the back of it. He tugs my keys out of my hand and hits the button to unlock the doors. He opens my door for me and leans against the open door, waiting for me to get in. I climb inside and start to buckle. Before closing the door, he leans in and his lips meet mine. He pulls them away before I can even kiss him back. At my puzzled look, his lips curl up into a devious smile as he explains, "There's time for more later."

I can't help as my own lips curl up into a smile as he closes my door and walks over to his car.

At my apartment, I quickly throw together a bag of PJs and clothes for the next day. I grab a toothbrush, my hairbrush, and my makeup bag from the bathroom and toss them in the bag. Grayson waits for me in my living room. I didn't exactly invite him in any further, but he seems content just waiting on the couch. When I get closer to him, he stands and then grabs the bag from my hands. Taking a look inside, he hands me back my makeup bag.

"You are way prettier without this crap," he says as an explanation when he reads the confusion on my face.

"How do you even know what's inside it?"

"I have a sister, who has a girlfriend. Trust me. I know it's full of makeup. Makeup you don't need." To prove he's right, he grabs it back from my hands and starts to unzip the bag. He rifles through it. "Yep. Not necessary," he adds. He shoves it back in my hands and tells me to go put it away.

I take it back from him and walk it back down the hall. Truth of the matter is I hate makeup. I've never been really good about knowing what colors suit me nor how to apply it correctly.

When I've returned, he's still got my bag in my hands. "Ready? Nat just texted wondering where we are."

"Let's go." I lock up behind us, and the minute the door is locked, he grabs my hand in his again. *I could get used to this,* I think to myself. Aloud, I ask him how long he's known Natalie.

"More than half my life," he explains. "I think we met in fourth grade, maybe third, I don't remember exactly. It was shortly after we moved here to Maine. I found her at recess when she fell off the swing, and we've been friends ever since."

Even though I know Natalie told me they've never been intimate, I needed his confirmation of it. "You ever have feelings for her?" I throw out there casually.

He stops walking in the middle of the hallway. "You're kidding, right?"

I shake my head. "No?" I squeak out.

He laughs and shakes his head. "No, as much as I love her, as a friend, she and I wouldn't ever work romantically. Not that we ever tried to know for sure. She's like my other sister, and the feelings are mutual on her part." He puts his hands on my shoulder and his eyes find mine. "I think your jealously is cute."

"I'm not jealous," I stammer. He's so right. I am jealous, and I wonder if I have the right to be envious of their relationship.

He laughs at me with a "yeah, right." "There's nothing to worry about with Nat. Besides, she and Caleb are together."

"Okay, just checking." I start walking down the hall to the exit, a sigh of relief escaping my lips.

When we get outside, he leads me to his car, tosses the bag in the back seat and climbs into the driver's seat.

"You aren't going to open the door for me this time?" I tease. He starts to climb out, but I stop him. "I'm only kidding. I'm perfectly capable of opening up my own door." I climb up into the car. He starts it up, the engine choking a bit, and pulls out of the spot.

On the way to the diner, I learn that he's twenty-eight, Bella is three years younger than him, making her my age, his parents don't live in Maine any longer, and he's a Scorpio. I ask him a lot of questions and get a lot of one-word answers. It's a bit like pulling teeth to not only get him to answer at all, but to elaborate as well. Part of the reason I ask about his life is because I don't want to share about my own. He manages to get in a few general questions: what I do for work (adjunct college professor), if I have any siblings (just the brother who lives in Illinois), and if I grew up here (born and bred).

When we pull up to the diner, after parking, he quickly hops out of the car before I can get out so that he can open my door for me.

"Such the gentleman." He gives me that smile that I'm learning to adore. As if he can't get enough of me, he grabs my hand as we walk inside. It's crazy to me how much I already crave his touch and there's no weirdness between the two of us. Whatever IS going on, it's totally comfortable and not forced. I'm almost tempted to ask if we can skip dinner and just go back to his place, but in reality, I do want to get to know his friends more. And well, I'm starving.

We find Caleb and Natalie huddled with their heads together in a back booth, sitting across from each other. Grayson gently pulls me behind him as he leads me over to the table. When we get there, he just stands there and clears his throat. Natalie breaks her glance from Caleb and looks up at us. Giving us a big smile, she moves out of the bench and takes a seat next to Caleb on his bench. Once she's vacated the bench, Grayson motions for me to climb in.

"I'll be right back," I tell him, suddenly needing a breather before I sit even closer to him. I leave him standing there, mouth agape as I hurry to the bathroom. Inside, I hide away in a stall, and soon afterward, I hear the bathroom door open and close.

"It's Natalie," I hear from behind the door.

"I'll be right out."

"Are you okay? Did something happen?" There's a hint of genuine concern in her voice.

I shake my head and when I realize that she can't see me, I respond quietly, "No."

"Which question are you answering?" she asks in that same voice.

"Nothing happened. I just needed a moment." I flush the toilet and open the door. She's standing in front of the door, a look of concern on her face. Before I know what's happening, she's wrapping me in her arms, enveloping me in a hug. From out of nowhere, tears form in the corners of my eyes. I really can't explain why. Not understanding any of my emotions, I squeeze her tighter and then go limp in her arms. She pulls her head back so she can gauge my state.

"Oh, sweetie. What is it? What's wrong?" she asks, worry adding to the look of concern on her face.

I shrug, then laugh. "I have no fucking clue! I've never felt this way. It's like, I'm overwhelmed and consumed by something, but hell if I know what it is." I wipe my eyes, wiping away the one tear that has slipped out. "I've known him less than forty-eight hours. How the hell do I feel this way about him?"

She smiles. "Don't take this the wrong way." Taking a deep breath, she continues, "I love Grayson; he's a great guy, but he doesn't make everyone feel this way. In your case, I think it's a great thing. Girls don't make him feel the way you make him feel. Not only can I see it for myself, but Caleb let a few things slip that they discussed on the trip."

My ears perk up at her confession. All of it. I try hard to grasp the meaning of everything she just told me. I don't even know which part to focus on.

"You must think I'm an idiot," I manage to blubber out.

"Nonsense." She laughs, shaking her head. "If the two of you feel this way after such a short amount of time, I can't wait to see how you feel in a few months."

I think about what she says, but I don't allow myself to go a few months down the road. Yet. I need to get through the night first.

Natalie wraps her arms around me one last time. "Come on, our boys are waiting for us out there."

I quickly wash my hands, all the while thinking about her statement. "Our boys" has a nice ring to it, something I could totally be on board with about Grayson. I smile at that thought as I head back out to our table.

6

GRAYSON

I'm not going to lie and say that I wasn't disappointed when Ainsley ran off to the bathroom. I thought she was feeling the same connection I was and if she wasn't, I wish she had said something. Without prodding, Natalie jumped up and followed her to the bathroom, making me appreciate her that much more.

When Natalie comes back, alone at first, she doesn't say anything, but her smile conveys what I need to know. She gives my hand a gentle squeeze before pecking Caleb on the cheek.

Since I'm so focused on my two friends, I don't notice at first when Ainsley comes sauntering back up. She's got a smile plastered on her face, and she slides herself into the booth next to me. Following suit, she pecks my cheek, and when I turn to look at her, she winks at me. I reach over and pull her in to me, and she melts into my side. I place a kiss on the top of her head, inhaling her scent. She reaches her hand down under the table and grabs my dick and gives it the tiniest squeeze. In my ear, she whispers, "Later tonight," and it takes all of my self-control to hold it together. Thankfully, Caleb asks Ainsley a question and her attention is drawn to him.

I quickly adjust myself under the table. When I look over,

Natalie's got the biggest smirk on her face. My cheeks redden, knowing that she witnessed that entire interaction. I reach into my water glass and grab an ice cube to toss in her direction.

"Hey!" she yells.

"Dude," Caleb adds, his attention drawn to Natalie when she yells.

I shrug. "She started it."

"She started it," Natalie accosts, pointing to Ainsley.

Ainsley smirks and shrugs her shoulders. God, is it possible to like her even more? Natalie whispers something in Caleb's ear and in turn, he brings his hand up and requests a high five from Ainsley, which she obliges. He flashes her his boyish smile, the one he used to give to women he was trying to hit on before Natalie came into the picture. Before I say anything, I notice that it doesn't do anything for Ainsley so I let it slide this time. All she does is smile back at him, but it's not the one of hers that makes my heart beat faster.

Natalie asks, "So what was wrong with the boat?" just as the waitress drops off the appetizers Caleb and I ordered while the girls were in the bathroom.

"The heater." I make myself a plate of food.

She raises her eyebrows. "You cut your trip short because you had no heat?" she asks incredulously.

Caleb snaps his head over to her. The look he gives her shuts her up.

Ainsley takes in the exchange and though she's clearly confused, she doesn't ask any questions. She just continues to munch on the nachos we ordered.

"I'll call Ben on Monday and see when he can get a new one ordered and installed. It's probably going to cost an arm and a leg, but it is what it is." I take a slow sip of my water when I finish speaking.

"When has the price of something stopped you from getting what you want?" Natalie asks.

"NAT!" Caleb hisses out.

She looks at him. "What? What is up with you two?" She shakes her head but appears to give up. And changes the subject. "So, how are the plans for Bella's wedding coming?"

I groan. "I don't know. I try to stay out of all of that and leave it up to Bella and Kylie. I told them just to tell me when and where I need to show up and what to wear, and I'll be there."

She nods. "I told Caleb that we are getting a hotel room for the night of the wedding so we don't have to drive home."

"Yeah, that's probably a good plan. Get me a bed. I may need a place to crash."

"No man. Not happening," Caleb grumbles. "Get your own room." He gives me the stink eye.

"When's the wedding?" Ainsley asks.

"About four months." I don't ask aloud if she wants to be my date. I can always add her as it gets closer.

"Are they excited?"

"Yes. It's practically all Bella talks about. I'm surprised she didn't mention it the other night."

"You've already met Bella?" Natalie shrieks.

Ainsley nods. "She's the one who sent the drink over to me at the bar the other night."

I look at her dumbfounded. "You knew she sent it?"

"Of course I knew. I just didn't know why she sent it because she appeared to be hanging all over you so I couldn't understand why she would send it on your behalf."

Natalie looks over at me. "Wow, Gray. Getting your sister to pick up the ladies for you now, huh?" She laughs at my expense.

Luckily the girl sitting next to me doesn't join in, but rather inquires, "Gray?"

"It's what his friends call him," Natalie supplies. "Well, and Bella and Kylie, too."

"Oh," is all she manages.

There's a lull in the conversation and somehow my hand finds her thigh. She doesn't even flinch when I start rubbing it up and down. I'm still shocked at how natural all of this feels, especially so soon.

Over dinner, the four of us continue to chat and get to know Ainsley a little better. She seems relaxed and appears to really enjoy herself, and the conversation flows effortlessly even though she doesn't know the history of our friendship. She asks questions here and there and lights up when Natalie tells stories from when we were younger. As usual, Caleb stays quiet, only joining in on things he deems important or to argue with Natalie about something. I'm pretty sure by the end of dinner, Ainsley and Natalie have plans next weekend for a girls' night.

Once the bill is settled, we say our goodbyes to Natalie and Caleb and head out to the parking lot. This time, she grabs my hand and traces little circles on my palm with her finger.

Walking over to the car, I think nothing of the man striding toward us, but as soon as Ainsley gets a look at him, her entire body tenses up. She almost stops walking, so I look over at her. Before I can ask if she's okay, the guy is jogging over to her. She lets go of my hand as if it was burning hers.

"Hey, Ains!" he calls out in a chipper voice. "Long time no see." When he gets over to us, he completely ignores me and wraps his arms around her. Her body stiffens even more and it takes all of her energy to bring her arms around him to return the hug. He's got a smug smile on his face, while her face looks almost sad.

"Jordan. It's been a while for sure," she responds curtly.

"I think my parents are at your parents' house tonight."

"Yeah, I was there earlier. Your mom told me your news. Congratulations." Her monotone voice conveys the lack of emotions she is giving this guy.

"Thanks? I wish I could introduce you to Maggie, but she's feeling under the weather. Some other time. Is your number still the same? I'll give you a call sometime so you can meet her." Ainsley nods. "Sweet. Well, it was good to see you. Take care." He continues on his way into the diner.

Ainsley's gaze is focused on the ground. Not only has her body language completely changed, but her face has lost some of that spark. Trying to bring her out of her funk, I call out to her, "Hey."

Surprised by my voice, she seems to have forgotten I was still standing there. I try again, this time, placing my hand on her shoulder. "Hey, you okay?" She doesn't back away from my touch, which I take as a good sign.

She shakes her head no. "Can we go?" she whispers.

I mentally berate the guy for taking away the happy girl I've spent the evening with. "Sure thing." Before leading her back to the car, I envelop my arms around her and pull her in close to me. Her body is still stiff and doesn't melt into mine like it had earlier tonight, although she does allow me to hug her for a few long minutes. Before pulling away, she looks up at me, a hint of sadness in her eyes.

My breath stops; I'm afraid the look she's giving me is going to be the brush off, and if that's the case, I'm going to more than mentally berate that Jordan guy. I need her to come home with me, even though I can't explain why.

When she finally starts talking, I'm hoping with everything I have that she's not going to ask me to drive her home.

"I'm not sure if there were expectations for tonight, but maybe I can take a rain check?"

Well, she hasn't asked me to drive her home, but I still ask for clarification. "Expectations?" I ask, having an idea of what she means.

She doesn't answer but instead, starts walking to the car. When she gets to the passenger side, I haven't unlocked the doors yet. She leans her back up against the door, sighs, and lays her head back against the car.

"Expectations....of sex," she clarifies when I'm close enough to hear her.

"Do you want me to drive you home?" I ask, hoping she doesn't hear the disappointment in that loaded question.

"No," she quickly states. "I want to go home with you. But, seeing Jordan, killed the mood for me, so I will understand if you want to bring me home. But I don't want to be alone either." Her gaze falls back to the ground, her toe digging in the dirt.

I appreciate her candidness and how she can say what she wants, regardless of whatever answer I give her.

"Hey," I say, tipping her chin up to meet my gaze. Her eyes are wild and filled with distress. "I won't lie and say I didn't have expectations for tonight." I pause and take a deep breath. "But if you coming home to my place, even just to sleep, is still on the table, I would want nothing more than that tonight." Her eyes soften and her lips curl up into a small smile. To lighten the mood even more, I add, "I don't usually put out until the third or fourth date anyway." That garners a laugh from her. "Although with you, I could have been coerced to make an exception."

"Is that true?" she asks quietly.

"Which part, darling?"

"That you don't sleep with girls on the first date." Reluctantly, I nod my head yes. "Wow," she says. "So, you've never slept with a girl you just met?"

"Nope," I tell her. "You?"

"Considering I've never slept with a girl, that would be a no for me too," she replies, not missing a beat. And then she lets out a little giggle.

"How about a guy?" I ask, not sure how I feel about the answer.

She hesitates a moment. "Yes. And before you ask, it's been more than one."

"You don't go around kissing guys you just met, but you sleep with them?" It comes out a little harsher than I intended.

She looks at me like I'm crazy. "Please don't tell me you've never slept with someone just for sex?"

"Of course I have, just not someone I didn't know."

"Oh right." She's quiet for a moment. "Does it bother you that I've slept with men I didn't know?"

She's looking up at me, for an answer, her eyes pleading with me not to care and not to judge her. "It's in the past, so there's no reason to let it bother me," I tell her as nonjudgmental as I can convey.

"Is it going to be a problem?" she prods further.

"No," I state adamantly. "Come here." I pull her into me again. She lets me hug her for a little while. When she pulls herself out of my arms, she looks up at me, a quizzical look on her face. "What?"

"You are so unlike other guys I know, other guys I've been with." I want to ask more, but she continues, "Take me to your house now." She digs the keys out of my front pocket, just barely grazing my dick. She hits the unlock button, opens her door, and climbs in. I walk around and get in. Holding out my hand to her for my keys, she proclaims, "Thanks for dinner. And pool. And for not judging me."

"You're welcome, for all of it. Thank you for coming home with me." I start up the car and drive us to my house.

It takes about fifteen minutes to get to my house. On the ride, she's pretty quiet. About halfway there, I lay my hand on the console between us, and she quickly places her hand in mine.

"Grayson?"

"Yeah?"

"How old were you when you lost your virginity?" When I look over at her, she's staring out her window, but her fingers are tracing shapes in my palm.

"Do want the truth or the answer I tell girls?"

She snaps her head to look at me. I knew that would get her attention; it always does. It's a line I started using a while ago just to see girls' reactions to the question. I know that Ainsley isn't "any" girl, but I knew it would get a rise out of her.

"I want the truth," she answers.

"Sixteen," I tell her, which is the truth.

"And the answer you tell other girls?"

"Last year."

She raises her eyebrows. "And girls fall for that?" she asks incredulously.

"There have been a few. You should see some of their faces when I say it, straight-faced. One girl wouldn't let it go. She was so annoying."

"Did you eventually tell her you were kidding?"

"Nope. I had her so convinced it was the truth that no matter what I told her after that, she wouldn't believe me." I laugh at the memory. "How about you? How old were you?" "Seventeen. It was my senior prom. So cliché, right?"

"Hope he at least sprung for a hotel room."

"Oh, he did. At the motel on Route 68. It was quite romantic." I look over to her because I can't tell if she's serious or not. "Dead serious," she declares with a shudder.

"Not a good time, huh?"

"No, not the best. And it wasn't even his first time! But I was naïve and didn't know any better, and by the time we ended things, he got his shit together. In the bedroom at least." She pauses for a minute. "Is this conversation awkward for you? Like, I feel like it should be, but it's kind of not."

"It's less awkward than other times I've discussed my virginity," I state honestly.

"Have you discussed it often? I have to say, most guys don't want to know my history."

Again I glance over at her. "Seriously?" She nods. "I find that most girls want to know the when and where of it but not so much the how. That's my experience at least."

"Okay, so where?"

"Her bedroom. Her parents were out of town."

"Was she your girlfriend?"

"At the time, yes. She wasn't my first girlfriend, just the first girl I slept with."

"Was she your girlfriend for long after the first time?"

I haven't thought about Rylee Denvers in a very long time. I shake my head. "Maybe like six months. Her family moved out of state and despite her persistence that long-distance relationships can work, they can't. At least not at sixteen."

"I hear ya," she exclaims. "Not that I have any experience with that; I've never tried to make that work."

She goes quiet again. Despite the deep topics we are covering tonight, it's not an awkward silence.

"Your prom date. Was he your boyfriend?" I ask to break the silence.

"Yes, for about a year before prom and two years after."

"Wow, that's a long time for high school. Why did you break up?" She shifts in her seat, the movement conveying the slightest bit of uneasiness in her demeanor. "You don't have to answer if you don't want to."

"No, it's okay. We both stayed in Maine for college, even though we chose different schools. We made it through freshman year together, but it turns out, he wasn't really good in a crisis, and it just drove us further and further apart until he eventually went his own way, and I went mine."

I don't ask about the "crisis" because if she wanted me to know what happened, she would have told me. Instead I ask, "Did you love him?"

She's quiet for a moment. "I thought I did. But what does a teenager really know about love?"

"I couldn't tell you," I answer.

"Have you ever been in love?"

Since we are pulling up to my house, I choose to ignore the question. I hit the button for the garage and after it opens, I pull the car in. Once it's parked, she goes to hop out, as she notices the other car in the garage. She squeals. "Oh my god! You have a '67 Mustang? That's like super cool."

I literally stop in my tracks. "What did you just say?" I ask her, knowing I couldn't have heard her correctly.

She looks over at me for clarification. "What? It's a Mustang, right?"

"The other part."

"That it's super cool?" she asks, shrugging.

"How the hell do you know it's a '67 Mustang?" Okay, seriously. This woman is the woman of my dreams.

"My grandfather was super into cars. He worked at the Ford Factory for like fifty years or so."

"Hold up," I tell her, crossing to meet her where she stands. I lay her bag at her feet. "Like *the* Ford Factory? In Detroit?"

"Yep. The one and only."

"I will be so jealous if you tell me you have been there."

"Only a handful of times. He retired when I was ten, but we visited at least once a summer every year before that."

Now it's my turn to squeal. She puts her hands over her ears. "That was way too girlish of a scream, Grayson."

"Visiting the Ford Factory has been on my bucket list since I was five. FIVE! Please tell me it's as cool as it looks on the Internet."

"If you like cars, especially Ford cars, it's super awesome. But the part that's not open to the public is even more awesome."

I throw my hands over my ears. "Stop talking. I don't need to be any more jealous of you right now."

She laughs. "So, is this your car? Better yet, do you drive it?"

"Yes, and yes. It was my dad's, but he passed it on to me. I've had my eye on getting one of the newer ones, but I just haven't bitten the bullet yet. One day soon I will."

"If it's a nice day tomorrow, can we drive this to breakfast? Please?" she practically begs.

"Sure. Let's go inside." She picks up her bag and follows me inside. Once we get inside, she drops her bag in the mudroom, kicks off her shoes, and ventures into the house. I hear her squeal again as I'm taking off my shoes and hanging up my keys. I have to wonder what she's squealing about now.

I find her in the kitchen, practically molesting the countertops. I stand in the doorway, taking in the view. After she feels up the countertops, she makes her way to the stainless steel fridge. She runs her hand along the handles and then pulls open the side-by-side doors. I always keep the fridge well-stocked, and I see her admiring what's inside. As I watch her, I'm regretting the "no expectations" discussion we had earlier. This girl is seriously turning me on right now. In the fucking kitchen. With fucking appliances.

She closes the fridge doors, pulls open the freezer for good measure, then moves on to the stove. She runs her hand over the cooktop. When she gets to the oven, she pulls the door open and peers inside. When she notices the second oven underneath, she squeals again. She turns on her heels to face me. "Please tell me that you use this kitchen and that it's not just for show."

"It's not just for show." I nod my head over to the door on the left. "Open the door."

Giddily, she jogs over to the door. Throwing it open, she stumbles, almost falling to the floor. She walks into the pantry and I imagine she takes a look around, since I can't see what she's doing. The sounds coming from the pantry lead me to believe she's touching things and moving things around on the shelves. She's in there for a good five minutes. Finally emerging, she saunters over to the island and hops up. Oh fuck, I think. She motions me over, batting her eyes at me. I walk over to her and hop up next to her.

"Can I please amend my comment from earlier?"

Having a good idea of which comment she means, I play dumb and ask, "Which comment would that be?"

She licks her lips and pulls the bottom one into her mouth before she answers. "The one about not having sex."

"And what would you like to amend it to?" I ask, brushing the strand of hair that's fallen in her face away.

"I'm putting it back on the table," she states nonchalantly. She reaches her hand over my leg and palms my dick. She leans into me and in the sexiest voice I've ever heard, she whispers, "The pantry or the island. Where should we start?"

I hop down off the island and instantly regret losing the feeling of her hand on my dick. I stand between her thighs, pushing them apart to fit myself in. Once I'm there, she wraps them around my waist. There's a hunger in her eyes, begging me to do things to her.

As slowly as I can, I find the button to her jeans. She senses what I'm doing and tries to hurry me along. I remove my hands and she pouts. When I make no move to continue undressing her, she puts her hands in the air, and I resume my work. I manage to unbutton the jeans and slide the zipper down. I'm met with the sight of cream-colored underwear with roses on them. Copping a quick feel, the satin is cool to the touch. I lift her ass off the counter and she helps me shimmy the pants down. I sit her back down, her pants now resting on her thighs. Taking a few steps back, she's forced to unhook her legs. She places her hands on my shoulders to steady herself, as I slowly tug her jeans down her legs and when they are finally off, I toss them to the floor.

Stepping back in between her legs, I tug at the hem of her sweater and slowly push it up her abdomen, making sure my hands keep in constant contact with her skin. When I've bunched the sweater up to her armpits, she raises her arms in the air, and I push it over her head and up her arms, again not losing contact with her skin. Once it's off, I toss it behind me. With only a quick glance at the white lacy bra, my hands reach around her back to unclasp it. Once it's unclasped, the straps fall down her arms. She wiggles her arms a bit so it slides even further down. I grab a hold of it, drag it the rest of the way off and fling it behind me. Glancing down at her chest, I'm met with the sight of the most flawless breasts. Although they are on the smaller side, their perkiness and near-perfect shape make up for what they lack in size. I grab the nipples in between my fingers, tugging gently as they harden in my grasp. I so want to lick them, but I know if I do that, I'll be a goner for good, and I'm not quite ready for that yet. I'll take them in my mouth when we are in my bedroom later tonight.

As I'm exploring her breasts, she lets out the slightest moan. She wraps her legs around my waist again and pulls me in closer to her. Her hands go around my neck and find the back of my head. She lets one hand float a little higher, and it knocks my hat off my head.

"You seem to be wearing too many clothes," she rasps out, already slightly out of breath.

"Whose fault is that?"

Since I've granted her permission, she grabs the hem of my shirt and starts to hastily pull it over my head. Because of her angle, it gets stuck on my one arm, so I help her out and pull it off. She ogles my bare chest up and down and then runs her hands over it. "Damn," she mutters when she gets to my abs. She pays them special attention, trailing her fingers up, down, and sideways. Her hands find the button of my jeans, but I push them away. There's no way I'm letting her take off my jeans right here.

She questions my action with a look. I take a deep breath. "Ainsley, I'm super happy you put sex back on the table for tonight, and as much as I want to fuck you right here on the island, and in the pantry, unless you have a condom that you can reach from where you are sitting, it ain't happening."

She contemplates my comment and her face falls momentarily, but then it's quickly lighting back up again. "You mean to tell me you don't carry a condom in your wallet?" Her lips turn up into the smallest smirk.

"Sadly, I don't make it a habit of carrying them around in my wallet." But boy do I wish I did right about now. Her smirk is replaced with a look of disappointment. "Let me finish what I've started."

"Okay," she whispers. Without even hesitating, she lifts her butt in the air and shimmies her underwear off and down her legs. She even manages to kick them off herself.

I grab her by the waist and bring her bottom half closer to the edge of the island. "Lie back," I instruct, pushing her chest gently. She obeys. She props herself up on her elbows, licks her lips, and then just waits for me to make my move.

I don't hesitate. I push her thighs apart a few inches more and then trail my fingers up her left thigh, across her sensitive area, and down the right thigh. Placing my left hand on the counter on the outside of her leg, my right hand finds her clit. As if on autopilot, my thumb starts circling it so that my fingers can trail lower. I don't need to push inside to know she's wet and ready for me. I find her opening and drive one finger inside.

As my fingers work below, Ainsley leans back even further, letting her head fall back, almost touching the counter. Every now and again, little moans escape her mouth. My gaze travels to her abdomen. She's completely bare above where my fingers are working, and I notice that her stomach muscles begin to tighten and twitch ever so slowly. When I up the intensity of my finger, pushing it in and out at a faster pace, the muscles tighten a little more. My thumb continues to circle her clit; I can feel it harden as well.

I add in another finger and almost immediately, she's screaming my name as she comes on my fingers, her thighs tightening and closing together with my hand in the middle. I continue to move my fingers around inside her for a few more minutes while she comes down off her high. My erection is pushing against my jeans, more so when she sits back up. While this look suits her well, I can only imagine how incredible her "just fucked" look will be.

I remove my fingers and pop them into my mouth. Yeah, there will be more tasting later this evening.

She slides herself down off the island, gives my abs one more once over, and then her eyes meet mine. "Two questions," she pants, out of breath.

"Okay..."

"One, where do you keep your condoms?"

"In the top drawer of the nightstand," I answer.

"Two, which way to your bedroom?" She bats her eyes at me, daring me to take her there.

"Follow me," I order, practically dragging her behind me as I make a beeline for my bedroom.

7

AINSLEY

*F*uck me! That's what I'm thinking as Grayson drags me to his bedroom. As he pulls me along, I try to take in his house, but it's hard to do as he's practically running, and I'm almost sprinting to keep up with him. I do take note that we go upstairs and there are a few doors in the hallway as we make our way to the bedroom.

Once inside the bedroom, Grayson instructs me, "Bed." I hop up on the bed as he grabs the condoms from the drawer. There are a bunch of pillows sitting up against the headboard, at least one with the pillowcase askew. The blanket and top sheet are thrown haphazardly at the end of the bed. The sheets are really soft, like T-shirt material, and I can't help but run not only my hands along them, but the rest of my body as well.

Before he joins me on the bed, he kicks his legs out of his pants and boxers. Once he's completely devoid of clothing, he crawls up the bed to where I'm lying, coming on the side of me, the condom package hanging from between his teeth. His brown eyes are full of hunger and lust, like he can't get enough of what he knows we are about to do.

He stops his head directly above my stomach and lets the package fall; I quickly snatch it up. As I'm holding it in my fingers, he puts his mouth back on the package and starts to rip it with his teeth. I hold it steady so he can get it open. Seriously hot!

Once it's in my hands, he rips the package out of his mouth and tosses it over the side of the bed. He pushes up to his knees, runs a hand through his hair, and grabs the condom out of my fingers. And that's when I get a good look at his erection. My hand shoots out to touch it, but he pushes it away before I can do anything to it. His dick is long, like at least seven inches, if I had to take a guess. I wouldn't call the girth "big," but it's definitely not tiny either.

Before he expertly rolls the condom on to cover himself, I notice a bit of pre-cum on the tip. As if on autopilot, my tongue slowly licks my bottom lip. Oh what I wouldn't give to lick it off.

Once he's hidden away his goods, I focus back on his face, only to find him watching me as I ogle his junk. I give him a small smile, which he returns with one of his own. "You approve?" he asks coyly.

"It will do."

With that, he pushes me down onto the pillows. He swings his leg around so that his legs are straddling me. Kneeling above my thighs, he squeezes his thighs together which squeezes mine in turn.

Staying in the same position, he brings his arms down to my chest and fondles my breasts in his hands.

"These are some perfect breasts. You know that right?" he asks, pinching the nipples between his thumb and finger.

"I don't have many to compare them to, but I think they are pretty perfect myself. And of course, other guys have told me that. Although I'm sure that some of them would have said that to get into my pants."

He shakes his head at me. "Ainsley, let's not bring other men into the bedroom, okay?" He looks a little hurt. When I try to apologize, he puts his hand over my mouth and doesn't let me.

To gauge his reaction, I gently bite down on his palm. He

mumbles, "Cute," and then goes back to playing with my nipples, his face hard set.

As if I wasn't worked up enough already, the attention he is showing my boobs hypes me up even more. I feel my breathing start to quicken. And then he about does me in right there when he brings his mouth down to my left boob and takes it in his mouth. He continues to play with the other one, as his tongue does circles around my hardened nipple.

"Grayson," I manage to moan out before my head falls completely back against the pillow and my eyes close on their own. I fist the sheets next to me because this guy knows how to use his tongue. Just thinking about his tongue on my clit, with his scruff rubbing against my leg, causes me to stop breathing for a second.

He pops my left breast out of his mouth as he makes his way over to the right one, trailing his tongue along the middle of them. I'm so tempted to interrupt him so that he can fuck me already.

As if he can read my mind, he straddles his legs wider and pushes mine open as well with one arm. Not stopping his loving of my breasts, his tip finds my clit, and he circles it a couple of times with the head. I'm blissfully aware of how little stimulation I need down there to send me soaring over the edge as my hips thrust upwards, my back arches, and my toes curl, as my orgasm hits me fast and hard. My stomach muscles tighten as the world goes black for a few seconds.

When I come down from my high, I let go of the sheets and just lay there for a few moments, soaking in the effect his body is having on mine.

He picks his head up off my chest and his lips make contact with my neck. He starts attacking it, although it's very gentle, as he glides his dick inside, an inch at a time. As he gets further in and begins to fill me up, I pick up my head off the pillow. I place my palms on either side of his face, forcing him to look me in the eyes.

His eyes are on fire, the brown a deeper shade as he continues to enter me. In that gravelly voice, he rasps, "Holy fuck, girl." He wipes the hair that has fallen in my face away, brushing his fingers on my sweaty forehead. I continue to hold his gaze as he pushes himself inside me. I know he's all the way inside when his balls slap against my ass, and then just like that, he's thrusting in and out.

I lift my hips to match him, thrust for thrust, my legs writhing underneath the weight of his body. I allow my eyes to close when for the third time within the hour, I feel myself climbing to ecstasy again. As his thumb finds my clit, his voice breaks me out of my trance when he commands, "Open your eyes. I want to watch your eyes as you come."

They fly open, just in time for him to watch me come undone. Even though this orgasm hits just as powerfully as the others, all I can manage to do is squeak out his name. It takes all of my energy just to get that out, since my eyes are still locked on his and my body is now sated.

In a matter of seconds, his orgasm pummels through him, causing him to thrust deeper inside. My body shifts backward slightly with the movement. His eyes close as he comes, my name emanating from his lips in a moan. Carefully, he lowers his body on top of mine and just lays there for a few minutes. His labored breathing matches my own, our heartbeats slowing as we both come down from the sexual high.

After several minutes, he pulls himself out of me and quickly removes the condom, tying it off in a knot. I push myself up to a more seated position and drape the covers over my lower half, more for warmth than to conceal anything. He brings his face to mine. "I'll be right back. You want or need anything?" he asks and then places the gentlest of kisses on my cheek.

"Some water, please," I answer. Before letting him go, I grab his face in my hands and bring his lips to mine. I pull his bottom lip into my mouth for a few seconds and then let it go with a pop. His eyes go wild as he pushes himself off the bed.

He collects his boxers from the floor and steps into them

before leaving the bedroom. I watch as he walks away. His ass is sexy, especially when naked, but even covered by the boxers.

When he's gone, I take a visual tour of his bedroom. Despite the unmade bed, everything else in the room is neat and tidy. A fairly large TV sits atop one of the dressers. The other dresser contains a few frames of photographs. I mentally make a note to check those out later. The bed is king-sized, and I barely take up any room in it. The door to the closet, which I'm guessing is a walk-in, is just slightly ajar. Next to that, the door to the bathroom is wide-open but from my vantage point, I can't see anything but the tiled floor. The gray curtains and shades are drawn on the two windows, both on the far wall and the one straight ahead of me. Turning my attention to the nightstand, there's a pile of about three books, his phone charger, remotes for the TV, and a small notepad. I smile when I see my name written on the top sheet in a neat print.

I only notice Grayson is back when he clears his throat from the doorway. He's leaning up against the doorjamb, his arms crossed across his chest, watching me. Damn is he sexy. His boxers sit low on his hips, and those abs. I want to trail my tongue along the contours of them. He's also sporting the arm porn, especially since his arms are crossed and a bit flexed.

"Are you coming back to bed?" I ask him, hoping he hears the pleading in my voice.

He doesn't move right away, just continues to stare at me, taking in my naked body as he does so. Finally, he starts moving in the direction of the bed. He's got a bottle of water in one hand, and he tosses it on the bed next to me. He walks over to his dresser, opens a drawer and grabs out a T-shirt. I watch his every move-ment like a hawk as he comes over to the bed and climbs on. He sits on his knees, straddling my thighs again, the hunger from before now a bit more satisfied. As I'm about to ask if we are going for round two, he pulls me up off the pillows and slips the T-shirt over my head. *What the fuck,* I think to myself.

He takes in my pissed look. "It's purely selfish reasons," he begins. I soften my look a bit, just to question him. "I can't possibly sit here with your nakedness in my face and not get hard again."

"And getting hard is a bad thing because?"

He settles next to me and motions me to lay my head on his chest. His chest is almost bare; he's got a little hair, but what he does have, it's soft on my cheek. He lets what's left of my hair out of the ponytail and entwines some locks around his fingers and tugs gently.

"Because I don't want tonight to be all about sex," he responds in a low voice.

Not that I needed more confirmation, but Grayson isn't your typical guy. Comments like this confirm that for me, and it only makes me crave him even more. And not just in a sexual way, although no complaints in that department.

I run my fingers along his abs again, because clearly I just can't get enough of them.

I realize as we lay here, this is what's missing in my life. It's been a long while since I've not only had a connection to a guy, incredible sexual chemistry, but this as well. It's been a long time since I've even wanted to cuddle after sex, but with Grayson, I'd be disappointed if we skipped it.

"Grayson?" I ask cautiously.

"Yeah, darling?" he answers, as he continues to twirl my hair around his fingers.

"Don't think I forgot that you didn't answer my question before."

His body tenses beneath me, and his fingers stop moving briefly, his body defying his voice when he asks, "Which question was that?"

"Have you ever been in love?"

He's quiet for a long while, definitely several minutes. He takes a deep breath before he answers, "Yes."

Hiding my slight disappointment, I pick my head off his chest and turn to look at him. His expression is hard to read. "You're a man of few words."

"So I've been told," he counters.

I lay my head back on his chest, debating whether to ask him more about his answer. I want to know more, but it's not a topic to be discussed casually.

"Why did that guy call you Ains today?" he asks quietly. He shifts his body slightly.

Crap. I was really hoping he hadn't heard that. I always hated that nickname, ever since Jordan started calling me it back in high school.

"Way to divert the conversation to me," I retort, rather than answer the question.

I'm getting the sense Grayson is a man of few words—silence in a conversation doesn't seem to bother him, as he goes silent quite often. However, I also realize that most guys would have distracted me with sex by now, rather than discuss their feelings, past history, and such, or allow me to discuss these things, though Grayson isn't so much "discussing" stuff as asking questions.

While I have no intentions of rehashing my history with Jordan, more so than I already shared earlier, I do answer his question, somewhat hoping it will get him to open up as well.

"I've always hated that nickname," I start, after taking a deep breath. "I don't remember when he started calling me that, but no matter how many times I asked him not to, he didn't listen. I guess some habits die hard."

"Duly noted. Clearly you and he have a history," he states rather than asks.

I nod. I peer back up at him. "I thought you didn't want to bring other guys into the bedroom?" I joke.

"I don't," he states but the serious expression on his face doesn't change.

Knowing we need a change of subject, I ask, "Do you cook?" His seriousness fades into something lighter.

"I do."

"I love a man who can cook." Realizing what I've just said, I quickly add, "And I love your kitchen. It's so awesome. I mean, you've got the stainless steel appliances, the double ovens, the spacious granite countertops. Oh, and your pantry!"

A smile creeps onto his face. "Is it because you just want to fuck in there or are you impressed in general?"

Love how he nonchalantly asks the question. This guy gets me. "I'm pretty sure it's a combination of the two. Have you ever..."

He cuts me off before I can finish my question. "That would be a no," he answers emphatically. "Happy for you to be the first." I'm giddy with excitement. "Are you always this excited about kitchens?"

"Just when they look like yours. I could do some serious damage in that kitchen downstairs. And by damage, I mean make some damn deliciousness."

"I take it you like to cook."

"Really?" I glower up at him. "You think I only *like* to cook, based on what I've just told you?"

"Based on your reaction upon seeing the kitchen for the first time, no. It's more than a 'like' to cook," he amends.

"Thank you. Actually, I love to cook. It sucks cooking for just myself, especially because I have to clean up after myself too, but I love to have people over for an excuse to cook."

"What do you cook?" The way he asks the question, he's genuinely waiting for my answer.

"The better question is what don't I cook."

"Cocky much?" he jeers, playfully punching my arm.

"I like to call it confident. But I'm very secure in my cooking skills."

"I like your confidence, and not just about your cooking skills." He's somehow managed to sit up against the pillows, and he tugs me in closer to him. I melt into him as much as I can, especially when he places a kiss on the top of my head. "I'm glad you decided to come home with me," he says, his voice barely above a whisper.

"Me too," I answer truthfully. "You're a good lay."

Knowing what his reaction would most likely be, he pushes me off of him, flips me on my back, and hovers on top of me, supporting himself on his forearms. His face has a wild look, and it amuses me to rile him up like this.

"You really want to go there?" I nod, smirking at him. He shakes his head from side to side, muttering something under his breath. He gets his face as close to my ear as he can, and he rasps, "I've changed my mind. Taking sex in the pantry off the table." With that, he pushes up off of me, gets off the bed, and starts to walk out of the room.

"I hate you," I yell after him.

"I'm fine with that. It's an empty threat." His voice trails off as he gets further away from me.

When he doesn't return in a few minutes, I kick off the covers and get myself out of the bed. If this were anyone else, I would be infuriated right now, but with Grayson? Not only am I highly turned on, I actually want him to continue to tease me. And that scares the shit out of me. This man could be my undoing.

8

GRAYSON

*N*ever in my life have I ever felt the connection I feel with Ainsley. She's already broken down some of my barriers, and I have the feeling I'm going to let her knock down more. I had to get out of the bedroom before she tore down all of my defenses in one night. I wasn't lying when I told her I'm not the guy who sleeps with girls on the first date. Hell, I'm not even the guy who brings girls home to my house this soon. Three days in, and this girl is under my skin, and hell if I don't want her there.

I make myself a cup of coffee in the kitchen, and while it brews, I pick up the clothes that are strewn around the kitchen. Raising Ainsley's sweater to my face, I inhale deeply, relishing in the intoxicating scent of her. Once the coffee is ready, I take a seat at the island. The island that needs to be wiped down, but hell if I want to wash any part of Ainsley away.

After a little while, I hear her padding into the kitchen. She takes a seat next to me, grabs my cup and takes a sip. I glance her way, just to get a look at her. She's still wearing my T-shirt and the sight of her alone is enough to make me smile.

Her lips turn up in a smile in return. "What?" she asks innocently.

"This is a good look for you."

"You should approve; you picked it out," she retorts with a giggle. "But I really like it too." She glances up at the clock on the microwave. "Is it really midnight?" she asks not believing the time. "Do you have anything sweet for a snack?"

Goading her, I tell her, "Check the pantry. I'm sure you can find something in there."

Unfortunately, she doesn't take the bait. "Oh, I'm all set with the pantry for a while."

"I'm sure there's ice cream in the freezer. Or you could make something."

Her face lights up. "I make a mean brownie. Want to help?"

Suddenly, there's nothing more than I want to do than bake with Ainsley, regardless of the late hour. "Yes. I'll get the ingredients from the pantry. What do you need?"

"Some sort of pants or undergarments would be helpful," she delivers in a monotone voice.

"Coming right up. Make yourself at home and get started." I shoot off my stool and take the stairs two at a time to get to my bedroom. In my drawer, I pull out a pair of Steelers PJ bottoms as I smile to myself. I grab myself a pair of pants and throw a T-shirt over my head.

Walking downstairs, I have to control my laughter at the scene I can envision when I get back to the kitchen. Wiping away my smile, I arrive in the kitchen and halt dead in my tracks. Ainsley's reaching for something on the top shelf of the cabinet. My shirt is riding up as she reaches up, showing off her bare ass in the process. What I wouldn't give to put my mark on her and bite that ass.

I cough and clear my throat, alerting her to my presence. She turns around abruptly. "How long have you been standing there?" she asks, not even bothering to cover up. Her confidence is smoking hot.

"Just a few seconds. Here, I got you some pants." I toss them over to her, trying as best as I can to contain my laughter.

She catches the pants and when she sees the symbols on them, she drops them as if they are on fire. "Hell no, Grayson. Nuh uh. Not happening." She frowns and kicks the pants with her feet, trying to get them as far away from her as possible.

Her reaction is even better than I imagined it would be, but I'm not done yet. I step out from behind the counter, and when she sees that I have clothes on, she shrieks. Not because I'm wearing clothes, but because of what I'm wearing.

"You think you are so funny, don't you? Asshole." She turns away from me, anger clouding her features.

I sidle up behind her and throw my arms around her waist. "You want these?" I ask, pointing to my pants.

"You know I do."

"What are you willing to do to get them?"

She maneuvers her body so that she's facing me. "Anything. You. Want." There's a craziness in her emerald eyes. She places her hands on my shoulders, and my body warms with just her touch.

"Anything?" I raise my eyebrows at her.

"Yep."

The words coming out of my mouth surprise even me, but once they are out there, I realize that I wouldn't take anything back. "Spend the whole day with me tomorrow, including another sleepover."

She pretends to think about it for a minute. "Deal. Now hand over the Eagles pants pronto."

I take a few steps back, step out of the pants and hand them over to her. She quickly pulls them on, rolling them at the waist a few times so they don't drag all over the floor. She walks over to the Steelers pants and kicks them in my direction, shuddering as she does so. Her animosity towards a pair of pants turns me on. I pull on the pants.

She hops up on the counter and drags me to her. I go willingly. "Don't we have brownies to make?"

"In a minute." She hushes me by placing her hand over my mouth. Placing her hands on my shoulders, she locks her gaze firmly on mine. In a more serious tone, she adds, "It's so refreshing

that you didn't automatically ask for sex. I mean, I'm not saying sex
would be a problem, but I like how whatever this is, it's bigger
than just sex for you. Because I feel the same way." She lowers her
voice. "You are overwhelming me, Grayson Abbott, in the best
possible way." She plants a slow kiss on my forehead. Before I have
a chance to respond to her declaration, she gently pushes me out
of the way, hops down off the counter, and announces, "I need
flour and cocoa powder from the pantry. Thanks, dear."

Shaking off the fact that she can switch topics so effortlessly, I
go to the pantry and grab the items she requested, as I think to
myself, I could get used to this.

* * *

*A*insley whips up a batch of brownies from scratch. While
she measures and mixes, I watch her attentively from my
perch on the island. I love how she's so at ease in my kitchen. She
quickly figures out where the measuring spoons and cups are and
when she can't find something, she doesn't hesitate to ask. Even
though I'm supposed to be helping, she's taken control of most of
it. It's rare for me to sit back and watch someone else be the cook,
especially in my kitchen; however, I find that I'm completely
content in giving up the control and just watching her.

While the brownies cook, she sits close to me on the island,
resting her legs on top of mine.

"A penny for your thoughts," I ask her, pulling her out of her
daze.

Looking over at me, she smiles. "Just thinking about what else
I can make in this kitchen. Not tonight, of course, but some time in
the future." She leans her head on me, not quite reaching my
shoulder.

Her comment catches me off guard at first, only because of the
nature of the word "future." I'd be lying if I said I didn't already
picture her making good use of the kitchen again sometime soon.

"That can certainly be arranged," I tell her, wrapping my arm around her and bringing her in closer to me. "So, what do you want to do tomorrow? Well, later today I guess."

She picks her head up off my chest and stares incredulously at me. "You mean, besides having sex in the pantry, right?" she asks, her tone of voice somewhere between serious and sarcastic.

"Of course."

She shrugs and then lays her head back down on me. "Haven't really given it much thought. We'll need food, so I figure we can still do breakfast at the café."

"Sure. Tell me what you would be doing if you hadn't enmeshed me in your life with that kiss at the bar."

"Let's see. On Sundays, sometimes I go grocery shopping for the week or I clean my apartment. Other days I spend it at my parents' house or with friends. There's always TV and books and crossword puzzles, stuff to keep my mind stimulated, and grading papers or planning lessons is a given. My commonplace Sundays don't usually consist of hanging out at the homes of hot men, just in case you were wondering." She giggles.

I shudder at her last comment. I choose not to think about her spending time with any other men at this moment, hot or otherwise.

"What about you? How do you spend your Sundays?"

"I'm on the boat as much as the weather allows," I answer, finding my hand entwined in her hair again. "I usually end up at Bella's house for dinner, or she and Kylie come here. I've been known to sit on the couch and binge-watch Netflix on rainy days. I like to take the Mustang out for drives, too, especially in the fall weather. It's my favorite time of year, especially in Maine."

She's quiet for a while, so I revel in the closeness and just listen to her breathe. She hops up off the counter when the timer goes off to signal the brownies are done. She carefully takes them out of the oven, placing them on the stovetop to cool. She resets the timer for ten minutes. "Bathroom?"

"Down the hall, first door on the left," I instruct. As she exits the kitchen, I watch as her hips sway back and forth and can't help but notice the way my pants sit low on her waist. Even though they are rolled up, the bottoms drag on the floor.

Needing something to do, I start to wash the dishes she's piled in the sink. Most of them go in the dishwasher, so it's not all that difficult. With the water running, I don't hear her return until she squeals. I fucking love that sound.

Shutting the water off, I turn on my heels to face her. She's got her hand thrown over her chest and her eyes are lit up. "Be still my heart. A man who knows how to load a dishwasher. I bet you make your mother proud."

My body tenses, but I let her comment slide for now. I turn back around to the last of the dishes. She comes up behind me, wraps her arms around my waist, and lays her head on my back. When she speaks, I feel the vibrations in my back but can barely make out the words she's saying.

"I'm so glad I kissed you at the bar. This has been the best first date I've ever had."

I shut off the water and close up the dishwasher; she somehow manages to keep her arms around me, but I feel her head lift off my back. I spin myself so that I'm facing her.

"I'm glad you feel that way." It's all I say because it's extremely hard for me to capture my emotions of how I feel right now with words. Instead, I bring my forehead down to hers, finding her gaze. Her eyes reflect what I'm feeling; she gets my message loud and clear.

Once the brownies have cooled for a bit, she cuts us each a piece. I pour us a glass of milk and hand her two plates. She carries the brownies to the table, and I follow her lead.

I take a bite first. Damn, she was right. These are delicious! After inhaling the entire brownie, I tell her, "These are delicious."

She beams. "Thanks. Everyone agrees," she adds with a giggle. "You want another one?"

"No, I'm good." Stifling a yawn, I get up and put the dishes in the sink. "Ready to hit the sack?"

She nods and goes to retrieve her bag from the mudroom.

When she comes back, she's the one yawning. "Damn, I'm tired. Hope you don't snore. I need to sleep!"

"I don't; do you?" I parrot her question back to her.

"Nope. Come on." She leads the way upstairs, where she proceeds to quickly strip down and change into some skimpy shorts and a tank top. I notice she leaves the underwear off.

"Oh, Ainsley. This is your sleeping attire?" I ask her, as a small moan escapes my lips.

"Is there a problem with it?" She crooks her head and bats her eyes.

"Not at all," I reply, turning around so she can't see me adjusting myself.

She snorts. "Yeah, okay. Keep telling yourself that." She goes into the bathroom for a few minutes, I assume to brush her teeth and do whatever else she needs to do. When she's done, she comes over to the bed. "Which side do you sleep on?"

"The side closest to the bathroom."

She crawls her way to the opposite side of the bed, settles on the pillows and brings the covers up so she's partially covered. I hit the bathroom, and when I'm done, turn off all the lights before climbing in next to her.

Her breathing is labored, and she appears to already be asleep. Since she's facing away from me, I slide in behind her and throw my arm over her. She doesn't stir.

Closing my eyes, I whisper in her ear, "Is it too soon to think I could possibly love you?"

9

AINSLEY

*H*e thought I was sleeping, but I heard every word. It took everything in my power not to react in even the slightest way. It should have freaked me the fuck out, him uttering those words. No one is more surprised than me to realize that I pretty much loved the words he confessed. I have never felt this overwhelmed before, not that I have much experience in the "love" and relationship areas. I've never felt this comfortable with a guy before, let alone this quickly into a relationship. I feel like I've known him forever, but then there are so many things I can't wait to learn about him because in fact, I've only known him a very short while. It's been merely days.

When I wake up in the morning, I'm lost for a minute or so. When realization hits of where I am, I roll over to find Grayson's spot vacant. Feeling a tad disappointed, I push up off the bed and go in search of him.

I find him in the kitchen, reading the newspaper at the table. His hair is tousled from sleep, his eyes a deep chocolate brown, and he's wearing just the PJ bottoms he slept in. His torso is bare, but I can't see much of it because he's slumped over the table. I lick my lips in anticipation of seeing his abs again. Did I mention they are picture-worthy?

He picks his head up as he hears me approaching. "Hey, darling. Sleep well?"

I smile and nod. "Best night's sleep I've had in a long time." *Or ever,* I don't voice aloud. "You?"

He gestures me over to him and when I get there, he pulls me onto his lap. He moves the hair off of my cheek and places a tender kiss on it. He nods his head. "So well," he agrees.

"How long have you been up?" I ask him, running my hand through his thick locks. I place my palms on his cheeks and before he can answer, pop a quick kiss on his lips.

"A little while. Shall we get ready for breakfast?"

"Yes, please. I'm famished."

"I'll set you up in the guest room's bathroom to shower." When he sees the disappointed look on my face, he quickly adds, "Just so we can both get showered at the same time and be on our way faster." Laughing, he shakes his head at the wild look that comes over my face. "Another day," he declares knowing what I want without me having to ask it.

"Promise?" I ask, keeping the pleading to a minimum but giving him my best pout.

"You've already made plans to cook again, and when you do that, you're bound to need a shower at some point."

"Good point. Okay, let's go before you have to eat me for breakfast." His eyes go wide in shock. I feel him harden underneath me. "Yep, time to go," I tell him, hopping off his lap.

* * *

*B*reakfast is fun. He opens up a little more about his job —the fact that he's a trainer explains his abs. Besides Bella and Kylie, he doesn't really talk about his family. He seems to want it that way, so I don't push him. God knows I hate to talk about my mother and brother.

Since it's a nice day, we take the Mustang for a drive and hit up a farmer's market in Portland. Even though his fridge and pantry are stocked well, he ends up buying some more fresh produce, freshly baked bread, and some chicken to cook for dinner.

After the farmer's market, he drives to a nearby park with hiking trails, and we spend some time exploring. He holds my hand the entire way up one of the trails and despite my heart beating quickly in my chest, I'm somehow able to keep my hands from becoming too clammy or sweaty in his grasp.

As we are hiking down the last trail, I realize that I haven't pulled my phone out all day, except to take some pictures and the obligatory selfie at the top of the trail. I haven't checked my email or Facebook once all day, a rarity for me. I also realize that I don't miss it because spending this day with Grayson has been damn near perfect.

Once we get back to the car, in a shy voice, he asks, "Bella wants to know if we want to do dinner with them. That loosely translates to them coming over to my house and me cooking. It's totally up to you..."

Before he finishes speaking, I'm nodding my head and answering yes. "That sounds good. Did we buy enough chicken?"

He nods. "Yeah, and if not, I have more at home I'm sure. Are you sure you are okay with this? They can be overpowering at times."

"I'm okay with it. I want to know them better. And plus, I know that Bella will tell me stories about you that you won't share."

He cocks his head to the side. "Oh really?"

"Definitely," I confirm. "I'm almost positive."

He huffs and then starts up the car. Before pulling away, he hands me his phone and tells me to text Bella to come over around six.

Taking his phone out of his hand, I look back over to him. "Are you sure you trust me with your phone?" I question. "I could totally creep it."

"There's nothing noteworthy on it but feel free to creep away." His voice has lost some of the jovial tones, so I just text Bella and put the phone on the console between us.

I peer out the window. "I enjoyed myself today. Thank you."

"Me too," he agrees. "But thank you for choosing to spend the day with me. Hopefully we have time to fulfill the only item on your to-do list when we get home." A slow smirk spreads across his face.

"I can text Bella back and tell her to come a little later..." I trail off and reach for his phone.

"Are you staying the night?" he asks instead of entertaining my thought.

"It *is* a school night, but I really would like to."

Stopping at the red light, he looks over at me. "I'd really like you to also."

"Well, in that case, I must."

He doesn't talk for the rest of the ride, but his hand finds my thigh, and he rubs it up and down the entire way to his house.

Back at his house, he unloads the groceries and sets to work on dinner. I'm a little bummed that he's focused on dinner, but when he hands me a bunch of veggies to peel and cut, I get to work and after only a few minutes, I find that chopping veggies next to Grayson doesn't feel like work at all. Since he's standing next to me, prepping the chicken with all sorts of spices, he keeps bumping his hip into mine. When I bump him back, he pushes back a little harder each time. He's trying really hard not to crack even the tiniest smile, but when he thinks I'm not watching him, his armor cracks.

"Music?" I ask.

He abandons his chicken prepping, washes his hands, and goes into the other room. In a few minutes, he's back with a Bluetooth speaker and an iPad. He cues up Pandora and the first song that booms through the speakers is Luke Bryan's "I Don't Want This Night to End."

"Love this song," I croon, starting to sway my hips to the beat. He comes up behind me and grabs a hold of my hips, pressing his body against mine. My heart starts to beat just a smidgen faster.

He sways in time with the music and when he leans in to kiss my neck, I almost drop the knife I'm holding.

Just as quickly as he came behind me, he moves away. *What the heck,* I think to myself, but go back to my prepping duties.

We work for about ten more minutes. He puts the chicken in the fridge to marinate and then grabs the veggies I've prepped, sprinkles on a few spices and adds them next to the chicken. He takes about five minutes to clean up the mess, and then he disappears from the kitchen.

Not knowing what to make of it, I figure I will take this time to explore more of his house. Did I mention his house is expansive? And I've only seen like three of the rooms.

The kitchen opens up to a large family room. There are two couches and a recliner that face the TV that's mounted on the wall. On one wall, there's a tall bookshelf that houses many books along the shelves. Perusing them quickly, I notice some about Ford cars, physical training, and then a hodgepodge of classic and contemporary fiction. Picture frames adorn a few of the shelves containing mostly pictures of Grayson and Bella, a few with Kylie added in, some that show he likes to travel, and then one of a couple who I assume are his parents. While Grayson appears to be the spitting image of his father, I can see his mother in him as well. I notice there aren't any family photos of the four of them but don't dwell on it.

Walking down the hall, there's the bathroom that I used last night. Even though it's only a half bath, it's fairly spacious. Across from that is a guest bedroom. There's a queen-sized bed, covered in a plain white comforter, along with a tall dresser and its matching nightstand. The guest room upstairs is more inviting than this one.

Rounding out this hallway downstairs is a closed door. Not wanting to be a total snoop, I resist the strong urge to open the door and peek inside.

I make my way back to the kitchen to the glass sliding doors. They lead to an incredible deck, complete with a grill and a patio set. Beyond the deck, there's a firepit, and not one of those portable ones either. This one is circular in shape, the cinder blocks stacked three levels high in an alternating pattern. In the far corner of the yard sits a shed.

As I'm looking out at the backyard, Grayson comes up behind me. He doesn't say anything; he just brushes my hair off my neck with his fingers and leans in to start kissing it again. My eyes close, and I start to sway on my feet. I'm suddenly aware that the music is still on, playing Lee Brice's "Love Like Crazy." He moves to the other side of my neck, nibbling every so often. A small moan escapes my lips, and I lay my palms against the door to steady myself as I rock back and forth.

His hands find the hem of my T-shirt. He makes his way underneath and palms my stomach. Inch by inch, his fingers make their way higher until they have reached my boobs. He's still kissing my neck, but they are getting longer and more drawn out, in contrast to the feather kisses he started with. He leans in closer to me so he can cup my boobs, and I can feel the beginning of his erection against my backside.

"Grayson," I whisper-moan.

"Ainsley," he parrots back in a similar tone.

My body temperature rises, my breathing deepens, and then I hear his "Fuck me." His tone of voice does not suggest he's actually looking for me to do what he says but rather voicing his frustration.

He doesn't drop his hands, but his kisses stop, and he drops his head to my back. I'm about to question his motives when I hear the garage door opening. Well, that's poor timing, I think to myself.

Knowing I have only seconds before the guests will be in the mudroom, I quickly turn my body around to him, causing his arms to fall from my breasts. His face shows pure frustration, which I know is reflected on mine as well. Standing on my tippy-toes so I can get closer to his face, I put my palms on his chest. His pulse is racing, possibly even faster than mine.

Looking up into his eyes, I say the only thing I can think of right now.

"I know she's your sister, but is it rude to kick them out right after dinner?" I wink at him.

In response, he lifts me off my feet and carries me to the kitchen. He sits me down on the island. Can I mention how much I am loving this island!. In an almost out of breath voice, he rasps, "Two, three hours tops, and they are gone. I will literally throw them out if I have to." He puts a quick kiss on my lips, bringing his tongue out at the very end to lick them. "And whatever you do, do *not* bring up the wedding," he manages to get out just as we hear the door to the mudroom open.

"Hey, we're here," I hear a female voice call out, but I can't distinguish who it is. Grayson quickly pushes away from the island and gets the food from the fridge. I hop down and head to the bathroom to compose myself.

10

GRAYSON

I love my sister. I love my sister. I love my sister. I repeat this thought over and over as I finish getting the meal ready to throw on the grill. Not only did she and Kylie cockblock me, they brought up the wedding five minutes after they arrived. And the worst part? They are dragging my girl to the dark side. No, they aren't converting her to lesbianism, but they are filling her head with stories from when I was younger. And they are not all pleasant stories. But the smile plastered all over Ainsley's face is enough to let it all slide.

You think I don't know I called her "my girl?" Yeah, I know all right. She's weaseled her way under my skin in the best possible way and hell if I can't get enough of her. Even just watching her from afar as she listens to stories told by Bella and Kylie makes my dick start to twitch. But I'm happy to report that the feelings are not purely sexual. She's got my emotions on a roller coaster ride as well and while I'm just a passenger along for the ride, I hope that it doesn't end anytime soon.

"Ainsley, help me carry these trays out to the grill please?" I ask, beckoning her over to me.

She's quick to hop down off her stool at the island, but Kylie beats her to it and grabs a tray before I can stop her. Damn her.

Ainsley gives me a small shrug and look that says "sorry." There's a small look of concern on her face but Bella quickly manages to get her talking about something else. She's the queen of changing the subject.

Kylie and I make our way to the preheated grill. I throw the veggies on one side, the chicken on the other. Kylie monitors my movements and then takes a seat at the table. Shutting the grill, I take a seat next to her and set the timer.

"She's really cool, Gray," Kylie states.

"That she is." I take a deep breath, not really wanting to have a conversation with Kylie but knowing it's practically inevitable.

"She seems really into you, too."

I'm sure she doesn't mean anything by the comment, but something about the way she says it irks me. "What does that mean?" I ask, deepening my tone just a bit and raising my eyebrows at her.

She puts her hand on my arm. "Relax. I just meant that the feelings you seem to have for her are reciprocal."

"Oh. And my feelings for her are that obvious?" I don't know how I feel about that. I mean, I know how I feel about Ainsley but didn't realize that I was wearing them on my sleeve. I rake my hands through my hair and stare down at the ground.

"Look at me," she instructs. I pick my head up. She's got a genuine smile on her face. "Gray, I've known you for about ten years now. I've seen you around many girls, including Molly." At the sound of her name, I cringe. "You've never been this interested in a girl this fast. Hell, I could go so far as adding you've never been this interested in a girl period." She doesn't let me interrupt even though I start to say something. "We'll come back to Molly. Let me finish." She takes a deep breath and her eyes dart around us, making sure we are alone. She leans her body in closer to me. And what she says next floors me. "Gray, you already broke your cardinal rule. Shouldn't that say something?" She winks at me.

I don't know who to be pissed at. And it takes me a minute to realize I'm not even pissed, more so taken aback. I'm content in the fact that I did sleep with Ainsley on the first date and it was most likely the best sex I've ever had. And I can't wait to do it again.

"Did she tell you that?" I'm not mad, just curious.

"Not directly, but she let something slip about your sheets being so comfortable and how they might need to be washed."

I smile at the memory of watching her come in my bed. Those damn emerald eyes. And knowing she hopefully didn't tell them about the island. That's between her and me.

Then she tells me something else I didn't know. "You know, you taught your sister well. She didn't put out until our sixth date. And I couldn't even get her pregnant!" Her face lights up, and she hoots with laughter.

I smile. "Sometimes she listens well."

It's not just about the pregnancy, but that is a big factor. It's more about protecting my heart.

The timer goes off indicating I need to flip the chicken. I get up and mix up the veggies and flip the chicken. When I go back to the table, Ainsley and Bella are coming outside with a pitcher of some sort of yellow drink and cups.

Bella puts the pitcher down and proceeds to pour four glasses while Ainsley takes a seat in the chair next to me. I slide the chair closer to me and put my hand on her thigh. I give it a loving squeeze, garnering a smile out of her.

She leans in close so that no one else can hear. My breath hitches in my chest in anticipation of what she might say. "I love your sister," she whispers all raspy in my ear.

I push her back from me. "That's what you whisper in my ear?" I ask incredulously, more so to get a rise out of her.

She looks taken aback. Then, because she's Ainsley, a smirk creeps across her face. "Oh Grayson, if I whisper the things I want to say, the things you want to hear, the semi you're sporting would be a full hard-on." Just for good measure, she gives it a tap, her smile getting even bigger.

It's at that moment the timer goes off indicating dinner's ready. Knowing I'm sporting wood, I can't stand right up. "Bella, check the food, will you please?" I call out to her. I do my best to adjust myself while working my erection back down.

She walks over to the grill and checks it all. "It needs about two more minutes. That long enough to compose yourself?" She giggles.

"Ass," I toss in her direction, feeling myself blush.

"Ainsley, I love how you rile him up. You will fit right in with me and Kylie."

I watch Ainsley's face at Bella's words. It doesn't seem to faze her one bit, which makes me smile. She *will* fit right in with all of us, but this kind of thinking is not helping my situation.

I finally get myself in check, by thinking about football players tackling each other, and get up and check the food. Since it's all cooked, I take it off the grill and plate it on the serving tray. Ainsley appears next to me and grabs it and starts to carry it over to the table. Once she places it on the table, I wrap my arms around her and place a kiss on her cheek. "Just so you know. I share Bella's sentiments." This time, it's my turn to leave her hanging. I let her out of my embrace and walk away, her mouth and eyes wide in shock.

Kylie serves the dinner and everyone agrees it's delicious. I wasn't too much worried about it, but I'm glad Ainsley especially enjoys it.

Before taking a sip of the drink, I look over to Kylie. My sister is known for her liquid concoctions that are less than stellar. Thank goodness Kylie and I are in cahoots in our agreement about our displeasure. "What is it?"

Ainsley answers. "Spiked lemonade. I helped her out." She wiggles her eyebrows at me. I have to wonder if she somehow had to taste test something before this one was concocted.

Pushing my chair back, I ask, "Anyone need anything inside? Going to grab a water." They all shake their heads no, but I don't miss the questioning look Ainsley gives to Bella.

Back outside, as soon as I'm back in my seat, Ainsley questions me with a hopeful look in her eyes, "Did you even try it?"

I shake my head as I chug my water.

"Why not?"

"I'm not a big lemonade drinker."

"Liar!" Bella calls me out. "He doesn't drink much since..."

Kylie's "BELLA!" cuts her off, which I'm grateful for. Bella gives Kylie the stink eye, but all Kylie does is shrug her off.

"She's going to find out eventually," Bella tries to start again.

"When Grayson wants her to," Kylie replies to shut her up.

I watch Ainsley as she takes in the exchange between the two of them. Confusion doesn't even begin to explain the perplexed look that's plastered on her face. Truthfully, I hate the look, but I can't get into the reason I don't drink right now, and my usual one-line explanation will make the look worse. Buying a little time, I tell her, "I'll explain later." Her look eases up a little. And then the next sentence out of her mouth causes me to almost lose it.

"It's okay. You can tell me when you are ready." She reaches her hand out and gives my arm a squeeze, a smile filling her incredible lips.

Between the genuine words and the loving gesture, I fall hard, harder than before. And realize I'm seriously fucked.

To prove how perfect this girl is, she looks over to Bella. "How did you and Kylie meet?"

I swallow. "Kylie tells it way better."

I listen as Kylie tells the story of how they first met. Not only was I a witness to their meeting, but I've heard the story a bunch of times. I watch Ainsley as she listens, laughs at the most appropriate times. Her eyes are full of happiness and her smile takes up her entire face. At one point, she looks in my direction, and if possible, her smile grows bigger. I match her smile.

After dinner is carried to the kitchen, I offer the girls Ainsley's brownies. I kind of hint they are from a box. Ainsley plays along.

"Wow, these are really good for a box mix," Bella says in between bites. "What's your secret?"

"These are not from a box," Kylie argues. "No way."

Ainsley can't contain her laughter and she gives in and confirms what Kylie thinks. "No, they are from scratch."

"Damn, Gray. This girl could give you a run for your money in the kitchen."

"I'm okay with that," I tell her, reaching for a brownie myself. "At least I would have help."

"Hey! I help," Bella whines.

Kylie snorts, shaking her head. "Ha! 'Helping' is more than just getting ingredients out of the cupboards. Or sitting there looking pretty."

I steal a glance over at Ainsley. She's had her fair share of animated conversations to watch today. This one just makes her smile.

"Kylie and Bella only eat homemade food at my house," I explain. "Kylie is just marginally better than my sister at heating meals from the freezer, but they are both great at ordering takeout."

Changing the subject, what she does best, Bella asks, "Firepit tonight?"

Oh shit. I should have factored this into the plan. Without missing a beat, Ainsley pipes in with, "I have an early class to teach tomorrow. Can we do it another day? I was just admiring the pit earlier, and I can't wait to roast marshmallows in it."

There's not even a hint of insincerity in what rolls off her tongue. Not that she's lying, but that's not her motive for passing on the fire with them.

"Ok cool. Another day." Bella looks slightly disappointed and doesn't take the hint. Thank god that Kylie gets it.

"Bells, I think that's her subtle way of telling us to leave so she can get it on with your brother."

Ainsley doesn't even blush. It turns me on even more. God, this girl!

"Ohhhhh," Bella draws out. "Yeah, okay. We can do that. I'm pretty sure I promised you sex tonight, too."

Comments like this don't faze me anymore. I'm just glad Bella found someone as comfortable with her sexuality as she is. Some of the other girls she dated had a hard time with how open she is about sex—her own and others too.

Hugs are shared. Both Bella and Kylie whisper their own secrets in Ainsley's ear. She takes whatever they say in stride. Only Kylie offers me a comment as she leaves.

"Bella already invited her to the wedding. She says she's not sorry." She hugs me tightly and when she pulls away, with a smile on her face, she adds, "Seriously though, she seems like a keeper."

"Thanks Kylie. Love you. See you soon."

She practically drags Bella away from Ainsley to get her to leave.

"Bye Gray. Love you...." Bella calls out as she's yanked out the door.

Once the door clicks shut, Ainsley looks over to me, a hunger in her wild eyes. "I get you all to myself now?" she asks, sauntering her ass over to me, hips swaying back and forth, her fingers twirling her hair. When she reaches me, she grabs my hand and drags me to the pantry. Since we're alone, she doesn't bother to shut the door.

"Darling, you're forgetting one thing."

She shakes her head. She reaches behind the flour and produces a box of condoms. She's got a wicked gleam in her eyes and her smile matches it.

Without wasting any time, her eyes boring holes into me, she commands in a mischievous voice, "Clothes off now. I've been wet since dinner. Make me come."

Fuck. Me.

I waste no time complying with her request.

11

AINSLEY

*G*rayson hastily strips off his clothes. His eyes watch me the entire time I'm shimmying out of mine, his heated stare causing jitters all over me. As I pull my shirt over my head, I glance around the pantry. It wasn't the size alone that drew me to the pantry, but it's huge. It may even be bigger than the kitchen in my apartment. It's a walk-in one, with counters—yes, like kitchen counters—attached to the wall on both sides. There are shelves above the counters and pullout drawers down below. Almost all of Grayson's small kitchen appliances and the pots and pans are stored here. And the thing is stocked with food. I'm pretty sure I could cook with the food in here and not have to restock for at least a month. Now that I've finally gotten a naked, and very erect Grayson ready to pounce on me, the whole appeal of the pantry has me even hotter and bothered. And pounce he does, before my shirt actually hits the floor.

Leaning in close, he instructs gravelly in my ear, "Turn around and put your hands on the counter." As I turn around to follow his orders, he's pushing a few items out of the way. Like all aspects of his house, the pantry is tidy and organized. The only things "out of place" are the ingredients we used for dinner and dessert.

I lay my palms flat on the counter and just wait for further instruction. Grayson slides up behind me and spreads my legs wider. My pulse quickens in anticipation; my body knows this will be good. "Damn, girl, you're wet." His voice at my neck sends shivers down my spine. "Actually soaked," he amends as his fingers enter me. He slowly starts to move them, just enough to tease me. Grayson seriously must have superpowers because I've already reached that point where having his fingers anywhere near my wetness causes me to moan and then my eyes go closed. Since he's behind me, I figure he doesn't need to see me come. Because that's what I'll be doing. Very soon.

His fingers push in and out, hitting that deep place inside. It takes only a moment to rise to my toes, the power of the orgasm rocking me to the core. It makes my legs quake, so much so that I can barely stand. My feet lower to the ground and once they hit the floor, my arms sag with the weight of my body and I'm falling toward the counter. Grayson pulls his fingers out of me and wraps his other arm around my waist. In no time, he lifts me off the ground and sits my ass on the counter. It's not nearly as spacious as the island, but since I'm hyped up on pure adrenaline and Grayson, I don't notice it so much. My head falls back to rest against the cabinet, and when I finally pry my eyes open, Grayson's watching me.

"That's one," he exclaims, "but not done yet."

I can't even think or move before the guy is kneeling on the ground in between my thighs. He uses his shoulders to widen them slightly, giving himself a better view of me. Noting the desire in his eyes, I figure he's going to attack at any moment, so I'm temporarily caught off guard when he starts trailing gentle kisses up my right thigh. I know I shouldn't be selfish; I mean, he did just get me off, but I'm insatiable for him. And somewhat impatient.

As if sensing what I need without me having to ask—or beg, if the case might be—he quickly finishes up his kisses, ignores the other thigh completely, and hones in on my clit. I swear, with one lick of his tongue, it drives me back to the top of the ledge. Again, it won't take much to make me topple over.

Placing his hands on my inner thighs, Grayson continues to devour me with his tongue. Like he's tasting the best food in the world. His tongue glides in and out of the place his fingers were not moments ago, but I'm done for when he takes my clit into his mouth and sucks. Hard. However, the pain is masked by the pleasure I get as I not only slip over the edge but come barreling down the other side as I ride out another intense orgasm.

I can barely speak, let alone breathe, as Grayson attempts to apparently lick me dry. Once he's satisfied, he pulls his head out and with a grin says, "That's two, darling. How about a third?"

I nod my agreement as I continue to catch my breath. When I'm finally able to speak, I tell him, "You too this time." I'm not sure if he was waiting for permission or if it was his plan all along, but he's grabbing a condom out of the box and sheathing himself just as quickly. "Well, that was disappointing." A small chuckle escapes. His eyes find mine, questioning my words. "You just rolled that on like nothing. Where's the sexy like last night?"

Knowing my meaning behind the statement now, he wiggles his eyebrows and his lips curl up in half a grin. Instead of answering me, he proceeds to lift me off the counter and lays me on the floor, making sure to cradle my head and neck as he does so. Even in the sexy times, he's so darn sweet. Happy with my position, he lies down on top of me, supporting himself on his forearms. With a tender sweep of his tongue across my lips, he makes his move, lining his dick up with my opening. I pick my head up off the ground so I can watch him. With his head right above my breasts, his eyes pore over my body slowly and he licks his lips. I'm about to ask him what he's thinking, and maybe tell him to get moving too, when he suddenly thrusts inside me with no warning.

"Oh," manages to escape my mouth before my head falls back toward the floor, leaving my neck exposed. While moving in and out below, he takes the opportunity to kiss and suck on my neck. "No marks," I squeak out as a warning to him. In understanding, he moves his mouth away from my neck and onto my breasts. *No one will see those marks,* I think with a smile.

I can't focus on anything else but Grayson thrusting in and out and his sucking on my breasts. He moves from one to the other in a rhythmic way as his dick hits deeper and deeper inside me, filling me completely. Almost without warning, my orgasm pummels into me and I'm shouting Grayson's name. I have never come so hard. Ever. "Seeing stars" doesn't do this orgasm justice, possibly ruining me for all other orgasms for the rest of my life. Yeah, that's a bit of an exaggeration, but this guy knows what he's doing.

I don't even have time to recover as I hear Grayson's "Fuck-kkkkk," emptying himself into the condom. Spent, he falls heavily on top of me, matching my breathing almost breath for breath. A few minutes pass, he pulls out, does something with the condom, and then he's shifting us so that I'm now on top. I lay my head on his chest, listening as his breathing starts to even out. The combination of his breathing and the three orgasms leave me in a hypnotic state; my eyes shut as I try to process my feelings of what this man does to me. His fingers find my hair and he begins to twirl, a habit I've come to enjoy the past two days. I'm not sure I ever want him to stop.

"Hey," Grayson starts, bringing me out of my thoughts, "when did you put the condoms in here?"

"While you were cooking on the grill. I knew there was no way we were going to want to go up and get them after the others left."

"Genius. And that was totally worth the wait."

"Um, totally," I say with a laugh and then try to stifle a yawn.

"Come on. Let's go up to bed." He waits for me to move off of him before he pushes himself off the floor.

I lead him into the kitchen. My heart sinks a bit when I realize that the dishes still need to be done. He must notice them at the same time when he declares, "Ah crap. Oh well. I'll do them in the morning."

He follows close behind me upstairs. We both throw on PJs, brush teeth and get ready to hop into bed.

Noticing the bed is made, he looks over at me. "Do you always make your bed?"

I shake my head. "No, just when I change the sheets."

"You changed my sheets?" His tone is hard to read, as are his facial expressions.

"Yes?" I pose it as a question. "Is that okay?"

He pulls me into him. "Yes, of course. It just caught me off guard that it would be something you would do. I love the feel of new sheets, especially when I don't have to make the bed."

He lets me slide in first and then he comes up behind me. It's been a long while since I've had someone to cuddle with. I love how he tucks his arm underneath me, under the pillow.

He's quiet for a few minutes and just when I think he's asleep, I hear him whisper, "Ask me now."

The drinking question.

I meant what I said to him earlier about him telling me when he was ready; I wasn't planning on asking him, especially tonight. I'm glad he's willing to talk about it though.

"Why don't you drink?" I question in a low voice, almost hesitantly even though he gave me permission to ask him.

He takes a couple of deep breaths before he answers. His answer is not something I'm expecting.

"My parents were killed in a car accident by a drunk driver. That day, I promised myself I would never let myself get to the point of being the reason why someone loses a loved one."

He goes quiet. I'm not sure how to respond. I know I gasped with the initial declaration. There are so many questions I want to ask him, but not sure that he will answer all of them.

"Oh Grayson, I'm so sorry." I turn my body to face him. His face shows little emotion. "When?"

"Five years ago." His eyes are the only piece of him that reflect any emotion. The deep brown of his eyes is slightly lighter, softer in a way.

No wonder he doesn't talk about his parents. I want to wrap him in my arms and never let him go. Before I get a chance to do that, he pulls me in closer to him, my head being almost swallowed by his chest.

I think back to something he said that first night on the phone. "Rich is a relative term." It's clear Grayson has financial means, but it must have come at the cost of losing his parents. How horrible for him!

My eyes start to dampen. Luckily they are still buried in Grayson's chest.

In a move so unlike the Grayson I know, he starts to tell the entire story. How his parents were his whole world, along with Bella. Where he was when he got the call. How Bella took the news. The funeral and the aftermath of having to deal with everything, moving back into this house, taking care of Bella and Kylie. How Bella shut down for a few months, and he was afraid he was going to lose her too. How Bella copes by drinking, sometimes too much, but Kylie always makes sure she never has the keys. He gives me all of it. And when he's done, I'm a sobbing mess, and he's the one comforting me.

I manage to squeak out an "I'm sorry" but it's more for my behavior and lack of composure than about him. I follow that up with a "thank for you sharing." He probably thinks less of me now that he knows how I deal with devastating news.

I fall asleep in his arms. When I hear the faint buzzing of the alarm the next morning, I realize I'm still entangled with him. I find it really hard to make my body move and pull out of his embrace. Grayson starts to move as he slowly wakes up. He finally manages to shut off the alarm, but once he does that, he comes back to cuddling with me.

"As much as I don't want to get out of this bed, we should probably get moving. You need to drop me off at home before work."

He groans and pulls me closer to him. "Five more minutes."

I sink back further in his arms and when they wrap around me, they are somehow lighter.

When more than five minutes have passed, I drag myself out of his arms. "Come on lazy bones. We need to get showered and moving."

He quickly pops up, flips me on my back and hovers over me, supported by his forearms. Even though his face is so close, I can't help but admire his bulging biceps. They give the term "arm porn" a whole new meaning. As I lick my lips and stare, he catches me watching. Instead of calling me out, he pushes down lower on his arms and makes them pop even more. He does ten push-ups over me, as I stare, openmouthed. Every time he comes down, he places one kiss on a different part of my face. The last one ends with a kiss on the lips, and I'm forced to close it as he massages my lips with his tongue.

After he does one last push-up, he pushes himself off and flops down on the bed next to me. "Your turn," he instructs. "Let's see who's the lazybones."

I take the same position over him and pretend that I can do push-ups. I can't get traction on the bed and my arms are too wide, so I end up flopping on top of him. He's clearly enjoying watching me struggle, the evidence written all over his face. He wraps his arms around me and squeezes me in a hug. "You should work on that," he tells me in my ear then flips us both over and pushes up off the bed. "Come on, lazy bones. I believe we have to get moving." He saunters into the bathroom, disrobing as he goes.

"You're such a tease!" I yell after him, trying to catch my breath.

I hear his mumbled "so I've been told" come from the bathroom as the water turns on.

Shaking my head, I get off the bed and decide there's no way I can join him in the shower. I must make myself go to the guest room bathroom. We don't have time for any wet distractions right now, not only of the shower variety, even though I'm certain I've got one going on already. I force myself to leave his bedroom and go down the hall to the guest bathroom. Before I can even get my clothes off, Grayson appears, still wet from the shower, a towel hanging low off his hips. He looks taken aback to find me here.

"Don't give me that look," I start as his lips curl into a pout and his eyes look like a sad puppy dog. "We don't have time for distractions."

"What time do you need to be on campus?" he asks, lifting my shirt over my head. Once it's off, he leans in and kisses my neck.

"Eleven," I manage to moan out.

In response, he lifts me off my feet and carries me back to his bedroom, trailing kisses up my neck the entire time. He sits me on the vanity in the bathroom—yep, it's that big—and removes my pants. He practically throws me into the shower, under the warm stream. Just when I think he's going to step in, he closes the door and walks away.

"Grayson!" I shout, wiping the water off my face.

He appears in the doorway, wearing just his boxers, looking all smug. And damn cute. "We don't have time for distractions, Ainsley," he pretends to scold. "Wash yourself up." He walks away again.

"Payback's a bitch," I call out. "Just remember that."

He reappears again, this time wearing a T-shirt and mesh shorts. "I missed that. Care to repeat yourself?"

"Nope." I grab a loofah, dump body wash on it, and start rubbing my chest and abdomen. Just for effect, I close my eyes and make sure I go low enough, between my thighs.

"Fuck, Ainsley," he warns.

I turn around so he can't see me, but it's more for myself than his benefit. He huffs and sighs, and then I'm fairly certain he leaves. I finish my shower quickly and resist the strong urge to relieve myself of the ache between my legs, which takes almost all of my control.

When I emerge from the bathroom, Grayson is nowhere to be found. I throw on my clothes and grab my hairdryer. I dry my hair and leave it down for now.

I toss all my toiletries and dirty clothes into my bag and go downstairs.

Grayson is standing in front of the stove, flipping pancakes.

"You made breakfast?" I ask, dropping my bag and taking a seat at the island.

"I took a chance you like pancakes. With chocolate chips," he replies with a smile.

"Love them actually. Coffee?"

He turns his back to the stove and grabs something off the counter. When he turns back around, he's got a steaming cup. "There's milk in the fridge and sugar in the pantry."

"Black is good." I pause before I continue. "Can I ask you a question, since we aren't in the bedroom?"

He shrugs. "What do you want to know?"

I hesitate for a minute. I'm not sure how to pose it, but the wanting to know has been weighing on my mind since the other night. "I get the sense, from you and Bella and Kylie, that having girls sleep at your house isn't typically you." I pause, working myself up to ask the question. I lower my voice when I finally get the nerve to ask it. "So why me?"

He ponders it a minute while he plates the pancakes. "Truthfully, I don't know. I felt a connection to you from the minute you walked in the bar, and that's never happened to me." I wait for him to add more, but he doesn't. Typical.

"Yeah, I felt it too. So weird, but so good."

He looks up at me as he passes me a plate of pancakes. "You want to do dinner tonight?"

"Only if I can cook for you," I rattle off. "But here at your house. Your kitchen makes mine look like a cardboard box."

"Okay," he chuckles. "Let me know what you need, and I'll stop at the store on my way home from work."

"You fucking grocery shop?" I ask in shock. And then tone it back. He clearly must since his pantry and fridge are stocked. "Sorry. You're just the total package." I throw my hand over my mouth. "Oh my god. I'm shutting up now." To make sure I take my own advice, I start to eat the pancakes, which are mouthwateringly delicious.

He smiles at something I've said or done. Then he grabs

himself some pancakes and takes a seat next to me.

"These are really good. Where did you learn to cook?" I ask in between bites.

"My mother. She was excellent and when she realized Bella had no interest in learning, she taught me everything she knew. I've always enjoyed it and loved that I shared that bond with her."

"That's sweet. I feel the same way, but my dad is the chef in my family. My mom sucks." *In more ways than just cooking,* I don't add aloud.

He seems to pick up on my implied comment about my mom. "You and your mom aren't close?"

I shake my head. "Nope. My brother is and always will be her favorite. Not that I'm bitter or anything. I have my dad and that's cool with me." I stop talking and go back to eating. I don't want to share more and now I definitely see the advantages of Grayson's "less is more" with words.

He changes the subject and I'm grateful for the distraction of having to even think about my mother. "Do you need to go home before work?"

"I need to get my car. And I should probably throw some makeup on my face."

"Don't," he says. "I told you already. You don't need it."

I blush. "Thanks, but I still need my car."

He goes quiet for a few minutes, and we each enjoy our break-fast. In a quiet voice, he breaks the silence with, "I could drop you off to work and pick you up."

I swing my face around to gauge his intentions. "Are you serious?" He nods. "Is this like some sort of possessive fetish you have? Or a way of making sure I come back tonight?"

"Just a part of the package," he returns with a smile. And hell if that smile doesn't make me fall harder for this guy.

"Okay. You can do that, but I do need to stop at my house for my work bag."

It's like I've told him he's won the lottery. His face lights up with a smile so huge, it causes tiny fine lines around his eyes to appear.

"Ok cool," he replies, as if he's hoping to diminish his excitement. "And maybe grab some more PJs and clothes."

Before I can react to *that* comment, he goes back to his breakfast. I don't miss the smirk he's not so conveniently trying to hide.

We finish breakfast, and I clean up the dishes as he finishes getting ready for work. And by that I mean, he brushes his teeth and puts a hat on and slips his feet into running sneakers.

"What time are you done with work?" I ask him as we pile into his Explorer.

"My last client is at two so by three-thirty I should be out of there."

He didn't really go into detail about what kind of "clients" he services or anything about the gym he works at.

"What time do you need to be picked up?"

"My office hours end at four-thirty so I should be good to go by five."

"Okay, I'll stop by the grocery store before I pick you up. Text me a list of what you need."

"Do you have any preference on what I make or anything you don't eat?"

"I'm good with pretty much anything. Make me something that you enjoy eating."

Under my breath, I mutter, "I could fucking get used to this."

I guess it wasn't low enough because quietly he mumbles, "So could I."

12

GRAYSON

*a*fter cooking me dinner and spending the night in my bed —who knew I could be a cuddler—Ainsley insists she has to go home. Despite my persistence to try and make her stay, she wins the fight. We go a few days without seeing each other, and damn if I'm not going out of my mind because no matter how hard I try, I can't get her off of my mind. I keep flashing back to her on the island, seeing how hungry she was for me, how she came so quickly, like she was ready and waiting for me. The stupid smile that creeps over my face won't leave. I feel like it's pretty much permanently plastered there now because she's permanently plastered in my life. In about a week. How the hell did she do that?

As if she knows I'm thinking about her, my phone buzzes with a text.

> Hey, so I'm kind of stuck at the moment and I need a huge favor. I didn't know who else to ask.

Curious, I immediately text her back.

> Anything, darling.

I see the bubbles start, indicating she's replying, but then they stop. They start again but quickly vanish. I keep my phone out of my pocket, anxiously awaiting her message.

After five minutes, she still hasn't texted back. I'm about to text her again, but before I can hit send, my phone is ringing. When the first few beats of the chorus of Lee Bryce's "Love Like Crazy" start playing, I'm startled. Then that damn smile is back on my face; she must have programmed the ringtone in for herself. The irony of the name of the song isn't lost on me. Nothing is truer in my life right now than "loving like crazy."

"Hey," I answer, but she quickly cuts me off.

"Are you busy?" She seems frazzled and out of breath.

"I'm meeting a client in about ten minutes. What's up?" Seven p.m. is later than I liked to schedule clients, but this particular client needed the extra time this week so I made it work.

"Oh okay." I hear her voice drop off, a bit disappointed.

"What do you need?"

She hesitates for a bit, which is unlike her. Then she sighs and takes a deep breath.

"Darling, is everything okay?" My heartbeat starts to quicken, but I'm unsure as to why. Something just seems off with her. Even though I haven't known her long, I feel like what I do know about her isn't jiving with how she's acting right now.

"I need a ride home," she finally articulates.

I can't quite make out what I hear in her voice. Desperation? Regret? Guilt?

"Where are you?" I ask, trying to get more information out of her.

"At the bar," she whispers.

Ah. Tipsy Ainsley, so we meet again.

"Are you alone?" She mutters something, which I don't catch. Before I can ask what she said, the phone sounds like it's been dropped. I hear a muffled "Oh shit" as she struggles to pick it back up. Making a rash decision I hope I don't regret later, I type out a text to another trainer at the gym asking him to cover my client. I know it's a shitty move, but I don't have the best feeling about the whole Ainsley situation. I hope that my client will understand.

When I hear her breathing in the phone, I ask her, "Which bar are you at?" I hurry to the front desk of the gym, clock myself out, and toss a "Thanks" to my buddy who has agreed to take my client. By the time I'm outside, she's finally talking again.

"Um, I don't know the name. It's down the street from the post office."

"Okay, I will be there in less than ten. Stay there and wait for me." Not sure why I add the last part; it's clear she's not going anywhere if she called me in the first place.

Before I hang up, I hear her mutter, "I'm sorry." The line goes dead. I'm not sure if that was for me or someone else, but I pick up my pace getting to my car.

When I pull up to the bar less than six minutes later, the parking lot is crowded. I finally find a spot at the very back of the lot. As soon as my feet hit the pavement, I'm jogging towards the front entrance. Once I get inside, I realize it's going to be a little harder to find Ainsley because there are people packed in everywhere. Trying to waste as little time as possible, I fish my phone out of my pocket and shoot her a text asking where she is. "Bathroom" comes her reply a minute later.

I look around the place. It's been a long while since I've been here, and I don't remember the layout well at all. I head for the back because that's usually where the bathrooms are located. People dancing jostle me every which way, and I have to push a few people out of my way who just literally stop walking in front of me. I get a nasty look from one guy, but I don't let it stop me from walking toward where I think Ainsley might be.

I finally find the bathroom in the back left corner. The hallway is dimly lit, but at least there aren't many people waiting; it's a narrow space. Not knowing whether I should go in, even though it seems like it's a one-person stall, I send her a text instead that I'm outside the door. It goes unanswered for about three minutes. In those three minutes, I put my hand on the door about ten times, but each time I hesitate and don't push the door open. As I'm about to barge in, the doorknob turns, and the door opens slightly. I push my way inside, not knowing what to expect from Ainsley.

The room is dark, the only light coming from a dim, lone light-bulb hanging from the ceiling. Ainsley has backed herself to the side of the toilet, head hanging down, her hair shielding her eyes from me. My heart stops for a beat and my breath catches in my throat. I hardly know this girl, yet my heart aches for her, and I don't even know what's wrong with her.

I clear my throat and slowly start walking toward her. "Ainsley," I start in a whisper. "Are you okay?"

She makes no notion to move, no reaction to me whatsoever.

I feel out of my element here, not being able to see her face and not knowing why she's locked herself away in the bathroom at the bar.

She finally picks her gaze up from the floor, and I see that her eyes are wet, like she's been crying. My feet clear the few feet of space between us in a second, and I'm wrapping my arms around her. I go to speak, but she cuts me off.

"I had a really shitty day at work, and I came for one beer. Then that one beer turned into two. Then I decided that a nice cosmo would be a good idea. Don't ask me why I thought that because I don't even know. But as I downed it, I remembered why I was drinking in the first place, and I kinda spilled my guts to the bartender, and he poured me a shot of something." She shudders before she continues. "It didn't feel good going down, but it felt worse on the way back up. Although it wouldn't have been so bad if I had stopped after that shot. But that's not how I operate. And then..."

I interrupt her, grabbing her face in my hands and pushing it back slightly so I can look into it. "Ainsley, love, are you going to be sick again?"

She stares at me for a minute, her brows crinkled as my words register then slowly shakes her head no.

"Okay, then let's finish this story on the way home."

Her face goes blank, almost as if what I just said was harsh. And maybe it was harsh, but I don't want to be in the bathroom anymore. I need to get out of there; I need to get her out of the bar. She rests her head back on my chest and inhales. "I'm sorry, Grayson. I didn't have anyone else to call."

Ah, shit. Damage control time. I rest my chin on the top of her head. "I'm not mad. I'm glad you called me to help. But I just want to get you out of here. That okay?" Reluctantly, she nods her head yes in agreement. "Do you have a tab you need to pay or any items at the bar?"

"I don't know," she whispers. When she finally pulls out of my arms, she looks on the verge of tears again.

"That's okay. I'll figure it out." I turn to the paper towel dispenser and pull one out. I tenderly wipe away her tears. When I'm done, she gives me a weak smile. I grab her hand in mine and head out of the bathroom.

When we get back out to the open area, I push our way to the bar and flag down the bartender. He comes over, takes one glance at Ainsley, and reaches for something under the bar. He pulls out her purse and hands it over to me. I hand it over to Ainsley and get my credit card out of my back pocket and give it to the bartender. He rings her up and passes me the slip to sign. After signing it, he mouths, "Take care of her" to me before going over to a new customer. I pull out a twenty and put it in the tip jar. When I look over to Ainsley, a look of horror washes over her face. Not knowing what the look means, but hope it has to do with my actions and not the fact that she's going to be sick again, I gently push her in front of me and guide her to the door.

Once outside, she grasps tightly onto my hand, not so much to steady herself, but as an anchor to me.

Confirming my initial thoughts, she says, "I'll pay you back. Just let me know what I owe."

"Not necessary," I tell her.

She wants to say something but thinks better of it. Instead, she mumbles, "Thanks."

At the car, I make sure she's okay for me to drive before I even get in the car. "I'm fine. The burger helped settle my stomach."

"You can finish your story now," I suggest as I pull the car out of the parking lot.

She's quiet and fidgety. "I'm sorry." Her tone is full of regret, and it has to be the fifth time she's said that since we got off the phone.

I look over to her. "For what exactly?" I keep my tone light and judgment-free.

"For starters, for drinking. I know how you feel about it..." she trails off.

"Whoa, nuh uh. You don't apologize for drinking."

She whips her head around to me, and I glance quickly over at her. Confusion is written all over her face. "But you said..."

"I make the conscious choice not to drink. That's my choice. But I have never told anyone else they couldn't drink nor begrudged them when they do. I'm sorry if I gave you that impression."

"Oh," she whispers, then goes quiet. "I thought you would have been all mad at me for drinking, especially to the point where I got sick on the bar."

Did she just say *on* the bar? Despite my own hesitations about drinking, I meant what I said to her. My friends and family all drink. It only ever bothers me if they decide to get in a car and drive after drinking. I feel bad for the girl. I mean, who gets sick *on* the bar? And if that's the case, how is she even this composed?

I realize I haven't said anything in a few minutes. Hesitantly, I ask, "Did you say you got sick on the bar?" She nods. "Man, that must have sucked." I don't mean for it to come out sounding judgmental, and when she snorts, I realize she doesn't take it that way.

"You have no idea. I swear, one minute I was talking to the bartender, and the next, vomit was spewing out of my mouth. It came out of nowhere, almost like the time I had..." She cuts herself off and takes a breath. *Okay, odd.* "The one saving grace was that the bar wasn't as crowded as it was when we left. And I'm pretty sure the bartender thought I was flirting with him. Well, up until that point at least."

Now it's my turn to whip my head around. She was flirting with him?

"Wow, jealous much, Grayson?" *Yes, yes I am.* "Relax, I wasn't flirting with him. I swear." She giggles. I guess I should be happy she finds this amusing now. She continues. "Even if I was flirting, as soon as I spewed vomit in his direction, he was turned off."

Well, she has a point there. And when she goes all quiet, I realize that she's still upset about the whole situation. I don't know if I've helped make it any better or if I've just made it worse.

"If I say thank you one more time, can we pretend none of this happened? Please?"

Here's my chance to redeem myself in her eyes if there's been any wrongdoing on my part. Casually I say, "Consider it forgotten." Just like that, it's done.

"Grayson?" she asks hesitantly.

"Yeah?"

"Can I stay over your house tonight? I don't want to be alone after everything that happened. I'll sleep in the guest bedroom." This girl's got more guts than I do, a quality that I admire in her. I'm highly certain that I'd been begging to go anywhere. Alone.

Raising my eyebrows, even though she's turned toward the window, I drawl, "If that's what you really want. If I were you, I would sleep in the bed upstairs; the sheets are comfier." I await her reaction. If she truly thinks I would allow her to sleep anywhere but my bed, she's got another thing coming.

She's quiet the rest of the ride home. When I pull into the garage, she hops out and heads inside before me. When I reach the kitchen, she's got the coffeemaker turned on and is reaching up for mugs. I can't help but notice how comfortable she is in my kitchen, despite just offering to sleep in the guest bedroom.

"You want a cup?" she calls over her shoulder, turning to look at me.

"Please."

After the coffee has brewed, she carries both mugs over to the table where I'm sitting. She places one in front of me and one in front of the chair across from me then slouches down into the chair. She sighs, then lays her head on the table. She mumbles something incoherent.

"Try that again, please."

She doesn't sit up, but she moves her mouth so that I can at least understand her. "You must think I'm crazy."

Aside for Bella, she's probably the craziest person I've ever met, and that's saying something for the short amount of time I've known her. But there's something about her brand of crazy that totally rocks my world. I didn't even know what was wrong with her when I dropped everything to be at her beck and call. And truthfully, I don't regret it. I'm glad I was the one she called, even if the situation was a lot out of the norm for me.

"Hey," I call out to her, reaching my hand to tip up her chin to me. She pulls her face up, but her eyes stay downcast. "Ainsley, look at me," I command. And then add, "Please."

Ever so slowly, she brings her emerald eyes up to mine. And I can see the regret swimming in them. At least they aren't wet with tears anymore.

I tread lightly with my words. "I've pretty much thought you were crazy since the moment you threw yourself at me. So you had a little too much to drink tonight; it's not the end of the world. And I'm glad that you called me to rescue you."

Her eyes soften and the corners of her lips hint up into a smile. "Thank you for coming to my rescue. You didn't even know what I needed, and you dropped everything you were doing. For me." She adds that last part as an afterthought. Like no one does things for her. Then her face changes to an expression of concern. "Oh no. Weren't you supposed to be meeting a client? I'm so sorry. I could have waited until you were done."

I shrug. "It's all good. As I said, I'm glad you called me."

She tentatively slides her hand across the table and when her fingers reach mine, she wraps them tightly around mine.

"Do you want to talk about your shitty day?" I ask, suddenly remembering it was the reason why she was drinking tonight.

She shakes her head. "Don't even want to think about it anymore. Thank goodness it's over and done with." Her fingers tickle my palm as she rubs them up and down it. The simple gesture makes my heart beat faster and makes my dick pay attention. It will have to admit defeat when I let it know that he won't be seeing any action tonight.

"Did you eat dinner?" Ainsley asks, breaking the silence after a few minutes. "I'm kinda starving. The burger really wasn't enough of a dinner, especially since it ended up all over the bar." She chuckles and then goes silent. "I really am a mess some days, and you didn't even see the worst of it," she adds quietly.

"We all are, darling," I retort.

She laughs at that. "I'd like to see Grayson Abbott's mess."

There are so many comebacks to that, but instead I go with, "So dinner?"

"Please," she pleads. "Something quick and light."

"Cinnamon sugar toast? Peanut butter and jelly?"

"Yeah, okay," is her reply.

"Which one, darling? There were two choices there."

"Oh right." She thinks for a minute, a slight wrinkle appearing between her eyes as she furrows them together. "Toast?" she asks rather than says.

"Coming right up."

I push up out of my seat to go make dinner.

I hear her mumble something under her breath, but this time, I catch every single word. "Some days, I wish I could keep you." All I can do is smile at the sentiment. My thoughts exactly.

After dinner, Ainsley takes a shower. I cuddle up on the couch and choose a movie for us to watch. When she comes back down, her hair is still damp, curling more than usual. She's wearing my Eagles PJ pants and a loose-fitting tank. Again, my dick takes notice. Maybe her idea of sleeping in the guest bedroom isn't so bad after all. And then I laugh at the insanity of that. No way this girl ain't sleeping in my bed.

As if I need more proof of that, she grabs the blanket off the couch and cozies herself up to me, tucking us both in the blanket. I'm lying on my side, my head propped up on my elbow, and my legs spread out on the couch. She lays down next to me, getting as close as she possibly can, and practically burrows her head in my chest. "Comfortable?" I ask, because I sure as hell am.

"Very," she answers.

My fingers gravitate toward her hair and before I know what I'm doing, I've got a strand of her hair wrapped around my fingers. She doesn't even flinch, and if I'm not mistaken, the tiny moans that escape her lips are not from the movie we are watching.

I bring my lips down to her ear. "Still want to sleep in the guest bedroom?" I rasp.

Her eyes close and her breathing quickens. "Nope," she mutters, popping the p. She brings her face around to meet mine, and when she parts her lips slightly, I move in for a kiss.

I can taste the mint toothpaste as my tongue explores her mouth. She gently tugs my bottom lip into hers, then releases it with a pop. Her tongue massages the underside of mine and when I pull mine back slightly, a tiny moan escapes her lips. My finger is still twirling her hair so I gently let it go and push her shoulders down on the couch, never letting my tongue leave her mouth. She adjusts her back and shoulders on the couch but keeps her mouth trained on mine. She wraps her arms around my back and pulls me in closer to her. I'm supporting myself on both forearms but when hers travel lower down my back to my ass, I almost slip. Thinking it's quite funny, she begins to laugh against my mouth.

I pull my mouth off of hers and push myself back up to sitting, breaking out of her grasp. Her laugh quickly fades, and she tries to pull me back to her, but I don't give in to her. "Grayson, I'm sorry."

Before she can continue speaking, I hop off the couch, click off the TV, and scoop her off the couch into my arms. The confusion on her face quickly fades as she realizes what I'm doing, and then you guessed it, she fucking squeals. And I had every intention of being good tonight. Oh, Ainsley Bradford, what are you doing to me?

* * *

*A*fter the night with the bar scene, I'm not ready for Ainsley to leave my house. And if I'm truthful with myself, that would be I'm not ready for her to *ever* leave my house. Okay, maybe I'm really the crazy one.

This time around, she doesn't put up any fight. We settle into a routine that consists of work, making meals, eating, having sex, and cuddling, not necessarily in that order. I love how we work so well together in the kitchen and I have to say, she's an excellent cook. It's been a long while since I've had someone to cook for, let alone cook with.

One Friday a few weeks later, we decide to have a cook-off. It comes on the heels of a competition that we had in the bedroom Thursday night. Not bragging, but it feels good to be the victor. I invite Bella, Kylie, Natalie and Caleb for dinner.

"So remind me again of the rules," Ainsley questions as we drive home from the grocery store.

"Whoever's meal gets the most likes wins. Simple, right?"

"And what does the winner get?"

"What do you think?"

She contemplates her answer for a bit. "Not going to lie. These last few weeks have been amazing, and I could totally just go for more of this."

The simplicity of her answer floors me. I've learned this week that she's low maintenance and the little things in life make her day. Like notes in her lunch. Or the chocolate cupcakes I made with extra chocolate chips.

"Can we agree that this request is a given?" I ask, somewhat hopeful.

"Yes," she chirps out. "So what do you suggest?"

Without missing a beat, I tell her, "Two days on the boat. If I win, we go fishing. If you win, you choose what we do."

"YES! Like two days as in tomorrow right?" she asks, using that voice that tells me I better say yes to that.

"Oh crap. I forgot I have to work the afternoon shift tomorrow." I steal a glance in her direction to watch the excitement fall off her face.

"Next weekend?" she asks, a little less hopeful this time.

"Just kidding. We can leave tomorrow."

She slaps my arm. "I hate you."

"I know, darling. Enough that you want to go home?"

"NO!" she states emphatically.

She mumbles something under her breath. I don't ask her to repeat it because I'm highly certain I know what she said.

When we get home, I let her unload the groceries. She leaves almost everything we need on the counters. "What time did you tell everyone?"

"Seven. That give you enough time to get your chili ready and cooked?"

"Plenty," she says and then adds, "and make a batch of brownies too. I'm going to try black bean ones, that okay?"

"Sure. Whatever you want."

Natalie and Caleb are the first to arrive. Natalie practically accosts Ainsley when she sees her, throwing her arms around her. Ainsley squeals. I'm grateful she never does that in the bedroom because I'd be in some serious trouble. Well, even more so than I already am.

I laugh as I watch them interact and revel in the fact that they get along so well.

"Hey man, how's it going?" Caleb asks me with a pat on the back.

"Great," I reply, stirring the chili.

"She seems happy." He motions over to Ainsley.

"That she is." I steal a glance in her direction. She's got her hair swept off her neck, but she left one strand out so she can twirl it.

And me too. She's wearing her skinny jeans and a new top that apparently still had tags on it from when she bought it. I learned she doesn't like socks, even in the winter, and she brought her slippers from her apartment so she doesn't have to walk around barefoot all the time.

"Grayson! You are going on the boat tomorrow and you didn't invite us? Did you get the heater fixed?" Natalie asks in what is not an indoor voice.

"No. It was a more complicated fix than what I initially thought, and the damn part won't be in until later next week, but yes, Ainsley and I are going on the boat tomorrow. And no, you are not coming."

She pouts. "Aren't you going to be cold?" She looks to Ainsley and then to me. A smirk creeps across her face. "Never mind. I get it."

"Get what?" Bella asks, walking into the kitchen.

"How Gray and Ainsley are going to keep warm on the boat," Natalie answers, walking over to give her and Kylie a hug.

"Oh yeah. They won't have a problem with that," Bella states. "You know he broke his own rules with this one, right?"

Natalie's eyes bug out of her head. "Shut the front door!" She swings around to stare down Ainsley. "And you didn't text me, girl?"

"Why is this such a big deal to everyone?" I ask, but it's purely rhetorical. Everyone thinks it's a big deal I don't sleep around, even some of the girls. It just proves my point of why I like to get to know someone before I sleep with her.

Ainsley comes up behind me and lays her head on my back. I turn around so I can face her. "I'm not sorry you broke your own rules. With the right person, rules are meant to be broken." She palms my dick. She goes up on her tippy-toes but still has to pull my face to hers a bit so she can whisper in my ear, "Ever have sex by the firepit? 'Cause that would be so hot tonight after everyone leaves." She plants a kiss on my cheek and sidles away. And I'm suddenly regretting inviting our friends over tonight.

I adjust myself as I watch everyone interact. I again relish the fact that Ainsley fits right in with the people I care about most in this world.

I hear Natalie yell again, even though I have no clue who she's yelling at. "What do you mean she's coming to the wedding?"

"Caleb, calm your woman down," I say to him with a laugh. Then I add, "Dinner's ready." Where do you think Bella learned to be so good at changing the subject?

Ainsley comes to stand next to me. "Okay, there are two types of chili. Grayson made one and I made the other one. And no, you do not get to know which one is which," she adds before anyone can ask. "You need to take a small portion of each and whichever one you like better, wins."

"What does the winner get?" Bella asks with a gleam in her eyes.

"Grayson wins a fishing trip on the boat for the weekend and I get to pick what we do, which won't involve fishing."

She doles out the bowls, and we all take the meal out to the deck.

I try hers first. Damn, it's delicious. It's got just the right amount of heat. There's agreement all around that both are really good. We let everyone finish both before declaring the winner.

As we go around the table, it's obvious Ainsley's is the crowd favorite. She does a victory lap around the table and it's when she starts swaying her hips I realize that I have fallen in love with her. In a matter of weeks.

Deal with it. I am.

"You have until tomorrow morning to decide where you want to go," I tell her, pulling her onto my lap as she dances by me.

"Okay, I'll let you know," is what she states aloud, but she whispers this in my ear, "I don't really care where we go; just get me out on the water and make me come. I'll be a happy girl."

See what I mean?

In. Love.

"Where have you been all my life?" I ask her in a more serious tone.

As if anticipating the question, she looks deep into my eyes and exclaims, "Just waiting until you were ready for me."

The words almost slip out of my mouth. It takes all of my self-control to keep them in my head. I start to twirl her hair in my fingers, and she lays her head against my chest. I sense that she can feel my erratic heartbeat, but she kisses her palm and places it over my heart.

I make Bella and Kylie clean up the entire kitchen while Caleb and I build a fire. Ainsley and Natalie are off somewhere in the house.

I get the supplies we need to build the fire.

"So you want to admit how you feel about her, bro?" Caleb asks me as we build the fire.

"What are you talking about?" I ask him incredulously but not bothering to look at him.

"Dude, I see the way you look at her. Do I need to spell it out for you?"

"You think I don't know?" I reply, my gaze finding his.

He lowers his voice. "I guess I'm just checking to see how you are doing with it."

"Shockingly, better than I've been in a while," I tell him honestly. His eyebrows raise, like he doesn't believe me. "Trust me, I get where your concern is coming from. You know me. I don't fall for girls in this way. But maybe that's because no one has ever been *this* girl. She gets me, she challenges me, she wants me. We're connected in every way, which is rare, especially for me. I can't explain it, but I don't know that it needs to be explained nor that I want it explained. I'm taking it one day at a time, and those days just happen to be fabulous."

"If you're good, I'm good. And you know Nat's judgment is impeccable." He laughs, implying the way Natalie chose him.

"The fact that Natalie seems to love her makes whatever this is that much easier to accept."

In a minute, all the girls join us. Bella has a pitcher of sangria, Ainsley has the brownies, and Natalie has the makings for s'mores. Caleb and I drag out the chairs from the shed, but I make sure that Ainsley takes a seat on my lap once she's passed out the brownies. Bella passes the sangria out. Everyone but Kylie and I take some.

"These brownies are better than your last batch," Kylie tells Ainsley after shoving the entire thing in her mouth.

"Thanks." Ainsley beams with pride. "These are made with black beans, but you would never know it."

"I never would have guessed that," Kylie says. "Do you do cupcakes? We need some for our shower."

I can tell she's half-joking, but Ainsley gets all excited. "Yes, how many do you need? And when? I would love to make them."

Kylie's about to tell her she's kidding, but Bella pipes in with, "OMG. Yes. Gray can help you if you need help. His cupcakes are pretty incredible."

"Agreed," Ainsley states with a smile.

"Okay seriously. How are you two this close in like what? Twenty days?" Natalie is practically teeming with jealously. Secretly, I love it.

"Twenty-two, but who's counting?" Ainsley giggles.

"Oh, let's play I've Never," Natalie suggests.

Caleb is about to stop her, but I encourage it. "I just need coffee. Kylie, you want coffee?" She nods.

"I'll help you," Ainsley offers.

We go inside and while we wait for the coffee to brew, she looks nervous. "Hey, what is it?"

"You aren't worried you might find out something about me you don't like?" she answers in a voice just above a whisper.

"Nah, should I be?" I'm not really serious but her expression gets even more worrisome. "We could skip it."

"No, it's okay. Besides, I'm kinda curious to learn stuff about you that you haven't shared yet."

"Okay." The coffee finishes, and we head back outside to our friends.

"Anyone not know how to play?" Natalie asks. Everyone implies they know the rules. "I'll start, with an easy one. "Never have I been in love."

Everyone but Ainsley drinks. Natalie looks over at her. "I have a feeling that will change real soon," she enlightens her and then winks. Ainsley takes it in stride and just smiles. "Okay, Caleb, you're up."

"Never have I smoked."

He brings his cup up to this mouth as Natalie shouts, "Smoked in general? Like anything?"

He nods. "Never have I smoked anything." He drinks, as does Ainsley, Natalie, and Bella.

I look over at Ainsley questioningly. "I stole one of my brother's cigarettes when I was like fifteen. I took one puff and practically coughed up a lung. Decided that smoking wasn't worth it."

Bella's up next. Of course hers is sexual. "Never have I had a threesome." She's the only one to drink. Big shocker there.

While Kylie may be comfortable in her skin about her sexuality and others, she plays it safe tonight. "Never have I kissed a person of the same sex." Obviously she and Bella drink, but Natalie's the wild card.

Caleb's mouth opens in shock. "Why am I just finding out about this now?" he declares, more turned on than pissed. "This will be discussed later tonight."

I'm up next. Not wanting to call Ainsley out, but wanting to call her out at the same time, I offer, "Never have I had sex in a pantry." Before she drinks, she glares at me. She eventually takes a sip of her drink, her cheeks flushing from either my question or the alcohol.

When I finish my sip, the other four are staring at us. Bella is the only one who can speak through her shock. "In *this* pantry?" she squeaks.

Ainsley nods her head, then holds up three fingers. Natalie looks like she's about to lose her shit. "OMG!" she screeches. "Girl, we are SO going out for girls' night one day this week. You have a lot of explaining to do." Ainsley merely smiles.

"Okay, my turn. Never have I kissed a person I just met."

Ainsley's the only one to drink on this one. "Seriously? Not even you, Bella?" Bella shakes her head.

"Grayson has some tough standards to live up to," she says with a shrug.

"Wow. I'm impressed, but truthfully, Grayson is the only guy I've kissed when I didn't know him."

"Well, that makes me feel much better," I tell her, pushing her hair out of her face. And then I add my own confession. "Well, technically, I did kiss you back and I didn't know you."

"And then you chased her down for another kiss," Bella adds. "Drink, Gray." And so I do.

The game continues. Some of the girls' questions get a little out of hand, but it's all in good fun. As the girls' get drunker, Ainsley admits to sleeping with guys she didn't know—thankfully we had discussed that before—and also saying "I love you" to someone because it's what he wanted to hear, not because she loved him.

She doesn't learn much more about me because the questions are more relevant to the girls. Until what ends up being the last question.

Natalie and Bella are beyond wasted, and Ainsley's definitely tipsy. Slurring her words, Natalie asks the question. "Never have I gotten a girl pregnant." Her stare is focused on Caleb, almost as if she's goading him. Even in her wasted state, Bella's eyes fly to mine. Ainsley misses that, but she doesn't miss the fact that I'm the only one who drinks.

"Well that's...interesting," she declares. "Care to share that story, Gray?"

I notice everyone looks away from us or down at the ground, even though Bella, Kylie and Natalie are the only ones who knew that. I also notice the fact that she's called me Gray.

Taking a deep breath, I'm about to start, but Ainsley cuts me off. "Actually, I don't want to know right now." She's pissed. Her eyes are darting back and forth and she's huffing. She pushes herself up off my lap and stumbles as she tries to walk away. She waves off my help and heads back inside.

Caleb announces that he's going to take Natalie home. Before leaving, she wraps me in a hug. "Gray, she'll come around. Don't screw this up." Even in her drunken state I know she's serious and this will be the one thing she remembers from the night.

"I have no intentions of screwing it up," I assure her.

"I'm pretty sure that girl loves you," she states, her voice softer now.

"Yeah, I know." I sigh. "I'll make it right." Feeling a little frustrated, I run my fingers through my hair.

She smiles up at me and then removes herself from my arms. Caleb shakes my hand, they say goodbye to Bella and Kylie and then leave.

I sit back down in my chair. "You want us to stay?" Kylie asks in concern.

"No, it was going to come up at some point. Just figured I would have more time and that I would be the one to bring it up." I hug Kylie. "Get my sister home safe."

"Always," she replies, squeezing me a little tighter.

I hug Bella, but her eyes are starting to close. "You need help walking her to the car?"

"Nah, I got it. Go get your girl." Kylie hugs Bella into her side, and Bella slumps into her. Even though she's pretty light, she's deadweight when she's drunk. Somehow Kylie manages just fine to get her to the back door and through the house, I imagine.

I take a few minutes to collect myself, and my thoughts, before I plan to head inside. I watch the flames dance around in the fire a bit, finishing up my coffee. Before I have a chance to make it outside, Ainsley comes back out with a blanket and a cup of coffee.

She's exchanged her jeans for a pair of PJ bottoms and the shirt for a hoodie. She's piled her hair on the top of her head in a messy bun. Her face is devoid of most emotion, except what appears to be sadness. She halts in front of my chair and looks down at me. "Can I sit on your lap?" she asks in a small voice.

"Of course." I pull her down onto my lap and pull her close to me. She lays her head down on my chest and in that moment, I realize I can tell her anything, that she deserves to know all my truths.

I'm about to start when I hear her ask, "How old is your kid?"

"Huh?" I ask, confused.

"Your kid. How old?"

It takes me a minute to realize she's missing so much of the story. I also don't miss the fact she doesn't seem angry I haven't told her any of this yet. "I don't have a child," I start. She lifts her head off my chest, her eyes questioning. "She had a miscarriage at eight weeks. But let me start at the beginning."

I take a deep breath and start. "Molly and I were together for three years. She's the one I was in love with. She's the reason I started the rule about not sleeping with people I don't know. Not that I slept with people I didn't know before her; it just became part of my history after what we went through. I was twenty-two and she was twenty-one. I had just finished college, and she had one more year of school. We stopped using condoms early on in our relationship because we both knew we were in love, and she was on the pill. She failed to mention that when she was ill for about a month, she stopped taking the pill because it was making her feel worse. When she got better, she had forgotten to fill her prescription, but we weren't that sexually active anyway because she was still getting over the illness." I take a minute to catch my breath. Ainsley's still got her head on my chest, but she brings her legs up and curls them under her. I grab the blanket and wrap it around her so she stops shivering.

"Fast forward about two months when she shocks me with the news she was pregnant. Besides for shock, I was pissed because I felt like we had both agreed to stop using condoms because she was on the pill. I blamed her. I was pissed because this totally could have been avoided. Did I love having sex with condoms? No, but I would have started using them again to prevent this from happening."

Instinctively, I take a strand of Ainsley's hair out of the bun and begin twirling it around my fingers.

During my brief pause, Ainsley asks, "Did you consider abortion?"

I shake my head. "No, neither one of us wanted that, even though we knew it was going to be hard to raise a kid. And we vetoed adoption as well. My parents were supportive to an extent, although hers were against us having the baby. I always looked at it as a blessing in disguise that she miscarried. It kind of solved our 'problem' so to speak without us having to make the decision.

"After we lost the baby, she fell into a depressed state. She dropped out of school and stopped going out. Heck, she barely got dressed. I tried to help her out, but she eventually shut me out too. She ultimately got better, and we started talking again. I thought we may have been able to overcome everything, but then my parents died and I couldn't focus on her at all. My focus shifted to Bella. And well, she didn't take that too well. She couldn't handle that I couldn't put her first anymore, even if it was only temporary."

"How awful of her," Ainsley pipes in. "You were dealing with the death of your parents and having to take care of your sister."

"She didn't see it that way, but it was another blessing in disguise. I didn't realize she was so mentally unstable, but it never would have worked out for us."

I finish the story there.

"Did she get the help she needed?" Ainsley asks, her concern for this stranger evident in the tone of voice she uses.

"Honestly, not enough. She spent some time in a mental hospital, but she checked herself out. I was glad when she decided to move out of state. When she ran into Bella, she accused her of taking me away from her. Bella didn't let on that it bothered her, but inwardly, I know it took its toll on her. Fortunately, Kylie was there to support her. Natalie, too."

"Thank you for sharing this. I'm sure it wasn't easy."

"This isn't an excuse, but I would have told you on my time. It's a lot to burden a person with in the first few weeks of knowing someone."

"I get it. And neither one of us knows where this is heading anyway."

I shudder at the thought of this not going in the direction that I see it going, but realistically, she's completely right. It's been just over three weeks, and I'm sure there's more of Ainsley that she hasn't shared with me.

"Are kids something you see in your future?" she asks quietly.

I've given this question a lot of thought, especially given everything that happened with Molly. "Yes," I answer truthfully. "Because once I got over the initial shock, there was a small part of me that was excited to welcome a child into this world. The timing was just shitty then, and well, so was my choice of partner, as it turns out. I feel like I matured a bit since then, especially with the death of my parents on the heels of that tragedy, and well, I've gotten smarter about protection. I haven't had sex without a condom since the time Molly got pregnant."

I realize it's a lot for Ainsley to absorb, especially this late at night and with her still being inebriated. "What about you?"

"Yes. Despite my rocky relationship with my mom, I've always wanted to be a mother."

At least we are on the same page there, I think to myself, and then criticize myself for going down that path right now. I'll just file it away for future reference.

I watch as the fire starts to dwindle and debate whether to add more kindling and logs. It's then I notice that Ainsley is asleep in my arms, her breathing slow and even. Making a snap decision, I carefully maneuver myself out of my chair, holding her steady against my chest. I shift her so that her legs are dangling from my arms, her head still tucked into my chest. She doesn't stir, even as I climb the stairs to my bedroom. I lay her down and pull the covers up around her. Her eyes flutter open and she whispers my name before she closes them again, turns over, and falls back into a deep sleep.

I go back outside and douse the fire in water before returning inside. In my room, I change my clothes and crawl into bed next to Ainsley. As I drift off to sleep, I hope she's the only girl I have to tell that story to.

13

AINSLEY

When I wake up, I am disoriented and have a raging headache. I don't remember everything from the night before, including how I got into Grayson's bed. I remember him telling me his story. As he was telling me, I couldn't look up at him because the tears that pricked the corners of my eyes would have been unleashed, and I couldn't let him see me cry again.

As he poured his soul out to me, I couldn't even bring myself to tell him my story, the one that's so similar to his, only with a different path to the same outcome. I know he's not a judgmental person by nature, but I've never come to terms completely with my decision six years ago. Last night proves that. Plus, I didn't deem it appropriate to burden him with my story when he just unloaded his. I know it will come up eventually, but as I said last night, we don't know where this is going. I know where I would like it to go, a place where my heart has pretty much already gone.

I feel him stirring next to me. Without opening his eyes, his strong arms reach out and pull me closer to him. "You feel okay?" he questions with a gentle tone.

"I didn't pass out, did I?"

"No, you fell asleep in my arms, but you were so cute, I couldn't wake you. It's so convenient to just carry you inside and tuck you into my bed." He still hasn't opened his eyes, I've noticed.

"I'm not complaining." With that, he pulls me closer to him. I nuzzle my head into his chest. "I could use some ibuprofen though," I say, more to myself. Pulling out of his grasp after a few comfortable minutes, I ask, "Where do you keep it?"

He pops up off the bed and hustles to the bathroom. He's back in a minute with a bottle of ibuprofen and a cup of water. He hands me both and takes off for the bathroom again. Sitting up in bed, I shake two pills out of the container and down them. Before Grayson gets back, I settle back down in the bed.

He's back in a few minutes and when he climbs in next to me, he resumes our cuddled position, pulling me back into his chest. "You still up for our boat excursion?" he asks.

"Um, yes." I can't wait to get on his boat and just be on the water. "I need to stop at my apartment and grab some warmer clothes before we go."

"Okay. It's a good thing you don't have any pets. Or plants. They would all be dead by now." He chuckles at his own statement and grabs a strand of my hair to twirl in his fingers. I love that he feels comfortable enough to do this. I've intentionally started leaving strands out for him to play with when I pull my hair back.

"Yeah, that wouldn't be good."

It's only been a few weeks since I've been with Grayson, but lying here in bed with him makes me forget what I used to even do on Saturday mornings. I already feel like this is what my Saturday mornings should consist of, maybe minus the hangover. I close my eyes, hoping to alleviate some of the pain that's taken over my head.

The next thing I know, it's about two hours later, and I realize I fell back to sleep. I sit up, a little too quickly, but some of the pain has subsided. Grayson's still in bed, but he's playing games on his iPad.

"Hey, sleepyhead. Ready to rejoin the land of the living?"

"Not particularly," I complain. "As if this king-sized bed wasn't comfortable on its own, you have to be in it too." I look up at him, a smile on my face. He places a tender kiss on the top of my head and then smiles at my comment. "How's the bed on the boat?"

"It's not as comfortable as this one," he replies, going back to finish his game. "But for one night, I think we can make do."

"When do you want to leave?"

"There's no rush."

"You shouldn't tell me that. I'll go back to sleep..." I cuddle closer to him, sneaking myself underneath his arm.

He puts his iPad in his lap. "Darling, you in my bed or you on my boat makes no difference to me."

"Where should we go on the boat?" I ask, willing myself to get some motivation to get out of bed.

"I was thinking we could go over to Bar Harbor. I don't think it will take too long to get there, but I can map it out. We can spend the day exploring it. Bella loves the shopping there, or so she says. Have you ever been?"

I shake my head. "No, but I've always wanted to go to Acadia National Park. Can we work that in?"

"You won, so you get to pick, silly." He tousles my hair.

"Then we are doing that. And I'm getting out of bed. Right. Now." I finally will myself out of bed to get the day started.

* * *

*A*fter a brief stop at my apartment for warmer clothes and to bring in the mail, Grayson drives us down to the marina where his boat is docked. It's a short drive, but as we get closer and the boats come into view, it's quite fascinating. He parks the car in the lot for overnighters, and we unload our bags and food. At his insistence, Grayson makes easy work of carrying all our stuff. He grabs my hand as he leads me down to the docks. We pass by several boats of various sizes, but the closer we get to his, the bigger they get.

When we reach what appears to be his boat, I gasp at the sight. "This is seriously your boat?" I ask in amazement.

"Yep, she's a beauty isn't she?"

"Yes!" I whip out my phone to take a few photos of it, including a selfie in front of it. Grayson hops aboard to get everything ready while I admire the boat. The boat is named *Gray's Bells*. "Who came up with the name?" I shout up to him.

"My father. He wanted a piece of both of us."

It's then that I realize he only has this boat because of his parents' death. Shaking off the sad feeling I won't allow to creep in, I start to climb aboard. Grayson reaches his hand out to me and helps pull me over. "Welcome to my home on the sea," he states, pulling me in for a hug. "I just need to make a few adjustments and then we will be on our way. Feel free to look around."

While he does whatever he needs to do, I take the grand tour. We climbed on the back, which has a two-seater couch. I descend the stairs first. Down below, there are two rooms, each with a double bed. I throw myself on one of them, the one that appears to be Grayson's room. The bed seems comfortable enough. There's a tiny bathroom to the left complete with a stall shower. It will definitely be cramped for two of us should we decide that's something we want to do.

The other bedroom is similarly decorated, but it lacks that comfortable feeling. I think it's solely because knowing Grayson's room is the other one has me drawn to it. There's a bathroom right outside the door to this bedroom.

I take a peek in the room with the engine and "boat parts" but as soon as I see that's all it is, I quickly move on. There's a storage room as well down here. It contains some of the necessary supplies for fishing, including tackle boxes and fishing rods. I run my hands along the rods and imagine Grayson behind me, teaching me how to fish.

I continue my tour back upstairs. The kitchen is small. There's a tiny amount of counter space, a stovetop and oven, a sink and a fridge. Opening up the one cabinet, I find a few mismatched pots and pans.

The dining area is directly across from the kitchen. There's a table attached to two benches. It will easily seat four adults comfortably. I can't help but wonder who Grayson has entertained on the boat as I make my way to the back of the boat, where we climbed aboard, and where Grayson is doing something. I take a seat on the couch and ogle him. He looks like he's taking notes on a clipboard, and then I realize he's on the phone.

"Okay, great. We'll be there in about a few hours or so." He hangs it up, makes one final note on the clipboard, and takes a seat next to me. "So, what do you think?" he asks, eagerly awaiting my answer.

"It's incredible. Thanks for sharing her with me."

He nods. "Of course. I'm glad you agreed to come along. You ready to hit the open water?"

"Yes, please."

He gives me one last hug before pulling me up. He grabs my hand and leads me to the helm. There are two white, comfy-looking chairs. In front of one sits the steering wheel and controls for the boat. He takes that seat and motions for me to take the other one. Happily, I sit my ass down in the chair and tuck my legs underneath me. Looking out the windshield at the water, all I see are boats. I know that will change soon, once we hit the open water.

He starts up the boat, clicks the lever into drive, and slowly eases us out of the boat slip, leading us away from the dock. I watch Grayson as he drives. He's extremely comfortable standing in front of his chair, one hand on the wheel. He clearly knows what he's doing, as if he's been doing it for a long time.

"How long have you had a boating license?" I ask him curious to know.

"First off, here in Maine, it's not a license. It's a Boater's Education Card. I've had it since I was first able to, at sixteen. We had a smaller boat then, and my dad taught me how to drive it when I was young, probably around eight or so. I couldn't officially get my card until years later, but I've been driving boats longer than I've been driving cars. And I started that before I officially had my driver's license." He peers over at me with a smirk.

"Cute," I tell him. Because well, he is.

In less than ten minutes, we are out of the marina and onto the open water. It's absolutely breathtaking, not only the view, but being beside this handsome man who I can't keep my eyes off of. The ride to Bar Harbor takes a couple of hours, and we keep conversation to a minimum. Grayson focuses on the navigation system to make sure we are on track and heading the right way to the marina at Bar Harbor. He's made reservations for us to be able to dock the boat overnight when we get there.

Once Grayson has pulled the boat into the dock, it's about all I can do not to jump his bones. He is seriously so sexy driving the boat. The entire ride over, all I wanted to do was shove my hands down my pants and relieve the ache that resided between my thighs. His flirty winks didn't help much either.

"So, can we go check out the bed now?" I ask in my most pleading and sexy voice, laying on the charm.

"You realize you aren't so subtle, right?"

"Of course I do. I'm not trying to be subtle. I'm trying to ease the throbbing that is lodged between my thighs right now." He's sitting in the captain's chair behind the wheel, so I try to climb into his lap.

"Downstairs," he commands. "Meet you there in two." He practically tosses me to the ground to get out of his seat. I scurry to the back of the boat, down the stairs, and make my way to the bedroom. I strip my clothes off and climb under the covers.

When he comes into the room, he wastes no time undressing. I hold up the blanket so he can crawl in next to me. He reaches his hand in between my thighs and smiles at how saturated I already am. "Damn, girl. Love that you are ready for me." He fingers my clit, circles it a few times, and then slips one finger inside. My body reacts instantly to his already familiar touch. It's not going to take much to bring me to orgasm, especially when Grayson starts breathing heavy.

He shifts his body so he's more on top of me, rather than sitting next to me. I watch as the veins in his arm pop out as he slips another finger inside. His other hand cups my breast, his fingers circling my nipple and then tugging gently. My hand finds my other breast and I mimic his movements. My head tips back against the pillow, exposing my neck. He brings his head down and feathers kisses down one side.

When I hear him whisper, "Let go, darling," I obey his command. I let my orgasm wash over me, the heat filling me up with ecstasy. My hips lift off the bed as he continues to slip his fingers in and out. He moves his lips to the other side of my neck and this time kisses up my neck. I wrap my arms around his back and allow myself to come back from the brink of pleasure.

As he kisses my neck, he removes his fingers and drags them up to my clit. He circles it a few times before he hops off the bed. I lay on the bed, massaging my breasts while I wait for him to get the condoms.

I hear him rummaging through the bags. "Hey, did you pack them?" He lifts his head over the bed.

"Nope, that's your job," I tell him, flicking my taut nipples, feeling myself beginning to rise again.

"Fuck," he moans, drawing out the last part of the word. Before he climbs back up on the bed, I notice the pre-cum on the tip of his dick. His face is pensive, as if he's contemplating something, clearly about to break another one of his rules.

Looking him straight in the face, I tell him, "No." I let my hands fall from my breasts. "Use your mouth."

He shakes his head and pretends to pout. "How exactly does that help me?"

His comment surprises me because he's not selfish when it comes to sex. At all.

"I'll let you come on my breasts," I quickly offer, sliding my ass back towards the pillows to sit up.

He starts to stroke his dick, as he hovers over me. "You're on the pill. I'm clean, you're clean. It will feel so good." He drags his dick along my stomach, getting awfully close to my groin area.

"No," I assert again, more adamantly this time. I don't want to remind him of what he told me yesterday, but that's not the only reason why I won't do it. "You want me to suck you off? I'll even swallow," I add with a smile.

"Tempting, but maybe later." He continues to stroke himself, but I can tell he's not satisfied.

"Let me stroke you," I tell him, adding my hand on top of his. As I try to push it out of the way, he shifts his body so I can't reach it from my position. As I watch him, I realize how aroused he's making me. So much so that my hand finds its way down my abdomen and in between my legs. I hover above my clit for a few seconds to determine his reaction. When his eyebrows go up, I find my clit and start rubbing. My eyes automatically close as I'm already keyed up.

"Eyes open, Ainsley," he instructs.

When I force them back open, he's sitting back on his knees continuing to stroke himself. His deep chocolate eyes bore into mine, and it spurs me on. My fingers attack my clit at a faster pace, and he picks up the pace for himself as well.

I lick my lips at the sight of the pre-cum leaking out. Trying to focus my attention on him as well as my pending orgasm, I lose the battle as my orgasm hits hard. My eyes close for the briefest of seconds as my insides tighten and the rush of pleasure overtakes my body. I remove my hand from my clit and lay it against my stomach.

When I'm able to open my eyes, I watch as Grayson's orgasm hits, the cum shooting all over my chest and stomach.

When he takes in what he's done, his eyes widen and he exclaims, "Shit. That was fucking hot." He hops down off the bed to grab a towel from the bag. He comes back over and gently wipes me down.

"Have you never done that before?" I ask him.

"Never," he replies, "but I'm adding that to my list to do again."
His lips turn up into a smile as he continues to rub me down. Then
his face gets more serious. "Have you done that before?" he asks,
and then quickly adds, "You know what I mean."

I shake my head with a giggle. "Nope, but feel free to do it
again."

He finishes cleaning me up and throws the towel on the floor,
then lays against the pillows, and hauls me up onto his chest. He
takes my hair down and slips the hair tie on my wrist. I get more
lost in him when he starts twirling my hair and almost miss what
he says. "We can get some condoms when we go to town in a bit.
I'm sorry I forgot them."

"I'm not," I respond honestly. "That shit was hot."

He nods in agreement. "I love watching you come."

And I love you, I almost voice. Where it comes from, I'm not
entirely sure, but damn it if it isn't true.

"Are you hungry?" he asks.

"A little." I look back at him. "Don't take this the wrong way
because you know I love your cooking, but can we go out to eat?
Like a real date?"

"Ainsley Bradford, are you asking me out on a date?" he asks
with a chuckle.

"Totally. Will you go out with me?" I wonder playfully, taking a
piece of my hair and tangling it around my fingers.

"Only if I get to kiss you at the end. With my tongue."

"Whoa there, buddy. Slow down. Let's get through the meal
first and then we can see where it leads." I can't contain my amusement, and by the end of the statement, I'm full-out laughing.
Grayson joins in, and then he starts to tickle my feet. Since my feet
are extremely ticklish, I get a little too close to kicking him in his
still uncovered sensitive areas, so instead, he tackles me to the bed.
There's a wild look in his eyes, and as he gazes down between my
legs, I know what he wants.

"No. I'm taking you on a date." I push him off of me, unsuccess-
fully, because he weighs more than me, and he's as strong as an ox.

"Grayson, come on," I plead with him, but he puts more pressure on me to hold me down.

"You said 'come' so I must obey."

I roll my eyes at him, telling him, "You're ridiculous." When his face finds me wet and ready to go again, I give up. "Food can wait," I manage to stutter out as I feel my stomach start to tighten.

* * *

*a*fter two more orgasms, he finally relents and lets us get ready to leave the boat. We shower separately because it's way quicker. And quite frankly, I'm starving.

I throw my wet hair in a braid because Grayson won't let me dry it. Just for that, I make sure to tuck in all the strands. Tight. It's the first thing he notices.

He looks my head over carefully. "Yeah, that's not going to work for me," he informs me, as he tries to pull a strand out.

"Hey! Cut it out. Leave it be or you will not be getting your kiss after our date."

Like a toddler, he pouts and is about to complain again, but thinks better of it. "I hate you," he tells me, sticking out his tongue.

I smirk at him. "Prove it to me later so that I actually believe you." I pat his abs—because who can ever get enough?—and walk away, leaving him standing there with his mouth wide open. I smile, knowing how much pleasure I get in the playfulness we bring out in each other.

He catches up to me and throws his arm around my shoulder. When he pulls me in closer, he places a kiss on the top of my head. As he pulls his face away, he mumbles something. Five words. Five little words that have an impact so big that I stop walking.

"What did you say?" I whisper. I grab his wrist and try to pull him back to me. Thankfully, he comes willingly.

He puts his hands on my shoulders, and I can't help but look up at his face. It's there in his eyes, what he just said.

He takes a deep breath. With his gaze locked on mine, he states slowly, "I think I love you."

As if the confession isn't enough, he crashes his lips to mine. It hits me full force, making me stumble. He steadies me without removing his lips. As he takes my bottom lip into his, I can't even close my eyes; he's shocked them wide open. I feel like I can't breathe as I start to sway back and forth, and he's still got his lips on my mouth. Feeling way too overwhelmed, I pull my lips away from his and fall into his chest. Trying to steady not only my breathing but my pounding heart as well, I hear him question, "Ainsley?"

Tears catch at the corners of my eyes, and I burrow my head deeper into his chest, wrapping my arms around his back. He embraces me in his arms and squeezes me tightly. And it's all I can do to just stand steady on my feet for a few minutes. I'm grateful that he just holds me.

When minutes pass, although no clue exactly how long, I squeeze him one last time and then pull out of his embrace. His face is worried, so to reassure him I'm okay, I push up on my tiptoes and plant a tender kiss on his lips. Looking up into those eyes of his, I have to clear my throat before I can speak.

"I'm sorry," I start, clearing my throat once again. "You caught me off guard. My emotions are all over the place. *You* have my emotions all over the place. I'm so not a crier, and yet, I've cried twice in the time I've known you. And they are tears of happiness because you make me so incredibly happy. I've never been so consumed by someone before, and well, it's overpowering in the most incredible and indescribable way. It's because I don't think; I know." I don't want to steal any of his thunder, nor do I want to say it because he said it to me. Even though I'm sure he wants to hear it, I want him to *know* I mean it too, that I'm not merely parroting his words.

I place one hand over his heart and the other one over mine. "It's yours," I whisper. "You're the first. Tread carefully." And I laugh because I need to lighten up the mood. Because as good as this feels, it's so deep that it's too heavy to deal with all of it.

Apparently it's too heavy for Grayson, too. He shakes his head side to side, glancing down at the ground, muttering something. When he picks his face up, his look is less serious than before. "Damn it, girl. Why do you have to go and say shit like that? Here I thought I was doing okay, telling you I love you, and you fucking go and ruin me. This?" He indicates the space between us, my hands still on our hearts, and he puts his hands on top of mine. "I feel it, too. Don't think I'm giving your heart back to you."

All I can do is smile. He's the first to remove his hands, just so he can wipe away the tear that's fallen down my face. I grab his hand in mine and start walking along the dock. "Come on. I owe you a date."

"After that, I'm pretty sure you owe me more than just a date." His smile sneaks across his face, and he winks at me. He brings his mouth down to my ear. "I'll collect later, darling."

"I wouldn't expect anything less."

14

GRAYSON

I had zero intentions of telling this beauty by my side my true feelings for her, yet I find myself having bared my heart out to her tonight. At least she doesn't think I'm crazy, and heck, she feels the same way. Not that I thought she didn't; I just wasn't sure if she was ready to admit it to herself or to me. I got a little nervous at her initial reaction until I realized she was just feeling how big this thing is between us and that's how she reacted.

We find a small café for our date. She's so cute when she pulls my chair out for me before I sit. She hands me my menu and asks, "What will it be today, Mr. Abbott?" She can't contain her amusement and starts to laugh playfully right away. I love watching her eyes when she laughs. The green actually lightens up to match the lightness on her face. I sit back and stare at her. She knows I'm staring; as she looks over the menu, her smile gets bigger and bigger without even looking up.

"Stop," she hisses at one point, catching me staring. She looks back to her menu, her brows furrowing.

Sitting up taller in my chair, I grab my menu. "What?" I ask her.

"I can't decide what I want. Everything looks so good."

"Let's get a few and split them," I suggest. "We'll work them off later." I wink, which makes her grin again. It's smaller this time, but the sentiment is the same.

"I bet we will," she responds. "Oh, we need to get condoms."

"Or not."

She stares up at me, a look of determination on her face. She doesn't get that I'm serious, but I am. I'm aware of the consequences, but I want to get inside her with nothing between us. She's more adamant than I am. "No, Grayson." It's not what she says, but how she says it. Her tone is hard, not exactly harsh but tougher than usual. And I get it, especially with what we talked about last night. I'm not ready to go down that route again, but she's on the pill. I know she takes it every day; the situation is way different. But I'm not about to start an argument, especially on our date, so I drop it.

"Okay, so what are you in the mood for?"

Well, I don't completely drop the subject. "You?" I ask.

"Grayson!" she whisper-yells. "Focus. On the food." Then she licks her lips. Because she knows she can.

"Do you trust me?" I ask, grabbing the menu from her hands.

"Yes," she says slowly.

When the waitress comes over to the table, she asks if we are ready to order. I motion her over to me and lean in and whisper our order. I watch as her cheeks blush, but what I'm saying is purely to get a rise out of Ainsley. She gives me the evil eye and after the waitress walks away, she stares me down.

"What did you just tell her?" she asks, somewhat hesitantly.

"I ordered us some food. You said you trusted me." I flash her my smile, the one that she can't resist.

"You are impossible sometimes. You know that, right?" She smiles as she shakes her head.

"Just when you tell me."

We chat, mostly about the things we are still learning about each other. I love how our conversations aren't forced and the conversation flows easily between us.

The waitress brings over our food, a grilled cheese and bacon sandwich, cheese fries, and an order of wings. Ainsley actually gasps when she sees the food. I've noticed that she tends to eat on the healthier side when we've cooked at home, but she eats almost anything. I'm totally taking her out of her normal comfort zone, but knowing Ainsley, she will roll with the punches.

As she takes half of the grilled cheese sandwich, she declares, "One night of sex is NOT going to work off all these calories, but I'm digging in anyway." She takes a hearty bite and the cheese drips down her chin. She swipes at it with her napkin and digs back in. Once she's eaten her half, she looks at me. "I'll just have to join you at the gym on Monday. Will you be my personal trainer?"

"You want to come to the gym with me?" I ask, surprised.

She nods. "Yeah, is that okay? It's been a while since I've actually been to a gym, but I think I could handle whatever you throw at me."

"You think, huh?" I ask skeptically.

"Maybe?" Her tone lacks the confidence from a moment ago. "You can take it easy on me."

"Yeah, sure. You can join me sometime." I finish up half of the grilled cheese sandwich and enjoy some wings which Ainsley hasn't touched. "You don't like wings?" I ask, licking the sauce off my fingers.

"They aren't my favorite," she replies polishing off the fries on her plate.

"Filed away for future reference." She smiles at me, then reaches into her bag for her phone. I can tell it's ringing but can't tell who's calling her. One glance down at the phone has her smile quickly fading from her face and a total frown replacing it.

"Shit," she mumbles under her breath. "No thanks. Not now." She dismisses it, puts it back in her bag, and looks back at me, anger still evident on her face.

"Who's that?"

"My brother."

She doesn't elaborate, and I don't want to push her. I get the whole "less is more" mentality.

"Okay." I finish off the wings and eat a few more fries. When the waitress comes over to ask if we are done, I nod because I can tell Ainsley is ready to go. I hate that she shuts down when she's upset or frustrated.

"Were you and Bella always close?" she asks in a voice just above a whisper.

"For the most part, yes. Since my parents died, we've definitely gotten closer, but it helped that we had a good foundation to build on." I want to ask her about her brother, whom she's only mentioned in passing. Her brother and her mother are the only pieces of her life she doesn't share. She's regaled me with stories of her father, but they always are about her and him only.

"That must be nice." She sighs. "Drew and I used to be close but not so much anymore. As I get older, it bothers me more and more because he's the only sibling I have." She tugs on the end of her braid, eyes downcast toward the table. The phone vibrates again in her bag, so she pulls it out. "Ugh, now he's texting me." With the frown still plastered on her face, she reads the text, getting more frustrated by the second. "Fuck! He's coming for a visit next month." She doesn't text him back but instead puts her phone away. "Can we go?" she asks quietly.

"Um, did you pay for our food yet? Remember, this was your date to me." I smile.

Her demeanor doesn't change. "Oh, crap." She digs in her bag for her wallet, but I toss some money on the table, enough to cover the meal and the tip. "No," she says, trying to hand the money back to me.

"It's on me, darling. Let's get out of here." Before she can protest anymore, I grab her arm and drag her out of the restaurant. "Can we walk?" I ask, treading lightly because I'm not exactly sure what's going on in her head.

She looks up at me, her face now reflecting sadness. "Yeah, okay. I would like that." She rearranges her fingers with mine. "He says he has big news to share, that's why he's coming. He's probably getting married. Oh, my mom is so going to love this."

"Where does he live?"

"He's in Illinois, right outside of Chicago. He comes to visit like four times a year, and my mom goes to see him a few times, too. Sometimes my dad goes and sometimes he stays here."

"What does your brother do?"

She laughs. "Ha. That's a funny one," she starts. "Basically, he does nothing. He pretends to be in a band and he pretends to work in a coffee shop. And by pretends, I mean he hangs out in the coffee shop all day long but doesn't get paid."

"How does he live then?" I ask, curious.

"I really wish I had an answer for that one. I'm highly certain my mom sends him money every month, but she would never share that information with me. And if I ever tried to live like that? HA!" She guffaws. "My mother would be up my ass so fast..."

"You'd let your mother up your ass?" I interrupt her, feigning shock.

She playfully jabs me in the arm. "You know what I mean." When she laughs, I know my joke worked, if only for a little bit. Looking around, she squeals and squeezes my hand. "Gray, a candy store. Come on. Let's go inside!"

Okay, seriously? Between the squeal and my nickname, it's all I can do to actually follow her into the candy store and not pick her up and race back to the boat. But then I change my mind. Because she is like a kid in a candy store. Literally. The girl is giddy. She grabs a bag, tosses one to me, and says, "Fill it up. Choose your favorite ones, and we can share later." She wastes no time walking up and down the aisles, adding a few pieces—or a lot of pieces in some cases—to her bag. By the time she's done, candy is practically jumping out of the bag. I take more time, methodical in my selections. The store carries a lot of lesser-known candies, ones I haven't had in years, so I want to make sure I get all the ones I want. She waits, not so patiently, for me to make my selections.

Once I'm satisfied, we bring them up to the register and weigh them.

"Twenty-five bucks for candy?" I ask in horror.

"It will last us a while," she assures me, taking out her wallet to pay. She eagerly hands over the money to the sales clerk, a girl of about seventeen. Once she's paid and is about to walk off with her loot, she casually tosses out, "Where can we get condoms?" She motions her head over at me. "It seems he forgot to pack them."

The girl's face goes bright red but she squeaks out, "There's a CVS on Main Street. It's about a five-minute walk."

"Thanks!" She grabs my hand and drags me out of the store, as I mouth a "sorry" to the sales clerk.

"Can you get the directions to CVS please?" she asks me as we walk back along the street. I pull out my phone, find the address, and plug it in.

"Why are you so adamant about getting the condoms?"

"Why are you so adamant that we don't need them?" she counters with a glare in my direction.

"Because I want to know what it feels like to fuck you bare," I state honestly.

She shakes her head. "No."

"You didn't answer my question."

She stops walking. When she glances in my direction, I can feel her eyes bore into mine. "I refuse to become a Molly," she affirms emphatically.

"That could never happen," I promise her, wrapping her up in a hug.

"Yeah, well, let's make sure we don't let it." She pulls herself out of my embrace and keeps walking, hands by her sides.

"Are you mad?" I ask tentatively.

"No, just standing my ground," she replies more softly.

I grab her hand and when she doesn't push me away, I entwine my fingers with hers as we continue to walk.

* * *

*A*fter we hit up CVS, we walk around the harbor a little more. When we finally head back to the boat, I can tell she's tired. I lock up everything and join her in the bedroom. She still has the braid in her hair, but she's changed into her PJ bottoms and a tank top. She's lying on the bed, her eyes half-closed.

"Hey, you okay?" I call to her as I shed my clothes, leaving just my boxers.

"I'll be better when you're next to me," she replies, but her emotions remain fixed.

"Be right there." I make a stop in the bathroom then fling myself on the bed, crawling up to where she's laying. "Hey," I say trying to cure her bad mood, kissing her breasts through the tank.

"Hey." She runs her fingers through my hair, tugging at the ends. "I'm sorry," she whispers.

"No apology necessary," I tell her, then I pull down her tank with my teeth, exposing her right breast. A slight moan escapes her lips. "You ready for this round?" Slowly, she nods her head yes. She's got it thrown back on the pillows and her eyes are closed.

I carefully lift the tank up her arms and over her head and when I go to shimmy her pants down her legs, I find her bare underneath.

"Oh, Ainsley, you little devil, you." She lifts her head; her smirk couldn't be bigger if she tried.

15

AINSLEY

*G*od, he's so gorgeous. He's barely touched me, and I'm already soaking wet in anticipation. It's more than just his looks; it's the way he makes me feel, it's the way he looks at me, like I'm the only girl in the room. The waitress was pretty tonight, but he barely acknowledged her, except when he whispered our order in her ear. Even then, his eyes were locked on mine. It feels good to be adored; it's been a long while, I almost forgot that I deserve it.

Grayson brings his mouth back to my breasts, sucking on each nipple for a short time, leaving them hard. He swings his leg over to straddle mine and even through his boxers I can feel his erection as he hovers over my groin. My arms lay at my sides, my fists gripping onto the sheets.

He flutters kisses up and down my abdomen, and when he hits my inner left thigh, he lingers there and sucks. *That's going to leave a mark,* I think to myself. Fortunately, he moves on to the other side and adds a matching one. When I think he's going to lower himself down to my sex, he surprises me by bringing his face up to mine. He grabs my lower lip into his and pulls it into his mouth. He does this a lot, not just during sex.

"Grayson," I moan.

He lets my lip go and pushes up onto his tiptoes, his legs making a V above mine. "Boxers," he rasps out. I reach up and slide his boxers down his leg, freeing his erection. He brings his knees down to the bed, still straddling my legs. He sets himself up at the perfect angle to enter me. As he drags his dick along my clit, I sit up.

"Grayson, stop!" He shakes his head, his dick inching closer to my entrance. "No." I try again. He picks his head up from where he's licking my stomach and gives me a pleading look.

"You make me want to break all my rules," he blurts out. "I'll pull out before I come."

I do a very quick calculation in my head. Against my better judgment, and the annoying nagging in my head, I give him the okay. With a smile and a wink, he gets back to work.

As soon as he's inside, I let go of all those fears; it feels pretty fucking amazing with no barrier between us. So much so that as soon as he starts moving in and out, I feel the fluttering in my stomach. I fist the sheets next to me as he takes me higher and higher toward my climax.

He thrusts in and out in a steady rhythm, and my hips lift to give him a better vantage point. I feel my legs tighten, my toes begin to curl, and my orgasm hits, making stars appear in my eyes.

I lower my hips down as he continues to grind against me. He's close, I can tell, and as I'm about to remind him to pull out, his orgasm hits, and he empties himself. Inside of me.

"Fuck, Grayson," I yell, louder than I meant to, but I'm pissed. Using both arms and all my strength, I push him off of me. He stumbles back a bit, first having to pull himself out of me.

"Ainsley, I'm sorry."

"I don't want to hear it," I tell him, rushing off the bed to the bathroom. I don't care that his cum is leaking down my legs or that I'm most likely getting it everywhere. All I care about is getting out of his sight for a while.

Once in the bathroom, I grab a towel and frantically wipe myself down. I lean up against the door, sliding down. When I hit the ground, I hug my knees into my chest. I drop my head to my knees and try to ward off the impending tears.

I hear Grayson moving around in the room but luckily, he lets me be. I contemplate telling him why I'm pissed, but I decide against it. I can't get into that right now, especially because I'm pissed at him for not respecting my wishes. Even though it was fucking incredible. And I'm on the pill. And time-wise, I should be fine.

I take a small amount of comfort in knowing that the fact that Grayson wanted to have bare sex shows his commitment to me. He knows the consequences and took the chance anyway. However, for me, it's the cavalier attitude that he dismissed my feelings and took what he wanted. And then the tears are unleashed because I'm having an inner war with myself and hell if I know which side is going to win. *You should tell him,* a voice whispers in my head. Picking up the towel, I wipe my eyes, then wrap it around me, even though it's dirty. The floor is kind of cold, making me shiver.

I open the door a crack and jump a little when I realize he's sitting on the opposite side of the door. From his position, he whispers, "Can we talk?"

"Get me my pajamas, please," I respond instead, a curt edge to my voice. I hear him get up and within a minute, he returns with them in his hands. He doesn't hand them over right away.

"After you put these on, please come out." His tone is regretful, but he sticks my clothes through the barely open door. I grab them from him and quickly shut the door again.

I pull on my pants and tank and sink back to the floor. I know I can't hide in here forever, but I'm too pissed to care at the moment. "UGH!" I yell. "Why did you have to do that?"

I don't really expect him to answer, but I hear him clearing his throat. When he doesn't start with "I'm sorry," I decide to hear him out. "I honestly don't know, Ainsley. And if that sounds like a cop-out, it's not. You know my history. It's not something I do, but I had this...this compulsion to take you bare. It's like I couldn't stop it, I couldn't help myself. And I heard you say stop and no, but something bigger was at play. And you know where I'm coming from; this isn't one-sided on my part. But I should have listened to you, and for that, I apologize."

And just like that, my anger fades, and the side of me that enjoyed the sex wins out this time. I can't even be mad at myself because he is everything. Everything I've ever only imagined I deserved and everything that's been missing in my life. Every. Damn. Thing. But I still can't open the door. So instead, I scrunch up the towel and lay down like it's a pillow.

He deserves the truth, my conscience whispers. And deep down, I know she's right. She's *always* right, that damn bitch. But I can't tonight. It will be enough just to be able to go out there and face him. Which I'll do in a few minutes. I close my eyes to help me steady my breathing.

I awake huddled on the bathroom floor and have no idea what time it is. When I realize I must have fallen asleep in here after Grayson's confession, I quickly pee and then open the door. Grayson's curled up on the floor next to the door. His eyes are darting back and forth under his closed lids, but his breathing is steady and even. I make a quick decision to wake him, and when I place my hand on his shoulder, he bolts upright.

"Huh?" he asks, rubbing the sleep out of his eyes.

"Let's get in bed," I tell him. I start over to the bed, hoping he will follow me. I crawl under the covers while I hear him padding over to the bed. He climbs in next to me and when he wraps me inside of his arms, any leftover anger I possessed completely dissipates.

"For what it's worth, I am sorry," he starts, but I cut him off.

"I know. Me too. We'll talk in the morning."

I'm facing the wall, and he's spooning me from behind, his arm draped across my body. Before I drift off to sleep, I hear him whisper, "I'm damn sure I love you."

* * *

I wake up to an empty bed, but I take a minute to revel in the silence, especially after last night's events. Grayson deserves the truth about my past. I need to explain why his actions caused me to act the way I did. I'm not even sure how to tell him at this point. "Hey Gray, so I had an abortion six years ago. You okay with that?" sounds way too flippant, but I'm not sure I want to make a big deal out of it. I mean, it *was* a big deal at the time, but it's in my past. I'm hoping he will just accept it like he did with my past sexual behavior, but deep down, I'm terrified to tell him and scare him off. And so begins the war within myself yet again.

When I finally decide to get up out of bed, I make a quick stop at the bathroom and then go in search of the man, the man who's captured my heart.

I finally find him sitting out on the stern. His hair is rumpled, he's thrown on a T-shirt and a pair of loosely fitting jogging pants. He's staring off in the distance, lost in a trance or another world. Not wanting to startle him, I quietly call out, "Hey," as I make my way over to him.

He breaks his stare and turns to look at me, his lips turning up into a smile that just about reaches his eyes. I can't help but smile back at him; his smile is infectious. He motions me over to him and pats his legs for me to have a seat on his lap. When I do, he puts a kiss on the top of my head and takes a long inhale. He pulls me in closer to his chest as he wraps his strong arms around me. It's at this moment that all thoughts of sharing my past are pushed to the deepest part of my mind for now. I don't want to ruin this trip.

"Morning, beautiful. How was your night?" he asks me.

"Mine was wonderful, with you by my side," I repeat back to him, the words to a country song. He doesn't get it at first, but then his face lights up with recognition.

"Kenny Chesney?" he guesses.

"Steve Holy," I correct, "but good guess." He reaches over to the table and grabs his mug of coffee, which he offers to me first. "Mmm, thanks." I take a sip and allow the warmth of the beverage to course through my body. I hand it back to him. "So what's our plan for the day?"

"Whatever you want, my girl."

I look up at him. "'Your girl?'" I question incredulously.

"Too soon?" he asks, a hopeful expression on his face.

"No, I kind of like that actually," I tell him, allowing the meaning of the expression to sink in.

"Good, because you are." He wipes the few loose strands out of the way and then kisses my temple. "Can I take you shopping today?"

"Um, yes please. But I must warn you. I'm not much of a shopper, and I loathe trying on clothes. Just a warning." I bat my eyes at him.

"I bet I can get you to try on some clothes," he disputes with a laugh.

"Oh, I'm up for that challenge." He tugs my braid, pulling my head back to him.

"You better be. Come on. It's my turn to take you out on a date. Go get yourself dressed and meet me back up here in ten."

"Wow, who is this bossy man and what has he done with the Grayson I know?" I ask, reluctantly pushing myself out of the comfort of his lap.

"Oh, he's still here. He'll be back later. Now scoot." He smacks my ass, pushing me on my way.

Smiling, I go down to the bedroom. I dig my sundress and leggings out of my bag and change out of my PJs. I let my hair out of the braid, run a brush through it, and let it all hang down around my face. I snicker to myself as I look in the mirror, knowing it will drive Grayson wild. I grab my purse on the way back up to Grayson.

He's standing in the kitchen, finishing the last of the coffee. He changed his clothes to a pair of cargo shorts and a long-sleeved T-shirt. My eyes ogle him up and down, and I lick my lips when I catch sight of his calves. And they may have just replaced his arms as my favorite body part. Holy muscles!

He catches me staring, but then it's his turn to stare. "Fuck me, Ainsley," he grumbles, shaking his head from side to side.

"Later, big guy. You owe me a date." I flip my hair and walk away from him, but I'm not quite fast enough for him. He grabs me around the waist and pulls me closer to him. I can feel his heart beating fast, his breathing labored.

"You drive me wild, you know that right?"

"Of course. Now we are even." I force myself out of his grip and walk away; sometimes I can't trust myself with his man.

He lets out a slow, low groan as I feel him watch me walk away. I make my way to the outside deck and wait for him. Just when I think I could get used to this routine, my phone vibrates with a message. I take a peek at the sender; it's Tara to Kelcie and me. And there goes my mood. I don't even get a chance to read the message before Grayson is grabbing the phone out of my hands. He shoves it in his back pocket.

"I don't know who that was and I don't care, but I'm not going to let this phone ruin another day for us. You can have it back at the end of our day."

"Thank you," I whisper. "I hate how I let people get to me."

He drags his fingers up my neck, tickling it as he tips my chin up in his fingers. "Today, I won't let them." He brings his lips down to meet mine and brushes a soft kiss on my lips. "Come on, love. I owe you a date." He gives me one last hug and then we head off the boat and into town.

* * *

*G*rayson takes me to Serendipity, a resale clothing store. He literally tells me to go find a dressing room and he will do the shopping; I just have to try the clothes on. And anything HE likes, he's buying for me.

I wasn't lying when I told him I'm not a shopper. I hate it. I usually buy my clothes online, but I'm really curious to see what he will pick out.

I find a dressing room and take a seat. Well, I wouldn't call it a dressing room. More like a stall with a curtain for privacy. He has my phone so I can't even stalk Facebook or check my emails. So I sit and wait. And wonder what he's doing out there, what he's finding.

In a few minutes, I get impatient and peek my head out of the curtain. I spot Grayson towards the front of the store, a young girl laughing at something he's saying. She goes so far as putting her hand on his arm, just to cop a feel I'm sure. Hey, I get it, even though I wouldn't touch a stranger who's clearly here shopping for a girl. I smile when he retracts his arm quickly from her touch. That's right, bitch. Hands off! He's mine!

I watch a few more minutes but then see him coming to the dressing room so I take a seat.

"Are you decent?" comes his bellow from outside the stall.

"Does it matter?" I ask with a chuckle. "You've seen it all."

He pushes the curtain out of his way and barrels in with a shit-load of clothes on his arm.

"No! I am not trying all these on."

"Humor me," he retorts as he throws them in a pile on the stool. He takes a seat on the floor and looks over to me. "These clothes aren't going to try on themselves, darling. Get to it."

So I do. And I don't even pretend to have fun. Because it is not fun. At all. He's brought me dresses, skirts, pants, shirts, and a very random sweater.

About halfway through the pile, I whine and tell him I'm done, but he just stands up and literally starts dressing and undressing me.

"I could make so many sexual comments right now," I start, as he draws his fingertips up my abdomen, "but seeing as how I hate this, I will refrain."

"That's really too bad. It's not every day I get to dress and undress a hot woman."

"Can we move this along if I promise you sex in your bed later tonight?"

"Make it every day this week, and you've got yourself a deal."

"Are you ever letting me leave?"

"If I say no, will you be mad?" He stops what he's doing for my reaction.

I pretend to contemplate it for a minute. "I suppose," I say, drawing out the suspense, "there are worse things in the world."

His face lights up. "Then nope." To make sure I know how happy he is, he lifts me off the ground and spins us around. When he puts me down, he throws my dress and leggings at me. He starts separating the clothes with tags into two piles. "Did you want anything in particular?"

I shake my head. "No, but I certainly don't need all these clothes."

It's like he doesn't even hear me; he keeps sorting the clothes, even going as far as moving some from one pile to the other and back again. He's finally satisfied with what he wants and grabs the piles and stalks off to the register.

After I'm dressed in my clothes, I meet him up at the register, just as the sales clerk is ringing him out. To the tune of over three hundred bucks!

"Grayson!" I exclaim in protest. "This is way too much!"

"Hush," he chides, handing over the cash. All of the store's proceeds are donated to the Food Pantry; he likes to "do his part," as he puts it. The clothes are bagged, and he grabs them. The sales lady gives him her biggest smile. In return, he throws his arm around me, staking his claim. "Come on, darling. Let's go home."

"Thank you," I say once outside. "I don't even know what you bought, but I'm grateful for your generosity."

"No need to thank me. Everything I bought is actually for me."

"Interesting." We continue to walk around, the bag in his one hand, mine in the other. Every so often, he places a kiss on my temple. "What time do we have to head back?"

"I figured we could get lunch and then make our way to the boat to leave for home." My heart flutters with the word "home."

"Sounds good. I want a burger for lunch. I know that's random."

"That can be arranged."

"Awesome. I love you," I toss out casually.

Without missing a beat, he returns, "Where's the fanfare with that statement?"

I shrug. "I'm pretty sure we've had our share of fanfare already. You know, when I asked you to marry me after you kissed me back the night we met? You're a fucking amazing kisser. Anyone ever tell you that? And I've kissed a lot of frogs."

He ignores my first question, choosing to focus on the second part of it. "A lot of frogs, huh? Like how many is a lot?"

"Oh I lost count after fifty," I tell him sarcastically.

He laughs. "So does that make me a prince then, since you said I was a fucking amazing kisser and then mentioned frogs?"

"If the shoe fits," I retort smugly. Then I lower my voice. "But truthfully, I think you are pretty much a prince."

He doesn't react. Or at least he doesn't appear to react.

We do a little more shopping before we grab lunch. He buys us matching hoodies, a souvenir from Bar Harbor, and a pair of PJ pants for me. We circle back around to the candy store from last night and he tells me to fill up a bag "for the road." Because there are so many of my favorite candies here, I don't hesitate to grab a bag and fill it to the brim. I throw in some of his favorites too, the ones I gleaned from when he filled his bag last night.

The burger hits the spot and soon we are walking back to the boat. "Let's start a new tradition to come back here," I suggest as we are nearing the marina, walking hand-in-hand.

"Whatever you want, darling."

Back at the boat, Grayson makes the last-minute adjustments before we sail out of the marina and hit the open water. The ride back is just as comfortable as the ride there, but there's less sexual tension. I can tell Grayson's tired, yawning every so often as he drives the boat, one hand on the wheel, the other in my lap or rubbing my thigh. Between the view, the company, and his constant touch, it's the perfect ending to a great weekend away, especially since we both totally avoid what happened last night.

16

GRAYSON

A month or so into what some might call a relationship with Ainsley, I still love her. What, you thought I wouldn't? Ye of little faith. I've yet to meet her parents but that's happening this weekend, along with Bella and Kylie's shower. Ainsley stood by her promise to make the cupcakes for the event and because I apparently can't say no to any of the women in my life, I'm helping as well. One hundred Black Forest cupcakes with a cherry ganache frosting. Since she's basically made herself at home in my house—only at my constant persistence—she moves flawlessly around the kitchen, grabbing ingredients, running the mixer, popping cupcakes in the oven. The kitchen is her domain, well after the bedroom of course. I could literally watch her cook or bake all damn day, as long as there were breaks for sex. I ordered her an apron from some personalized crafting site, Etsy, or some shit like that. It reads "Kiss the Chef" in big, bold letters, and then in smaller letters, underneath is written, "But only if you're Grayson." She wears it all the time.

I'm sitting on top of the island, admiring her work. I told her that I would help, but for once, she refused my assistance, at this stage at least. She said that she wants to do most of the work on her own, as her gift to Bella and Kylie for being so welcoming of her into the family. I pointed out that I was also extremely welcoming of her, which garnered me an eye roll.

"Gray, grab me another stick of butter please," she calls out from the pantry.

I hop down and grab a stick from the door of the fridge and set it on the counter. "How many more do you have to make?"

"One more batch should do it, and then I will frost them all tomorrow. I'll need your help with that please." She bats her eyes at me.

"Yeah, okay. Before dinner at your parents' house?"

"We are not talking about that tonight." Her face falls a bit, even though it was a simple question.

She shuts down every single time her brother or mother come up. Every damn time. And I hate that she feels that way, so I try not to ask. She also shuts down when her friends text her. Again, I haven't pushed her because truthfully, it's heartbreaking to watch her happy self be dragged down. Some of her students get to her too. I've learned when to avoid talking about work. I can usually tell by her mood when she gets in the car if I'm picking her up or when she walks through the door.

Changing the subject, I ask what she wants for dinner. "Um, pizza? From the place up the street. Please."

"I'll call it in and have them deliver it. Not in the mood to go back out. The usual?"

"Of course. Thanks, love." She tosses a smile my way and goes back to measuring ingredients.

She takes a break from the cupcakes to scarf down her pizza. As soon as all the cupcakes are cooled, she lets me know she's calling it a night. I think her day was a little rough, even though she won't talk about it. Well, that and the fact that she's dreading seeing her brother and mother tomorrow.

"Okay, I'll be up in a little while. I just want to clean up the kitchen."

"Oh thank goodness. I really have no desire to clean it up, even though it's completely my mess. You are the best." She plants three kisses on my face. "I love you."

"Love you too. Keep my side warm for me, please." Whenever she goes to sleep before me, she always cuddles up on my side.

"Will do," she tosses my way as she exits the kitchen.

She'll be asleep before I get up there, so I take my time getting the dishes done.

* * *

*D*espite an easy morning of frosting over one hundred cupcakes, when we pull up to her parents' house, Ainsley is downright nervous. I've actually never experienced this side of her before. Her eyebrows are all scrunched together and her breathing is fast. She keeps rubbing her palms on her jeans. Instead of twirling her hair, she's been nervously tugging at it the entire ride.

Before we go in, I rest my hand on hers, which is resting on top of her thigh. "Hey, look at me." Slowly, she lifts her head to face mine. "What's your worst fear about tonight?"

She's quiet for a minute. "That my mother is so horrible. To you. To me. To everyone."

"And so what if she is?" I ask quietly. I empathize with her because I have no idea what it's like to have a mother like hers.

She shrugs. "You don't deserve that." It's a whisper.

"Neither do you," I state emphatically. "You know that, right?" She shrugs again. I pull her into me. "You don't, and whatever damage your mother may inflict tonight, I will undo later tonight in the bedroom." She at least cracks a smile. "Come on. Let's get this over with."

I get out of the car—we made sure to bring the Mustang—and go around to her side. She hesitantly gets out of the car. "I love you. Keep that on repeat throughout dinner." I close the door behind her and we walk up the driveway, hand-in-hand.

At the front door, she walks right in. "Hey, we're here," she calls out.

I take in the surroundings. The house is nice, not huge or overwhelming, but well taken care of and not too modest. To our left is a formal living room, which Ainsley already warned me to not even set foot in there. To our right, is a hallway that leads to the kitchen. In front of us is a set of stairs leading to the second floor with the bedrooms and an office, if I remember correctly. She promised she would show me her childhood bedroom before we left.

She leads me down the hallway to the kitchen and family room. She lets go of my hand just as we enter the room. There, we find four people, her dad, mom, brother, and a younger woman who is hanging all over Drew so she must be connected to him in some way. All four heads turn in our direction. A smile starts to spread on her dad's face when he sees us coming in. He starts to get up but is interrupted by her brother.

"Ains! Long time no see!" Drew calls out to her in a jovial manner. He gets up and comes over to her, wrapping his arms around her. She's stiff at first but eventually becomes a little more comfortable in his arms. His hair is browner than Ainsley's but the color of their eyes is exactly the same, as is the shape. He's a little shorter than I am but has way more weight on his frame.

After Ainsley pulls herself out of his grasp, she motions me over to them. "This is Grayson. Grayson, my brother Drew."

I reach my hand out to him with a smile. "Nice to meet you."

He returns the smile. "Same here. I've been wanting to meet this mystery man of my sister's." The woman comes up behind him.

"Baby," she whines.

Yes, whines. In a nasally voice that I can only predict will be high pitched as the night progresses. Taking a look up and down, she's on the petite side like Ainsley, but that's where the similarities end. While she may not be "ugly," she doesn't have much going on in the looks department. Her hair, a dyed shade of deep red, is stringy at the ends and looks a little ratty.

"Oh, right," Drew says, as if he forgot she was in the room with us. "This is my fiancée, Claudia. This is my sister, Ainsley, and her..." he trails off.

"My boyfriend, Grayson," Ainsley finishes for him. "It's nice to meet you. Congrats, I guess." Ainsley offers her hand, which Claudia limply shakes.

"Thanks." There's no sense of appreciation or happiness in her tone of voice.

I start to reach out my hand to her, but she turns back to Drew. "Can we eat now? I'm starving! This baby needs food."

Wow! *Shotgun marriage?* I think to myself.

"Huh?" Ainsley asks, confused. "You're pregnant?"

"Yes, we wanted to share all of our news in person. Isn't it so exciting?" Drew appears to be beaming; the girl, not so much. She awkwardly places her hand on her stomach and gives a small, forced smile.

"Congratulations," I tell them. Ainsley seems to be stuck in the spot she's standing.

"Wow. And you're keeping the baby?"

Drew's happy expression fades. He glares at Ainsley. "Yes," he hisses. "It's a good thing. That's why we are getting married."

"Well, yeah. I suppose Mom wouldn't want it any other way," Ainsley retorts. I'm not sure who this girl is, but she certainly isn't the Ainsley I know and love.

"Better than repeating the past," he throws back at her. Now it's her turn to glare.

I watch the interaction between the two of them and am all sorts of confused. It's like they are speaking another language. Thankfully, their dad finally bellows out, "Agee! You're here!"

Ainsley's face, just sheet white a minute ago, regains its color, and she breaks out into a smile.

"Hey, Dad," she calls out to him, walking over to him. He holds his arms out for her and she burrows into them. I see the resemblance between father and daughter; it's almost uncanny how much she looks like him, only a softer, more feminine version. He's got the same eyes as his children, color and shape, and Ainsley's facial features are identical to his. "Dad, this is Grayson," she tells him, letting herself out of her embrace. "Grayson, this is my dad, Bob."

His hand shoots out first and when I grab it, it's a hearty handshake, not like with her brother. I say, "It's nice to meet you. Ainsley's told me so much about you, especially about how you share her love of cooking. You've taught her well. I've never met anyone who could rival my skills in the kitchen, and well, she does." And there's the girl I know, beaming with pride.

"Yes, Agee's told me all about how you both love to cook."

Her mother chooses this moment to come over from the table. I reach my hand out to her and say, "Nice to meet you. I'm Grayson." Not that I have to use it often, but I give her my "mother-approved" smile. She weakly reaches out her hand and shakes mine.

"So I've gathered." She turns to Ainsley. "Ainsley, nice of you to come."

Wow. And now I get it. So many questions swirl around my head, questions that won't get answered until we are out of here, if at all.

"I wasn't given a choice," Ainsley counters.

"There's always a choice, dear. You should know that." Frostily, she smiles. She looks nothing like Ainsley. While she's pretty in a way, she doesn't possess that natural beauty that radiates off of Ainsley. She's quite uptight. Her blondish-gray hair sits perfectly in its tight bun at the base of her neck and her painted nails have no chips. Her eyes are blue but not that blue that everyone wants, just blue.

The visit continues in much the same manner: Kim throwing jabs at Ainsley at almost every comment, Drew joining in, but when Ainsley turns the tables on him, the mother protects him. While Bob does stand up for Ainsley occasionally, the constant negativity grates on her. I understand a little more about what makes her tick and why she's done some of the things in her life she has.

When dessert comes out, I can tell she's not only had enough, but she's physically exhausted as well. I'm sure having to bake and frost one hundred cupcakes doesn't help that fact, but the couple hours we've spent here have seriously taken their toll. It will be an early night for her.

"Grayson, this is the one dessert my mother makes. Luckily, she's perfected it over the years so they are delicious," Ainsley tells me as she puts one on my plate. I wait until everyone is served before digging in. Not that I doubted her, but Ainsley's right. The caramel cookie is delicious. The caramel center melts in my mouth and the cookie part is soft and chewy.

After I swallow my bite, I look over to Kim. "These are delicious, Kim."

"Thank you, Grayson." She gives me a smile, the most genuine I've seen all night. And then casually slings this out there. "Despite my daughter's culinary skills, hers never quite compare to mine."

I don't even have time to react before Ainsley is pushing up out of her seat and telling me it's time to go, shooting daggers in her mother's direction. She kisses her father on his cheek and tells him she will call him later in the week. She tosses a "nice to meet you" in Claudia's direction and a "safe trip" to Drew.

When we are almost out of the kitchen, Kim calls out to Ainsley. On instinct, Ainsley turns to face her mother. "Forgot to tell you, dear. We received the invitation to Jordan's wedding in the mail. I guess you were right about one thing. It is over between the two of you. I guess it's a good thing you made that *choice* all those years ago."

Ainsley stumbles as she tries to will her feet to carry her outside, to get away from this house. I grab onto her left arm so she doesn't completely fall over and only catch a glimpse of the emotions on her face. I hear her muttering under her breath.

"Don't let them see you cry. Don't let them see you cry."

"I got you, love." She looks up at me, trying hard to keep herself together. We're almost to the door, and when we reach it and walk outside, her face crumbles and she throws herself at me. I stumble back but then catch myself and wrap my arms around her, pulling her into me as tightly as I can. She starts sobbing against my chest.

After a few minutes, she pulls herself away from me, with heavy eyes and tear-stained cheeks. I swipe across her cheeks with my thumbs to wipe the remaining tears away. "Take me home, please," she begs in a small voice.

"Let's go." We walk down to my car, her huddled into my side. I open up her door for her and she climbs in. I shut hers and walk around to my side. Before I pull away, I glance over at her. She's got her head thrown back against the seat, her eyes closed. She's not crying, but her face conveys all of her emotions. The girl I love is nowhere to be seen; instead she's been replaced by this imposter, a girl who has taken one too many jabs to have any confidence left in herself. I lay my hand on her thigh; she doesn't even respond. "Guess I have a lot of damage control to do tonight." It comes out jokingly, an attempt to lighten the mood. It garners a small smile from her. It's enough to let me know that my girl's still in there.

As soon as we pull into the garage, Ainsley hops out of the car and sprints inside. I figure she's going right upstairs, so when I find her in the pantry muttering under her breath, I'm surprised.

"What are you doing?" I ask her, leaning against the door of the pantry.

She's got a wild look on her face and is frantically searching for something on the shelves. "Do we have any caramel candies, like to bake with? I can't find any, and I need some." She looks over at me but when I shrug, she goes back to scouring the shelves.

And it hits me exactly what she's doing. Her mother's words ring in my ears: *hers never quite compare to mine.*

"Ainsley," I call out. "You have nothing to prove." She ignores me. I try again, a little louder this time. "Ainsley, stop." She stops and looks over to me, and I think she's going to stop. She doesn't. I walk over to her and put my hands on her shoulders, which she tries to shake off. So I get in her face. "STOP!" That gets her attention, and a shocked look creeps over her face.

"You don't get it."

"You're right. I don't. But your mother was right. Yours can't compare to hers." She gasps and looks like she wants to hit me. "Because yours could only be WAY better!" I quickly add before I wrap my arms around her like a straight jacket and hug the crap out of her. It takes her a minute to loosen up and melt into my arms.

"I don't deserve you," she murmurs. "You don't know...."

It's sad that she truly believes that. Because this girl deserves so much more. But I don't think I'll get through to her, not tonight at least, so we just stand in the pantry, me holding her.

Later that night, she heads up to bed, while I lock up and make us some coffee. When I finally join her in the bedroom, she's lying in bed on her back with her eyes closed but she's not asleep. I place the mugs on the nightstand and crawl into bed next to her, not even bothering to change my clothes at the moment. I tuck my hands behind my head, cross my ankles and stare up at the ceiling.

After a few minutes of silence, she starts speaking in a low tone. "Well, tonight was a shit show. I'm sorry you had to witness that, but I can't thank you enough for coming with me." I'm about to answer her, but she keeps talking. "I know you have to have questions about what you witnessed tonight. So, have at it."

She's right; a million questions are saturating my brain right now, but I need to tread lightly because I can't let her shut down. So I start with an easy one.

"Agee?" I ask, glancing in her direction.

She opens her eyes and smiles. "I'm Ainsley Grace. My dad's always called me that for as long as I can remember. My mother hates it, so secretly I love it even more." At the mention of her mother, her demeanor changes and she stops. So I change the subject.

"So, can we talk about your brother getting married and having a baby?"

"Ugh, could we not?"

"Okay," I give in. We are both quiet for a bit. "Who's Jordan?"

She sighs and I don't think she's going to even answer. "There is no easy answer for that question. And plus, I'm not allowed to discuss other men in the bedroom."

"Oh, it's okay, considering he's totally over you and this is *our* bedroom now." It comes out a little more sarcastically than I meant it to, and I hope she doesn't shut down.

"Jordan was the guy that day at the diner."

I think back to that first date at the diner. "The one who called you Ains, like your brother?"

She nods. "He was one of Drew's friends, but he was also my first."

It takes me a minute, but I am finally able to come up with who he is. "The one who took you to the crappy motel and didn't know what he was doing?" I didn't mean it to be funny, but she chuckles anyway.

"Yep." She turns on her side and props herself up on her elbow, facing me.

"But there's more to the story I don't know, I'm assuming."

She nods again. Her face falls and she becomes that "ghostly" representation of who she was again. "A lot more."

I would have never guessed what she's hiding behind the usually confident façade she portrays.

17

AINSLEY

SIX YEARS EARLIER

I was staring at a positive pregnancy test. What it meant was not sinking in. It couldn't be true. It couldn't be positive. No way. That would mean I was pregnant. And there was no way that was true. Yeah, I was a few days late but that wasn't all that uncommon, especially lately with the stress of college and trying to juggle classes and Jordan.

I closed my eyes, took in a deep breath, and willed the result to be different. I looked again. No such luck. Still positive.

"Fuck," I swore under my breath, then said it a little louder. "FUCK!"

Images of that night about two weeks ago flashed in my memory. His dorm room. The fact that I said no, not tonight and him not listening. At least he had the decency to wear a condom, all the good that did.

Karma really was a bitch. I could only blame myself for putting off going on the pill. Our "sex life," if you could even call it that at this point, was almost non-existent and when I first tried the pill, it made my hormones worse, and I was an utter bitch. Well, according to Jordan. And my mother. So I stopped taking it, and he had to wrap it up.

"FUCK!" I yelled again to the empty room. I pulled out my phone and texted Jordan.

> We need to talk. Come over tonight.

His response was immediate.

> I have a frat meeting tonight. Can it wait until tomorrow?

> No

Even though I was still going to be pregnant tomorrow, I needed to tell him tonight.

> Ok, I'll c what I can do

> Thanks

I put my phone down on the bed beside me and lay down. I was still in shock. I couldn't even begin to imagine myself with a baby. Jordan's baby, no less. My mother was pretty much going to kill me. And Drew would kill Jordan. It was going to be fabulous. Not to mention the fact that I was going to HAVE A BABY!

I closed my eyes for a second and before I knew it, I had fallen asleep. When I woke up, I was disoriented. Until I saw the positive test and it all came flooding back to me. I was pregnant!

I heard the door to my dorm room opening so I hastily shoved the test under my pillow. My roommate, Kelcie, came barreling in.

"Ainsley!" she called out, a little loudly since she was clearly past tipsy. I looked over at the clock. At 4:30 in the afternoon. She stumbled a bit, almost falling over, which caused her to fall into a fit of laughter.

"What were you toasting today?" I asked her. Every day she started drinking earlier and earlier because there was always something to "toast." Yesterday it was because she was first in line at the dining hall. One day last week it was because she actually woke up for her eight a.m. class.

"Brett Anderson winked at me!" she replied with gusto.

"Right," I said, my voice heaping with sarcasm. I rolled my eyes. "Well, he is cute."

"Not nearly as cute as Jordan," she gushed.

Again, I rolled my eyes. I will admit. He was good-looking, but it got old, especially from Kelcie who told me every day.

She flopped down on her bed. "You want to go out tonight? A couple of people from my Arts Society class are going to hit the bar on campus."

I shook my head. "Jordan's coming over tonight."

She smirked. "Ohhhhhh. In that case, I'll stay out."

"It's not like that," I insisted.

"Right," she replied, in that same tone I gave her before.

"Whatever." I threw myself back on my bed. "Have fun."

"Oh, I will!"

Of course she would. How could I be so silly?

That night, Jordan was set to come over at seven, so he still had time to go to his meeting with his fraternity.

As usual, he was late. At around 7:30, he finally strolled through the door.

He placed a quick peck on my cheek and took a seat in the chair at my desk. "So, what's so urgent?" He was wearing his signature outfit: jeans, a U of Maine sweatshirt, his running sneakers, and his stupid Pirates baseball cap. There was nothing but a smile on his face. That would soon change with my news, I thought.

Way to get right to the point, Jordan.

I had practiced what I was going to say in the mirror as soon as Kelcie had left. Now that the moment was here, I just blurted it out. Dropping my eyes to my bed, I simply stated, "I'm pregnant." After the words were out, I looked over to him to watch his reaction.

The smile was still there. The enormity of my words hadn't sunk in yet. And when they finally did, he laughed. "You're kidding, right?" At the shake of my head, the smile faded off his face. "Fuck. How?"

"Really, Jordan?"

"No, I mean I know how, but we've been careful."

"Guess the condoms weren't as effective as we thought."

He ran his fingers through his hair and then stood up and began pacing. He started talking quickly, saying things about how this was going to affect his college career, how he'd have to give up the fraternity, things like that.

"I'm fine, by the way," I said sarcastically.

He stopped walking. "Oh, right. How are you really?" he asked, pretending to care because it was expected of him.

"Shocked, pissed, terrified. Those are the emotions I've had for the past few hours since I took the test. I'm sure more will hit me later."

"What's your plan?" He resumed his pacing.

"MY plan?" I squeaked out. "This is a 'we' thing, Jordan." I got off the bed and forced him to stop his pacing and look at me. "We got into this together, and we will both make the decision."

Truthfully, I had no intentions of raising this baby by myself, but maybe I overreacted just a tad.

"I'm sorry. My emotions are a little off-kilter right now."

"You think?" he asked sarcastically.

I shot daggers at him.

"Whoa, calm down. We both need time to process this. Think about what you want to do and I will too. Then we will make the decision. Together." His voice got softer at the end, and he loosely draped his arms around me for a hug. Well, a pathetic excuse for a hug.

Before he released me, he plopped a kiss on my forehead. "I have to go, babe. I'll call you tomorrow so we can make our plan. Love you." And he walked out of my room.

I flopped down on my bed. I felt like I should cry, but no tears came. And now I had to make the biggest decision of my life, pretty much on my own. There was no way I was going to my mom about this. I couldn't even imagine what words she would have for me.

Feeling exhausted, I lay down and stared up at the ceiling, studying it like it held the answer to my problem. I knew what I should do. No way was I ready to be a mother, but even more, Jordan was not ready to be a father. I closed my eyes for a moment and fell into a fitful sleep.

I stop the story there. When I look over at Grayson, he's sitting upright, a pissed look on his face.

"Seriously, Ainsley. You've kept this from me? Even after you knew my history?"

"Don't be mad. Please." I plead for his understanding.

"Mad doesn't even begin to cover how I feel right now," he says even-keeled.

"Let me explain why I never told you."

"Where's your kid?" he demands.

"I don't have a kid."

"Explain." His face softens the slightest bit. It doesn't last long.

I have to look away from him. "I had an abortion," I stammer out. It never gets easier to say it.

He's quiet for a few minutes, then he gets off the bed and leaves the room.

I get it. I should have told him this before. I've had so many opportunities.

Tears prickle the corners of my eyes, and I cry silently. Because not only is the guilt all flooding back, I may have fucked up the only good thing in my life. Ever.

I don't even know how long I cry or lay in the dark hoping Grayson will come back. I must have eventually fallen asleep because when I wake up, the clock reads 2:46 a.m. Not surprisingly, the bed beside me is still empty.

Making a rash decision, I scribble a note to Grayson, throw a sweatshirt over my PJs, and quickly throw my stuff in my bag. Hoping I've gathered up all my belongings, I go in search of my keys. I find them on the island in the kitchen. How fitting, I think as I swipe them. Luckily my car is in the driveway and not in the garage. I catch sight of a lump on the couch. I debate with myself if I should go over to him. My emotional side wins.

I tiptoe over to the couch. Even in his sleep, he's gorgeous, even with his face looking conflicted. I'm half tempted to climb in next to him or at least, leave him with a parting kiss goodbye. I settle for a "Goodbye, Grayson. For what it's worth, I love you. If I could go back and change things, it would only be to tell you sooner. We had something special, and I will likely never get over you."

I blow a kiss in his direction, tears falling down my cheeks again. I somehow make it to my car and drive myself back to the place that I called home just a few weeks ago.

I awaken to a pounding at my door. Since I didn't make it to my bed last night, the sound is ridiculously loud.

Falling off the couch in near exhaustion after a shitty night's sleep, I make it to the door. I don't know who I'm expecting to find at the door, but it certainly isn't Bella.

"What the fuck is this?" she yells, stomping past me into my apartment. Her hair is piled atop of her head in a messy bun and she's wearing yoga pants and a tank. She's waving some sort of paper at me. When I don't answer her, she shoves it in my face. It's my note to Grayson. The one in which I told him that he needed to deliver the cupcakes to the shower and to tell Bella I was sorry I couldn't do it myself, among other things I had written.

"How did you get that?" I squeak out.

"From his counter. I had to make a stop there." Her face loses some of the wildness. "What did he do?"

"What?"

"What did he do to make you leave?" she asks.

"Oh. Nothing." I hang my head.

"Then why did you leave? He loves you, you know that right?" There's a hopeful look on her face as she takes a seat on the couch.

I sit down on the other end, tucking my legs under me. "I know," I tell her quietly.

"You love him?"

"So much." I'm surprised she can even hear my response, it's so low.

"Then what the hell is the problem?" she asks incredulously.

"I had an abortion." It just kind of falls out of my mouth.

Her eyes bug out. "WHAT?" She's yelling now. "He got you pregnant?" She gets up and starts pacing, shaking her head from side to side. "Stupid boy," she mutters mostly to herself.

"No. It was years ago."

She stops, caught off guard. "Oh. So what's the problem?"

"I didn't tell him until last night. And I'm pretty sure he was pissed about the whole abortion thing."

"Did he tell you that?"

"Well, not in so many words. He was pissed I never told him I was pregnant, especially when he told me about him and Molly. And then when I dropped the other bomb, he took off for the other room and slept on the couch."

"Boys are stupid," she says after absorbing what I just told her. "Thank god I'm a lesbian." Her comment makes me laugh, and she cracks a smile too. "I don't accept this though." She waves the letter again. "You're coming to the shower. I'll make him deliver the cupcakes though, for two reasons. One, he owes me. Two, they are damn delicious because I sampled one this morning when I found your note."

"I really don't think I should. You're his sister."

"Shut up." She cuts me off. "It's my shower. Well, Kylie likes to pretend it's hers too, but we know the truth." She laughs at that. "You come as *my* guest. I can handle Grayson."

"Are you absolutely sure?"

"That I can handle Grayson?" she questions.

"Well yeah," I snicker, "but also that I should come? I don't want it to be awkward."

"For who? You and I, well and Grayson and soon Kylie, are the only ones who know this note exists. Kylie will agree one hundred percent with me. On her own because I know she wants you there too. And Grayson will deal. He's only coming to deliver the cupcakes and to help with presents at the end. You can avoid him."

I think for a minute. I really want to go. I've become really close to Bella and Kylie since I started hanging out with Grayson. They're the sisters I never had. "Okay, I will. On the condition that I avoid your brother."

"Done!" She comes over to the couch and hugs me.

Pulling out of her embrace, I say, "Can I ask you a question?"

"No I will not be your lesbian experiment," she replies straight-faced, looking so much like Grayson. It has the intended effect, and I can't help but laugh. A slow smile creeps onto her face. "For real, what?"

I take a deep breath and swallow before I start to speak. "Did I totally fuck it up with him?" It comes out in a complete whisper, and I can't be certain she even understood what I said.

She contemplates the question before she answers. Her face gives nothing away. "Grayson's a very forgiving person. There's not much you could do that he wouldn't forgive, short of killing someone." I cringe. "Oh crap. I didn't mean that," she adds when she sees my face. "That man is crazy about you. I could have told you that the first night in the bar. He can be stubborn so it may take some time and work on your part, but he will come around. He's not about to let the best thing in his life walk away from him. He's not dumb."

Her words give me a little comfort. And a glimmer of hope that I didn't screw this up.

She keeps going. "You have to let him come to you. It has to be his idea." She pauses a moment, pondering her next thought. "You want to take bets on how long it takes him to come to you?"

"That would be kinda fun," I tell her, smiling her way.

"I knew I liked you," she says with a chuckle. "Okay, I bet by tonight he'll be knocking on your door, tail between his legs."

"No way! You didn't see how mad he was."

"Did the vein in his forehead appear?"

I think back to the look on his face. I shake my head. "No, not that I recall."

"Then he's not that mad. But word to the wise. When you do see it, text me. Kylie and I have a guest room."

I can't help but crack up with laughter. Then I get serious again. "If he doesn't come around, can I still keep you?" I'm sure I sound desperate, but it's how I feel. It would be like losing a best friend.

"Definitely! That would piss him off even more, and besides for sex with Kylie, messing with Grayson is what I love most." She looks at her watch. "Shit. I have to go. I'll see you later. At two, not a minute after." She hugs me again, whispering in my ear, "It's going to be okay."

"Thank you. For everything." She smiles as she walks toward the door. "Oh, crap. Your present is in the closet at Grayson's house. Feel free to grab it when you are there next."

"I'll get it the next time you cook me dinner. In Grayson's kitchen." She winks at me. "See you soon." The door opens and then she shuts it behind her, leaving me alone again.

I can't wallow in my misery all day, so I change into workout gear and go outside for a walk. The warm weather, the sun beating down and just being in the fresh air definitely helps lift my mood. I try not to think of Grayson.

I'm not successful in the slightest.

* * *

*T*he shower is being held at a local restaurant, fortunately not one Grayson and I had visited together. Before I can even take in the decorations and look of the place, Natalie grabs my arm and drags me to a table. She pulls me into a hug and then lets me sit down. Despite all the plans we had to meet for girls' night, none of them ended up panning out.

"Girl, we so need to catch up. I haven't seen you in ages. How are things going? Better question, how is he in bed?" Her face lights up, and she cracks a huge smile as she waits for my answer.

I know she doesn't know about last night, but the way she's quasi-interrogating me feels like she does. And I have to swallow down a huge lump in my throat before I can answer her. I start with the question that I can answer truthfully, but it also happens to be the one she most wants the answer to.

"It's the best sex I've ever had. Like ever. And every time is better than the last."

"I knew it! He's like good at all parts of it, right?"

"More than good," I confirm.

"I'm so happy for you guys. You deserve each other."

I can't correct her, so I just give her another smile. She seems satisfied with that. She pulls at my hair. "I love your hair this way. I bet it drives Grayson wild too."

"That it does. He likes to play with it a lot. It pisses him off when I have it all tied back. He somehow always manages to pull out at least one strand. Secretly, I love it."

"Seriously, there isn't another woman on this planet who is better suited for him. I hope he realizes that."

"We'll see," I reply with a shrug. Fortunately, Kylie comes over to our table so I'm saved from having to answer any more Grayson-related questions.

"Ainsley! So glad you could make it." She makes me stand and then grabs me in for a hug. In my ear, she whispers, "I'm really happy you came. And Bella's right. He'll come around." I notice her face light up as I pull away. "And thanks for making the cupcakes. I hear they are delicious. I can't wait to try one."

"I hope you like them, but I'm not too worried." I lean in closer to her. "Are you drunk?" I've never seen her drink more than one since she's always the one who is taking care of Bella, but she's definitely had more than one.

She nods with a giggle. "Shh, don't tell Bella."

"Don't tell Bella what?" Bella asks, coming up behind us.

"Nah-nothing," Kylie stutters out.

"Jeez, woman. How many did you have?"

"Two, maybe three so far. But I'm not done yet. This is my shower, and I'll drink if I want to. Ainsley can drive me home, right?" She tries to wink at me but is unsuccessful and ends up blinking both eyes.

"Sure thing, Kylie. Drink away."

Bella gives me the stink eye. "Don't encourage her. I told you, this is *my* shower." She can't help but snort, which makes all of us join in.

The shower is a fun time. Kylie gets more than a little wasted and ends up spending some time in the bathroom. At least it was after they both opened up the gifts. Bella stayed pretty sober, surprisingly. The cupcakes are a huge hit, not that I'm surprised. I made sure to take some pictures of the display. Grayson can not only make an appetizing cupcake, his are visually appealing as well. No one can tell I didn't frost them all myself.

I say my goodbyes before everyone else has left so to avoid Grayson. I make sure that Bella will get Kylie home safe, a habit that I picked up from living with Grayson, although truthfully, it's just nice knowing someone is watching out for you. I promise Natalie a more thorough catch-up within the next few weeks.

When I get home, I change into more comfy clothes and figure I will order takeout for dinner. It seems like forever since I've had to eat by myself, even though it's only been like six weeks. It's amazing how life can change in a short amount of time, and then one wrong move can make it change again.

I spend the rest of the afternoon and evening lounging on my couch, vacillating between reading, watching TV, and grading papers. I order myself a pizza, which I eat in front of the TV. It's not nearly as satisfying as eating it with Grayson, on his couch, while watching chick flicks—always his choice. The memories make me smile and then somewhat melancholy. In some ways, I'm thankful it was only six weeks.

In the middle of some movie with Channing Tatum—in which he doesn't play Magic Mike but is still quite sexy—my phone vibrates on the couch next to me. Putting down my pizza, I pick it up. To say I'm surprised by the sender is an understatement.

GRAYSON

Let me in

Please

Then there's a knock at my door. When I slowly open it up, he's standing there, looking as un-Graysonlike as he possibly could.

18

GRAYSON

I knew I screwed up the minute I walked out the bedroom door after Ainsley's confession. I listened to how she told me about being pregnant; that was shocking enough. But when she threw in the line about the abortion, it floored me. I can't even explain the feeling; it rocked me to the core. It all stemmed from the fact that she didn't tell me about it, especially after I shared my history, because we shared so much in general. Abortion wouldn't be a route I would go, but given her circumstances, I can tell why she chose that. Six years later, the decision clearly still haunts her, and I had to go and make it worse.

I was mad, more so at the fact that she felt the need to hide it from me. I hate that she must think I judged her for having an abortion when that's so far from the truth. But I made my bed and shouldn't have been all too surprised to find her note the next morning.

I was truly surprised that with her hasty exit, she didn't leave anything behind that had been hers before we got together, just stuff I'd bought for her. If she had asked, I would have told her to take it, that she deserved it. But if she had asked, I would have told her not to go. So there's that.

When Bella came by and saw the note, she didn't say a word,

just grabbed the note and stomped away. Before the shower, she sent me a text.

> FIX. IT.
>
> TONIGHT!

>> You're so demanding.

> It's all part of my charm. Love you!

After delivering the cupcakes to the restaurant, I spent some time on the boat, at the marina. I couldn't get Ainsley off my mind, and I could picture her everywhere. It didn't help that I found something of hers in the bedroom. And then I remembered the last time we had sex on the boat and how I didn't stop myself. Now that I knew her history, no wonder she freaked.

I am so messed up. I fucked this up, big time. Bella was right; I had to fix it. There's no way I can let this girl walk out of my life. She's the best thing I've ever had. I have to plead my case; even if she doesn't take me back, at least she'll know I wasn't judging her. She at least deserves that much.

I found myself at the bar with Caleb. When Dan brought over my obligatory beer, I drank it all and ordered another one. And then one more. I was by no means wasted, but there was no way I was driving either, so I had Caleb drop me off at Ainsley's. I'd figure the rest out later; for now, I had to see her and explain.

>> Let me in.

>> Please.

When she opens the door, it's about all I can do to not wrap her up in my arms, get her to drive us home, and make sweet love to her all night long. Instead, I go with a casual, "Hey."

"Come in," she tells me, opening the door even wider. She's looking me up and down, taking in my rumpled appearance and the fact that I'm not walking entirely straight. "Have you been drinking?" she asks quietly. When I nod, she goes sheet white. "Please don't tell me you drove here."

I reassure her I did not. She seems quite relieved and asks if I want something to eat or drink.

"Coffee, please. I need to sober up for what I have to say to you."

"Sit on the couch," she instructs before walking away. She's nervous, but underneath the nervousness, there's a hint of happiness. I take in her appearance. Her yoga pants hug her ass and the tank is stretched across her chest, offering a nice view of her perky nipples.

I sit on the couch and look around at the surroundings. I've only been in her apartment a few times, waiting for her to grab her things. I've always been the kind of person who is most comfortable at my own house, even growing up. Since Ainsley's never had any issue with us spending so much time at my house, we never spend time at her place. In fact, I've never seen her bedroom or used her bathroom. Quaint is a good word to describe it. She keeps it tidy, everything has its place. The off-white walls are bare, save for one photo of the quad where she went to college or where she works. There's a lone bookshelf in the corner with about two shelves filled with books. There's also one photo of her and her dad. It amazes me how little personal effects she has here. It makes the statement that this place isn't permanent.

She carries two mugs over to me and hands me one. "Thank you," I say as I accept it and take a sip. It's been a little while since I finished the last beer so it won't take too long for the coffee to kick in.

"How was the shower?" I ask to make small talk about a subject that shouldn't be too uncomfortable. "Bella said the cupcakes were a huge hit. And she may have mentioned Kylie was drunk."

She smiles. "Kylie was so drunk. She was puking in the bathroom when they brought out dessert. Don't tell Bella though." She laughs. "It was nice to see a different side of each of them. Kylie's a fun drunk, and Bella was toned down a bit, still funny as hell, but watered down. And yes, the cupcakes were a huge hit. Thanks again for helping me frost them. I may have been commissioned to make some for a birthday party in two weeks and a baby shower at the end of the month. It's a good thing they are smaller orders; it would be hard to make eight dozen in my tiny kitchen."

That one stings a little, thinking she won't be back in my kitchen.

In true Ainsley fashion, after she's quiet for a bit, she asks, "Grayson, why are you here?" She looks at me, her eyebrows scrunched up in a quizzical look.

I take her underwear out of my pocket. "I found these on the boat and figured I should return them." I don't hand them over right away. I finger them in my hands, loving the feel of the satin against my fingertips.

"You came here to return my underwear?"

"Getting to return your underwear solidified my decision to come over," I start. And then I go for broke. I move closer to her on the couch. She doesn't flinch when I put my hand on her thigh nor when I tip her chin up in my fingers. I look into her eyes. They reflect what I'm sure mine show: regret and sadness. "I came to apologize. For walking out of the bedroom last night. For letting you think I was judging you. For being pissed." I take a breath. Before I can continue, she speaks.

"I wanted to tell you so many times. I tried, I really did. The night you told me about Molly. The last night on the boat. You deserved to know; I shouldn't have kept it from you."

"You were worried I would judge you." She nods. "And you think I did." She nods again and then casts her gaze on her thighs. "Hey, look back at me." Slowly she lifts her head and finds my gaze again. I scoot closer to her. "I can't judge you for a decision you made six years ago, a decision you made for yourself that was best at the time. I've been in shoes very similar to yours, just on the guy's side. Just because I made a different decision doesn't mean that yours is wrong, or if I were in a similar circumstance to yours, maybe I would have made the same decision you did." I take another deep breath. "I need to ask you a question, and I want an honest answer. Can you do that?"

"Yes."

Giving it some thought, I realize it's more than one. "Actually it's two questions. Hope that's okay." Her mouth forms a small smile. I take that as my cue to continue. "I mean, it may be three. Let me see." I pause for a moment, assessing the situation and once I'm satisfied with her expression, I ask my first question. "Do you regret your decision?"

"The easy answer to that question is no. I don't regret making the decision not to be a mom at nineteen." She stops. "But I have regrets."

"You regret the act itself?" I ask, confident I'm correct in my thinking. I find her eyes again.

"Yes," she whispers. "I've never gotten over it completely, and honestly, I don't know if I ever will. In some ways, it was an easy decision to make because I didn't want to have a baby at nineteen, but I also didn't want to be pregnant so adoption wasn't really an option. But in other ways, it was so damn hard. It *is* so damn hard to live with that decision." The questions are taking their toll on her as I see the worry lines begin to appear around her eyes and lips.

"Okay, one more for tonight." This one requires another deep breath. I place both of my hands on her thighs. "If I had been the father, would it have changed your decision?"

She doesn't hesitate in her answer, and her gaze never falters from mine. Her emerald eyes lose some of their sadness. "Yes." This time, it's not a whisper.

She throws herself at my chest, wrapping her arms behind my back. I pull her onto my lap and return the hug. I close my eyes, inhaling her scent. "I'm so sorry," I whisper in her hair. "Not just for my behavior last night."

"I know," she responds. "I'm sorry I didn't tell you."

"We're okay?" I ask hesitantly. I need her back in my life, in my house. The hours she was gone only today were far too many.

"Yes. I was so worried I fucked this up by not telling you. I would have been mad at myself forever."

"You were worried?" I ask, pushing her back so I can see her expression. She's startled at first. "I figured I would be the one who would have to grovel to get you back. I was so afraid of losing you. AM so afraid of losing you."

"I feel like this whirlwind, whatever this is, should seem crazy to everyone, because let's face it, I've known you less than two months and you all but moved me into your house. However, all of your friends and family think we belong together. And I gotta tell you. I agree." Her face radiates happiness.

"You do not know how happy that makes me when you say shit like that." My voice conveys my enthusiasm.

"I think I have a pretty good idea." Teasing me, she takes one strand of her hair and starts twirling it around her fingers, smirking all the while. "Oh, by the way. Bella was right."

"About what?"

"She said that you would come around by tonight."

"That bitch! She set me up."

"Why doesn't that surprise me? What did she do?"

I take my phone out of my back pocket and cue up Bella's messages. I hand it to her so she can read it for herself. She chuckles when she reads them. "Oh, she totally set you up. She sent these messages right after she left my house." And then her smile fades just a little. "You're lucky you have her."

"Every day, I'm grateful she wasn't in the car with them. Every. Damn. Day." I swallow back the lump that's forming in my throat. "I love you, Ainsley. So damn much, it hurts. You get that?"

"Yeah, I pretty much do." She takes one of my hands and places it over her heart and then places the other over my heart. She places one of her hands on top of each of mine and lightly squeezes them. "I wouldn't have it any other way." She gets that sparkle in her eye, the one that I can't ever get enough of. She leans in close to me. "Want to see my bedroom?" she whispers, her voice full of sexual undertones.

"If by 'see your bedroom,' you mean 'have sex in your bedroom one time before you don't have the bedroom anymore,' then yes, by all means, let me 'see' your bedroom."

She jets off the couch, giggling the entire way down the hallway. I'm not even sure she caught what I said to her, but I don't care. I sprint after her to "see" her bedroom. I don't actually "see" anything, just Ainsley who gives me the best makeup sex in the history of makeup sex.

Twice.

* * *

We both call in sick to work on Monday. We spend the day alternating between packing up her apartment (luckily that doesn't take long) and having sex (luckily that does take long). Around dinnertime, there are boxes galore and almost everything is packed. Ainsley decides she will bring her stuff to my house and store what she doesn't need in the attic. She's not quite ready to get rid of the apartment just yet, and her lease is paid up until the end of summer so the bed will stay. For now.

Sitting on the couch, I watch her as she finishes packing a box of her books. "I want to cook you one last meal here," I tell her. "I bet no one ever cooked for you here."

She glances in my direction. She looks so cute, thinking hard about my statement. "I believe my father made me soup one time when I was sick. He may have just heated it up. There's not much here to work with," she says, joining me on the couch.

"Finish packing, and I'll run to the store and grab what I need. I just need to borrow your car."

"Keys are on the table by the door. Keep her safe." She kisses me on the cheek. "I love you."

"Ditto. Be right back."

When I get to the store, I grab the ingredients I need to make lasagna, one of Ainsley's favorite comfort meals. Back at the apartment, she's asleep on the couch, her students' essays from her summer school class strewn around her on the floor and couch. Her hands are tucked under her chin, looking fucking adorable. I place a quick peck on her forehead, but she doesn't stir. *That's about right,* I think. She's exhausted. There wasn't much sleep going on last night. I get to work on dinner. She's going to be starving when she wakes up.

Ainsley wakes up as I'm putting the lasagna in the oven. "How long was I asleep for? And did you make lasagna?" She takes a seat at the only table in the kitchen.

"You've been sleeping an hour or so, and yes, it's lasagna."

"I guess I've dropped enough hints about that one, huh?" she asks with a laugh.

"You sure did. But I actually happen to really like lasagna too, so it's a win-win for both of us."

"This kitchen kinda sucks compared to yours, am I right?"

"OUR kitchen," I correct her. I take a seat across from her and grab her hands. "What's mine is yours, darling."

"Babe, you have a '67 Mustang in OUR garage. I'm pretty sure that's 'yours' and not 'mine,'" she responds.

"I've been meaning to get myself another one."

"Yeah, you keep mentioning that. Any year in particular you want?"

I think for a minute. "I think I like the 2015 model the best. I guess I'm just waiting for the right time to buy it." Although lately, I think there's less of a 'right' time and more of a 'things happen when they are supposed to happen' time." Like meeting Ainsley that night at the bar. There's been no doubt in my mind that I was supposed to be in that bar that night to meet this incredible beauty who has captured my heart and soul. It's only a matter of time before I make her mine officially. Because the way I feel about her, that only comes around once in a lifetime, and I'm holding on to it for dear life and never letting go.

19

AINSLEY

I've learned that when Grayson makes his mind up or makes a decision, he commits to it. One hundred percent. Like when he told me I was moving into his house. Luckily I didn't have too much stuff to pack and move and by the end of the week, I was completely moved into his house. Our house, I suppose. We christened every room before the week was over. It's too bad jobs get in the way of sex.

Three weeks or so before Bella and Kylie's wedding, the girls and I go out to celebrate. Both girls insisted on not having a bachelorette party and opted for a night out at the bowling alley. It was apparently where they had their first date and wanted to commemorate it one last time before they get married.

I'm sitting in the kitchen, waiting for Natalie to pick me up. "Hey you," Grayson says, startling me as he walks up behind me. "Are you positive you have to go tonight?" He pouts his lips and gives me puppy dog eyes. Before I can even shoot him down, he tries another tactic. He throws his hand over his forehead and feigns illness. "I think I'm sick." He coughs, really playing it up. "I need you to take care of me." He grabs my hand and places it on his forehead. "Feel me." He coughs again and then groans.

I hear a beep from outside. I push off my stool, straighten out my skirt, and place a kiss on his cheek. "Gotta go, babe. Feel better. Love you!"

If only it were that simple. He manages to grab hold of my skirt and pulls me back to him. He pulls me into his chest and wraps his arms around me. "I'm going to miss you." And for dramatic effect, his lips turn into a frown. And he sniffles.

I push away from him. "Grayson! I'm going to be late. I will be home in a few hours. You'll be fine." I crash my lips to his, because that's what he really wants. I linger there way less than he likes, but Natalie beeps again. Reluctantly, he lets me go. I peck his cheek one more time. He slaps my ass before he lets me walk away. I turn and throw a glare in his direction and follow it up with a smirk before grabbing my bag and heading to the front door.

"Behave, Ainsley," I hear him call out.

"I always do," I call back to him. "Don't wait up!" And then I'm out the door.

Natalie waves to me before I can get to the car. When I climb in, she reaches over and pulls me in for a hug. "Hey girl, how's it going? He give you a hard time about leaving?"

"Yes! But he's so cute when he's being all pouty so I will give him a pass." I buckle up. "So excited for bowling. I feel like it's been forever since I've bowled."

"Yeah, me too. It's going to be super fun. And I'm so getting wasted. I already told Caleb he's coming to pick us up." She grins, as she starts to back down the driveway.

"Grayson warned me not to let the girls both get wasted tonight. Not sure that's really going to happen."

She laughs. "I love how he's so overprotective of them."

"They are all he has."

She glances my way. "Add yourself to that list, my dear."

"Yeah, I know. Sometimes it's still hard to believe it because it all happened so fast, ya know?" One hundred twenty-five days. That's how long I've known Grayson. Some days it feels like I've known him forever and other days, I'm grateful we still have so much to learn about each other. Like yesterday I learned he sucks at strip Scrabble. Or he was putting on an act to suck at strip Scrabble. Yeah, it's probably the latter.

"Never been my experience but totally see how it works for you guys." She smiles, keeping her eyes on the road. "How long until he asks you to marry him?"

"What?" I spit out. "No way. We haven't even talked about that, like ever. No. Not anytime soon."

"Honey, you've practically been living with the guy since your first date. You think he's going to wait much longer? Not going to happen." She sighs. "I'm going to ask the girls what they think. I bet they agree with me."

"No! This is their night. Do not bring my relationship with Grayson into it." I hope she can hear the pleading in my voice.

She smirks, her eyes twinkling. "We'll see."

Ah, fuck.

When we get to the alley, Bella and Kylie have already claimed the last two lanes. There are pitchers of soda, water, and one half-filled with beer. They each have a cup in their hands, downing their drinks. And they aren't filled with soda or water.

Great, I think, pulling out my phone to text Grayson.

> Don't shoot the messenger, but both of them have already started drinking. Will do my best to keep it at a minimum.

His answer is immediate.

> Thanks. Text me before you get too wasted and I'll come pick everyone up. They can crash here.

> Love that you know I will be drinking. I'll text you. Love you.

> Love you, my girl. BTW, are you as good at bowling as you are at pool?

> Wouldn't you love to know. MUAH!

SMH.

I slip my phone in my back pocket and pour myself a cup of water. I'll save the drinking for later. Natalie comes up and pours herself a beer. "Cheers!" she calls, clinking my cup to hers. We drink.

The girls come over and hugs are exchanged. Kylie takes a seat in the chair. "Thanks for coming, ladies. Everyone else backed out so it's just the four of us. Hope that's okay."

I feel like a mother hen. I want to ask her if she's eaten anything before she started drinking. Before I can ask, a tray filled with bowling alley, fried-fat appetizers, is delivered to our table. *Perfect timing,* I think. My inner Grayson agrees.

Bella hands us each a mozzarella stick and motions for us to "clink" them together. And so we do. "Cheers," we whisper-yell, and shove them in our mouths. Kylie is the first to swallow and break out in a fit of laughter.

"This is why I love you, Bella. I can't fucking wait to make you my wife." She reaches over and grabs her hand, squeezing it.

Bella swallows up her food, and tosses out, "I can't wait to rip your dress off and fuck you senseless on our wedding night."

Natalie and I break into hysterics. "Can I just tell you how much I adore all of you girls? And by being with Grayson, I have instant girlfriends, girlfriends whom I actually love spending time with."

I hear someone clear a throat behind me. And then a voice calling my name. And I freeze.

Ah, fuck.

I plaster a fake smile on my face before turning on my heels. "Tara!" I exclaim with feigned enthusiasm. "So good to see you." I don't even attempt to move.

"Yes. It's been quite a while. I guess you've been....busy." She looks around at the other girls. "Wait, I remember you from the bar that night." She points to Bella. "And you too." This time, she points to Kylie. "That's the night you stuck your tongue down that guy's throat." She pauses and rolls her eyes. I hear a few gasps behind me.

"Yeah, it was." I merely confirm what she says; my tone stays steady.

"How did that work out for you?" she asks with an undertone of sarcasm in her voice.

Before I can answer, Natalie comes up behind me and throws her arm around my waist. "Not well," she exclaims, leaning in closer to me. "For him." And then she takes my face in her hands and plants a kiss on my lips!

It catches me off guard, my eyes going big, but then I play along. I lean into her, and whisper in her ear, "I think I may love you. Not like I love Grayson, but close. And if our boys could see us now!" I can't help but giggle; Natalie soon joins in. "Is she still standing there watching?" I stammer through my teeth.

"Nope, she just stomped away." Natalie doesn't let me go right away; she's still hugging me close.

"That was priceless," Bella exclaims. "Simply priceless. I wish I had captured the look on that bitch's face when Nat kissed you. And I wish I had gotten that kiss on camera. My brother would about die."

I pry myself out of Natalie's grasp. "You will not tell him. He will never let this go. Please," I plead.

"She's right, Bell. He would make them reenact it every time they are together. But that was badass, Nat." Kylie holds up her hand for a high five, which Nat obliges.

"I love you too," Natalie turns to me and says. "And if I were into girls, since Bella's already taken, you would be my first choice."

"Hey," Kylie whines. "What about me?"

"So not my type." Natalie hoots with laughter.

Kylie pouts. When she looks up, she says "oh shit," and we all turn to see Tara walking back in our direction, Kelcie on her heels.

"Ainsley!" Kelcie feigns shock. "What are you doing here?"

Knowing Tara has filled her in on my antics, I grab Natalie's hand and explain, "Out celebrating our friends' upcoming nuptials. And you?"

"Just came to bowl with Tara and the guys. We must catch up soon. Dinner next week?"

Knowing full well I'll cancel, I say, "Of course. Text me."

"Perfect. Well, have fun and see you around." That comes from Tara, who is clearly jealous of the fact she thinks I have a girlfriend now. She's always such the bitch. It's even clearer to me now that I have friends like Bella, Kylie, and Natalie. Not sure why I even hung on to the idea of "friendship" with Kelcie, especially since she's so tight with Tara, whom I never could stand.

"Bye." I give them my best wave and don't wait for them to walk away before I turn back around. It's not a goodbye for now; it's more of a final goodbye to the toxicity of having a "friend" like Tara, which I certainly don't need in my life.

I pour what's left of the beer into a cup and chug it. "We are going to need more of this," I call out to no one in particular, but it garners a laugh from my friends.

"Come on kids. Let's bowl." Kylie motions to the bowling balls and pins.

I dig my phone out of my pocket and shoot a text to Grayson.

> Let the drinking commence! I love you. And Natalie too. Think Caleb will share?

I know his response would be immediate.

> I DON'T SHARE

> But it could be fun

> Never going to happen. Now get back to bowling

> Yeah, okay

> Get their keys now please

On it. Love you lots

I don't bother asking either Kylie or Bella for the keys. I simply go into Kylie's bag and grab them out and put them in my bag. Bella would never get in a car to drive after she drinks, and I'm sure Kylie wouldn't either.

"Okay, here's how we play," Bella informs us. "Every time your ball goes in the gutter, you drink. Simple enough."

Kylie comes over to me as Bella enters the names into the computer for scorekeeping. "Grayson's good to pick us up?" she asks pleadingly.

"I just have to text him later."

"He's such a great man. You and Bella are blessed." She hugs me.

"He would do anything for Bella and whomever she loves. Just trying to keep everyone safe."

She pulls out of the hug, and I think she's done. Looking a little wistful, she starts, "I don't have a family. Bella and Grayson are it. I fell in love with Bella the moment I laid eyes on her. There's something special about those Abbotts." She pauses, catches her breath and continues. "He's not going to let you go, you know."

"Told you!" I hear Natalie say from behind us. When I turn to face her, she's got a huge shit-eating grin on her face.

"Told her what?" Bella asks.

"That Grayson's going to ask Ainsley to marry him sooner rather than later," she replies, still wearing her grin.

Bella looks over to me, a hard look on her face. I think she's going to be upset; I mean, we are here to celebrate her. "Oh, he totally is, and you'd better say yes!" Her grin matches Natalie's.

All I can do is laugh.

"Come on, let's bowl." Bella grabs a ball and throws it down the lane. At the last minute, it knocks down one pin. You would have thought she bowled a strike, the way she celebrates.

As I watch her take her next turn, I contemplate what they've said. Grayson and I have never talked about marriage or long term, not that I don't see this heading that way. It is. I'd be a fool to give up the connection I have with Grayson, and I know he feels the same way. That we have talked about. I would be so lucky to be Grayson's wife. He truly is the perfect package.

When it's my turn, I shut off my thoughts and just bowl. Fortunately for me, I am a good bowler, and Grayson's question about the comparison to pool isn't far off the mark. So I don't get to drink much, but the others do.

Of the three, Natalie is the least wasted, but there's no way she can drive. I see her attempting to text Caleb so I take her phone and help her out.

Kylie and Bella are lying down, stretched across a few chairs, arms over their eyes. I had texted Grayson earlier to let him know when he should come, so I was surprised he wasn't here yet.

I check my phone and realized I missed a text from him earlier.

> You could so kick my ass in bowling too, woman.
> PS: your ass looks sexy in that skirt.

"So sexy," I hear him murmur in my ear as he comes up behind me. He nips at my neck, and a small moan escapes my lips in reaction as I turn around.

"Hey, Gray." I find his lips and plant a kiss on them. He climbs over the bench where I'm sitting and sits down next to me.

"Why don't you look like them?" He points to the other girls.

"Because I don't suck at bowling," I complain. He looks confused. "We were only allowed to drink when the ball went in the gutter. Mine didn't go in the gutter so much." I shrug.

His arm wraps around me, and he pulls me into his side, letting his hand linger on my breast. "And I was so looking forward to drunk sex with you tonight," he guffaws, shaking his head.

"I can remedy my situation."

"Nah, darling. Sober sex works."

Our moment is interrupted by Nat's shouts of "Baby!" She sits up a little straighter in her seat, but as soon as he's close, she slumps against him. "Take me home and take me to bed," she slurs. I can't help but snort when she tries to wink at him.

Caleb scoops her up, and her eyes close as she lays her head against his shoulder.

"Have fun with that, bro," Grayson tells Caleb. He grunts his response, gives a little wave, and walks away.

Before he gets too far, Natalie pops her head up. "Ainsley, don't forget what we talked about!" she yells back to me. "We forgot to take bets!"

I feel myself blush and will her to stop talking. Grayson's eyes bore into the side of my face, but I won't meet his gaze. He misses nothing, that one.

"What's she talking about?" he asks, begging for an answer.

"Nothing," I stammer out and quickly change the subject. "How are we getting these two home?" I point to Kylie and Bella.

As if she heard me, Kylie pops up from the chairs. "I'm okay. Just get me a cup of coffee from Dunkin' to sober me up." She looks over at Bella. "Yeah, she sucks at bowling." She giggles. "Ouch, not a good idea." She rubs her temples as the smile fades.

Grayson looks at me. "Are you okay to drive?" He doesn't need to give me the intense stare he's giving me, but I know he's just keeping everyone safe.

I nod. "Yeah I only had one beer at the most, and it was over an hour ago."

Handing me his keys, he directs, "Okay, you take Kylie to Dunkin' in my car, and I'll take Bella in the girls' car and meet you at our house." He walks over to Bella and picks her up effortlessly. The way his arms flex and make his muscles pop doesn't escape me. He looks right at me as I lick my lips, adds, "Later, darling," and my face starts to get hot.

Even in her drunken state, Kylie takes in our exchange. She tries to whisper, but she's louder than she means to be. "Oh yeah. Totally saying yes."

Grayson whips his head around. "Keep moving," I instruct.

"Nothing to see here." As he passes by, I smack his ass. "Love you, babe." His expression still looks confused, but he blows a kiss in my direction, shaking his head.

This is the moment that Bella chooses to pop her head off his shoulder and yells out, "Two weeks. At the most!" And just as quickly, she replaces it on his shoulder as he carries her off, looking more confused than ever.

"You guys are killing me tonight, you know that, right?" I ask Kylie as we make our way over to the desk, carrying everyone's shoes to be returned.

When we get to the desk, I turn in all the shoes and get my money out to pay. When I turn in the lane paperwork, the cashier tells me, "You're all set."

"Huh? Kylie, did you already pay?" I look back to her, who looks as confused as I feel.

"No, and I'm pretty sure Bella didn't either."

I turn back to the cashier. "Lanes thirty-five and thirty-six. You're sure we paid?" I ask him still confused.

"Yep. The guy who carried your friend out took care of the bill. You want the receipt?"

"No, we're all good. Thanks!" I smile in his direction and then turn back to Kylie. "Grayson paid."

"Ah, I should have known," she responds, like that sums it up.

Walking to his car, I look at her. "Can I ask you a question?"

"I love Bella and don't cheat, but I'm flattered you're asking.." She gets most of that out with a straight face but then cracks up at the end. "I'm kidding. What do you want to know?" She tones down the laughing but keeps the smile on her face.

"You and Bella are meant for each other. Not that I didn't know that already or that you need to know it." I pause for a minute, contemplating how best to ask the question. "How loaded is Grayson exactly?"

She considers my question for a moment, the lines above her eyes coming out as she draws her brows together. "Truthfully, I have no idea. He keeps it pretty hush-hush, and since he handles most of Bella's finances, she doesn't really know either. We live comfortably with our two salaries, but occasionally an extra couple thousand dollars ends up in our account. And he totally paid for the entire wedding. Well, he just gave Bella his credit card. He hasn't once said she's spent too much. He pretty much doesn't deny her anything money-wise if she asks nor does she take advantage of him. He paid for her engagement ring too, but she doesn't know that. And he won't let me pay him back."

"Wow, he's so generous."

"He's more than generous for the people he loves."

"And yet, he drives this beat-up Explorer. What's up with that?"

She looks at me, a wistful look in her eyes. "His dad bought it for him, and he can't part with it. Bella teases that he's going to drive it to the ground and then keep it in the backyard forever. Truth is, she's probably not far off the mark."

We get into the car and as I start it up, I ask, "What were their parents like?"

"They were the best people you could ever meet. Jack was very much like Gray, a man of little words but with a heart of gold. And Diana, well she was just lovely. She was the mom everyone talked to and wished she were your mom. She and Bella butted heads over a lot of Bella's choices, but I like to think that Bella's grown up into a woman she would be proud of."

"Were they okay with Bella being gay?" Not only is Kylie so easy to talk to, she's a great listener too. And I've found that she has great perspectives on Gray, different from what Natalie offers and even different than Bella since he's not her sister.

"Right from the beginning, even though Gray outed her. She didn't speak to him for a week, according to him. I didn't know them then."

"I wish I knew Gray as a teenager."

"You should have seen Bella as a teenager. She was wild!"

"*Was* wild?" I ask curiously.

"She's tamed since I've met her. But I fell in love with her wildness so she can't lose all of it." She smiles to herself. "You're really perfect for Gray, just in case you ever have any doubts. I've known both of them a long time, and he's never, ever been this happy."

"Me either," I whisper. "Me either."

When we get home, Gray has already tucked Bella into bed in the guest bedroom, and he's sitting at the table. Kylie hugs him and says, "Thank you for bowling and for keeping her safe. We are both lucky to have you."

"Anything for you girls, you know that," he responds, pushing the hair out of her face. "Good luck with her tonight. Just shout if you need anything."

We both watch as she climbs the stairs to the guest bedroom. I take a seat in the chair next to him.

"Coffee?" he asks me.

"Yeah, I'll get it in a minute. I need some food, too. Is it too late to cook?" I look over at the clock. It's only eleven.

"What do you want to make?" He scoots his chair closer to me. He turns his hat around on his head, puts his hands on my thighs, and starts massaging them with his fingers.

As much as I can, I ignore the way his fingers dig into my skin and how he is turning me on. "Pizza," I moan out.

He brings his lips to mine, but instead of kissing me, he leans into my ear and rasps, "I'll order you a pizza to be delivered and as we wait, I'm taking you upstairs for appetizers." He doesn't wait for my answer but scoops me out of the chair and sprints upstairs to our bedroom.

"Grayson! The girls will hear us," I call out as he slams the door and tosses me down on the bed. His eyes are full of hunger. Hunger for me.

"I'll make sure you stay quiet," he tells me, running his hand up my skirt. He stops when he gets to the top of my thighs. His eyes go wild. "Um Ainsley, where's your underwear?"

"Oops, must have forgotten to put them on before I left." I

smirk at him. Forgetting about my hunger, I pull my skirt up around my waist, giving him the full access he craves.

"Girl, I could not love you any more," he exclaims, getting to work.

At least he keeps his promise to help keep me quiet.

20

GRAYSON

*I*t seems like the summer passes by in a blur. By the time fall rolls around, Bella's wedding is finally here. The Friday before the wedding, I get home before Ainsley. Okay, I actually never left the house. I canceled my clients last night so that I could get started on the cake for the girls' rehearsal dinner tonight. But I didn't tell Ainsley. She thinks we are going to bake it when she gets home. She only has one class on Fridays for this fall semester so she's done by eleven. Usually she stays on campus, but she is heading home right after class today.

She's having a hard time this semester, even though it's only a few weeks into it. Her schedule is horrible, and she has a bunch of one hundred level classes, which are a lot of work for her. She's really looking forward to the wedding and getting away for the weekend, even if it's just to a hotel close by. We have her brother's wedding next month in Chicago, and then maybe we can take a real vacation.

"I'm home," I hear her call out, slamming the door behind her. "God, my day sucked. Care to make it better? Where are you?"

"In the kitchen," I call back to her.

She appears in a minute, looking a bit disheveled but still sexy as ever. Since I don't want her to know I started the cake yet, I keep her away from the island. "What happened?" I ask, grabbing her into me.

"I don't want to talk about it. Plus, we need to make the cake for dinner tonight. And then we have to shower." She takes in my appearance and her face falls. "Did you already shower? Why aren't you all sweaty?" I ignore her questions and distract her with a kiss. "Mmm," she mumbles against my lips. "I see what you're doing. Don't think I'm not onto you." She slips her tongue in my mouth, licks the underside of my tongue, and pulls out. "Come on. We have a cake to bake." She walks to the pantry and goes in for the ingredients she needs. "Gray, we don't have any flour. Shit."

"It's on the island."

I watch as she comes out of the pantry and finds the empty flour container on the island. Anger crosses her face when she takes in the flour spilled all over. And then her eyes go big when she sees what I've done. She gasps and puts one hand over her mouth. Her eyes fly to mine, then back to the island, and then back to me. "Gray?" The shock on her face is reflected in her voice.

"Believe it, love." My face erupts into a huge smile as I pull the black box from my pocket. And for entertainment purposes, I get down on one knee. I ask the question I had written in the flour. "Ainsley, marry me?"

She smiles just as big, only stopping when it reaches her eyes. There are tears at the corners of her eyes and one manages to escape down her cheek. "Yes," she croaks out. "Yes!" Her eyes start to twinkle. "OMG, yes!"

I push up and lift her off the ground. I crash my lips to hers and kiss her like I've never kissed her before, letting all my love for her pour out through my lips. She responds with a serious kiss of her own, making me see stars. Guess that's really a thing.

I break the kiss so I can slip the diamond on her finger. With Kylie's help, I picked a ring that I thought she would love. Slipping it on her finger, it fits perfectly, and she can't help but gaze down at it. "Grayson! This is huge. It's gorgeous. I love it. But it's huge!" The smile hasn't faded from her lips. "Did I mention it's huge?" she repeats as she peers down at it.

"It makes your finger sparkle. It's the perfect size."

"You would think so." Then she gasps and her smile fades. "I CANNOT wear this tonight! It's your sister's rehearsal dinner. No way." She starts to slide it off her finger, but I stop her.

"Don't you dare," I tell her. "Do not take that ring off, you got me?" I stare down at her, letting her know how serious I am.

She shakes her head. "Grayson, you don't get it. You aren't a woman. I'd be PISSED if someone showed up at my rehearsal dinner wearing this. I will not be that person. I love you and this ring, but there's no way I am wearing this tonight."

She has a good point. I can only imagine Bella's reaction if she DID show up wearing the ring. Not because of its size; just because of the meaning behind it. Reluctantly, I give in. "Okay, I get it." I slip the ring off her finger and back into the box. I hand it to her. "As soon as the wedding is over, that ring goes back on your finger, you got me?"

"Understood," she tells me, pecking my cheek. "I love you."

"I love you. And I can't even tell you how much more I love you by making me realize that my sister's happiness is more important than you wearing my ring. For the next two days, just so we are clear. That's so selfless."

"I just wouldn't want it to happen to me, so I can't do it to someone else. If that makes me selfless, then so be it. And you will not speak of this until after the wedding. Now, we have a cake to make!"

"Will you be mad if I told you I already baked the cake?" I ask, my tone pleading for her understanding.

Her face loses the elation for a minute, then it comes right back as she says, "Oh thank god. After the day I've had, I have no desire to bake. That's insane, right?"

"Wow, that bad, huh?"

"You ever have one of those days that you think to yourself, 'man, if I didn't need this job, I would so quit right now?' That was my day today."

I'm quiet for a minute. Ainsley and I never really talk finances. She knows I have the means to support the lifestyle we lead, but she has no clue how far they stretch. "So quit." I don't say anything else as I wait for her reaction. I'm almost certain she'll think I'm crazy.

She looks at me, her face giving nothing away. "Okay," she challenges me, shrugging her shoulders. "I will." There's not even a hint of sarcasm in her voice.

I know she's waiting for me to challenge her back, but I'm not going to. I'm serious that she should quit. "Dead serious, love. Quit. Your. Job."

"Grayson, I said I will." The green in her eyes gets a little lighter as she cracks a smile.

And I thought I loved her ten minutes ago! "You're seriously going to quit your job because I told you to?" I ask incredulously.

She nods. "It's not so much because you told me to; it's because you respect me enough to support my decision to quit. I don't love my job; I never have. I thought that when I became a professor at a college, my mom would be proud of me. Yeah, not so much. I'm done doing things for people who don't appreciate my talents and my skills. I want to do something I love, something that makes me happy to do every day, something that doesn't feel like work."

"You want to bake," I supply for her, grabbing a hold of a strand of hair and twisting it around my fingers.

"Every damn day. Except for right at this moment," she says with a laugh. "But I can't do it without you. And I don't mean just your financial support. I want you to 'work' with me because we make an excellent team in the kitchen. What do you say?" She looks up at me, her eyes pleading with me to say yes. "Well?" she asks after a minute or two of silence.

"There's nothing I would rather do than help you bake. Every damn day."

Her face is giddy with pure joy. "You sure know how to make a girl's day improve. An engagement, a dream job. What's next, a baby?" She lets out a laugh, but it's a nervous one.

"Well, that's the next logical step, isn't it?"

She nods her head, but when she looks back up at me, she's lost some of her happiness. "Not right away," she starts, her voice barely above a whisper. "I can't wait to have babies with you, but considering how fast we came together, there's so much of the relationship left for us to explore before we bring kids into it. I want to enjoy you, just you, for a little while longer."

"I'm on board with that. You let me know when you're ready to share me. And, babies, plural?"

"Oh yes, there will be more than one," she utters, the smile returning to her face. "I'm guessing you're okay with that?"

"Yep."

Changing the subject, she asks, "Did you frost the cake?" When I nod, she looks at the clock. "Now we have plenty of time to shower." She puts her hands on the hem of my shirt, tucks her fingers underneath, and trails them across my abs. "Come on, let's go shower." She leads me by the shirt and begins to make her way out of the kitchen. She stops abruptly at the door. "You took a picture of the flour?"

"Of course I did," I tell her sarcastically.

She contemplates going back and taking a picture but thinks better of it. "It will be here when we get back," she voices aloud, confirming her decision to proceed upstairs.

"Good choice, fiancée."

* * *

"No, I'm not doing it," I protest for about the fifth time. "Grayson, you have to," Ainsley practically begs. "Bella wouldn't have asked you to do it if she didn't want you to. She knows you can do it." She places her palms on my cheeks. I try to shake them off, but she anticipates that and somehow manages to keep her hands planted and steady on my cheeks. She looks me in the eyes, and I take in hers: the emerald swirling around, a caring expression filling them. "I know you can do this. I'll be right there next to you."

For the life of me, I can't remember why I agreed to make the toast at the wedding. Oh right, there was Bella. And Kylie. And Ainsley. The three of them ganged up on me and wouldn't back down until I said yes. Ainsley and Kylie wrote the speech; all I have to do is get up there and repeat it. It really shouldn't be that difficult; it's basically a proclamation of how much I love Bella and Kylie. And I do. Love them. But I'm having a hard time breathing and my palms are all sweaty. So, I start pacing, as much as Ainsley tries to stop me.

Psyching myself up, telling myself I can do this, Ainsley comes up behind me, wraps her arms around me, and lays her head on my back. One of her hands finds my wildly beating heart, and she begins to tap my chest in a slow, steady beat. Between her calming breaths at my back and the way she's tapping my chest, I start to relax. When she's just about finally calmed me down, she whispers, "Deep breath, Gray. You got this."

I spin around to face her, taking in her appearance for the hundredth time today. The dress she picked, with Bella's approval, is form-fitting at the top, and while she doesn't have much in the chest area, Kylie managed to find her a bra that gives her a little more lift than usual. I trail my fingers along the swells of her breasts. I can't help myself but drop my head to her chest and trail my lips along them too, which makes her shiver. "You ready?"

"Getting there," I tell her, letting my tongue linger a little longer on the right breast. Not wanting the other one to feel left out, I slowly drag my lips over there.

"Grayson, you have two minutes until we need to be back out there so you can give your speech. Do not start anything you can't finish. That's what the hotel room is for later."

I pull my head up from her chest. "Thank you. I couldn't do this without you."

She meets my gaze, stands on tippy-toes, and exclaims, "You

won't ever have to do it alone." She kisses one cheek and then the other.

God, I love this woman. So damn much.

"One more hug," I insist, wrapping my arms around her, squeezing her as if my life depended on it.

"I love you too, Grayson. Now, get out there and give that speech." And then she adds, "Just think. The next time you have to do this, you'll be professing your love to the crazy girl that stole your heart the first time she kissed you and hasn't given it back since."

"Damn straight," I tell her. "Come on. We might as well get this over with." I grab her hand and lead her back to our seats at the reception.

We get back just in time for the toasts. Before she begins her "toast," Bella glares over at us, like we're late or something. She stands behind her seat at the table but passes on the microphone. It's a small venue, but she can make her voice carry regardless.

"First of all, thank you, everyone, for coming to share in our wedding. Kylie and I are so thrilled that you could join us. We can't wait to start our lives together.

"A huge thank you to my brother, Grayson. Not only for your continued love and support for both me and Kylie, but none of this would have been possible without your financial support. You gave me, I mean us, the wedding we've dreamed about. Mom and Dad would be so proud of the man you are."

As if I wasn't nervous enough, she throws out the last line. I find her gaze and mouth "Bitch" in her direction. She smiles at me, wipes a tear from her eye, and then continues. "I love you, Grayson. You're my rock, and I would be lost without you." She blows a kiss in my direction. "Your turn, big bro. Knock their socks off." She sits back down and Kylie whispers something to her which makes her smile and her eyes sparkle even more than they already are today.

I push up off my chair, heart beating faster. As I pass by her chair, Ainsley flashes me that smile I've come to love more than life itself. I lean down and pop a kiss on the top of her head as she murmurs, "You got this. I love you."

"Thanks, love. Hope I do you proud." I flash my smile and make my way to stand behind Kylie and Bella.

I pass on the microphone too because it would just shake in my hands. As I look around the room full of family and friends, my breath catches as I realize my parents should be here to share this moment with Bella. And then I realize they are here, just not how we would have thought. Taking in a deep breath, I begin. And I totally go off-script.

"I'm Grayson, Bella's brother for those of you who don't know me. Like Bella, I want to thank you for coming to help these two kids celebrate their love. They truly are the perfect pair, and I couldn't be happier to share my sister with you, Kylie. You make her so happy, you put up with everything she throws at you, and you tame her wild side. Well, you tame it more than anyone else could." I pause as the crowd breaks into laughter. "I'm happy to add you to our family as another sister. I love you."

I lean down and hug her. She wipes the tears from her eyes and mouths "I love you" and hugs me back.

I stand back up and try to garner the confidence to continue; it's not going to be easy. I steal a glance over at Ainsley. She puts her hand over her heart, and I match her movement in return.

I can't look at Bella as I continue. It will be too hard. So I stare at the back wall as I start. "To my Bells, I can't tell you how happy I am for you. You did it, kid. You found the love of your life and made it so that she loved you back. You've always been a fierce lover, and no one in your life ever deserved your love like Kylie does. She's seen you at your worst, and it was her love that saw you through your darkest days." I swallow the lump in my throat because I'm not quite done yet. "We don't always see eye to eye, but there's not another person in this world that I would want as my sister." The tears fall, but I have to finish. In barely a whisper, I continue. "There isn't a day that goes by that I don't thank my lucky stars you weren't in the car with them that fateful day. I know I had to take care of you, but you were the one who gave me the strength to get up and live during that time. You will never know how much you mean to me, and I'm positive that Mom and Dad are looking down, with tears in their eyes, at the woman you've become. I love you, Isabella, and am proud to call you my sister." When she hops out of her chair, I lose it. She wraps her arms around me and hugs me tightly.

"I love you, Gray. More than you'll ever know."

I rest my head on her shoulder to compose myself. And then I feel another set of arms around me. "Thank you, Gray. You will never know how much your speech meant to both of us," Kylie chokes out, tears streaming down her face. "Bella and I are the lucky ones to have you in our lives."

I'm not sure how long we stand there, but none of us care. Once I've composed myself, I pull out of their hold. They wipe the last tears that are falling and sit back down. "One more thing. I know you think it was me, but I didn't pay for the wedding." Bella shoots me a "WTF" look. "Dad had an account set up entitled 'Bella's wedding.' All I did was invest it wisely so I didn't have to finance your over-indulged choices. I mean, come on. I can't really deny my future wife the wedding she deserves because I had to pay for yours, right?" That garners another laugh from the crowd. Automatically my eyes find Ainsley's. She's wiping the tears from her eyes. "I love you so much," she mouths.

"Speaking of your future wife, when are you going to ask her?" I hear Bella call out from behind me. "Or do I have to ask her for you?" She stands up. "Ainsley, what do you say?"

I should have anticipated this; I mean, it's Bella we are talking about. But I'm pretty sure the shock I feel is reflected on my face. "Bella, sit down," I hiss. "Don't embarrass her."

Kylie tries pulling her down too, but she's up out of her seat and heading in Ainsley's direction. "I believe," she starts, "this is still MY wedding." The determination in her face and body language suggests she's not going to let this one go.

All eyes follow her to where Ainsley's sitting, a hush falling over the crowd.

I watch as she takes a seat in my vacated chair, right next to Ainsley. She takes both of Ainsley's hands in hers. Ainsley shoots me a look, a look that screams "HELP!"

"Bella," I spit out quite angrily. "Stop."

She drops Ainsley's hands and looks back at me, challenging me. "You going to ask her?" She's daring me.

"He already did," Ainsley states quietly.

Bella whips her head around to face her, an incredulous look on her face. "What? When?" She lifts Ainsley's left hand, her ring finger still bare. "I don't see a ring." And then a look of fear crosses her face and she looks like she's about to flip out and says, "Oh crap, did you say no?"

I reach into my pocket and dig out the ring box. I wander over to where they sit, and go up behind Bella, allowing me to still look at Ainsley, who is looking quite confused.

"You want to tell her what you said or should I, darling?" I ask Ainsley.

"I think we should make her sweat it out a little more," my girl says, playing along.

I look over to Kylie, who like the rest of the crowd, is sitting there speechless. "I bet you didn't think your bride would upstage her own wedding, did you?" Kylie giggles and shakes her head.

"No, especially because I specifically told her not to do this. Clearly I can see how well she'll listen as a wife." She shoots Bella a death stare.

Bella glares at her from where she's sitting. When she turns back to Ainsley, she tries to read her facial expressions. "Okay, the suspense is killing me. What did you say?"

Ainsley looks at me and gives me a slight nod, indicating I should share. "She said," I begin, pulling Ainsley out of her chair, a small gasp escaping her mouth. I take her left hand, slip the ring on her finger, and finish with, "Yes!"

Bella's eyes grow big, and her hands fly up to her mouth,

silencing her gasp. "Oh my god!" She hops out of her seat and pulls Ainsley into her. "I knew it! Two weeks, I was right!" And then she looks down at the ring. "Damn girl. That rock is HUGE!"

"That's what she said," I state with a smirk.

"Jeez, Gray. Overcompensating for something?" She leans against me. I drape my arms over her shoulders and place a kiss on the top of her head.

"Absolutely not," Ainsley exclaims, a smile appearing on her face.

"That's my girl." The crowd erupts in laughter again. I bring Ainsley into the other side of me. Giving each of them a squeeze, I know I'm the luckiest man in the world with these two, and there's not anything in the world I wouldn't do to let them know that every day.

21

AINSLEY

*W*ho would have thought Grayson would have so many opinions on our wedding? The venue, the flowers, the time of year, the fucking napkins. He was starting to drive me crazy with all of it so I started ignoring it. All of it. The planning of my wedding. I put it on the back burner and changed the subject every time Grayson brought it up. And the guy couldn't even get mad at me; after all, I learned that skill from him.

Even though it was the beginning of the semester, I up and quit my job. I regretted it for about half a second and then realized who was I kidding? I was never going back to the college world so if it looked bad on my part, it didn't really bother me. And well, Grayson more than made me feel better about it. The thing I found the most difficult was not having any "spending" money of my own anymore. Not that Grayson wasn't willing to pay for everything; he was, even transferring money into my account every week, which more than covered my needs. Except when I asked him for a semi-loan. He questioned and pestered me about what it was for, but I wouldn't budge. He eventually gave in and said he'd transfer the amount into my account, even though the amount was somewhat crazy.

You'd think with so much money, he'd be laxer about how and

where it was spent, but I'm learning he's not. He logged on to the accounts every damn day so I couldn't even hide any purchases that way. And by hide, I meant things I wanted to buy for him. I didn't care that he saw where I spent money or even how much. He never told me to stop spending the money or that I was spending too much nor did he make me feel like I couldn't spend the money any way I wanted. As much as Grayson isn't a "controlling" person, when it comes to money, apparently he is. Oh, and the wedding. But I'm still ignoring that right now.

At dinner one night, I hear my phone vibrate with a text. I push out of my seat and when I see that it's Kylie, I open it up.

> Are you with Grayson?

> > Yes, why?

> She's okay, but Bella's been in an accident.

Without realizing it, I gasp aloud. When I feel Grayson's stare on me, I mutter, "Fuck" and try to come up with a lie to cover up until I can get more info from Kylie.

"What's wrong?" he asks.

Thinking quickly, I say the first thing that comes to my mind, while furiously texting Kylie. "Natalie and Caleb had a fight. I may have to go out with her."

> > What happened? What can I do to help?

> A car barreled into hers. We're at the hospital and she's likely broken her arm. Waiting to hear if she needs surgery. Bella says don't tell Grayson anything yet.

> > Easier said than done.

> Please. Give us some time to find out what she needs and then she will text him.

> > I'll do my best but can't promise anything.

K. Thanks. I'll be in touch soon.

Do you need anything?

She stops texting for the moment.

I feel Grayson come up behind me and in my haste to put away my phone, it drops to the floor. "Shit," I say, trying to pick it up but having trouble since my hands are shaking.

"What the hell did Caleb do that's making *you* so nervous?" he asks me, trying to grab my phone.

"Huh?" I'm confused at first until I remember my lie to him. "Oh, she didn't even say. Just that he's being an ass, and she wants to go out for drinks."

"You seriously want me to believe that nonsense you just spewed out of your mouth?" he asks, his facial expression getting harder.

"Why do you think it's nonsense?" I stand by my lie. I do my best to convey it's the truth, but clearly he's not buying it.

He just stares at me, waiting for me to give it up. I stand my ground against him, even though he's so much bigger and taller than me. Until this comes out of his mouth. "Have it your way. You can tell me the truth about who you are texting or you can tell me why you need so much money."

"You already told me I could have the money," I plead. For about two seconds, I consider telling him why I need the money. But then I throw Bella under the bus because he's going to be so much more pissed about that than he is about how I'm spending the money. "Sit down."

"No, I think I'll stand," he argues with me.

"You might want to sit," I suggest as kindly as I can.

"Ainsley, tell me what's going on." His voice is deep, teetering on the brink of angry. "Now." And there it is.

"I don't know all the details, except that she's okay," I lead with. His face hardens with more anger because I'm not giving him what he wants. "Bella was in a car accident."

My words sink in fast. I know this because his face goes sheet white. And then it turns red with anger. "And you weren't going to tell me?" he practically yells in my face, his eyebrows furrowed.

"Bella didn't want you to be upset. She thinks it's just a broken arm, but they are waiting to see if she needs surgery." His face gets even redder as his anger starts to boil. I cower a bit when he starts speaking.

"Where is she?"

"At the hospital," I squeak out. He stomps his way to the garage. "Grayson wait." He stops moving but doesn't turn around. I run up to him. "She doesn't want you worried about her. Let's just wait until Kylie lets me know what's going on."

He spins around and stares me down, the anger radiating off of him. I've never seen him this angry, this unhinged. And it hits me that he's not angry; he's fucking scared shitless. I can't even begin to imagine the things that must be swirling around in his mind right now, so I won't even try. I interlock my fingers with his, and tell him, "I know."

"No, you don't. You have no clue," he replies, looking away from me. He tries to pull his hands out of my grasp, but I use all my strength not to let him.

"She's okay. Kylie said she's okay. It's just a broken arm."

He takes a deep breath and brings his eyes back to mine. The anger has been completely replaced by fear. And sadness. "They told me my mom was fine. Until she wasn't." He's fighting back tears, trying to hold himself together. "Can we go, please?" He's begging me.

Knowing there's only one answer to his question, I pull him into me, wrapping my arms around him, knowing it's not enough, but it's all I can give him. "I'm so sorry, Grayson. I didn't know." His body struggles against mine, warring with itself to either give in and accept my comfort or to pull away to get to his sister. The former part wins out, as I feel his body go heavy in my arms, his body wracked with sobs. As carefully as I can, I lower us down to the ground before I topple over with the weight of him. Once I manage to get us to the ground, he puts his head in my lap. I run my hands through his hair, trying to offer even the slightest bit of comfort.

I don't know how long we stay like that, but I don't dare move until he does. He eventually stops crying, his breathing returning to normal, even a bit slower than normal. I think he could almost be asleep, but he jumps at the sound of my phone vibrating. He lunges out of my lap for the phone, which is still on the ground. He hands it over to me, his hands shaking as he does so. I read the message.

"It's from Kylie. She doesn't need surgery. They are going to cast her arm and then she can go home. It will probably be about an hour or so."

"Text her and let her know we're coming to drive them home." It's not going to go over well with Bella, but I do as he asks. It isn't a suggestion.

Before getting up, he slumps down against the island. He looks my way, his face pleading with me for comfort. He's still scared, I can see it in his eyes, in the way his shoulders are slumped, in the fear he's trying to hide on his face. I slump down next to him, and he brings me onto his lap. I lay my head on his chest, and he takes my hair in his fingers and starts twirling like crazy.

"My worst fear is that I'll lose her," he starts, his voice barely above a whisper. "Had you not been here, I probably would have raced to the hospital, and stormed in, demanding to see her. And she would have been pissed. But she doesn't get it; she doesn't know what it's like to get that call, the call that changes your life in an instant. She doesn't know because I didn't tell her. I didn't tell her that our mother was alive when they brought her to the hospital, that only our dad had died instantly. She doesn't know that I got to the hospital thinking my mom was still alive, and when I learned she didn't make it, it broke me. Because by the time I told her, it was just easier to say they both died in the car. That was enough to break her; she didn't need any extra burden." He swallows hard. I can't see his face, but there's no way I can look at him now anyway. Tears fall rapidly down my face, crying for this man who has lost so much in his life, and yet has to be strong every day for his sister. He swallows once more before speaking again.

"Thank you, Ainsley, for being here. For loving me enough to know what I needed when I broke down. For seeing through my anger for what it really was. Fear. Fear of losing the one constant in my life since I was three years old. Since my parents died, I've always put Bella first in my life, above any woman that came into my life." He clears his throat again before he continues. "I realized tonight that as much as I love Bella, as much as I will always fear losing her, she's been replaced as number one."

He stops. The enormity of his words hit me hard. Like, so hard, that my breathing stops for at least a minute, as my heart stops beating. I can't move, I can't speak. And he senses it, so we stay huddled like that for a bit.

"Ainsley?" he asks quietly after some time has passed.

"Yeah?"

"Is it okay if we get up now? My legs are falling asleep." He starts to stand up, shaking out his legs.

I can't help but to let out a chuckle. I tilt my head up toward his, as he looks down at me. "I love you, Gray."

"Ditto," he replies, putting a kiss on my forehead. "Thanks for tonight. I hope you know I was never angry with you."

"I know," I reply honestly.

He hugs me one last time before he walks down the hall. Once he's back, he tosses keys in my direction. "I'm in no shape to drive, but I need to get to Bella."

"Come on. Let's go see what havoc she's causing at the hospital."

"One more reason why I love you, darling." He smiles at me as he follows me out of the house.

At the hospital, we hear Bella before we even get to the door of her room. From the sounds of it, she's yelling at someone. "Well, she sounds just fine," I say with a grin as we walk down the hallway hand-in-hand. Even though he's doing better, Grayson won't completely be okay until he sees for himself that Bella is okay. The worry he feels is etched on his face, and his hat is completely pulled down low on his forehead to shield his eyes from onlookers.

When we get to her door, Kylie's walking out, shaking her head. "Oh thank god," she declares when she sees us. "I need help with her. The pain meds are making her loopy, even crazier than usual. And they want me to take her home. Tonight! She may just drive me batty." She looks frazzled. Her hair is up in a messy bun, but strands are falling every which way. It's probably because she keeps tugging at her hair, even in the few minutes we've been here. Her clothes are wrinkled and her shoes are untied. She needs a hug, so without thinking, I wrap my arms around her and pull her in tight to me.

"Are you okay?" I whisper against her face. She shakes her head. I turn back to Grayson. "Gray, I'm taking Kylie for a walk. Go see Bella and make sure she's okay." His head nods slightly as he heads into her room. I turn my focus back to Kylie and just hold her for a few minutes. When she pulls out of my embrace, I tell her, "Let's go get some coffee." Her eyes are wet, but she gives me a small smile. I put my arm around her shoulder and her body melts into mine.

In the cafeteria, I sit her down at a table and go grab us some coffee. Returning with the coffee, she seems a little less frazzled, even if it's the tiniest bit. Before I can ask how she is, she looks at me, concern overtaking her face, and asks, "How's Grayson?"

"He's been better. He's scared, but it came out as anger."

"That's what I was afraid of." She looks down into her coffee cup.

"You've got enough on your plate. I'll take care of him." I lay my hand on her arm, and it seems to help calm her even a bit more. "How's Bella? What happened?"

"It was just a fender bender, but the guy that hit us, rammed into the car at a high speed and on impact, she hit her arm the wrong way, and it cracked. Luckily for her, well all of us, I guess, it was a clean break that didn't require surgery. Just shoot me now if that had happened." She laughs.

Without thinking, I ask, "Do you want us to take her home to our house? I'm sure it would actually make Grayson feel better anyway." I hope she takes my offer as purely a way to help her, not that she can't take care of Bella herself.

She contemplates her answer for a moment. "So, I don't know how to answer that." As she speaks, her eyebrows scrunch up in concern. "I don't want Bella to think I'm bailing on her, nor do I want to burden you guys with her, not that she's even a burden." She puts her hands over her face. "Oh my god. I can't even believe I'm thinking of sending her somewhere else. I truly love her, but she's not the easiest person to handle. And in this condition? Ha! She would kill me if she knew what I was saying." She starts to breathe a little heavier.

"Hey, calm down." Putting my hand on her thigh, I wait to continue until she moves her hands off her face, so I know she can process what I'm saying. Once her hands come down, I take them in mine. "It was just a suggestion. But I will totally tell Bella that it will make Grayson feel better, which isn't far from the truth anyway. She will never know what we talked about and how you feel, which is due to the stress of the situation." And then I quickly add, "You can come too. Grayson will totally cook breakfast in the morning. It'll be fun."

She seems to light up at that thought, but then the smile starts to fade. "Please. It's the least we can do." I try to convince her, knowing she doesn't want to be a burden. And then I get an idea. "Don't tell Bella, but he's giving me the money." A snort escapes my mouth.

Her eyes bug out. "Seriously? How did you convince him of that?"

I shrug. "I just flat out asked. And with a little convincing, none of which was sexual in any way, he finally caved."

"Wow. You are something special. I mean, you *are*, but damn. Although, I don't know why I should be so impressed. He's always so generous, and he would do just about anything for you. No, not 'just about anything'; he would do *anything*." She's quiet for a moment or so. "Bella's going to flip when she hears that he's giving you the money. Please let me be there when you tell her." Her lips curl up into a smile. "Yes, I think we will come home with you. But don't let Bella know I made the decision." She winks at me.

I pull her into a hug. "Grayson will be so happy. And it will be our secret." I push up out of my chair and grab the coffee cups. "Come on, let's go see what that wife of yours is up to."

When we get back to the room, Bella is sitting up in the bed, a cast on her left arm, and her head is resting on the pillows behind her. She looks like she's been through the wringer, a few scrapes on her face. Grayson's sitting on the edge of her bed. He looks a little more at peace now, definitely less worried, but his face still has that concerned look to it.

"Hey," I call out, coming up to stand in front of him. Almost on autopilot, his thighs move apart, and he grabs me into his chest, wrapping his arms around me. "Is she okay?" I ask against his chest, hoping she can't hear me.

"She's been better," Bella answers my question. I pick my head off Grayson's chest in time to see Bella pick hers off the pillow. She looks over at Kylie. "Can we go home now?" Her voice is about as un-Bellalike as I've ever heard. Kylie's face scrunches up, a look of worry coming over it.

"Bella, you want to stay at our house tonight? Grayson will cook for you." I feel Grayson's stare, so I give him a weak smile. I look over at Kylie. "You too," I say in her direction.

Kylie looks to Bella for her answer. She closes her eyes again. "Only if I can take a bath in Grayson's tub."

"Deal," I tell her as Grayson squeezes me tighter. "When can we spring you out?"

"She's all set," the nurse replies, entering the room. "The follow-up and discharge papers are in this folder." She hands the folder to Kylie who's standing at the entrance to the room. "Bella, take care of yourself." She gives her a wink which Bella returns with a grin. As she makes her way out of the room, she pats Kylie's shoulder. "Good luck to you."

"Hey, I heard that!" Bella shrieks. We all laugh. "Kylie, help me get dressed."

Grayson and I take that as our cue to leave the room. He grabs my hand and tells his sister, "We'll be right back to take you home." He leads us out into the hallway and once there, he leans up against the wall, pulling me next to him. His head falls back against the wall and his eyes close. He lets out an audible sigh and the breath he's been holding since I told him about Bella. "Do you know how much I love you?" he asks, his eyes still closed.

I push up on my tippy-toes and put a kiss on his cheek. "I have a pretty good idea," I reply with a giggle. I face him, straddle his legs, and wrap my arms around his waist, snaking them behind him as he still stands against the wall. I put my hands in his back pockets and lay my head against his chest. His heartbeat pulses against my cheek as his arms drape over my shoulders.

"What did I do to deserve you?" he asks quietly. I have no answer to that question, so I just shrug. "Well whatever it was, I'm glad I did it."

"Me too," I whisper back to him. I gaze up at him, but he's still got his eyes shut. The day-old stubble on his chin demands to be touched, and as I pull my hand out of his pocket to touch it, Bella and Kylie come out of the room.

"Jeez, guys. We'll be home soon. Can't you wait until you're back in your bedroom to get it on?"

"I see you are back to feeling like yourself, Bells," Grayson retorts, still not letting go of me. He opens his eyes. "You ready?"

She nods. She starts to walk down the hall and then abruptly turns around to face us. "Kylie and I will sleep in the downstairs guest bedroom tonight. I'm not drunk this time, and I'd prefer not to hear your bedroom shenanigans." Her face doesn't even crack a smile before she turns around to keep walking.

I look back up at Grayson, panic on my face. "I told you!" I screech. He just shrugs and cracks a smile.

"Darling, trust me when I tell you it was purely payback for years of Bella's bedroom antics I've had to endure."

From in front of us, without turning around Bella gives him the middle finger. "Love you too, Gray."

I can't help but giggle.

22

GRAYSON

*B*etween having to see her mother, her brother's upcoming wedding and the two-hour flight ahead of us, Ainsley was up half the night. I could handle her being a nervous flyer; I've always wanted to join the Mile High Club. But the stress she's putting on herself about her mother and the wedding, while totally warranted, is enough to make me want to tell her we can't go, only to spare her the stress. But since that's not an option, I just have to do my best to keep her as calm as possible. And not piss her off myself.

She makes me pull over twice on the drive to the airport. Her stomach is in turmoil, and my poor girl is nauseous as hell. When she gets back in the car the second time, she looks miserable.

"Darling, what can I do?"

She buckles up her belt and rests her head against the headrest. Her eyes close, and she tries to control her breathing, something that she's not too successful at. "Just drive. I'll be okay."

I rest my hand on her thigh. "Love, when? When will you be okay?"

"When this shitty ordeal is over with. When we get back home, and it's just me and you, and we can focus on our wedding." I can't help but laugh. Her eyes fly open. "Why is that funny?" she asks, shooting daggers in my direction.

"You've done practically nothing about our wedding."

She sighs. "Yeah, I know. It sounded good in my head. And it's something I should be focused on. I'll do better when we get home."

"Hey." Grabbing her chin, I force her to look in my direction. "There's no rush to get married. The only thing that's going to change is your last name."

"Yeah, about that." She casts her eyes away from me and down to the seat.

I wait for her to continue, but when she doesn't, I ask her, "What about that?" It's something we haven't talked about, but I always assumed she would take my last name.

She picks her head up and gazes into my eyes, a crazy look to her own. "Just kidding. I can't wait to be Mrs. Abbott." I sigh and squeeze her thigh, a little less tender this time. "Hey!" she shrieks.

"I hate you." Of course my comment just garners another laugh from her. And with her mood changed, I start the car up again and get back on the road to the airport. I leave my hand on her thigh; she puts her hand on top of mine and just rests it there.

When we get to the airport, I drive to the long-term parking lot and find a spot to park. She takes a few deep breaths before hopping out of the car. She grabs her backpack from the backseat, and I grab the rest of the luggage. Locking the car, I grab her hand in mine as we stroll into the airport.

The minute we get on the plane and are settled in our seats, she grabs my hand and squeezes it. Hard. Somehow her diamond gets flipped around, and it's digging into my palm. Right about now a smaller diamond would have been a better choice. She doesn't let go until after takeoff, when she finally relaxes a bit about the flying part. I try to convince her that joining the Mile High Club will ease her nerves, but she shoots me down, telling me that airplane bathroom sex isn't as easy or as sexy as everyone makes it seem.

That gets my attention. "Is this from personal experience?" I raise my eyebrows at her admission as I look over at her.

She hesitates a minute, which means yes. "Do you get to be a member of the club if you didn't finish the act?" she asks quietly.

"You didn't finish or he didn't finish?" I ask, feeling my body heat rising. I don't really know why this is affecting me this way. It's over and done with, and I got the girl. And honestly, I'm not the type of "sex in public places" kind of guy. Well, I never was. A girl like Ainsley sure can change a guy's mind about certain things.

"He certainly didn't, but neither did I. Well, I didn't finish with him."

"Keep going," I encourage, needing to hear the end of this story.

She looks at me, all traces of nervousness completely gone. When she starts to lean into me, I know it's going to be good. "That was when I learned how not to make any noise when getting myself off," she coos in my ear.

I love the things that come out of this woman's mouth. But I don't let her finish there. "Is that so?" She giggles and nods, her curls bouncing around her face. Then I lean back into her, and in her ear, I rasp, "This I have to see." I pull back and watch as what I've just said registers on her face. At first, she's shocked. Then, as nonchalantly as she can, she shrugs and moves her hand to the top of her waistband. Right before she slips it inside, I grab her hand. "You made your point, darling, but this isn't happening until your only audience is me."

"Suit yourself, big guy." As the flight attendant nears our aisle, she leans over again and whispers, "Aren't you going to adjust yourself, Gray? That show's for my eyes only."

I don't have to glance down to know what she's referring to, but she's right. I quickly adjust myself just as the flight attendant leans over to our row and asks, "Drinks?"

"I'll have a glass of wine and he'll have a Coke, please." There's no trace of the vixen, as if we weren't just having a discussion about sex on airplanes. That's my girl.

As soon as the flight attendant has turned her attention to the next row, I pull Ainsley in closer to me. "You, my dirty girl, are going to be the death of me."

Her face lights up with laughter. "You know you love it."

"There's seriously no place I would rather be right now than here with you," I pour out honestly. "I can't wait until you are officially, officially mine."

She pulls herself back for a moment to gawk at me. "Oh Grayson, I've been officially, officially yours since the day you made me kiss you in the bar. I just didn't admit it until later."

"I love when you say shit like that."

And then she full-out glowers at me. "I'm sorry. 'Shit' like that?" She puts quotes around the word shit.

"You know what I mean." I try to reel myself back in and not lose this moment with her, especially because I know once we land, my nervous girl will return.

"Oh yeah, I do. But I have to admit that Bella's right. Messing with you is quite hilarious." She lays her head on my shoulder. "Love you, Gray."

"Yeah, yeah," I tell her playfully and then add, "the feeling's mutual."

Her nerves are back even before the captain comes on and tells us to prepare for arrival. Luckily we have a few hours to kill before the rehearsal dinner tonight. 'm not totally convinced that she won't weasel her way out of it somehow, even though she really has no choice but to attend. And there's the added bonus of the wedding tomorrow.

Once we have touched down and are taxiing to the gate, she relaxes only slightly. We didn't check any bags so we head to the rental car counter to pick up our car.

"Abbott," I say when it's our turn.

The woman behind the desk smiles as she types some information into the computer. "Oh yes. The Mustang reservation. Let me just get everything set."

I cut her off, confused. "I'm sorry. Did you say Mustang? I'm pretty sure I reserved an SUV."

She looks puzzled as she looks back between her computer and me. "Hmm, maybe I'm looking at the wrong reservation." She studies the computer intensely.

And then I realize that this has Ainsley written all over it. When I look over at her, she's got her head down, trying to hide the smirk that's creeping over her face.

"Never mind. It appears my accomplice here has made a change. Mustang it is."

She looks back at me cautiously, then glances over at Ainsley. She hands me some paperwork to sign as I hand over my credit card. Once everything is signed and paid for, she hands over the keys. "It's in spot R-2, not that you could miss it."

"Thanks so much." I turn to Ainsley. "Come on, sneaky. Let's go." I grab the bags. She follows behind me, keeping a short distance between us.

When we get to the car, I unlock it, toss the bags in the trunk and climb behind the wheel. I look over at her before I start it up.

"Are you mad?" she asks hesitantly.

"Surprised is all. When?"

"Once I knew you wouldn't be checking your email again. It goes with the theme."

"The theme of what?" I can only imagine what this could relate to, especially with Ainsley.

"That I can't tell you." She smirks mischievously. "Yet."

"I bet Drunk Ainsley would let it slip," I tell her with a chuckle. "I'll liquor you up tonight."

"Pretty sure I'll have no problem liquoring it up on my own. You know, between my mother, my brother, and that woman he's marrying." Then she goes quiet. "I'm sorry. I hate how they bring out the worst in me."

"Me too, darling. You are so much better than them." I lean over and peck her cheek, but she grabs my face and assaults my lips with hers. She pulls away first, her cheeks just a tinge of pink to them.

"Come on. Let's go to the hotel. I need a nap." She winks at me.

I pretend to yawn. "You read my mind." I start up the car and navigate our way out of the airport.

After a couple of mind-blowing orgasms, we shower and freshen up for dinner. The rehearsal is being held at some restaurant in the heart of Chicago. As we drive there, Ainsley says, "I would love to know who is paying for this dinner and wedding. It sure as hell ain't Drew." She looks more pissed than nervous at this point.

"Why do you care?"

She sighs. "Because I do. I always have and it's hard to let go of that kind of thinking. And if my parents are paying for his, they should pay for mine."

"I already told you that I am paying for *our* wedding."

"That's not the point," she argues. "You shouldn't have to pay for all of it."

"It's not about what I should or shouldn't have to do. I want to pay for it. I want you to have whatever you want for the day. Well, what we want."

I feel her looking over at me. "Okay. I get that and appreciate it. Grayson, please pay for our wedding," she begs, batting her eyes in my direction.

"Done." Turning away to face the window, she mutters something under her breath. "I missed all that."

"That was the point." Changing the subject she adds, "Don't tell my parents I quit my job. I don't need to give my mother anymore ammunition against me this weekend."

"Sure thing." I contemplate my next question. I'm pretty sure I know the answer, but I need to know for sure. "Do you regret it?"

"Nope."

"Good." I don't face her but still smile.

When we get to the restaurant, I find a parking spot. She unbuckles but doesn't make any indication she's going to move.

"I'll be by your side the entire time," I remind her. "What did you decide about your ring?"

She hasn't told her parents yet. We had a heated discussion about telling them tonight. I think she should wait, but she's not worried about stealing anyone's thunder. I think it says a lot that she was adamant about not stealing Bella's thunder but doesn't care about Drew's or his fiancée.

"I'm wearing it. I believe a wise man told me not to take it off." She looks over in my direction, a twinkling in her eyes.

"Your call. Come on. Let's go." I get out and head over to her side and open her door. She turns her body to face me but doesn't get out.

"You think we can leave early if I feign sickness? You would have to cover for me. My mom can see through my lies." She looks up at me, her expression pleading with me to agree to her plan.

I put my arms under her armpits and lift her out of the car. "Not. Happening." I put her down on the ground. Her feet stay rooted in their spot. "I'll carry you in there, caveman style if you would prefer."

"I need one more kiss before we do this." She moves up next to me, wrapping her arms around my waist and letting her hands travel down to land on my ass. I grab the back of her neck and lean it backward. Then I slowly bring my lips to hers. She waits for them, instead of meeting me halfway. Her eyes flutter closed, and she parts her lips the moment mine hit hers. I waste no time slipping my tongue inside her open lips, finding hers waiting for me. She brushes the underside of my tongue ever so slightly and when the tiniest moan escapes, I wrap my other arm around her waist and pull her in closer to me. And then she assaults my tongue with hers. I match her greediness and attack back.

She's the first to pull away, breathless. I rest my forehead against hers. "Gray," she moans. "Guess I don't need the liquor." When I look at her, bewildered, she adds, "Keep kissing me like that, and I'll get drunk on you."

I smile in return. "I'm on board with that."

From behind us, I hear someone yelling "AINS!" Ainsley stiffens. "Fuck! Are you fucking kidding me!" She buries her head in my chest. "I may actually be sick."

I turn around and see the guy from the diner all those months ago walking up, a girl by his side. He picks up his pace a little, which forces the girl to keep up with him. She's having a harder time because she's in heels.

When he finally reaches us, Ainsley is still nestled in my chest.

"Darling, you can do this." I persuade, giving her another squeeze.

She shakes her head. "I can't."

"You don't have a choice. He's here."

I flash a smile in his direction and gently release Ainsley out of my arms, nudging her slightly. She pulls herself together, plasters the fakest smile on her face, and with feigned enthusiasm voices, "Jordan."

And then her past slaps me in the face. This is the guy who was the father of the baby. Who told her they would work it all out and then broke it off with her soon after she had the abortion. And as much as I want to kick the guy in the nuts, I realize I should be thanking him. For letting her go so I could keep her. With that thought, I pull her back into me. She comes easily.

The bastard watches my every movement, almost glaring at my actions. I notice that he's not even paying the girl with him any attention until Ainsley reaches her hand out to her.

"You must be Maggie. Congrats on your engagement." Another fake smile.

Maggie hesitantly reaches her hand out to Ainsley, as she sizes her up and down. "You're Ainsley?" she replies in shock. "Like *the* Ainsley?" She looks back at Jordan for confirmation. "You said she was pretty. This girl is gorgeous!" She frowns.

I can't help but chuckle. And then it only gets better.

"Oh my god!" She tugs Ainsley's left hand to hers. Ainsley just stands there, a look of shock on her face. "You're engaged too?

Jordan, her ring is huge!" she whines as she looks back to him. His expression hasn't changed much, even as he looks between his fiancée and Ainsley.

I lean down in Ainsley's ear. "Own it, darling."

"Yeah, Grayson and I are getting married too," she responds, pulling her hand out of Maggie's as if she were being burned. "It was nice meeting you. We'll see you inside." She flashes them both a smile and then grabs my hand, pulling me towards the restaurant. As we walk away, I notice they're standing there, mouths agape.

As we near the door, Ainsley glances my way and says, "The only thing that would have made that better was if my mother was a witness. Did you see the look on her face? Priceless!"

"I missed the look on her face because I was watching the look on your face. That, my gorgeous girl, was priceless." We get to the door and her hand squeezes in mine as she stills once again. "You got this, darling."

She takes a deep breath and exhales. "Here goes nothing!" I pull open the door, and she walks in, head held high.

After her run-in with Jordan, the rest of the night goes pretty smoothly. Luckily it's a sit-down dinner so there's little interaction between her and anyone else she doesn't want to speak with.

I didn't choose the size of Ainsley's ring to be show-offy. It wasn't to show other people how much money I have. It was the first ring I laid eyes on that reminded me of Ainsley so I bought it. I'm not going to lie and say that I don't enjoy the attention the ring gets. It's purely because it makes her light up and each time, her nervousness fades a bit, and the girl I love shines through more and more.

As we are saying our goodbyes, Drew, who's clearly had too much to drink, comes over to us. "You just can't help yourself, can you, Ainsley?" he spews at her.

"What are you talking about?" She holds her own, standing her ground, a determined look on her face. Despite her nerves earlier, she didn't really have much to drink.

He reaches out and grabs her hand. "You were flashing this all night long. It made Claudia feel bad. This is her night."

Ainsley rolls her eyes as she pulls her hand out of his grasp. "Is she jealous that mine's bigger than hers? Is that the real problem? Or is she just jealous that I got the better guy?" Rather than engage him more, she takes the high road and walks away, leaving him speechless and open-mouthed.

"Wow. She really is a bitch," I hear him mutter to himself.

Not wanting to engage him either but needing to stick up for my girl, I shoot him a look. "She's your sister. She came all this way to support you even though you never give her the time of day. I would watch what you say about her, especially in my presence. Do you ever think she acts that way because of how she's treated? Because that girl you just saw? She only shows up when you or your mother are around. It's too bad you don't know the real Ainsley. She's really quite amazing." And that's when I turn and walk away and run right into Ainsley's mother.

"Well she's certainly got you wrapped around her finger, doesn't she? It didn't take her long at all to land herself a man who can't see through her bullshit. It's never going to work out between the two of you. She will suck you dry before you realize what she's doing."

I'm too shocked at the words coming out of her mouth, the way the evil words spew out so easily, to come up with a retort to that. I'm sure the shock is registered on my face.

Before I can compose myself with a comeback, she tosses this out. "Please tell Ainsley we won't make it to her wedding, if there even *is* a wedding. After what I witnessed tonight, I can only imagine what kind of stunts she will pull for herself." She smirks at me, turns on her heels, and walks away, leaving me even more confused than before.

Pulling myself out of the shock, I go find Ainsley.

The smile fades off her face as I get closer. "What's the matter?" she asks, concern creeping on her once cheerful face.

"Your mother said she won't be at our wedding. She may have insinuated that there might not even be a wedding."

She hesitates, and I see the wheels turning in her head as she furrows her brows. "What about my father?"

"I believe she said we won't make it."

She looks down at the ground. When she looks back up, she's got tears at the corners of her eyes and one of the saddest expressions I've ever seen on her face. So of course I drop it. Because it's not an act.

"Darling, don't cry," I speak softly as I envelop my arms around her.

She looks up at me as one tear slips out. "She really said we? As in my dad too?"

I'm not sure at this point, and I'm at a loss at what to tell her so I go with the truth. "I don't know."

She pulls herself out of my grasp and starts running for the exit. I watch as she pushes herself through the throng of people and out the door. Quickly, I find myself following her outside. When I reach her, she's hunched over, trying to catch her breath.

"Ainsley! What's the matter?" I speed up a bit. When I get to her, I grab a hold of her shoulders and pull her up to standing.

"I c-can't," she stutters, breathing heavily. The expression on her face matches her breathing.

"You can't what? Can you tell me?"

She shakes her head no. "I need to leave. Please," she begs.

I grab her hand and walk her to the car. When we get there, I open the door for her and help her in. Before I can walk away, she starts to speak.

"You must think I'm crazy. I'm really not. It's just..." she trails off as she smiles weakly.

"On your own time, when you are ready. That's what you told me that night around the dinner table, and I fell hard right then. Take the time you need. But my girl, you are a little crazy. It just so happens that I love your kind of crazy." I lean in and place a lingering kiss on her forehead.

"I'm seriously the luckiest girl in the world."

"Nah, I'm the lucky one." I wander to my side of the car.

Once I'm inside, she tells me with a wink, "I'm surely not going to disagree with that logic. Let's go back to the hotel so I can show you just exactly how lucky you are."

"While I'm not going to argue with you, you show me every day, my love, how lucky I am. Every damn day."

"Yeah, I'm a pretty great catch." With her words, the smile I adore appears on her face.

I leave it at that and drive us back to the hotel.

23

AINSLEY

*A*fter the rehearsal dinner, the wedding was quite tame. I showed up, stayed sober, and watched my brother marry Claudia. She didn't even seem that into it; I'm not sure why I had to pretend to be. But I did, even if it was only for Grayson's sake. I'm finding that this man can pretty much talk me into anything, and not just things of a sexual nature.

Once we get back to the hotel after the wedding, I'm up half the night. I haven't done one thing about my wedding, yet here I am worrying about it. I just can't get over the fact that my dad won't be there. I tried to talk to him about it at the wedding, but every time I got the chance, my mother pulled him away from me. He just kept giving me a sympathetic smile and told me we'd talk later. I couldn't care less about my mother; Grayson told me what she said. I never realized how jealous she was of me until that comment. Thankfully Grayson knows the truth, because he's all that matters.

At 5:30 in the morning, I can't take it anymore so I get out of bed and head for the couch. Luckily Grayson is out cold so I don't have to explain anything to him.

I grab my phone from the charger and call Bella. As I dial, I'm slightly aware it's still pretty early in the morning for the girls, even if Chicago is an hour behind Maine. Kylie answers on the second ring. "Ainsley?" I hear the grogginess in her voice, knowing I've woke her up.

"My dad's not coming to my wedding," I blurt out before she can even put Bella on. And then the tears stream down my face. In an effort to contain my sobs so Grayson can't hear, I end up snorting instead.

"Oh, sweetie. What happened?" she asks, sounding a little more awake.

"Put it on speakerphone," I hear Bella call out in the background, her voice scratchy as if she was suddenly awoken too. I just need to talk to someone, someone other than Grayson.

"So apparently, I was 'showing off' my ring at the rehearsal dinner, and it upset Claudia. And my brother said some shit and Grayson let him have it. Then my mother made up some bullshit to feed Grayson about me being a gold-digging whore and said they weren't coming." It all comes out in one breath. And once it's all out, the tears start again. "Oh, and did I mention Jordan was there too? Yeah, that was fun," I blubber through my tears.

Bella is the first to speak. "Okay, all of that sucks. But, let it go, babe. You're so much better than all of them. And Grayson knows the truth. You must know that."

"Of course I do," I confirm, wiping my eyes. And I truly do. It's amazing how she and Grayson are so much alike sometimes.

"Okay, good. Then wipe those tears, pack up your shit, and come home. We'll be over for dinner tonight, but seeing as you are in another state, we'll bring dinner."

I love how she's so matter-of-fact about everything. All I can do is laugh. "Yeah, okay." I wipe the last of my tears and chuckle again. "Love you girls. Thanks for talking me off the ledge. See you soon."

"Love you, too," they both manage to say at the same time.

"Bye." I hang up. As much as it sucks that my dad won't be there, I guess I really can't let it bring me down at this moment, considering I don't even know when it's going to be. I have time to change his mind, once we are back home, and I can get in an actual conversation with him. If not, it's his loss. I have better things to focus on. Like actually planning said wedding. I was never one of those girls who planned out her dream wedding. I never fantasized about Jordan and I getting so far as marriage, and after him, there was never anyone else who got more than a few months of my time so thinking about a wedding and marriage was the furthest thing from my mind.

With Grayson, it's been so quick, like six months or so, and I wasn't lying when I told my friends Grayson and I hadn't discussed marriage. We really hadn't. His proposal came as a shock to me, not that I have ever regretted saying yes. I know for certain we are meant to be together. It's the whole "wedding" that has me caught up. I truly don't have many opinions one way or the other. Some days, I'm ready to just hand off the entire planning to Grayson who clearly has opinions on what he thinks we should have. And every time I'm just about to give in and hand him the reigns, something stops me, but hell if I can explain what it is or have any clue what I want for the wedding. In a way, I'm just glad Grayson has let me get away with ignoring it for so long so far. I have a feeling that's going to change once we get home.

On the way to the airport, I inform Grayson of the plans for dinner with the girls. He has nothing to say about it, not that it's a surprise. "Do we really have to go home today?"

"Um, one of us has a job to report to tomorrow. You know, someone has to work to support your lack of income." He smirks at me. He knows that I know he doesn't have to work. But he actually likes his job so he keeps it.

"Can you take a few days off soon? Like for a real vacation?"

"What do you have in mind?" He keeps his eyes peeled on the road, not bothering to look over at me.

"Somewhere tropical, where there are boats, colorful fish, beaches."

"You in a bikini," he drawls.

"That too." I chuckle. "So can you? Can we?" He's still focused on the road, but I turn to face him, giving him my best puppy dog eyes. Then I just go for broke. "Grayson, I don't work. There are only so many Netflix shows I can binge watch or books to read. So I get bored and research stuff for our wedding, new recipes, places to visit. In addition to all the porn I watch." His head whips around at that one. Luckily we are already in a spot to drop the rental car off.

"You do not," he mumbles, eyes wide, brows furrowed.

I smile and nod my head. "I have to keep up with you. You have quite the browser history when it comes to porn, Gray."

His eyes go wider. And then he denies it all. "I have no idea what you are talking about."

"Yeah, okay. Did someone else use your computer?"

And then he deflects. "What was wrong with your laptop?"

I'm actually surprised he's giving all this info up. I have no idea what's on his history. But clearly he watches the porn.

"So, yeah. I didn't know you watched porn, so thanks for confirming that." I chuckle to myself. And prepare for a verbal attack.

But it doesn't come; he stays silent instead. After a few minutes, I can't take the silence. "Really, Gray? Nothing? And I finally thought we were over the whole 'man of few words' thing."

He runs his hand through his hair. "I'm impressed, I gotta tell you. And yes, I do watch porn. Got a problem with that. He finally directs his gaze back over to me, although his expression gives nothing away.

"Absolutely not. I would be more shocked if you didn't."

He sighs audibly, saying "Come on," finally making a move to get out of the car. "We have a plane to catch and places to be."

He gets out of the car and goes around to grab the bags. Today's flight isn't nearly as difficult as the one the other day, but I still can't completely shake the fact that my dad isn't coming to my wedding. I'd be lying if I said I wasn't upset and disappointed. Clearly I'm having a hard time letting it all go. I guess once he's home from Chicago, I'll go over and have dinner and talk with him. It's the best I can do for now.

When Grayson comes over to open my door, he reaches in and grabs my hand to pull me out. As if he knows I need to be close to him, he wraps me in a tight embrace. "I love you, my girl."

"You always know when I need something." I nestle myself into the comfort of his chest.

"I just get lucky you happen to need what I need too," he tells me, kissing the top of my head. "Let's go hop that plane."

* * *

*W*hen we arrive home, Bella and Kylie are already at our house with dinner. Grayson takes our bags to our room as I share hugs with the girls.

"Bella invited Caleb and Nat too. Hope that's okay." Kylie looks a little unsure.

"The more the merrier, of course. Too bad it's too cold for a firepit."

"Well, that's probably not a good idea anyway." As she speaks, Kylie looks over to Bella for confirmation to go on. When Bella nods, she continues. "So, Nat may have been a tad bit hungover last night and Caleb wasn't too happy with her being hungover and when she puked all over herself, he let her have it. He's probably sulking at home and I wouldn't actually be surprised if they don't show. Bella already warned both of them not to come if they are just going to argue all night."

"Ugh, that sucks. Hopefully she feels better and can come for dinner."

"We'll see." Bella joins in the conversation as Gray comes walking back down. He's changed his clothes and I'm kind of wishing I hadn't agreed to dinner with our friends. I mean, his sweats are hanging low on his abs, his T-shirt pulled taut on his broad muscles. Licking my lips, I hear Bella clear her throat.

Loudly. I reluctantly tear my gaze away from Grayson and over to her.

"You woke me up at the ass crack of dawn this morning. The least you can do is have dinner with us without eye-fucking my brother." Her tone is serious, serious enough for me to question if she's kidding or not. Even Grayson's eyebrows rise as he watches our interactions. "Hell, who am I kidding? Eye-fuck him all you want, but I'm eating dinner." She makes her way over to the table and starts pulling things out of the bag. Kylie joins her as we hear Natalie and Caleb come in through the front door.

Kylie is right about Caleb. He's done nothing but snip at Natalie, grunt, and grumble, and he's been here all of five minutes. Natalie looks miserable. When I hug her, she says, "I'm sorry. I just need some coffee, ibuprofen, and some sleep."

"It's okay. It's not like I've never been in your situation before." I start to laugh but stifle it when she gives me a sad look. She looks like she's going to cry.

"What's wrong?" I ask, realizing there's more at play here.

"Not today," she returns, wiping at her eyes with her sleeves.

"Is everything okay?" When she shakes her head no, I pull her into me and feel her body shake with sobs. "Come with me." I throw a look over to Grayson and mouth, *Be right back*. He nods his head. I lead her into the closest room to us, which happens to be the bathroom.

Locking the door behind us, I turn to face her, and order, "Spill, girl."

She takes a breath. "Caleb and I had a fight yesterday. We both said some nasty things, and he got pissed. I walked out and ended up at the bar. I got more wasted than I ever thought I would." She stops talking, contemplating whether to say anything else. She lowers her voice as she continues. "I think I may have kissed a guy too. I can't remember."

I gasp, but if I'm truthful, she doesn't look remorseful. "Are you and Caleb having problems?"

She glances down at the floor. "You can't tell Grayson," she starts. She keeps her head glued to the floor and lowers her voice, even though it's only me and her in the bathroom. "There's this guy at work that's been flirting with me. At first, I thought it was just innocent since he knew I was with Caleb. But then he didn't stop, and I eventually stopped telling him to." She stops and looks at me. Her eyes are wet and definitely a little regretful now.

I hesitate a minute but have to know. "Did you cheat on Caleb?" I hold her gaze, hoping she tells me the truth.

"Not physically," she tells me, keeping her gaze locked on mine. "But emotionally I did." And then she looks back down.

I'm more than a little shocked but hopefully I hide it from showing on my face. "Does he know? Is that what your fight was about?"

She nods. "That was part of it." She pauses and when she raises her head again, a lone tear is slipping down her cheek. "Then we fought about marriage."

"What about marriage?" I question. But thinking that it really doesn't matter what the fight was about exactly, I quickly add, "That man loves you. He'll forgive you. If it's over with that other guy." Caleb and Grayson are very similar, and they are very forgiving people. "Wait, is he the guy you may have kissed last night?"

She slowly nods. "I so fucked up!" She buries her head in her hands. "I love Caleb. I want to fucking marry him, and I'm flirting with some guy at work. What is wrong with me?"

I don't know how to answer her. I've never experienced this Natalie before.

She lifts her head from her hands. More tears fall down her face. "What would you do?" she whispers.

Not wanting to give a knee-jerk reaction, I think about my answer for a moment. "I would be honest about my feelings. I think you first need to ask yourself why you flirted back. That's about you, not Caleb." It comes out a little harsher than I mean it to. But she's a big girl and can handle it.

"I know you're right. Thanks for not being judgmental."

I have no other words to comfort her right now, so I stay quiet about the subject. "Come on, let's get back out there and eat some dinner."

We wash our hands, Natalie freshens up her face as best she can, and we exit the bathroom. Back in the kitchen, I watch as Natalie looks over to Caleb, but he barely acknowledges her. Grayson takes in the same exchange with a perplexed look. "Not now," I mouth to him.

Grayson has made me a plate of food, and he makes me sit next to him, practically on top of him. As I look around the table at the people gathered here, I know I've finally found a place to truly call home.

24

GRAYSON

*A*fter everyone finally leaves for the evening, I find Ainsley curled up on the couch. She's on the brink of sleep, but when I sit down, she huddles in close to me. I can't help but instinctively pull her closer to me. Her eyes remain closed, her breathing is slow, and if I let her, she'd be asleep in a few minutes.

Despite my better judgment, I ask her, "What's up with Natalie?" While it's not my usual inclination to pry, Natalie was so unlike the happy-go-lucky person I know, it was kind of frightening. And Caleb was even quieter than usual except when he was snipping at Natalie, and that's saying something. I knew he wouldn't talk to me about it.

I can feel Ainsley still beside me, her breathing quickening the slightest bit. "Can we talk about it in the morning please? I'm really tired."

"Sure thing, darling. Come on, let's go up to bed." I gently coax her off me and push up off the couch. With her eyes barely open, she sits up, putting her arms out for me to help her up. Grabbing her arms, I help her stand up, but then I quickly bend down and grab her to toss over my shoulders. She lets out a tiny squeal on the way upstairs to our bedroom.

Before I can even toss her on the bed, she's wiggling in my

arms, trying to get herself down. I gently release her to the floor, and she shoots to the bathroom. When she returns, she's yawning and looking overly exhausted. Over the last months, I've learned the hard way that when she's tired, just let her go to sleep. There was one time that I made her feel bad about wanting to go to sleep, and well, it totally backfired in my face the next few days when she withheld sex. I've become smart and just let her go to sleep when she's tired because she will always make it up to me.

Just for shits and giggles, and not to rile me up of course, she climbs over me where I'm already lying in bed. After she gets herself comfortable, she cuddles in close to me. She brings my hand closer to her and puts it in her hair. Then she starts speaking.

"Fair warning, I'm tired and going to sleep, but just need you to know something." I go to speak, but she cuts me off as she continues. "There is no way I would have survived this weekend without you, Grayson. I most likely wouldn't have gone, and I wouldn't have regretted it, even though I'm sure it would have driven an even bigger chasm between both my mom and me as well as me and Drew. And I wouldn't have cared all that much; it's what I was used to. But you coming with me, I not only got to show up and walk tall, but I realized that no matter what happens from here on out, you are all I need."

She stops speaking. I can't see her face, but her voice is strong throughout her speech. My fingers are twirling her hair. Not wanting to ruin the moment, I bask in what she's just told me. It's by no means news to me, but I know she's still somewhat learning to share her feelings, especially when it comes to me. And while I know that I'm head over heels in love with this beauty, knowing how much I mean to her makes me fall even harder for her. And I can never figure out how that's even possible, so I've stopped trying.

In a few more minutes, I realize she's asleep but I can't help but whisper, "You are something special, darling. Don't you forget that." I let her hair slip from my fingers, wrap my arms around her a little tighter, and bring her closer to me.

"Love you," she mumbles, settling in even nearer to me. Kissing the top of her head, I close my eyes and try to find a way to get to sleep.

The alarm goes off way too early the next morning. Wiping the sleep out of my eyes, I gently push a still sleeping Ainsley to her side of the bed. Unlike most mornings, she doesn't just roll over but starts to get up with me. "It's early, darling. Keep sleeping."

"I'm making you breakfast," she declares with a yawn. "I'll be downstairs." She sashays out of the room. My eyes follow her until I can't see her anymore. With a shake of my head, I shed my clothes and go shower.

When I get downstairs, I'm met with not only the sight of a PJ-clad Ainsley but a tear-streaked Nat as well. Ainsley's got her arm on her back, gently rubbing it as they sit at the table. Natalie's a tired mess, which given the early time of day, I would figure she'd be tired, but there's more at play here. Nat's not a crier. I think I can count on one hand how many times I've seen her cry in all the years I've known her.

Taking in the scene, my first instinct is to ask what's going on, but as I try to take a seat at the table, Ainsley's eyes fly to mine, almost panic-stricken. She shakes her head and then says, "Your shake is in your mug. What time will you be home later?"

Well okay. This is how it's going to go down? I think to myself. Not knowing what to do, I answer her with, "Noonish. Thanks for the shake." I grab the shake from the counter, toss a, "Hey Nat" in her direction, and literally grab Ainsley out of her chair.

She protests. "Gray! Let me go." I ease up my grip slightly and once we are in the living room, I let her go completely. "What the hell, Grayson?" Her tone of voice is harsh, matching the hardness on her face.

"What do you expect me to think, Ainsley? She's here, crying, at 6:30 in the morning. If you can't tell me what's wrong, just tell me she's okay. That she's not hurt at least." I'm really at a loss of what's going on. I'll have to text Caleb later. Now that I think about it, he seemed off last night too.

"She's not hurt." Ainsley speaks, her face softening a bit. "But please don't ask me to tell you why she's here and crying. Please." In her voice, I hear the pleading. Against my better judgment, I know I have to respect her wishes.

"Okay," I relent, "but if it gets to the point where she's not okay, I trust that you will tell me?" I tip up her chin with my thumb.

She nods. "Thank you." She lays her hand over my heart and damn it if my sour mood doesn't just melt away. Without even trying, this girl knows what my heart needs. No matter how many times I try to explain it to her, she doesn't understand, how she could mean so much to me. So I stopped telling her and just show her now. It's really a win-win for us both; no arguing and just loving gestures.

"I'm going to go now. If you need me, text me. I'll be home around noon, like I mentioned. I'll make lunch when I get home unless you get to it first."

"Sounds like a plan. I may just veg all day, depending on Natalie. Thanks again for understanding." She pushes up on tippy-toes and plants a sweet kiss on my lips. Wanting more but knowing now is not the time, I let her walk away, loving how her short shorts hug her sweet ass and curves in all the right places.

Realizing I left my stuff in the kitchen, I follow her back in there. I make myself a cup of coffee to go as the girls are huddled at the table, intently focused on their conversation. Natalie breaks free for a moment and gazes up at me. She's just so sad and so unlike herself. Before I know what's happening, she's coming over to me. I truly don't know what to make of the situation but will surely be in touch with Caleb as soon as I'm out the door.

"Grayson." It's never a good thing when she "Grayson's" me. "Ainsley says you don't know what's going on."

"Nat, I have no clue, no clue what to think about you being here so early in the morning, crying no less. You're not hurt?"

She lowers her gaze to the floor but shakes her head no.

"Look, Nat," I start but wait until I know I have her attention. "Whatever is going on, you know you can talk to me. We've been friends practically forever. And while I'm glad you have Ainsley to confide in now, it's a little unnerving that you're shutting me out. You've never shut me out. And I'm pretty sure that you were the one who was going to kick my ass if I shut you out when all that shit went down with Molly. Is that how you want to play this?"

She's quiet, which again is surprising. She's so quick-witted that she usually has a comeback for everything. "I'm sorry," she stammers out and takes off running down the hall.

"Grayson!" Ainsley shrieks. "Really?" She's standing now, hands on her hips, a mad as hell expression on her face.

"What?" I ask. "How am I the bad guy in all of this? I don't even know what's going on!" My voice starts to rise, my anger fueled by the lack of knowledge of the situation. I dig my wallet out of my shorts pocket, take out a few bills and toss them in Ainsley's direction. "Do something that will cheer her up." With a shocked look clouding her face, I grab my stuff and blow out the door.

Opening the passenger side door, I toss my bag in but am more careful with the two liquid containers. When I get around to my side, I throw open the door and climb in, exhaling a deep breath. I put the car in reverse and back out of the garage, escaping from the drama inside the house.

Even though I'm slightly behind schedule, I send a quick text to Caleb before entering the gym.

> Dude, your girl's at my house. She's crying. Care to explain?

I'm not expecting a response being that it's still so early in the morning, but my phone dings with a text about two minutes later. I halt my steps and almost drop everything I'm carrying as I read his response.

> She fucking cheated. She can cry all she wants.

What the fuck, I think. This situation keeps getting worse. And interesting that Ainsley is keeping it from me, but now I know why Natalie's tightlipped. Suddenly, I know what I have to do.

> I'm done at noon. What time can you meet me at the boat club?

He doesn't respond right away, so I continue to the gym. Just as I'm about to ditch my phone for my clients, I see his reply.

> Pick me up on your way from the gym. I'll be home.

> K

My focus is off at work, which isn't good. Luckily I only have two clients this morning, ones I've worked with for a while so it's easy to maintain my composure with them. In my downtime, I spend the time in my office, contemplating what the fuck is wrong with Natalie. I never would have guessed that's what the problem is; Caleb screwing up, not screwing around, would have been my guess.

I shoot Ainsley a text letting her know I'll be home later than I planned.

She starts to write something but then stops. Then the bubbles appear again but just as quickly disappear. I place my phone on my desk and start to pack up my stuff. I'm thankful today was a light day, with just being back from vacation and now the whole Natalie fiasco. Yes, I said it; it's a fiasco. And it's not even my life! But I wasn't lying when I told Nat that she's probably my oldest friend, and we don't keep secrets from each other. Well, we never have before. And I hate to admit that she's seriously losing points in my book right now.

Before I can continue down this rabbit hole, my phone dings with a text.

> Ok

I know I shouldn't but I expect more from her, but when it doesn't come, I wrap up everything for the day, sign out at the front desk, and head to pick up Caleb.

He's standing on his front porch as I approach the house. He doesn't even let the car come to a complete stop before he's opening the door and hopping in.

"Thanks, man," he grumbles as he settles into his seat. I don't expect more, and well, I don't pry with Caleb, just as he doesn't with me. It's the way we work.

We drive in silence to the club and only once he's seated at the bar with a beer in front of him does he finally open up.

"I wish she would have said she was unhappy instead of fucking around behind my back." I knew he'd be angry and bitter, but he's almost beyond that to I don't even know what.

"She told you?"

"Not at first. I knew she was hiding something, knew something was eating her but she wouldn't talk about it. It's just so unlike her. I've never known her to be at a loss for conversation. She's always going on about this or that; hell, half the time she won't shut the hell up. But now? When I need her to talk? She clams up. Go figure."

He gulps his beer, practically sucking the entire bottle down in one swig.

I feel for the guy. Not that I've ever been in his shoes, fortunately for me. He's a disaster. His hair is standing up, sticking up every which way, his clothes are wrinkled, well more wrinkled than normal, and he's got the days-old scruff going on. By habit, he shaves every day. And well, it's a Monday afternoon and he's sitting in the bar drinking instead of being at work. Not that I can blame the guy, but my brain won't allow me to venture down this line of thinking as it applies to Ainsley. Nope, not going there. Ever.

"So what are you going to do?" I ask tentatively.

"I haven't a fucking clue. After we got home from your house last night, she may have gone back out. And when she wasn't home this morning, it didn't even occur to me that she'd be at your place. Not that I gave it much thought truthfully. I'm a little surprised she confided in Ainsley, truth be told, but well that girl of yours is special and has a knack for drawing things out of people." He pauses, deep in thought. I can only imagine what's going through his head right now. He finishes his beer, and promptly motions for another one. The bartender brings it over and he's already gulping that one down.

"Is it over with the other guy?"

"She refuses to answer that. She won't even confirm she actually cheated."

"Huh?" I ask, bewildered as I turn in his direction. "I thought you said she cheated on you."

"She says all she did was kiss him."

"And she thinks that's not cheating? Oh Natalie." I shake my head, mostly in disgust. Disgust at a girl who I consider one of my closest friends. And while I'm not a judgmental person by nature, I have certain moral standards I expect the people I love to live up to.

Caleb goes quiet, nursing his beer. I realize it's all he's going to say on the subject, and I have to respect him for it. After he pounds back three more beers, he tells me he's ready to go home. I pay our tab and notice he's walking with a slight hitch in his step, but nothing worse than I've seen before.

As we approach his road, he mutters, "I hate that she's put me in this position. The girl's been my rock for so many years. I'm not sure I know how to be Caleb without Nat."

Treading lightly, I state, "Just don't give her an ultimatum. It will never work the way you want it to." That's the only piece of advice I have to offer him.

He nods in agreement. "I still love her and nothing's going to change that for me right now, but I truly don't know if I can forgive her."

"Give it time, talk to her, see if she regrets her actions in a few days. Maybe she's just going through a rough time and needs to work some things out."

He shoots daggers my way. "Do not make excuses for her behavior. She made a conscious choice to cheat. She should have just talked to me."

"Calm down. I'm not making excuses for her. It was horrible what she did, but maybe ask yourself *why* she didn't talk to you."

"Yeah, you're right. Thanks for the beers. I'll talk to you later." His door is open and he's hopping out, all the goodbye I'm going to get. As I watch him stumble to the door, I can't help but wonder what path he's going to take and what the hell I'm going to say to Natalie about the situation, without allowing it to come between Ainsley and me.

Ainsley's car is in the garage when I get back. Grabbing my stuff and walking inside, there's a disaster in the kitchen, but the girls are nowhere to be found. I hear the slight murmur of the TV drifting in from the living room, so I follow the sound.

Ainsley's asleep on the couch, curled up into a ball at Natalie's feet. Nat is zoned out, staring at the TV but in no way absorbing whatever she's watching. I step right up in front of her to get her attention. Slowly, she drags her eyes up to meet mine, her face still covered in tears.

"I have to shower but when I get back down, we are talking. Don't you dare think about leaving." I know my tone is harsh, but I want her to know where I'm coming from.

My shower gives me more time to think and stew about what to say to Natalie, not always the best thing. Back downstairs, she's still in the same spot on the couch. Ainsley's still sound asleep. "Kitchen. Now," I indicate to Natalie. She begins to move, but it's at a snail's pace. Once there, I sit down at the table and motion for her to do the same. And then I let her have it. "What the fuck, Natalie? Are you seriously cheating on him?"

"Calm down, Gray," she dares to tell me.

"That's your comeback?"

"What do you want me to say?"

"I want you to tell me the truth."

She goes quiet and drops her head into her hands. In a voice barely above a whisper, she says, "Yes."

"Wow," is all I can manage. "You want to explain why?" I'm trying to decide why I'm so pissed at her. One, because Caleb doesn't deserve it. Two, she's not a cheater. In fact, she stopped talking to Bella when she cheated on one of her girlfriends, who she'd only been seeing for a few months. Natalie and Caleb have been together for years.

"You can hold your judgment and your lectures. I don't want to hear what you have to say. I've already given myself the lecture multiple times and yet, I can't stop myself. And I fucking love Caleb. I do. I love him, and I know he's so fucking hurt right now, and it's all on me, but I don't know how to fix it. Or even if I want to fix it at this point. You should have seen the look on his face last night when we got home. And I get it. I did this to him, to us. And I have no excuses so I'll at least spare you that." She manages to get all of that out in one long breath so when she stops, she has to catch her breath.

"Why? What made you do it?" I ask, because well, I have to know.

"I don't fucking know!" she practically shouts at me, finally looking back up at me. There's wildness in her eyes, a wildness I haven't seen since we were younger. "No wait, that's not true. I do know. I see the way you look at Ainsley, the way Caleb used to look at me, and I was jealous. Jealous of her and jealous that you finally found someone who makes you ridiculously happy. And you fucking deserve it, Gray. You deserve everything Ainsley offers you and then some. You truly are the best guy I know, and she's fucking perfect for you. And I fucking want that. I thought I had it with Caleb, but I started questioning it. And there was this guy, and he made me feel special. And I fucking slept with him. I'm a horrible person because I was so fucking jealous of my best friend."

I'm floored. I literally have no words. Thank goodness Ainsley walks into the kitchen. She takes one look at the situation and walks closer to Natalie. "You lied to me?" she asks, her voice unsure, quaky, her face bearing an expression of confusion.

Natalie looks in her direction and when she realizes Ainsley heard it all, she gets in her face. "I couldn't tell you the truth. I saw the judgment on your face; I saw how you thought what I did was so horrible. I couldn't risk you hating me anymore. So yeah, I lied."

Scratch what I said before; *now* I'm speechless. "Wow" slips out of my mouth yet again.

Looking over at Ainsley, she looks like she's going to start bawling. And I have to shoulder some of the blame here. I practically threw this new best friend on her and now, she's realizing that Natalie lied to her. The one friend she could truly count on.

"Wow." Ainsley echoes my sentiment. Taking a deep breath, she continues. "You cheating on Caleb has nothing to do with me, or Grayson. That's all on you. And until you figure out why you not only felt the need to cheat on that man but deflect the responsibility onto one of your oldest friends, you aren't welcome here. I'm sorry if you have nowhere else to go, but I really think you should leave."

Natalie's eyes go big as they fly up to Ainsley, shocked as the realization of her words sinks in. And then her armor cracks, and the girl I've known most of my life finally peeks through. "Oh my god. What have I done?" Tears spill from her eyes as she looks back and forth between Ainsley and me. She's muttering things under her breath, things I can't even begin to decipher. While she's doing that, I get Ainsley's attention and motion her over to me.

Once she reaches me, I pull her head closer to mine to whisper in her ear. "Is it wrong I'm highly turned on right now? Because that was damn sexy, you standing up for yourself." Ainsley pulls out of my grasp. Turning to face me, she glares in my direction. I'm about to ask her why she's upset, but Natalie's "ugh" distracts me for the moment. She's wiping her eyes with her sleeves. For the first time today, I really take her in. And shit if I don't finally notice what's really eating her: she's scared. Of what, I don't know, but her eyes are full of fear.

Looking back over to Ainsley, I say, "Darling, go upstairs and I'll be up in a few minutes. I need to talk with Nat alone. Say good-bye, or don't; that's up to you." I could add more, but I wisely decide to hold my tongue.

Ainsley looks back to me, her face plastered with confusion and still clouded by anger. "Yeah, okay." I can see in her face that she's torn over how to address Natalie, but in the end, Natalie's friend wins out. Tentatively she throws her arms around Natalie and whispers something in her ear that has Natalie nodding. Before she lets her go, Natalie says, "You're right, for what it's worth. It's all about me. I'm so sorry that I not only lied to you, that I dragged you and Grayson into my mess. And I'm sorry that I put you in a position where you had to choose to keep my secret from him. I'll give you a few days, but if you decide you can't forgive me, I will be crushed but will understand." She's extremely sincere; there's not one hint of the girl who was speaking before.

Ainsley chooses not to say anything more and instead walks away. There are so many things that I want to tell her right now, most of all how proud I am of her for forever choosing the high road when things get tough.

Once she's gone, Natalie turns herself to face me. She's looking at me for answers.

"He's pissed, Nat, and rightly so. And he's hurt. Truthfully, I don't know what I would do in his situation except to say that if it were Ainsley, I would demand the truth, demand to know why she didn't come talk to me before acting impulsively. And I'd want to know what I could have done differently, but this is all on you. If there's any hope of getting him back, you fucking take all the blame."

"I know. It's all on me. I just wish sometimes he was a little more forthcoming with his feelings and would talk to me more."

"Natalie," I warn. "That's a cop-out, and you know it. You know who he is; he's not going to change. You can't use his personality against him; that's not fair."

"Damn you, Gray, for being so smart. And sentimental. When did you get this sentimental?"

I shrug. "It may have something to do with the girl you tried to tear to shreds."

"Ah, fuck. I screwed up with her too. You going to have to do damage control?"

I shake my head. "Nah, not too much." At least I don't hope so. "But if you ever blame her for something you've done again, I won't be so nice." She smiles at that, and well, my friend is back. I cover her hand with mine. Startled, she looks up at me. "Fix it. Fix it soon, or I will sic Bella on your ass. And she will not be nice to you." She laughs a little harder.

"I love you, Gray."

"Yeah, yeah. You sure have a funny way of showing it lately. First you kiss my fiancée, then you go and cheat on your boyfriend, for real, and then you take your problems out on Ainsley and me. You're damn lucky I love you." I get up and drag her up to standing so I can hug the shit out of her. She's going to be okay, even if she doesn't work things out with Caleb. I'll check in with him in the morning. He needs more time to stew. "You going home?"

"I have nowhere else to go and well, I owe it to Caleb to at least try to explain where my head's been at lately."

"You okay to drive?"

"Yeah, I'm good, but thanks for checking." She squeezes me one more time and then pulls herself out of my embrace. "You're going to go have makeup sex now, aren't you?"

"You better believe it. That girl upstairs deserves it and then some. I'm sure she'll call you in the morning and fill you in if you want the details." I walk her to the front door.

"I'm perfectly fine without knowing," she giggles, "but tell her to feel free to call me. I'm pretty sure I owe her a better apology."

"Yeah, you do. Bye, Nat. Stay safe."

Walking out of the door, she glances back at me and throws a kiss in my direction. "I'm damn lucky I have you for a friend, Gray, but Ainsley's even luckier." With that, she dashes to her car, and I shut the door.

I avoid looking at the disaster that is the kitchen and head upstairs, shedding my shirt as I go. I stop halfway up the stairs to find a curious Ainsley perched at the top. Her expression is only a bit softer; she still appears mad. "You heard?"

"Pretty much everything." Without another word, she stands up and turns to head to our bedroom. As she's walking in the door, I hear her comment, "You can't have makeup sex if you haven't made up yet."

As I walk to the bedroom, I contemplate her statement. Clearly, she's still mad. I just can't understand why. Once I enter the bedroom, I find her already under the covers, facing the wall. We've never gone to bed angry, and hell if I'm going to let shit with Natalie be the reason that it happens tonight.

Taking a seat on the bed, I ask, "Care to tell me why you're mad at me?"

"Not particularly." She sighs heavily.

Well, that's interesting. "So, you're just going to go to sleep being angry at me?"

"Pretty much. If you stop talking so I can actually go to sleep."

"What the fuck, Ainsley?" Running my fingers through my hair, I sigh as I wait for some sort of response from her. I turn to look at her, but she doesn't stir. As she continues to ignore me, it fuels my anger. Besides her being mad at me, I don't even know why I'm angry.

After a few minutes of her silence, I push off the bed and finish getting ready for bed, hoping it will curb my anger slightly. It's hard to do when the entire time I'm brushing my teeth, I think about why she's angry with me and in turn, I just get madder. By the time I'm done, I think I've come up with a conversation starter. If she'll actually speak to me, that is.

I dig in my drawers for a pair of shorts to wear to bed. I'm by no means quiet with my actions. However, when I hear Ainsley's harrumphs, I know she's still awake at least. So I make my getting ready for bed a little more dramatic. And way more exaggerated than necessary. It's childish but effective when Ainsley practically shouts, "Grayson! Do you mind?" She doesn't move an inch but her tone is laced with ire.

"Actually I do." I bound onto the bed causing her to be jolted slightly. She quickly whips her body around to face me, her face hard set and her eyes shooting daggers.

She finally relents. "You want to know why I'm mad?"

"I think I've made it pretty clear that I do." I keep my tone as expressionless as possible.

"Nat needed you to be a friend today, Gray. And you weren't there for her."

I start to say something, something I'll most likely regret, so I decide to keep quiet. But really? She thinks I needed to be there for Natalie today? And how was I "not a friend" to her? I realize that my opinions on the subject matter too, and so I don't hold my tongue. "Truthfully, I needed to be there for Caleb today. She cheated on him. For no reason. That's not okay in my book. And she blamed you. And yet, you're defending her." I pause, wondering if I should say more of what's on my mind, to let her know more of how I feel about cheating, but she interrupts me.

"I'm not defending her actions. I'm just saying she needed a friend. Good people make bad decisions sometimes. It happens to all of us. We don't know why she did what she did, but who are we to judge her?"

Leave it to this one to be rational about the situation. Here I am, all emotional not only about Natalie's actions, but how it's affecting my relationship, and Ainsley's removed all emotion from the situation and focused on the part about Natalie needing someone to listen to her. I'm just about to tell her that, when she pipes in with, "Guess I know not to cheat on you, huh?" As soon as it's out of her mouth, she turns her face away from me.

That gets my attention. My mouth drops open. Before I can think about what I'm saying, the words are flying out of my mouth. "That's something you've considered?"

She sighs but doesn't say anything for the longest time. But now I need an answer. When she's still silent after a few more minutes, I settle myself into a more comfortable position for sleeping. It appears that tonight will be the night we go to bed angry.

It's only been about ten minutes, but the fact that we are sleeping with our backs to each other is not something I'm enjoying. Since that first night she slept in my bed, she's never not slept tucked into me. I flip over and just watch her. She's not sleeping; I can tell by the way she keeps moving her legs, almost as if she's trying to find a comfortable position. And then she finally speaks. It's just one word, in a whisper, but it's something.

"No."

Part of me wants to push her for more of an explanation, but the part of me that doesn't want to continue this fight tonight wins. With one last glance in her direction, I turn back around.

Despite how tired I am, sleep doesn't come easy. Not when I keep replaying the day's events in my head, wondering how I could have reacted differently to not be in this damn predicament I'm in now.

At 4:30, I give up trying to sleep. Ainsley finally fell asleep, but it was fitful for her too. Good to know she's affected by our situation as well. I quietly get dressed and then mosey on downstairs to make some coffee. At this rate, I'll need a few cups even before I make it to work.

Seeing the mess the girls left in the sink does nothing to help improve my mood. I'm not quiet as I clean it up, but there's still no noises coming from upstairs. Not that I expected any; it's extremely early.

As I drink my first cup of coffee, I look over my schedule for the day. I have three clients in the morning and then two after lunch. I groan as I notice who my last client of the day is. Not what I need after last night and such an early morning.

I make myself a protein shake and toss some lunch together. As I'm slipping my feet into my shoes, I hear the upstairs toilet flush. I contemplate what to do. Do I see if she comes downstairs?

Do I go back up there and talk to her? Do I just leave for work with the status quo? Having no clue as to what the "right" choice is, I stall for time to see if she's going to make an appearance. Just as I'm about to give up and leave, I hear her footsteps on the stairs. When she comes into view, she's surprised.

"Oh, you're leaving already?"

I take in her appearance and while her outfit doesn't look any different from any morning, nor does her usual morning hair falling around her shoulders, her face conveys it all: regret, sadness in her eyes, and no sign of last night's anger. And while my heart wants to pull her close to me, my head makes me stand my ground.

"When will you be home? We need to talk." Her voice is hesitant and if her fiddling fingers are any indication, she's nervous.

"Oh, now you want to talk?" My tone is clipped, harsher than I intended, but I'm not going to apologize.

She's taken aback by my words. She's about to retreat out of the kitchen, but then she's suddenly turning on her heels. "Fine, go to work. I'll be here when you get home to talk." And then she turns back and stomps in the direction of our bedroom.

Despite not wanting to fight with her, I have to admit that a pissed-off Ainsley turns me the fuck on. I smirk to myself as I grab everything I need for work and finally head out the door.

The day is slow. Like really slow. Knowing Ainsley's stewing at home leaves me unsettled. Not being able to text her doesn't help. And picturing her stomping away riles me up. In between clients, I get a workout in myself, text Caleb to check up on him, and make some follow-up calls. It's when the last client of the day shows up that the sour mood of the day rears its ugly head.

I always know she's here before I actually see her. Besides her chipper voice, it's her smell that alerts you to her presence. She must douse herself in her perfume. To come work out at the gym. I'll never understand it. Nor will I understand how I am the unfortunate soul who ended up as her trainer. She sounded so pleasant on the phone, like someone who really wanted to change her habits and needed to work out. Yeah, not so much. But her ex-husband pays her a shit ton of alimony and she clearly has nothing better to do with her time than parade herself around the gym as she pretends to work out. Today is no different.

She starts by calling, "Yoohoo, Grayson. I'm here." *No shit, Sher-lock. I smelled you the minute you walked in.*

Pushing up out of my chair, I plaster my work face on before greeting her. Sixty minutes, I tell myself. You can pull it together for one hour and then go home and deal with your personal shit with Ainsley. And by deal with, I mean *fix* the personal shit.

Taking a deep inhale, I greet Gretchen. As she runs her hands down my arm, I mentally begin the countdown. Fifty-nine minutes to go.

I take a quick shower before I leave the gym. I need to wipe away Gretchen's germs and her smell off me. She touched me no less than fifty times today but at least it was all above the waist. I shudder as I recall the time she grabbed my ass. "By accident," she sweetly said. *Accident, my ass.* I'm pretty sure I got more of a workout than she did, as she made me demonstrate every single move. You would think I'd be used to the attention from her by now, but it never gets easier. The only woman I want ogling me is Ainsley.

I do my best to wipe the day away as I go into the house. I'm about to call out to let her know I'm home, but I find her in the kitchen, elbow-deep in flour. It shouldn't surprise me that the kitchen looks like a tornado hit it, nor that there are dozens upon dozens of baked goods scattered on top of the counters.

She looks up at me from where she's mixing the ingredients and with a shy smile, some of my anger fades away. She must see it too because she quickly takes her hands out of the dough, rinses them off, and approaches me, some hesitancy in her body language. "Hi," she speaks, her eyes looking everywhere but at my face.

"You baked?"

She nods sheepishly as she glances around the room. "I didn't have anything else to do and I couldn't just sit and stew. I needed to be busy." She reaches her hand out like she's going to touch my arm, but I grab her wrist before it reaches me. My actions catch her off guard and her surprised eyes dart up to mine, questioning me. She goes to pull away, but before she can, I tug her into me and wrap my arms around her. It takes her a minute to understand my gesture but soon enough she's melting into my embrace. I hear a muffled "I'm so sorry" and she brings her arms around my waist. I revel in just holding her for a few minutes, inhaling her scent to erase earlier ones. With one final squeeze before letting go, I'm overwhelmed with the fact that no matter what comes our way, what obstacles we have to face that may drive us apart, even if only temporarily, I need this girl by my side.

"Sit," I instruct, pointing to the table once I've let go of her. "We're talking."

Without argument, she pulls out a chair and sits down. Then she grabs one of the muffins from the table and breaking off a small piece, stuffs it in her mouth. I take the seat across from her and grab a muffin for myself. Instead of mimicking her actions, I take a huge bite. Once I've swallowed, I say, "The banana flavor is strong in this one. Makes the muffin really tasty."

"Thanks. I added an extra banana to see how it would change it up. Glad you like it." She grins in my direction, then hastily adds, "I'm not used to navigating these kinds of waters, the friend versus the fiancé. And while I realize it's not you against her, I needed to be there for Nat yesterday. And with the way you were first judging her, you weren't there for her." She looks like she wants to add more but her mouth closes instead.

With a deep breath, I begin to speak. "Darling, I'm sorry. I'm not used to these kinds of waters either. All we can do is try to navigate them a little better and make sure we don't lose focus of what's important for us."

There's more I want to say, but she cuts me off, a finger to my lips. "I get it, Gray. I always get it when it comes to you. We both reacted poorly, and for my part, I'm sorry." When I think she's done, she quickly whispers, "I would never cheat on you, Grayson. It wouldn't ever cross my mind. I love you too much."

I close my eyes. Because once again, this girl has weakened my resolve with just her words. It's like I'm unable to stay mad at her. I slowly open my eyes. Between the look of remorse on her face, the fact that she's apologized, and the fact that my world has been unsettled since yesterday morning, I crack, and all of my anger slips away.

So without thinking anything else through, I ask, "Are we made up yet?" I waggle my eyebrows in her direction and she giggles. Her eyes scan the kitchen and the mess she's made. "It will still be here after we've officially made up." The girl goes to protest, but through gritted teeth, I state, "Leave. It. Upstairs. Now." With that, she doesn't hesitate.

25

AINSLEY

*I*t takes me a few days to truly forgive Natalie, but in the end, I realize that despite her recent actions, she's a really great person and one of the best friends I've ever had in my life. She's got a rocky road ahead of her with Grayson—and Caleb too—and I don't need to add to that burden. It hurts that she lied to me, but I'm over it. And she knows I won't be as forgiving if she ever lies to me again.

As for Grayson and me, I'm actually kind of glad Nat put us in the middle. I know everything won't always be smooth sailing between the two of us, and while I know this wasn't a huge fight, it sucked when his anger was directed at me. It's not something I need to be feeling again anytime soon. I'm just glad we are learning this together. Maybe I will even learn to let go of my need to hold grudges against others. Grayson can probably teach me that, as long as it's not him I need to hold the grudge against.

One night a few weeks later, we walk in the door around 9:30 p.m. after being out for most of the day. Grayson drops the bags in the foyer and comes into the kitchen, plugging in and turning on the coffee machine before doing anything else.

"I need a big mug, please Gray," I call out. I take a seat at the table and scroll through my emails.

Surprisingly, I don't have as many as I thought I would and by the time Grayson puts a steaming mug of coffee down in front of me, I've whittled my inbox down to twenty-five, one of which stands out, so I start with that one. The subject is "Cupcakes."

I slowly read through the email, and by my facial expressions, Grayson knows it must be good news.

"What has you smiling from ear to ear, darling?" He takes a seat next to me and starts rubbing my thigh. His head snoops over my shoulder trying to read the email himself. I flip it around so he can't read it. "Hey! Share the news then."

"It's a friend of a friend who was at the girls' shower. She wants me to make cupcakes." I can't help the even bigger smile that spreads on my face.

"That's great," he replies, as his hand moves closer and closer up my leg. I swat it away as I continue.

"Apparently, she's hosting some gala at an art museum and needs like two hundred fifty to three hundred cupcakes next month."

His face shoots up to mine. "And she wants you to make them all?" he asks, his face registering the shock he must feel.

"Yes. Isn't that pretty cool?"

"That's super cool. You okay with that many?" That's where his shock comes in. It's a big order, bigger than anything I've, no we've, ever done. "Can we handle that big of an order?"

Without letting the smile slip, I nod my head. "It will take some preparation and planning, but I know we could pull it off. You in?"

"Of course. I can clear my schedule for whatever you need."

"Thanks. You know how much I appreciate your help."

It's only been a few weeks since I quit my job, and I haven't baked every day. Pretty close to it, though. I've taken a dozen or so orders from people I know or friends of friends, for birthday parties mostly. Grayson's helped with all of the orders, following my lead. We did have one major tiff over the color of the frosting— he said teal and I said aquamarine and neither one of us were budging on our thoughts. Luckily Bella decided for us. I have to say, it was pretty hard to get the teal icing out of certain places after we made up.

The biggest order we've done remains the girls' shower so to have to make more than double that amount, should stress me the hell out. But for some reason, it's not. Like at all. And maybe that worries me just a tad.

"I will email her and get all the details. Maybe this will be the start of my new career."

Grayson stops his hand mid-stride, halfway up my thigh. "Yeah?" he questions. "Something you've been thinking about?"

I nod, placing my hand on top of his. "This is a big order and if this goes well, I want to look into finding ways to expand my hobby into more of a business. Maybe. It's just an idea I've been tossing around my head. I was waiting for an opening to talk to you about it, and this is the perfect one." I know he can hear the hopefulness in my voice. I don't have to say it; he knows me too well.

"I love it," he tells me, moving his hand again. "And I love you." He brings his face in to nuzzle my shoulder and quickly drops three kisses on my collarbone. He pulls his head away just to look at the clock. "Race you upstairs?" I don't miss the hungry look in his eyes.

I grab my mug and push off my chair. "Go!" I yell out as I shove my arms out, pushing past to block him to make my way up to our bedroom, not even stopping to care about the coffee splashing out of the mug.

* * *

So it turns out, baking close to three hundred cupcakes isn't as easy as I thought it was going to be. I'm up early to get started, like six a.m. early, the time Grayson sometimes leaves for the gym. He couldn't move his first two clients so he went to work while I got started.

My goal for the day was half. I figured that was doable. When Grayson gets home around eleven, the kitchen is not only a disaster, but I am as well.

He catches me muttering under my breath as he jumps up onto the counter to watch. That's right, just to watch. When I take a batch out of the oven and turn to him, he's got a wicked smile plastered on his face. "Hey," he rasps. "Need some help, love?" His left eye winks at me, ever so slowly.

"Why did I think I could do this? What possessed me to say yes? I can't handle this. I only have three dozen baked and I need like WAY more than that if I'm going to stay on track. This was a stupid idea. There's no way this hobby can turn into a business..."

He cuts off my ranting by hopping down from the counter and grabbing my wrist. Luckily, I have already put the tray down on the stove to start to cool. He brings me in close to him and wraps his strong arms around me, clasping his hands behind my ass. "Hey," he tries again, this time less jovial and more loving. I look up into his eyes, and I instantly calm. For the life of me, I can't figure it out, but I've given up trying. He makes everything better. Always. Just by looking at him, my cares and worries fade away.

He unlatches his hands and wipes my cheek with the pad of this thumb. "Flour." He chuckles when I question his gesture. "So, what were you saying? Something about you not being able to do this."

I nod and lay my head on his chest. "I severely underestimated how much time this order would take."

He shakes his head at me. "No you didn't. That's why you started today. You knew it was going to take a while. You planned it out. You've got this, love." And just like that, with those words, I know that I can do it. And do it, I will.

I wrap my arms around his back and squeeze him before pulling myself out of his arms. "Go shower and then come back and help." When he doesn't start to move, I bat my eyes at him and add, "Please."

He leans in and covers my lips with his own. When he starts to sneak his tongue inside my parted lips, I place my arms on his chest and push him away. "Later. We have cupcakes to bake." Reluctantly, he starts to move away, but not before he places a kiss on the top of my head. I watch as he makes his way to the stairs, staring way longer than I can actually see him.

Smiling to myself, I take in my surroundings. The counters are a mess, there's flour and sugar everywhere, well except the island. For some reason, I've never found myself using the island to prepare food. We eat there all the time; it's just never become a place for prep work. There are twenty-four cupcakes stacked on cooling racks, and twelve more sitting in the tray. There's a batch ready to put into the oven, so that's where I start. I pop that batch into the oven and set the timer. And then I set to work on making more batter.

When Grayson finally reappears after his shower, I push all thoughts of how he looks—and smells—out of my mind to focus on the task at hand. I grab his apron off the hook and help him into it, ignoring the playful look and small noises he's making, his version of a distraction. He tries one last-ditch effort at distracting me when he leans his head in close to mine to nibble my ear, but when I push him away once more, he harrumphs and then like a good partner, asks, "What do you need me to do?"

"A double batch of Salted Caramel."

Without another sound, he gets right to work, choosing wisely to stay out of my way.

About five hours later, we have about thirteen dozen cupcakes baked. They will all be frosted in two days, so we start to make room in the freezer for the already baked ones. Fortunately, the freezer capacity is quite large so after some creative rearranging, the cupcakes will all fit once they have cooled.

Grayson pours me a mug of coffee and as he's making me a grilled cheese sandwich, I say, "Sorry for panicking before."

He just shakes his head. "I expected that," he says, but quickly continues when he sees my fallen face. "Not in a bad way; just that

I knew it would be overwhelming at first, but there's no doubt in my mind that it wasn't something you couldn't handle."

This man! I know it shouldn't amaze me anymore, but it does. In all my life, Grayson is the only person who has ever "gotten" me. Ever.

"Okay," I offer back to him with a smile. It's all I can muster at the moment without cracking.

When he places the grilled cheese in front of me, he leaves a kiss on the top of my head. He goes back over to make a sandwich for himself and calls over his shoulder, "Hey, darling, you want to talk about our wedding yet?"

I freeze up, the sandwich halfway to my mouth. I have been avoiding talking about it, not because I don't want to marry Grayson, but because I don't know what I want. Well, I do know what I want, finally, but he doesn't want it to be just our immediate family and close friends. Crazy, right? He wants to have this big-ass wedding. Who he plans to invite is beyond me. And that's why I've avoided talking about it with him. Because he's not budging on his ideas in the slightest. I don't want to argue about our wedding, so I ignore it. At least he hasn't brought it up in a while, thankfully.

I look over to him, a hopeful expression on his face. "How about this?" I start. "Let's pick a date today." Hopefully that should suffice. For now.

"Let's hear your ideas."

I take a bite of the sandwich and once I've swallowed say, "How about April?"

He shakes his head and turns his nose up at that. "That's too far away," he chides.

"Let me finish." He shoots me a look and then zips his lips. "How about April twenty-fifth?"

He contemplates the date for a minute or two, and for a split second I don't think he's going to figure out why I've picked that date. And then his face lights up. "Yes, that works. I'm holding you to it." He grins in my direction, flipping his sandwich.

I smile in victory. It's a small one, but it's a victory nonetheless. Until he adds, "Okay, where?"

"Grayson!" I squeak. "I picked a date. Let me be for at least an hour, or a few weeks," I mumble under my breath.

He grudgingly gives in. "Okay. That only gives us like five months to plan so don't think we won't be discussing more of the details in the next few days."

"Fine," I concede, knowing that I will just put it off when he brings it up again. "How did you know about the day?" I'm really curious to why he agreed so rapidly.

"It took me a minute to figure out, not going to lie. I mean, of course I remember it was April when we met, but not the actual date. But then I remembered that my parents' wedding anniversary was on the twentieth and knew it hadn't passed that long ago when I was in the bar that night. So I just put two and two together. Smart, right?" He looks over at me, wanting confirmation that he is indeed, a smart cookie.

"So smart," I confirm. And then the enormity of what he just told me dawns on me. "Oh. We can pick another date if you'd rather, if it's too close to your parents' date." Selfishly, I don't want him to take it back. I want to marry him on the day we met, the day my life changed forever. The day our first kiss became my last "first kiss."

Not knowing whether he sees it written on my face or if he truly feels the same way I do, he shakes his head. As he walks over with his sandwich and sits down, he says, "I think it's a perfect date, Ainsley. Even if my parents were still here, it would be the perfect date."

"Okay, good." The relief I feel is evident in my tone. "Glad that's settled. I would have taken a few more weeks to come up with a date if you had said no." I can't help but chuckle.

He glowers over at me. "Real funny, Ainsley," is all he mumbles before scarfing down his sandwich.

The next day, we finish up the order for the cupcakes. I haven't quite figured out how we are going to deliver them, but luckily Grayson has the forethought to think it all through.

He manages to fit all three hundred plus cupcakes into the back of the Explorer. Once he's done that for me, he hands over the keys. "They're expecting you at the museum. Park around the back and go in through the back door. There should be a few guys there to unload them for you."

"You aren't coming with me?" I inquire, hoping he can hear and see my surprise.

"I have an errand to run."

"You can't run it after?" It's not that I need him for this, but I would love his help. Plus, it just means spending more time with him.

"Sorry. I'll meet you back home later tonight." He drops a kiss on the top of my head. "Love you." He tosses that out, almost as an afterthought. *So weird,* I think. Something's up with him.

Realizing that I don't have much time to get these cupcakes delivered, I climb up into the driver's seat and drive off to the museum.

At the museum, I follow Grayson's instructions and park around back. Before I've made it out of the car, Mary, the woman who placed the order, has come out of the back door and is walking up to my car. Even though I've never met her, she wraps her arms around me and pulls me into a hug.

"Ainsley!" she booms. "It's so great to finally put a face to a name. I can't thank you enough for baking the cupcakes and delivering them as well."

"It's my pleasure," I tell her. "Hopefully they'll be a big hit."

"I have no doubts that they will. Lydia can't stop raving about the ones she had at Bella's shower. It takes a lot to get her to rave about something." Her smile grows bigger.

As we are talking, a few men come out from inside the museum, one of them pushing some sort of cart. I walk around to the back of the car and open up the trunk. In a short amount of time, the cupcakes are loaded onto the cart and are being wheeled inside to be set up.

"Do you need my help with the display?" I ask Mary.

"No, we should be all set." She hands me an envelope with the payment. "Thank you again. I know I will be in touch with you in the future." She smiles at me.

"Thank you. Please send me a picture of the final display and email me any feedback about the cupcakes. I would appreciate it."

"Sure thing," she confirms. "It was a pleasure working with you."

"You too. Enjoy the event." I walk around to the front of the car, as she heads back inside the museum. I toss the envelope on the passenger's side, start the car up, and drive back home to wait for Grayson, all the while trying to figure out what's up with him.

When I get back home, Grayson isn't home yet. I go inside and take a seat at the table. Opening up the envelope, I squawk at the amount of the check. It is way more than what we agreed on. Like, a lot more. I don't have a chance to fully let it sink in before I hear the garage door open, and soon, Grayson is walking through the door. When he sees my stunned look, his face goes to concerned.

"What's the matter?" he asks, coming closer to me. He doesn't take a seat but leans up against the island.

I don't even have the words to answer him; I'm still in that much shock, so I just hand the envelope over to him. He peers inside but either the amount doesn't register or he doesn't even look at the amount. He looks back over to me. "What?" His questioning tone is one of confusion as well.

"Do you see how much money that check is for?" He looks back in at the check and yet his look still doesn't change.

"Yeah, so?"

I try as best I can to make him understand the shock I feel. "Grayson, that is way more money than she agreed to. Like *five hundred dollars more* than she agreed to. She didn't even look at the cupcakes when I delivered them nor did she taste them yet. They could be horrible!"

He comes over to the table and takes a seat on the chair next to me. Placing the envelope on the table, he motions for me to come onto his lap. When I don't move quick enough, he practically drags me up onto his knees. Well, that's one way to knock the shocked look off my face.

Once he settles me onto his lap, he brings his hands to my face turning it toward his, forcing my eyes to look into his. He runs one hand through my hair; the other gently caresses my face. Then he begins talking, all the while making sure that I am paying attention to him.

"Darling, one of these days I'm going to get you to truly understand your worth. You deserve that money, all of it. You worked damn hard to earn it. Even though it was more than what was agreed on, it shouldn't come as a shock to you that she gave you more. You are worth it."

As I listen to his words, I could argue. I could argue and tell him that I'm not, that despite what he thinks about me, I may never be worth it. But for once in my life, I try to let his words just sink in.

I lay my head against his chest, listening to the beating of his heart. I wrap my arms around his waist and his arms embrace me. "Okay," I whisper, giving in and letting go of the shock. I feel his chin rest on the top of my head as he takes a deep breath. After a few minutes, he unwraps his hands from around me and then untangles mine from him. He pushes me back slightly, a bemused look on his handsome face. I'm about to ask him what the look is for when I remember his "errand" from before. "Hey, what was so important that you couldn't help me deliver the cupcakes?"

The grin starts to fade from his face, but he quickly recovers back to being giddy. Without answering my question, he tips his face down and plants his lips on mine, barely giving me a second to realize what he's doing. I try to push him away, while I try to break the kiss, mumbling, "Not funny, Gray," but I'm not successful in the slightest. Instead, he's pushing back from the chair, wrapping my legs around his middle and carrying me away, all the while still sucking my face.

For the second time today, I give in to this man. The man who has stolen my heart in more ways than one.

26

GRAYSON

I wake up the next morning with a raging erection, but when I turn to face Ainsley, her spot is empty. Sighing, I roll onto my back, staring up at the ceiling. She's going to pester me about where I was yesterday, why I couldn't help her deliver the cupcakes we had worked so hard on. *Ha, there is the "hard-on" again*, I think, trying to decide what to do about my own. Maybe I can distract her with sex all day so she doesn't ask where I was. The smile quickly fades into a frown because I know I should tell her. But I'm not sure I want her to know yet. And then a light bulb goes off in my head and a plan formulates. My smile returns, just as my girl does.

Ainsley saunters back into the room, wearing nothing but my T-shirt. She's carrying a tray, with two mugs of coffee—bless her soul—and a plate of something. As carefully as she can, she places the tray on my nightstand, making sure that it isn't going to teeter off. Grabbing my usual mug, she commands, "Sit up." And obey her I do. I push myself up to sitting, trying as best as I can to conceal the situation in my pants. Knowing Ainsley, it will be the first place she looks once she climbs back in bed with me. I would grab her and pull her down, but she's handing me my mug so that's not going to work.

She takes the plate and her mug and walks over to her side of the bed. Balancing the plate on her overcrowded nightstand, she slides into bed next to me, careful not to spill her cup.

"What's on the plate?" I ask her as she settles down on her pillow.

"A new cookie recipe. I couldn't sleep so I've been baking."

I glance over at the clock. Eight a.m. "How long have you been awake for, darling?"

She shrugs. "Since 5:30. I didn't think you'd want the early wake up on your day off."

While she's right, I do like to sleep in on the weekends, she also knows that she can wake me up whenever she wants; it's never stopped her before. On several occasions, she's woken me up from a deep sleep for a variety of reasons, all of which involve some sort of sexual act. No, that's not true. Every once in a while, she has bad dreams and once she woke me up because the main character in the book she was reading died. A fictional character. And she was sobbing like she lost her best friend in the entire world. She's lucky I love her.

"Thanks, darling. I appreciate it." I bring the mug of steaming coffee to my lips and take a tiny sip, so as not to burn my mouth. Placing it back on the nightstand, I slink my way out of bed so I can use the bathroom. At least I had the good fortune of sleeping with my boxers on last night.

When I get back, my erection much less of a problem now, Ainsley's nibbling on a cookie. Throwing myself on the bed next to her, I swipe the cookie from her hand.

She immediately protests. "Hey! That's my cookie. Get your own."

With my mouth full of cookie, I mumble, "I believe you are mistaken. My mouth, my cookie."

She huffs as she turns herself to grab another cookie off the plate. After swallowing, I commend her recipe. "I like this one. There's a hint of orange?"

She nods. "Too much?" She hesitantly awaits my answer. I hate that she still doubts herself when trying something new.

"Nope. It's perfect."

"Phew. I made some notes so I can remember it for later when I need to replicate it. The first batch was a definite no. Those went right in the trash." She giggles.

Over the last few months, she's been way more adventurous in the kitchen. She has a lot of recipes in her repertoire, and she's really good at cooking without a recipe to recreate a dish she's eaten before. Lately, though, she's been branching out and creating her own concoctions. While everything might not taste great, at least it's mostly all edible, unlike some of the disasters I've tried to concoct to compete with her. My stomach howls in protest remembering one batch of a god-awful creamy pasta sauce. Yuck!

"Earth to Grayson," I hear her call as I snap out of my memories. I noticed she's finished her cookie and has put her mug down too. She cuddles up close to me, laying her head on my chest. She rubs her fingers over my chest, tugging gently on the light smattering of hair. No matter what her mood, the time of day, what we are doing, when she lays her head on my chest, even if we are standing, I've learned that she needs comforting.

"What's up, darling?" I ask, bringing my arm around her back.

She sighs, takes a deep breath and lets it out. "Where did you have to go yesterday?" she whispers.

Crap! I seriously didn't think it would bother her *this* much. I figured she wouldn't let it go without an answer, but her position, coupled with the fact that she's hesitant and whispering, lets me know it's *really* bothering her.

Before I can answer, my fingers find her hair and begin to twirl. "Are you okay?" I have to strain to even hear her.

It's been a while since I've had to do damage control. We've managed to avoid her mother since the wedding, and she hasn't said anything to me about whether or not she's spoken to her father about it. I know she wanted to talk with him once we got back from

Drew's wedding, but I don't know that she ever got a chance without her mother there. Besides the major fight we had about Natalie and Caleb, my bubbly girl has been in appearance lately.

"I went to see your father."

"Oh," is all she manages to squeak out. She continues rubbing my chest, applying a little more pressure now, so I know I have to tell her the whole story. Not that it's a secret because in truth, I know it will be a good thing for her.

"I had to ask him a question, a question I should have asked before I asked you to marry me. But I was too damn excited for you to wear my ring that I overlooked it." I pause for a moment. I know she's hanging on my every word and is willing me to continue, preferably as fast as I can get it out. "He was shocked."

I don't get to continue because she whips her head off my chest and is glaring at me. Maybe glaring is too harsh of a word; she's more gawking at me, wondering what the hell I'm going to say next.

"He's shocked that you had the decency to ask now?" she wonders.

I shake my head. "No, he actually didn't mind too much that I didn't ask his permission. He knows you are undoubtedly happy so there's no concern there. He just didn't know."

She's getting irritated at me, her face conveys it all. "Grayson, he didn't know what?" she asks, pouting her lips and furrowing her brows.

"He didn't know your mother told you they wouldn't be at your wedding."

She about jumps off the bed. "He didn't know that? How could he not have known that?" She's off the bed and pacing the floor, muttering to herself as I continue.

"He flat out told me that he wouldn't miss your wedding for the world. Like, nothing is going to stop him from walking you down that aisle."

She stops pacing, her face jerking in my direction. "He said that?" When I nod, her face softens the tiniest bit. "My mom?" she questions.

"We didn't talk about your mom. The only time I mentioned her was when I told him what she said about not coming to the wedding. I didn't even go into the other things she said because his face looked like, well like yours did a moment ago when you jumped off the bed."

"So, he's really going to come?" She's whispering again.

I get off the bed and walk over to her. I cup her face in my hands and look deep into her eyes. "Yes, darling, he will be there. No matter where, no matter when, your dad will be there. Heck, he even offered to pay for it." Her face, which looked so fallen and sad just a few short moments ago, now beams with joy. And there's no doubt in my mind that the tear that slips down her cheeks is one of pure happiness. And I can't help to feel responsible that I helped her get to this place because she so deserves this. If I have to spend the rest of my life making sure she knows this, then I will make that my mission. Because as happy as she is right now, she makes me infinitely happy, happier than I ever imagined I could be.

Out of nowhere, she's jumping into my arms. I manage to catch her before we both fall over. She lays her head on my shoulder, hanging her arms down my back. "Gray?"

"Yeah, love?"

"You realize you're stuck with me, right? Like, especially now that you have my father's blessing, I belong to you?"

Since I can't see her face, I can't quite gauge her reaction, but when her body starts to slightly shake, I confirm that she's laughing. Her response is just what we need to lighten the mood, so instead of answering her, I toss her down on the bed. Her cackles fade away as she matches me, thrust for thrust, showing me that not only does she belong to me, but that I belong to her.

* * *

*O*nce Ainsley knows that her dad will officially be at the wedding, she finally starts to plan it. And by "finally" I mean, she allows me to talk about it more than once a day. And by "plan it," I mean that every day, she picks one thing she wants. She actually doesn't have too many requests, but she damn sure has opinions about what she doesn't want. I think it only takes us about three months to make every last decision.

In the meantime, she has decided to start a blog, chronicling her passion and love for baking. My favorite posts are what she calls "Trashcan Treats" where she describes the mistakes she makes along the way, the food that ends up in the trashcan. She absolutely loves both the writing and the baking aspect of it; it's the perfect fit for her, and I can't but help to feel so proud of who she's become, the sense of worth this project gives her. I think she finally "gets" that she's worth the love and adoration that I not only have for her, but our friends and her father, too. We still don't talk about her mom, and well, her friends from her life BG, "Before Grayson," only come around once in a blue moon. However, the fact that she's ridiculously happy allows her to see the world in a different light, one with a more positive worldview.

As for me, I can't wait to make this girl my wife. About once a week, I think about giving in to her original wishes about a small ceremony, and then she does something that makes me change my mind. Like right now.

As much as I don't like to share her with others, when she's up in the front of a classroom of students, giving instructions on how to measure out the flour, the sugar, the chocolate, I want to invite everyone I know and then some to our wedding so that everyone and anyone knows that not only will she be my wife, but she is *my life*.

I watch as she moves to the girl in the back row. She's about nine and she can't quite seem to crack the eggs for the cupcakes they are making. With the utmost skill, Ainsley patiently demonstrates the best way to crack the eggs to avoid getting shells in the bowl. When the shy girl finally successfully completes the task, her face lights up. And while Ainsley couldn't be more proud of her student, I couldn't be prouder of her.

When she's done with the girl, she glances at me where I stand in the back of the room. It's where you'll find me every Tuesday afternoon, just watching her. She once asked me if I had a possessiveness fetish with keeping her close to me. I prefer to call it a devotion, but yes, when it comes to Ainsley, where she is, I'm bound to be close by. What can I say? She stole my heart the minute her lips met mine, and well, nothing in this world can ever make me take it back.

She blows me a kiss, mouths, "Love you," and diverts her attention back to the kids. Crossing my feet at the ankles and leaning against the doorframe, a smile creeps over my face. "Ainsley Bradford, you overwhelm me, in the best possible way," I whisper. I know she can't hear me, but she knows, she gets it.

And she's the only one who ever will.

EPILOGUE

AINSLEY

ONE YEAR LATER

I'm staring at a positive pregnancy test. Unlike last time, the meaning sinks in right away, and the smile I feel creeping across my face couldn't be bigger.

Grayson wanted to start trying even before the wedding, but I held back. It's not that I didn't want to be pregnant or have kids; I needed time to enjoy our life together. I needed time to enjoy my husband all to myself. Heck, I needed to enjoy just being by myself for a bit. Being without a job for a little while, meeting and marrying the love of my life in a matter of a year, I needed to just BE Ainsley for a while before I became someone's mother. Grayson never pressured me to stop taking the pill, never asked when we would start; he just let me have my time. He knew I needed the time and would come to him when I was ready. Even when I nonchalantly told him over dinner one night that I decided to stop birth control, he raised his brows, shrugged his shoulders and went back to eating his meal. It's what I love most about the man: he allows me to be me, gives me unconditional love and support, and doesn't ask questions when they aren't needed. He. Gets. Me.

He is going to be ecstatic, I think and in turn, my smile grows even bigger.

Before I can even decide how to tell him, I hear Grayson call from somewhere in the house, "Hey, darling. I'm back. Time to make the donuts."

I chuckle at his use of the phrase, but he's not wrong. It *is* time to make the donuts.

I shove the test into the pocket of my hoodie and wash my hands. Not wanting to give anything away, I wipe the smile off my face.

When I get to the kitchen, Grayson has the ingredients and supplies spread all over the counters. He's just come back from the gym and a morning of training clients. His back is to me, that toned ass that I can't ever get enough of, in perfect view. Well, second only to his abs. And after his arms. And those calves.

Lost in my head, I barely hear him clear his throat; he's caught me staring, yet again.

He's shaking his head at me as he begins to speak. "It's been four hours, Ainsley."

"And it will be way more than that until I can get you naked again," I retort.

He comes over to me and wraps his arms around me, planting a slow kiss on the top of my head. My eyes slip shut and a small moan escapes my lips. I can't help it. Even though we've been married a little less than a year, his kisses still make me swoon. *As it should,* my conscience bellows from inside. "Love you, Gray," I manage to pant out.

"Ditto." He lets me go and tells me, "Come on, these donuts aren't going to make themselves."

"Did you pull the Mustang in the garage? Or are we going to take it out tonight?"

He turns to face me. "His or hers?"

Yes, that's right. We each have our own Mustangs. Mine is the '67 I inherited from Grayson when he finally got his 2015 one. The one I picked out for him with the money I borrowed before our wedding.

When we got back from our honeymoon, I directed him to the Ford dealership. When he found out why we were there, his only reaction was a shake of his head and the words, "I guess I paid for my own wedding present." I'm lucky he loves me.

"Mine. You told me I could drive this evening and well, I'm still a little scared of yours being so new."

He snorts and mumbles, "But she's okay driving a classic one. Go figure."

"I heard that!" He shakes his head and heads to the pantry for supplies.

Grayson made good on his promise to help me achieve my dream of baking every day. Not only did he supply the startup money for commercial grade equipment and other supplies, he also got our kitchen licensed to be able to sell our baked goods without the "food police" coming after us. He's also in the process of finding me a small storefront. If I want. I'm still undecided. Don't get me wrong. I love baking, filling orders for the clients and customers I've earned over the year or so since I started this little side "business," but I don't know if I'm ready to branch out that much yet, especially with the news I learned mere minutes ago. I also love waking up, coming downstairs in my PJs and calling it "work." Having Grayson's help and support in all aspects just adds to how much I love my "job."

I also have the blog to think about. It's really been cathartic for me to write about the food that I'm baking and cooking, even the mistakes I make along the way. Sometimes, those are the most fun to write. I have a ton of faithful followers, and I love to read their messages to me about a recipe they've tried or just random baking or cooking questions. Of course, then there are the Grayson worshippers who just want more pictures of the man that I call my husband. It was just a stupid move to post the picture of him in the kitchen. I mean really, what did I expect? Of course followers are going to want more pictures of him; did I mention he's gorgeous? And all mine?

The blog has taught me that even though I'm not perfect, I am important, that I deserve what my life offers me. Grayson makes sure I know this every day, and I couldn't be more grateful.

"Earth to Ainsley," I hear. Noticing I'm still somewhat staring, he jokes, "Which body part got you this time?" He chuckles, if only to himself.

"Oh, it wasn't you this time," I lie. "Just thinking about getting to work on these donuts. How many do we need to make again?"

He finds the order form and scans it. "Three dozen glazed, with three different frostings. Some with sprinkles."

"That's not too bad. Okay, let's get to work. Start up the music."

Grayson and I long ago mastered the art of cooking in the kitchen together. It's a dance we know well, how to stay out of each other's way, silent tells that let the other one know what needs to be done or what ingredient is needed from the fridge or pantry. Sometimes we work in silence, with just the music in the background. Other days, we chat. The "man of few words" I met that night in the bar can be quite chatty when he wants to be. Today is one of those days.

"You want to take the boat out next weekend with everyone? I want to get Jack on the water as soon as possible." He's measuring and adding flour to one of the stand mixers on the counter. He looks over to me, awaiting my reply.

"Yeah, sure. That will be fun. He's kind of little though, isn't he? I don't know that Kylie will go for that."

Jack is Kylie and Bella's adopted son. He's just two months old, and Kylie is a bit on the overprotective side. I think in some ways, she has to balance out Bella's "fly by the seat of her pants" parenting style, but it's also a consequence of having to care for Bella all those years. They both love that boy fiercely; he will never be unloved.

"She'll be fine with it," he assures me. "Bella said it was okay."

"Of course she did." I giggle.

In just two months of his life, we've witnessed more quarrels between the two of them than in all the years I've known them, which I know isn't saying much given the fact I've only known them two years. If we thought their sexual chemistry was strong before, we were wrong. Pretty sure their makeup sex has to be smoking hot.

"Oh, and I talked to John at the real estate office. He has a few locations to show us if you want to go and see them. There's one that I really think will work."

I look over at him. His expression, while soft, conveys a look of wanting. Like he wants me to go see the spaces and like the one he's chosen. Ultimately, I know he would never push me into something I'm not comfortable with.

"I will go look at them, but I've told you before, I like our setup. We have a good thing going here and everything's familiar. Why rock the boat?"

He's still got the hopeful look on his face. "I get that," he starts, "but I just thought you would want to expand your business. In the next few months, we could grow it into something bigger, reach more people."

I start to walk over to where he is but am interrupted by a text message on my phone. It's on the table where I had it earlier, and Grayson's closer to it. He goes to check it and when he reads the name, I cringe.

"I don't even care what she has to say this time," I tell him, trying not to let my opinions and feelings about my mother detract from my happy news.

I will give her some credit that she's tried to make amends over the last year. She did attend my wedding. I don't know who was responsible for getting her there, but in the end, I appreciated the fact she was there to help me celebrate.

After Claudia had the baby, she softened slightly in her new role as grandmother. Then, when Claudia picked up and walked out of Drew and the baby's life, forcing him to move home, she eased up a little more. Drew and I made somewhat of a truce, just for the sake of Sadie, his daughter. I try to see her at least once a month, usually on my terms, taking her somewhere, even just to our house. Shocking, Drew isn't half bad as a father, although it's a good thing he has my parents to help out. I still avoid my mother when I can, but there's a part of me that thinks she knows she was wrong about Grayson and me but won't admit it.

Grayson puts the phone back down on the table and comes over to where I am.

"Don't let her get to you today, love."

I love that he knows what to say and what I need to hear. Knowing that her text won't be as bad as it once was, I try to push it out of my head temporarily; she will be there later.

"Anyway." It's my attempt at changing the subject back to the business and to sharing my news. "I do want the business to grow, but it may be more difficult over the next few months."

His look turns questioning. When I smirk at him, he asks, "Care to explain?"

I reach into the pocket of my hoodie and as best as I can, conceal the test in my hands. Without saying anything else, I grab his hand away from the mixer and gently slide the test into it. It takes a minute for the object in his hand to register, but once it does, a huge smile overtakes his face, and the next thing I know, I'm being lifted off the ground and he's spinning me around.

Once he's done twirling me around a few times, he gently places me back on my feet. He slips the test back in my pocket before grabbing a hold of my hands, placing them on my stomach. He lays his directly on top. Then in a whisper, he declares, "I didn't think it was possible to love you more." Then with his eyes full of love, his expression completely content and happy, he crashes his lips to mine, grabbing a hold of the back of my neck. While his tongue explores the inside of my mouth, he twirls my hair around his finger. To steady myself, I throw my arms around his waist, knowing that we will be here for a while.

When he finally pulls his mouth off mine, I see a lone tear at the corner of his eye.

"Gray," I whisper. "We're going to have a baby."

"Fuck yeah we are," he shouts, making me giggle.

Standing there, in the middle of our messy kitchen, the making of donuts put on a temporary hold, I wrap my arms around my husband, the love of my life, the father of my unborn child. When I look up into his eyes, seeing how happy they are, I don't have to wonder anymore.

This is happy.

This is where I'm meant to be.

This is the definition of US.

* * *

*I*s the baby a boy or a girl? Find out in a bonus scene.

*F*or more of the Abbott family, one-click Where Forever Leads, a single mom, parent/principal small-town romance.

WHERE FOREVER LEADS

One night. No last names. No strings.
That was the agreement.

It took one weekend getaway to fall in love with the quaint harbor town of Falls Village. Months later, needing a fresh start, it seems like as good a place as any to pack up and move me and my boys.

For a change, everything is smooth waters. Until it's time to register my kids for school.

It's just my luck my hot one-night stand happens to be the principal of the small private school.

The stakes are high for both of us—his job and my reputation. Not to mention the consequences it could have on my kids.

I shouldn't want him. But I do.
I should say no when he suggests exploring the connection between us. But I don't.
We shouldn't pursue a relationship. But we do.

With so many obstacles standing in our way, will we have a chance to discover where forever leads?

One-click Where Forever Leads

AUTHOR'S NOTE

Thank you for reading! In so many ways, it was so strange to write about new characters. I felt like I was "cheating" on Brayden and Claire. And while they will always be my first, I LOVE Grayson and Ainsley. I love them together, and I love them separately. I had such a fun time writing their story, when they would cooperate.

As usual, this story would be still sitting on my computer if not for the great people I have in my life.

Denise, it was SO difficult writing this and not letting you read any of it. There were so many times I wanted to say, "What do you think about this part?" and I couldn't because you hadn't met the characters yet. Selfishly, I was keeping Grayson all to myself for a little while. I finally let you in on the drive home from Philly. (That was an awesome trip and so looking forward to more book signings with you!) I can't even recall how much I had written at the time, but the final product is very different from that first conversation. Thank you for everything...reading it chapter by chapter, sharing ideas, making it better even at the early stages. Thank you for your "red pen" edits. Thank you for all the other edits after that as well (how many times did I force the Prologue on you?). Grayson may never be Brayden to you, but that's okay. Like I said, as long as his story is enjoyable, he doesn't have to be your favorite. Every time I hear "Body Like a Back Road," I'll think of Grayson (and possibly the pics of hot guys we text each other!) You have more Brayden coming your way, but then, the Storm will hit! And it's a doozy. So glad we are such good "book friends".

Missy, thank you for reading the story so quickly. It feels like forever ago when we were discussing how much you loved this one (even more so than *Waiting on Forever*) in the wave pool at Six Flags. I hope I addressed all the questions you had that I left hanging this time. Love you.

Laura, thank you for agreeing to beta read this one. I knew it needed another reader, and you were my only choice. Thank you for sharing and posting months before release. I'm thrilled that you love Grayson. That's a huge compliment coming from you! So glad we connected and can't wait until we can finally meet in person.

Jen, get reading!! If I promise you more Brayden, will you at least finish Grayson's story? In all honesty, I know how busy you are, and I'm grateful for all you do for me, whether it's talking books or nagging me about online dating. Thank you for being my friend and supporter!

Cathie, I'm so grateful that you read and thoroughly enjoyed the book. We always have so much fun together, but our book discussion about this one was just so awesome. I love how you "got" the characters, especially Natalie (her story is on the way soon, don't worry!) and how your insight was spot on. Panera date soon!!

Kelly, I think your "deadline" of July first has passed! By the time you finish this one, I'll have another one for you to read. Just kidding (or not). I love our "meme wars". Now that release of the book is almost over, I'll get back to my daily texts. #sistersarethebestfriends

Tanya, still my favorite cheerleader. Next time I see you, I'll get you your Nutella (that you somehow keep managing to leave with me), and set you up with the next sex scene. Ask Jen. I've stepped up my game in this one.

Aarika, I can't thank you enough for designing the awesome cover. I truly appreciate your offer to help and am in love with what you came up with. One day, you might regret your offer to help, but I hope not.

Megan, for the gorgeous new cover! It's so fitting for Gray and Ainsley. I love the logo for the series name. I adore working with you, seeing what magic you come up with for each new book. Thanks for making it such a nice working relationship. I can't wait to see what you create for future characters.

Jodi, thank you for your editing expertise. I loved reading your feedback and am excited that I wrote characters and a story that you loved. I'm so glad to have you as an integral part of my team. I know we will be working together again very soon.

Beth, thank you for all you've done to help promote this book through the Panda and Boodle blog. I simply adore your blog, your book recommendations, and the fact that you used "cheeky" in an email. It was so great meeting you in Philly last year. I'm so glad Denise and I stalked (I mean asked) you to be our Facebook friend. I don't know how you do all that you do, but the book world is better because you are a part of it.

Thanks go to other incredible indie authors who offer their expertise and wisdom to newbie authors or just let me crash into their Reader's group and share my work: D. Kelly, Amelia Stone, Melanie Harlow, Alessandra Torre, Kathryn Nolan, Brenda St John Brown, and K. Bromberg to name just a few. And to Lizbeth Hughes: thanks for being my sprinting partner. You best get moving on your book. I need me some Nolan and Quinn!

To my **readers and fans**: I love you. I truly can't say that enough. I love writing and would probably still need an outlet to get these characters' stories out of my head, but to know that there are people out there who have picked up my books and read them, that's like so awesome. Please continue to reach out to me; your messages make my day!

To the **blogging community**: you are wonderful! Thank you for all your hard work and effort that goes into reading and reviewing. A special thanks to all the blogs that participated in the Release Blitz. You make this book community come alive.

To my **parents**, especially **Mom**: thank you for your continued support. Mom, I love how when you knew a third book was coming, you had the Nook out for me to charge so I could load it for you. Here it is, a few months later. Hope I did you proud!

Lastly, to **E and A**, I think you are starting to get that I write. At the very least, you know I'm a voracious reader, especially when I say "just one more chapter and then we can watch American Ninja Warrior." I'm thrilled that I have passed my love for reading on to you. I love going to the library and "talking" books with you. I love you so much!

ABOUT THE AUTHOR

Taylor Delong writes small-town, contemporary romances full of heart and heat. Her cinnamon roll heroes protect the ones they love and will leave you swooning. She has been reading and writing for as long as she can remember. It's always been her dream to be a published author. She spends her days chasing after toddlers and her nights scribbling down stories and ideas the characters in her head dictate to her. She lives in CT with her two children.

Check out her website for more.

SCAN ME

Printed in Great Britain
by Amazon